KATE O'BRIEN

(1897–1974) was born in Limerick, Ireland, the fourth daughter of Catherine Thornhill and Thomas O'Brien. Her mother died when she was five and she was educated at Laurel Hill Convent, Limerick, and at University College, Dublin. Kate O'Brien lived in London for some years where she made her living as a journalist and began to write stories and plays. She also worked in Manchester, on the *Guardian*, and spent a year as a governess in Spain: a country she was to return to and write about often.

Kate O'Brien originally became known as a playwright, her first plays being *Distinguished Villa* (1926) and *The Bridge* (1927). But it was with the publication of her first novel, *Without My Cloak* (1931), that her work became widely acclaimed. Described by J. B. Priestly as a "particularly beautiful and arresting piece of fiction", it won the Hawthornden and the James Tait Black Prizes of 1931. This was followed by eight more novels: *The Ante-Room* (1934), *Mary Lavelle* (1936), *Pray for the Wanderer* (1938), *The Land of Spices* (1942), *The Last of Summer* (1943), *That Lady* (1946), *The Flower of May* (1953) and *As Music and Splendour* (1958). Two of these novels, *Mary Lavelle* and *The Land of Spices*, were censored for their "immorality" by the Irish Censorship Board. Kate O'Brien dramatised three of her novels, *That Lady* also being made into a film starring Olivia De Havilland; she wrote travel books: *Farewell Spain* (1937), and *My Ireland* (1962); an autobiography, *Presentation Parlour* (1963); English Diaries and Journals (1943) and a monograph on Teresa of Avila (1951). Her works have been translated into French, German, Spanish, Czech and Swedish.

After a brief marriage at the age of twenty-six Kate O'Brien remained single for the rest of her life. In 1947 she was elected a member of the Irish Academy of Letters and a Fellow of the Royal Society of Literature. She lived in Roundstone, County Galway until 1961 when she moved to Boughton, near Faversham in Kent, where she died at the age of seventy-six.

Of her work Virago publish *Mary Lavelle*, *That Lady* and *Farewell Spain*.

THAT LADY

A NOVEL

KATE O'BRIEN

With a New Introduction by
DESMOND HOGAN

PENGUIN BOOKS — VIRAGO PRESS

PENGUIN BOOKS
Viking Penguin Inc., 40 West 23rd Street,
New York, New York 10010, U.S.A.
Penguin Books Ltd, Harmondsworth,
Middlesex, England
Penguin Books Australia Ltd, Ringwood,
Victoria, Australia
Penguin Books Canada Limited, 2801 John Street,
Markham, Ontario, Canada L3R 1B4
Penguin Books (N.Z.) Ltd, 182–190 Wairau Road,
Auckland 10, New Zealand

First published in Great Britain by William Heinemann Ltd. 1946
First published in the United States of America under the title
One Sweet Grape by Doubleday & Co. 1946
This edition first published in Great Britain by Virago Press Limited 1985
Published in Penguin Books 1985

ISBN 0 14 016.105 8

Printed in the United States of America by
R. R. Donnelley & Sons Company, Harrisonburg, Virginia

INTRODUCTION

Why did'st thou promise such a beauteous day
And make me travel forth without my cloak?

Between her birth in Boru House, Limerick, on 3 December 1897 and her death in the Kent and Canterbury Hospital, Canterbury, in the afternoon of 13 August 1974, Kate O'Brien chose discretion and privacy as a maxim for her life. In her last book, a book of reminiscences, *Presentation Parlour* (1963), Kate O'Brien piquantly refers to an aunt, a nun, who expressed a desire to read her first novel *Without My Cloak* (1931) and was only given it with certain sections pinned by safety pins. The nun was amply satisfied with her censored read. In a way when one comes to look at it, unlike like those of many authors, certain sections of Kate O'Brien's life are closed off from us by safety pins. To know a little more one must construct from the pointers in her fiction, from her few autobiographical writings; one asks her friends, one delicately handles an heirloom of photographs.

My favourite photograph of Kate is one of her in her twenties, about the time of her short-lived marriage, in a shapeless many-coloured jersey. She has a face that resembles someone she quoted in *English Diaries and Journals* (1943), Katherine Mansfield. A face that is both serene and yet dogged by the fact of exile. It is an image that is premature in a final reckoning with Kate O'Brien because the image of her that seems to survive is that of the author of *That Lady*; her public portrait was finally completed with the success of *That Lady*, a middle-aged woman still with a twenties-style hair cut, her impressively-boned Limerick face a little solemn, her eyes aristocratic, challenging, but not arrogant. Having spent a while looking at Kate O'Brien's work my conclusion is that she was incapable of arrogance. Her life, like her work, was a supplication to a God who was partly provincial and partly a global traveller.

In her life Kate O'Brien knew the vicissitudes of poverty and wealth; she encountered international success and in the latter part of her life on The Street, Boughton in Kent, an eclipse from the public eye. In many ways the end of *That Lady* was prophetic of the end of Kate O'Brien. As Ana de Mendoza forfeits her Mantegna, a lifetime of refinement enshrined in it, so we can presume Kate had to relinquish her own precious works of art on selling her house in Roundstone, Connemara, (a house recently owned and vacated by Sting of the Police) and retiring to Kent. But prior to this fate, as for Ana de Mendoza, the mulberry trees had bloomed for Kate, the world of her time had chattered about her, as in the cases of Rose and Clare in *As Music and Splendour* she was more than familiar with the "symbols and augurs of total success".

Kate O'Brien's grandfather was evicted from a small farm just after the Famine; he headed towards Limerick city where by the 1860s he had established a thriving horse breeding business. In her first novel *Without My Cloak*, a grand gesture of an Irish novel not unlike Eilís Dillon's recent *Across the Bitter Sea*, Kate chronicled the emotional lives of an Irish bourgeois family through the nineteenth century. But Irish bourgeois families, as in the case of Kate's own, very often have their roots in recent poverty and catatonic acts of transcendance. Insecurity travels like a banshee through such families. In her second novel *The Ante-Room* (1934), a kind of *Lady Chatterly's Lover* without the release of the sexual act, Kate very brilliantly, very toughly denuded such a family of the romance and left us with images of the detritus of the Irish bourgeois family, the gardens, the garden-houses, the guns poised for suicide.

Kate's much-loved mother died when Kate was a child and she was sent to Laurel Hill Convent, run by the Faithful Companions of Jesus, which she left when she was eighteen. Kate loved the school, a school where Mother Thecla and the bishop were wont to converse in Latin in the garden, a school which bordered on the majesterial Shannon, and from it she coaxed the experience for her most perfect novel, *The Land of Spices* (1941), one of the most important smaller novels of the twentieth century. Youth is set against age. A girl on the threshold of life against a nun about to become Mother General of her order. There is love between nun and girl. But intercepting this love, in the nun's eyes, is an image of her father making love to a boy student in Brussels, a sight which initially drove her into the convent. The innocence of age and the innocence of youth is intercepted by an image of carnal love. The girl is walking into the world of such images. The nun is quietly withdrawing from the memory of the image. We can take it that Kate, on leaving Laurel Hill in June 1916, was walking into the world of these paradoxes, innocence inaugurated into experience. The nun was based on an English Reverend Mother who was at Laurel Hill in Kate's time, a woman who never smiled so alienated as she was by this grey city and this, to her, slovenly river, a woman of "Yorkshire bred and Stonyhurst men".

Already the duality of Ireland and England was established in Kate's personality. An American writers' directory of the 1940's tells us that on Kate's visit to the United States in the late forties she was without an Irish accent. I imagine those pinched "Stonyhurst" eyes looking with trepidation after Kate from a convent gate in 1916. Kate's father died in 1916. His business had already been in decline. In Dublin in her mackintosh "half starved by the holy men and the holy women" Kate walked among the ruins of an English-built city. An uncle of hers, Uncle Hickey, had wept when Queen Victoria, "our great little queen", had died. But Kate befriended many young and radiant revolutionaries at University College, a great number of whom, she tells us, had only a few years to live though that could not be suspected in a world which dazzled with ideas. Within a few years Kate had taken some of these ideas to Washington, working indirectly on behalf on the newly-declared Irish Free State, her American sojourn giving an authority to the final section of *Without My Cloak* in which Denis Considine hopelessly looks for his fugitive beloved in the half-lit late nineteenth-century world of port-side New York, a section where Kate, like some maverick folk-song writer, seems to have trapped all the acumen of an archetypal experience.

But before Washington Kate worked briefly on the *Manchester Guardian*, living in Manchester, and taught two terms at a London school. An incident there prepares us for the heroine of *Mary Lavelle* (1936). Kate's beauty and graciousness made such an impact on the girls she was teaching that a mother traipsed to the convent to see what was astir, to be met at the door by a nun who declared "Well the fact is the beloved is very beautiful." 1922–23 Kate was in another country. Spain. Which was to be the love of her life, a country from which she was barred from 1937 to 1957 for expressed Republican sympathies (*Farewell Spain*, 1937). In Bilbao in the rainy winter of 1922–23 Kate was acquainted with an Englishman who when she encountered him years later could only disdainfully recall the mud. Kate loved the mud for it reminded her of Ireland. In the Middle Ages there was constant commercial traffic between Spain and the West Coast of

Ireland. A dark people on the West Coast of Ireland, the street names of certain Irish towns—in Galway there are names like Madeira Street, Velasquez de Palmeira Boulevard—bear witness to this.

In 1922 Ireland had a new link with Spain. It exported governesses. Kate joined the misses, the "legions of the lost ones, the cohorts of the damned", the women who spoke English imperfectly and bided their time in cafés, hoping for the consummation of marriage. In *Mary Lavelle* there is a gesture of renunciation of Ireland, less publicised than Joyce's, but, for me, more tender, more universal. A young, already-betrothed, Irish governess, naked in the night, after seducing a young married Spaniard, realises she has sold "the orthodox code of her life", she has burnt her boats. "She would answer it, taking the consequences." Like Agnes in *The Ante-Room*, Clare in *As Music and Splendour*, Ana in *That Lady*. She accepts the lifelong totality of a single choice. In a way the night of lost virginity in *Mary Lavelle* dawns into the burning days under the Guadarramas in *That Lady*; Ana, older than Mary, still carries the struggle ensuing from the same choice. She knows she must let the consequences of her choice run their full gamut before she can connect again with her immortal soul. The landscape of Castile itself, eternal, unyielding, becomes a foil to the consternation within her. Mary in *Mary Lavelle* visits Castile for the first time and perceives it as "meeting place of Moor and monk", a land where the miracles of the New Testament could comfortably have taken place. Her persona as it is developed in the character of Ana de Mendoza is destined to seek the miracle of salvation here in spite of an adulterous affair she regards as a mortal sin.

In 1923 Kate married a young Dutch journalist in a registry office, cohabiting with him in a confined space in Belsize Park; often, Kate would recollect, the two would stroll in state into London, pretending it was for exercise, whereas in fact the real reason for these promenades was lack of money. The marriage lasted a year. *Distinguished Villa*, Kate's first play, produced in 1926, a study of the middle classes of Brixton, was very nearly a tremendous success but its run was ended by the General Strike. The British papers in 1932 were describing a remarkably comely Irish woman, whom many thought was just over from Limerick, going to collect the Hawthornden Prize. As long as English was so beautifully used by Irish people one paper gushed Ireland and England could never really be enemies. Kate's age was given as either thirty or thirty-one. In fact Kate's first novel *Without My Cloak* was published on her thirty-fourth brithday in December 1931. Kate's second two novels, *The Ante-Room* and *Mary Lavelle* are each a giddy leap ahead of the last. The first wavering of quality is her fourth novel *Pray for the Wanderer* (1938). But there is a remark that seems to have gathered force with the development of Kate's life. The hero, an expatriate Irish writer, briefly home on a visit to a grey, Southern, river-side city, reflects that "a life of absence predicates a life of absence".

Kate chose England for the war. During the war she published *The Land of Spices* and *The Last of Summer* (1943). Among the flying bombs she wrote her most structured novel, a novel which reveals itself like the panels of a painting, *That Lady*. Among the dramatic consternation of her time everything in the novel impels towards the inner life of Ana de Mendoza. She is a woman of middle age, the one-eyed, a little ridiculous looking, but to those who are intimate with her, magnetically sensual and emotionally calming. The post-war reading public loved her and *That Lady* sold more than half a million copies in its first few years of publication. The book was filmed. "I went to see it one afternoon" Kate says, "and there were lots of little boys in the cinema. They were booing and whistling and, of course, were absolutely right. I agreed with them and left the cinema."

On the proceeds from the book, film version, stage version Kate moved to Ireland; she was possessed by the old Celtic dream that one should die in Ireland; for her prospective burial she picked out a hill overlooking a beach near Roundstone. She purchased a house in Roundstone, one occasionally plagued by rats whom some local shop proprietors muttered were the Tuatha de Danann in disguise. But in spite of the magic of white beaches and mystic rats *The Flower of May* (1953), shows a diminishing of tension. Her next and last novel *As Music and Splendour* (1958), was not a success and though marred by languor it is iridescently memorable for its depiction of "complicated dusts and civilisations" and of lesbian love. Clare, a young Irish opera singer in Rome at the end of the last century, brings a Catholic sense of fidelity to a lesbian relationship only to be shattered to find that others are not inured to the same sense of fidelity even in something as extreme and as, to her, soul-risking as lesbian love. The end of Kate O'Brien's life in fiction is Clare walking into an uncertain and lonely life. A sense of sin, chosen and clung to, has a say in the last paragraph of *As Music and Splendour*.

Having sold her house in Roundstone in 1961 Kate moved to Boughton, near Faversham in Kent, where she secured a little house. In *The Ante-Room* an English doctor, Sir Godfrey Bartlett-Crowe, who realises that Dublin has at least a few good wine cellars in its favour, ventures into "the murderous and stormy South" to be taken aback by the elegance of the Mulqueen family. Sir Godfrey would have been equally surprised to find a member of such a family living in the South-East corner of England in the 1960s. Kate's family was always haunted by the fear of declining fortunes. Aunt Hickey, of Mespil Road Dublin, used to shopping in Switzers, on bankruptcy, trained her parrot to say "Damn Switzers" on which she would approve him "Good boy, Sam."

I don't know what Kate's attitude to her new relative obscurity was. Her books were following one another out of print. But she maintained a distinguished and acerbic poise in her column in *The Irish Times*. In *English Diaries and Journals* she quoted Katherine Mansfield "And when I say 'I fear' don't let it disturb you, dearest heart. We all fear when we are in waiting rooms. Yet we must pass beyond them, and if the other can keep calm, it is all the help we can give each other." One is reminded of the stolid devotion of Bernardina to Ana at the end, and of Ana's final isolation, from the world of glamour she was accustomed to, from the world of company, her last and only contact being her daughter. One is reminded of the anguish of Kate's last months in a hospital ward, deprived of her classical music and her Radio Four quiz programmes, forced to listen to the clatter of Radio One and Two. Two weeks after having a leg amputated she died. On her gravestone in Faversham cemetery is a simple epitaph from a childhood hymn of Kate's. 'Pray for the Wanderer.' In *The Flower of May* is a paragraph that compels with relevance.

Fanny looked about the beautiful wide table, at the gleaming glass and heavy silver, at the Sevres plates and dishes; she smelt and appraised the radiant fruits; she tasted her golden wine and looked with attention at the many splendid faces, ageing and young and very young, about her in the gentle lamplight. "It is a lovely scene," she thought, "all this civilisation, generosity and peace; all this blind, easy grace, this taking for granted of perfection in small things; all these radiant eyes, all this well-mannered affection, all this assurance, this polish, physical and even mental. But I belong to another place. I have dallied, I have dawdled. None of this is either mine or what I want. Mother, I am coming home.

Kate never finally got home or wanted to go home.

New Year 1969 Kate put these words in *The Irish Times*. "Private life remains—and cannot be taken away, except by death. Though, as Marvell reminded us very truly 'The grave's a fine and private place.'" *That Lady*, her most commercially successful novel, is about private life, Ana de Mendoza's attempt to preserve private emotions against the carnivorous demands of her society and her time and her attempt to preserve a knowledge of her soul against a passionate and very physical love affair. In *Teresa of Avila* (1951), Kate makes reference to a follower of Teresa, who after her death left his Carmelite order, and spent the rest of his life wandering as a tramp in North Africa. Ana de Mendoza is another such character. Her life a side-show of history. She stumbled out of "The Letters of Saint Teresa" for Kate, Teresa having had a run in with the princess. It is not the organisation of historical events and characters, the arabesque of place names that finally impresses but the imaginative totality Kate brings to the emotional life of Ana de Mendoza. Philip is the other character that is wholly palpable but despite his tangibility he is a wraithe-like character; time, the Nazis, what you will. Ana de Mendoza realises that once an action has begun—her affair—she must see it through against all other principles and when it has run its course she can connect again with the journey of her salvation. Not before. Kate O'Brien's theme can be summed up in two words. "Nunc Dimittis". The life of experience chosen and lived to the point you can say "Now I've lived; now experience has come to its logical conclusion and now I can tend again to the acreage of spiritual life within me and that alone."

Ana de Mendoza is a woman pitted against a time of manifold danger and much chaos; her reservoir of emotions is filled by the world her emotions must fight against; her triumph, and the book's, is that her persona transcends its time, its enemies, and time itself with the magnitude of its sensitivity and the depths of its intuitions. Ana is a child of any time when the idea of individuality is attacked, when inner life is under fire, when individuals must square up to the notions of their monomaniac kings. Ana's struggle against the king is, apart from anything else, a wonderful story; the king's final punishment a birth for her and a revelation for the reader. And the fact that Ana happens to be a sixteenth-century Spanish princess points Kate in the direction of lines by Marina Tsvetayeva:

Back to the land of Dreams and Loneliness—
Where we—are Majesties, and Highnesses.

Desmond Hogan, London, 1984

FOREWORD

WHAT follows is not a historical novel. It is an invention arising from reflection on the curious external story of Ana de Mendoza and Philip II of Spain. Historians cannot explain the episode, and the attempt is not made in a work of fiction. All the personages in this book lived, and I have retained the historical outline of events in which they played a part; but everything which they say or write in my pages is invented, and—naturally—so are their thoughts and emotions. And in order to retain unity of invention I have refrained from grafting into my fiction any part of their recorded letters or observations.

KATE O'BRIEN.

I

ANA did not wait for the king in the porch of her house. She stood above it, in her drawing-room, on the threshold of the central, balconied window. From there she could overlook the market-place, which was outside the open forecourt of her house, and she was spared the courtier-fuss of her son, Rodrigo. Her youngest child, a little girl of three, stood at the window with her and held her hand.

The October evening was brilliant and cool. Philip should have enjoyed the drive from Alcalá, especially perhaps the last few miles, through lands to which her husband's care had brought so much contentment. He had always cherished the humaneness of Ruy Gomez, and Ana had sometimes heard him muse enviously on what he called the latter's "curiously practical application of goodwill to life". She had teased him then about his adverb "curiously", pointing out that his own goodwill often took practical shape. And he had said that it pleased him to hear that from her, who was "no courtier". "No courtier, sir; only a subject who admires her king."

How long since she had said that to him? Seven, eight years ago? At least; because she had said it in the queen's presence. She remembered Isabel de Valois' soft, appreciative smile—and it was eight years now since that lovely creature's death. If she were alive still and on the throne, instead of this dull poor girl from Austria—why she would be thirty, incredible as it seemed. And perhaps even beginning to look something like a match for her middle-aged husband.

Ana, thirty-six herself, smiled on the word 'middle-aged', and let her glance pass over the market-place to the roof of the Colegiata church, where her husband slept, with round him

the small bones of four of their ten children. Life was moving
on indeed. They were dim now, the vivid, hopeful days
when she and the princess from France were brides together.
Spain had seemed impregnable then, the king was gay and
self-confident, and the tragedy of Don Carlos had not
advanced its shadow very far. Now there were many graves;
much blundering, war and trouble; the king worked like a
mole, people said, and court life appeared to have degenerated
into a cryptic, stuffy routine, directed by a few fanatical
canons from Sevilla, and some upstart clerks from no one
knew where.

Ana had not visited Madrid or opened her house there
since her husband's death. Nothing tempted her thither, and
she had learnt to love, with a constancy which sometimes
amused her, the exhalation of bright peace which rose to her
morning, noon and evening from this landscape of Pastrana,
which was both her home and her charge. It was indeed an
oasis in the proud poverty of Castile.

And she, very Castilian, had mocked the first efforts to
make it so.

"You Portuguese peasant," she used to say to her husband,
"would you mind telling me why two blades of grass are so
certainly better than one?"

But Ruy insisted that to starve was not essential to Castilian
character, and pointed out to her that she had grown into a
very true example of her own race on a lifetime of good
meals.

So the land which Philip gave them had been irrigated,
manured and planted. A colony of persecuted '*Moriscos*' had
been immigrated from Valencia and established in Pastrana,
to teach the people their good farming methods, and in
particular how to cultivate the mulberry tree and make silk.
Here they and their children still were, happy, tolerant and
tolerated. Pastrana was prosperous.

This was a commendable state of affairs, and sufficiently

remarkable in a Castilian village; and although Ana had jibed in her time at its bringing about, yet now that Ruy, the good landlord, was dead and that his king's new policies were making waste of his statesman-like work for Spain, she thought with pleasure sometimes that here at least in his own village the first Duke of Pastrana would be remembered for a generation or two as a man of goodwill.

Philip might be thinking similar thoughts as he drove past the stripped mulberry farms and the weavers' sheds. For the king was a faithful friend. She knew better than most how faithful. And knowing, wondered now what especial whim of avuncular fuss brought him all this way to-day to visit her. True, his happening to be the guest, near-by at Alcala, of the Marqués de los Velez, would appear to the court to minimise the great honour done to Ruy Gomez's widow—and Philip would undoubtedly think of that, for no one was more careful of appearances. Nevertheless, busy and tired as he was, to make this journey and risk the gossip of Madrid, meant that some aspect of her affairs must now have been worrying him for many months. For on principle he never examined any anxiety when it first arose to him. But having always held himself as, after Ruy, the guardian of her and her children, he kept informed about her, and during the early months of her widowhood had written her many fussy letters about this and that. And Ana, being herself incapable of fuss and unsympathetic to it, yet marvelled, as she read these letters, at his kind-heartedness, and his gusto for detail. She had once observed to Ruy that surely this latter peculiarity of Philip's must be ultimately destructive to him as a king, but they had agreed that it made him oddly endearing as a man and a companion.

It would be pleasant to Ana, even stimulating, to see Philip again after so long a time. His admiration of her was constant, and had always pleased her. Thinking of that, she glanced back over her shoulder towards the bad Dutch portrait of her husband which hung in the room. In the flat, conventional painting she could find no hint of the urbane grace and friendliness of the man who had so surprisingly commanded her life in thirteen years. She sighed a little and cupped her fingers over the black silk patch that covered her right eye. She reflected that, in regard to his marriage, Ruy had lived exactly long enough for the completion of his own devoted purpose—which had simply been, she used to tell him, to train her out of being herself. He had known, it seemed, when to dismiss himself, known exactly how much imposition of time and habit was needed to lacquer a wild heart.

Yes, you sleep in peace, she mused ironically to the portrait now, you sleep in peace because you know your *Tuerta* is growing old, and soon will be quite old, a very old woman in charge of a very tidy parish. You kept me safe, Ruy—you insisted on that—and now you know that even a King of Spain can do nothing against the attrition of the years——

Ana de Mendoza y de la Cerda, Princess of Eboli and Duchess of Pastrana, was the only child of the Prince of Mélito, and therefore heiress in her own right to the estates, privileges and titles of one of the greatest lines of the house of Mendoza, the leading family of Spain. This family, Viscayan in origin and now holding lands all over the peninsula, had nevertheless, at the time of Ana's birth in 1540, been Castilian in root and spirit for over three hundred years.

She was physically the expression of what that implied. Her beauty, for those who found her beautiful, was, paradoxically, of exaggeration and restraint. She was taller and thinner than is averagely considered seductive in a woman; her bones were narrow, and every feature, nose, chin, hand and foot, was a little longer than it should be. Her skin was thinly white, with blue veins showing on her temples and her hands. Her left eye was full of light, but over the socket of the right one she wore, as has been said, a black silk eye-shade, cut in diamond shape. She had worn this since she was fourteen. At that age she fought a duel with a page in her father's house, and lost her right eye.

So when Ruy Gomez de Silva returned from England and Flanders in 1559 to consummate the marriage which he had contracted six years before with the child-heiress of the Mendozas, he found her *tuerta*, one-eyed.

She made no drama of this. Her husband and her mother were allowed to call her *Tuerta*, as a caress, in private; but she preferred the disfigurement ignored as a rule, and no one had ever heard that it troubled her. She seemed to wear her black silk patch as naturally as her shoes.

Her husband had always thought her extraordinarily beautiful, and had understood well that many men envied him and thought his luck fantastic. For he was forty-two and she was nineteen when they first slept together, and yet the fourteen years of married life which he enjoyed with her had been warm and happy, in spite of a courtier-world which did not spare them spatterings of dishonour.

For Ana was not merely too rich and important to escape slander. She was, even under Ruy's guardianship, too careless. Also her husband was the king's favourite minister of state and, all through his life, was given every privilege and kindness in Philip's power. Therefore Madrid said again and again that Ana was the king's mistress, and by her husband's will. And Ana often smiled at the awkward perspicacity of gossips, who will often locate accurately enough what they might call a situation, but can seldom manage to interpret its truth.

But now she was forgotten by the chatterers of Madrid. And Philip, the once-handsome and scandal-giving king, was an over-worked and over-worried middle-aged man, concerned to breed a male heir who might be hoped to grow to manhood, and otherwise tortured by the repercussions from his own obstinate conception of kingship.

Such news as Ana heard in these days, from visiting relations, or from the echoes of Alcala University, picked up by her son Rodrigo, made it seem that Spain was facing grave trouble, at home and abroad. But what seemed to her most alarming was that no one, none of the great princes or captains of her own family, for instance, either knew or desired to know exactly what those troubles were, or how they could be met or avoided. Spanish policy was the king's business now, apparently. And all that was asked of the nobility was that it should live ostentatiously, practise its religion, marry and breed.

It was Philip's wily foreign father, Ana knew, who had so carefully altered the principle of Castilian government. After his defeat of the *Comuneros* he had directed himself to making absolute the power of the Spanish monarchy. And he had succeeded curiously well.

In her husband's lifetime Ana had often fretted to him disgustedly about the growing indolence and indifference of the Spanish nobility before the general question of Spanish destiny. Old lords and vassal-holders lived lazily on their estates and gossiped detachedly about the foreign wars and the religious troubles abroad; their sons commanded the king's regiments or ships as directed, and without caring why they did so—or they sailed for adventure to the western empire, to make fortunes, or they joined the Church, or they played the fool expensively in Madrid, and made fun of the vulgar new politicians who manœuvred portentously round the self-important and over-pious king.

But Ruy, a 'vulgar, new politician' himself, an 'upstart from Portugal', laughed at her, and said that it would do Spain no harm to have a rest from the *pundonor*, egotism and all-round posturing nonsense of the Castilian lords, and that Charles and Philip were men of executive power, good cosmopolitans, of whom the country had great need.

Provided the king's ministers were chosen well, this new method of government by Cabinet was safe, he thought, and assuredly worth trying for one or two generations. For Ruy believed in change, and in getting things done. But Ana, the Castilian, laughed at him and said that time often showed the great advantage of *not* getting things done, and that anyway ancient rights were ancient rights. To this her husband retorted that no one had withdrawn the ancient rights of Castile, and that if they *were* falling into disuse, was that any reason why Philip II should not proceed with the government of Spain?

But such talk belonged to the days when she had been near the throne and had inside news of great events. Now she was an obscure country widow, concerned with olive harvests, sheep-shearings and silkworms—and perhaps with her children too, she thought with a little laugh, looking down at the silky head of her baby daughter.

The *Colegiata* bells began to peal. The chimes of the convents took up the message, and lastly, the Town Hall bell threw in its pompous weight. A hum of pleasure rose from the crowd in the market-place. The little girl tugged at her mother's hand, and Ana picked her up and went on to the balcony with her for a moment.

"Yes, he's coming now, Anichu! The king they've been so boastful about!"

All the de Silva children except this baby Ana had met the king, though Fernando, who was only six now, could not really remember his one encounter with Philip II, which had taken place before he was two. But the four boys often teased the baby with this superiority of theirs, even making her cry. So to-day she was eager to catch up with them, and meet the king.

The buzz in the town soon became a cheer, and then a spreading and at last united cry of welcome. Ana could see the first horsemen coming up the street towards the market-place. She admired the easy way the people parted into a lane for the cavalcade. The cheers were warm but measured; they sounded a full welcome, but they were also contained within a border of etiquette. They suggested that Philip was immeasurably welcome to their town, but that they understood that he was here on private business and had no desire to force a state occasion on him. Ruy would have approved these cheers, she thought.

As the hoofs and wheels rattled into the market-place, Ana withdrew from the balcony and walked across the room to a chair near the chimney-piece. She set her protesting little daughter on a stool beside her, and laughed at her indignation.

"No, Anichu, we simply can't peep at him from overhead; that isn't etiquette, and Rodrigo would be furious!"

The clatter was in the forecourt now, and she could hear the king's carriage drawing up before the door. Poor little vain Rodrigo! She hoped nothing would go wrong with his beautifully polished speech of welcome. He was beginning on it now perhaps, with his three pretty brothers standing behind him—all nicer boys than he, in their mother's private opinion. Don Francisco, the chaplain, was ready with his speech too. And no doubt her secretary would get himself presented. And as many of the children's tutors as dared. But it was all worked out to a nicety, of course; Rodrigo would leave nothing to chance! And how delighted he had been when she had said that she would not be present in the hall for the king's arrival, but would leave him to do the honours, as second Duke of Pastrana. This was the kind of liberty that she could always take with Philip—and she hated official occasions. Besides, whatever Rodrigo thought, it was not to him, young peacock, that she was really entrusting the reception downstairs, but to her butler, Diego, whose poise was such that Ruy used to say at five minutes' notice he could have taken up office as *mayordomo* of El Escorial. And

Bernardina, her *dueña*, would take everything in very shrewdly, and report it all to her for her amusement afterwards.

But then, impulsively, and not, as Rodrigo would believe, with intention to exasperate or humiliate him, Ana over-threw the ordained plan of the king's reception, and picking up her baby daughter, ran down the stairs to welcome him herself. For as she sat in the upper room she realised that she was very glad indeed that he had come to see her and it occurred to her that he would be disappointed not to find her waiting for him with her sons. So she ran very quickly round the galleried corridor, and paused for a second at the top of the staircase, before descending into the patio.

"You mustn't giggle when you meet the king," she whispered to her delighted little daughter.

She could hear Rodrigo's clear, pretty voice fluting gracefully through his speech.

" . . . and also, Sire, on behalf of my mother, Her Highness the Princess of Eboli, who did not wish your first moments here, after travel, to be overtaxed with ceremony, and will be most happy to make her own obeisance of welcome and duty to Your Majesty at whatever later hour of this evening which it may please Your Majesty to ap-point . . ."

Ana had half-descended the staircase now, unnoticed by anyone save Bernardina, and the king. The latter's eyes, having found her, stayed upon her as she moved quickly round the group of welcomers and dropped on her knees between him and her astonished, speeching son. She placed her baby daughter also on her knees.

"Bend your head a little, Anichu," she said softly, and then looked up and smiled at Philip as she took and kissed his out-stretched hand.

"Your Majesty is most warmly welcome to this honoured house, and all that it contains is naturally yours and at your absolute service."

Philip smiled at her slowly and she rose as he drew up his hand.

"Thank you, Princess. It gives me pleasure to see you again, and your family and your people. Is this the little one, the last?"

He put his hand on the baby girl's head.

"Yes, Your Majesty. This is Ana de Silva, Your Majesty's most obedient and honoured servant."

The Princess stood aside then, on the king's left, and allowed her little sons and the other members of the household to make their bows and murmur their loyalty. But there were no more set speeches, not even Rodrigo's peroration. Instead the welcome came to life, and the king thanked them all for being so glad to see him, and laughed when Fernando, aged six, politely ventured to correct his assumption that this was their first meeting.

"Princess, I do not think that you know my Secretary of State? May I present Don Mateo Vasquez—Doña Ana de Silva y de Mendoza, Princess of Eboli."

The tall dark priest who stood behind the king came forward and bowed. Ana looked at him shrewdly as she returned his salutation. She had heard of him. He had taken unimportant office at the Court a year before her husband's death, but within the last twelve months his favour as a counsellor was said to have risen very high with the king. He belonged, Ana understood, to that party, or *amistad*, at court which her husband had led in his lifetime, and which stood for progressiveness at home, and tolerance and non-violence abroad. But she thought now that he did not look like a man of tolerance.

Mateo Vasquez was somewhat stiff in his movements.

"His Majesty does me a very great honour, Your Highness, in bringing me to your illustrious house." Ana thought that even Rodrigo would think this etiquette heavy. "I had the privilege to be in some measure acquainted with Your

Highness's late illustrious husband, His Highness the Prince of Eboli, whom we all still mourn as one of Spain's greatest servants."

The Princess of Eboli did not like the Andalusian accent.

"He's very likely a Moor," she thought flippantly. "What on earth's come over Philip?" And hardly troubling to hide boredom, she turned from the still speechifying Secretary of State, to greet Fray Diego de Chaves, the King's chaplain.

And now the doors of the house chapel stood open, and the whole group moved towards them, to offer the customary word of thanksgiving to God that his Majesty had once more enjoyed safe transit from one place to another.

Ana walked to the chapel by the king's side.

"I miss Ruy very much even now, Ana," he said to her. "Often when I'm overtired, I forget he's gone, and look forward to his counsel—and then——"

"I miss him too," she said.

Rodrigo offered the king holy water in a silver bowl. The king dipped his fingers and spoke once more to his hostess before he crossed the threshold.

"Last time I was in this chapel, it was to see Mother Teresa herself give the Discalced habit to two of her Pastrana novices." Philip said this very softly, and with a curious half-smile. But Ana winced. She did not like to be reminded of Mother Teresa.

"And now perhaps Your Majesty will pray for any so unlucky as to be disliked by that great woman."

The king smiled more broadly.

"They say that she's a saint, Ana."

"I have always thought so, Your Majesty," Ana whispered back, but the dropped voice did not relax its mockery.

"Te Deum laudamus . . ." Fray Diego was chanting.

Philip suppressed his smile and made the sign of the Cross as he entered the chapel.

II

An hour later one of the king's pages came to Ana's drawing-room. He said that His Majesty was taking a *merienda*, a light refreshment, in his own apartments, and, that consumed, he desired to give himself the pleasure of talking to Her Highness. He would like to come to this drawing-room, if that was agreeable to Her Highness?

It was agreeable.

It was dark outside now, so Ana had the great window shut and the curtains drawn. The fire was burning well, but the servants piled it still higher with logs and pine-cones; they lighted candles, and withdrew.

Ana was not quite sure if she liked her most recent re-decoration of this beautiful room. She had had it done early in the year under the influence of an access of gaiety and excitement, which she had half-thought she might express in a brief return to social life, by giving a house-party at Easter, or a banquet for Rodrigo's birthday, or—or something. That had been her mood then, restless, extravagant, but un-directed. But during Lent her mother, the Princess of Mélito, had died, and mourning shrouded the house. There was no party to justify the new paints and tapestries, which she imagined Philip would not care for. He had been fond of the room in its more austere days of plain white walls and dark red hangings, and would be bound to resent as too experimental this all-over design of gold acacia-leaves painted on white. Probably he would be right. But the heavy plain gold silk of the curtains was a triumph of the Pastrana looms, and so was the dark green velvet of the chairs and cushions. And the pictures were mostly favourites of the king's: a Giorgione landscape that always led him on to talk of Titian; a Clouet head of a boy that Isabel of Valois had given her; her own dark, sober portrait by Sanchez Coëllo; a Holbein drawing of a woman's head which Ruy had sent to her from England twenty years ago; Ruy's portrait, which Philip admired, by the Dutchman Antonio Moro; and, hung in a bad light, so as not to annoy her too much, a gift from the king, a "St. Peter Weeping" by Pantoja de la Cruz—a picture which bored Ana extremely.

To-night, however, whether or not Philip would approve of it, the room in which she awaited him pleased her by its lighted-up, expectant air. Returning to it from her bedroom now, and pausing on the threshold, she noticed this and her own irrational response of pleasure.

Anyone would think that something momentous was in the air, she thought, whereas actually I am only going to be bored by some wild-cat match-making scheme for one of the children, or a legal catch in Mother's will, or Heaven knows what! Still, she felt exhilarated by the room's beauty.

There were roses on an Italian table near the fire. They looked very beautiful there, but she wondered if they would get too hot and die quickly. However, as she stood and considered where else to place them, the great door at the north end of the room opened, and the king was announced and came towards her.

She dropped on her knees before him again, and by the time she rose the door was shut and they were alone.

He looked about him appraisingly.

"You didn't tell me you were making all these changes."

"Are your subjects really to worry you about their new wall-paint and cushion-covers?"

"I think I like it, Ana. Surprising and—worldly, for a country house. But—it suits you."

He gave her his slow smile, and sat down near the fire. Ana went and sat at the other side of the hearth.

"It's a long time since I have felt worldly," she said.

"Just as well for your immortal soul, I suppose."

"Your interest in the soul increases," she said demurely.

"It's an interest you were once inclined to force on me, Ana."

"I, Your Majesty?"

He laughed outright. When they were alone she used formality of address only to get effects of irony or innocence. The device amused him.

"Your virtue was a silent sermon to me on the importance of the soul. Indeed, Ana, it was a succession of sermons."

She heard him with a certain confusion which was novel to her. For this surely, memory said, was Philip in sensual mood, Philip riding up to the imperious question of his desire. And Ana had for years now regarded that Philip as a ghost, a departed lover, unsatisfied but appeased, the memory of whose subdued passion gave a peculiar interest and character to her relationship with the man who stood in his place, Philip the king, the family friend. However, she answered him as she thought best and kindest.

"Your affection for Ruy was your true censor, Philip. And as for my 'virtue'—I should hate to think that it preached 'silent sermons' anywhere, to anyone!"

The king had been pleased by the first part of her speech, but now he looked disturbed. He did not wish anything that he had ever desired to be made to seem cheap of access.

"I, for one, have always believed in it in any case—no matter what Madrid had to say about you, Ana."

She laughed at him.

"So well you might, Philip. Considering that Madrid's only charge against me was that I slept with the king!"

He looked a little startled.

"I had forgotten your free way of speech, my dear!"

"I'm sorry—does it annoy you now?"

He half-stretched out a hand towards her, and she, without taking it, noticed the ageing, thickened texture of its skin.

"On the contrary. It reminds me of good days—and it does suggest, Heaven forgive you! that death is not on the doorstep yet."

"You and old Death! What a surprise you'd get if he forgot you, Philip!"

"Forgot me?"

"Is it *lèse-majesté* to suggest it?"

Philip was sitting upright in his chair, his elbows on the arms of it, his hands clasped loosely together. He looked brighter of eye, more invigorated than when he had entered the room, Ana thought. And as he leant towards her, shaking his head in mock reproval of her flippancy, he was conscious of freshness and gaiety within himself. He recognised the sensation as her particular gift to him; always with her it had been like this. Always, sitting with Ana, he had felt confidence in himself, he had felt warmed and well. But he must resist this unsuitable comfort now—or at least resist awareness of it. It might introduce, or reveal, disingenuousness in him for the business about to be discussed.

"Your audacity has always amused me, and been permitted—as you know well, Ana," he said, "but I have travelled here in order to talk of serious matters."

"I know—it is extraordinarily kind of you. What are these serious matters, Your Majesty?"

He dismissed the mock-innocence of the query with a flick of his hand.

"You must return to Madrid, and take hold of your complicated family affairs."

Ana paused before she made an answer. This was a curious command from Philip. Hardly a year ago, when her father had pleaded with the king to make her return to Madrid for reasons of family convenience, he had deliberately refrained, and had reminded the Prince of Mélito of her husband's desire that she should live as much as possible at Pastrana, away from the troubles of the Court and her much ramified family.

"Has Father been getting at you, for some dark reason?"

"No. The Prince of Mélito isn't worrying about his daughter at present. He's preoccupied——"

He smiled, but Ana's face was contemptuous.

"So I hear. Courting Magdalena de Aragon, isn't he?"

The king nodded.

"And mother hardly cold! Disgusting old fool!"

"Ana! He *is* your father, and a great prince. He wants a male heir, and, after all, he still has time to get one." This was said with faint mischief, as Ana took free and full enjoyment always from her position as a great heiress in her own right.

"Still has time? He can't be much off seventy."

"Sixty-five, perhaps."

"Well then?"

"Five years older than Ruy would be, if he were still alive, Ana."

She laughed away the surprise of that.

"If that's true it makes no difference. Ruy was a man—and he managed to get the heirs he wanted in suitable time. Poor Magdalena! Will they really marry her off to father?"

"They'll be foolish if they don't," said Philip. "And indirectly it *is* this intention of your father's that brings me here. But primarily—have you heard that since your mother is dead without producing male issue, your cousin, Iñigo Lopez de Mendoza, is taking legal opinion on whether he has not an equal claim with you to the Mélito inheritance—since you are a woman."

Ana sat up very straight.

"What madness!" she said.

"Actually, no. It appears to be quite a point."

"Salic law—in Castile?"

Philip laughed.

"Well, a whiff of it here and there in some of our families!"

"How barbarous! Does Iñigo really think he has a case?"

"More importantly, certain lawyers think he has. But you

see, Ana, *if* he has, *and* if your father marries again and gets a male heir——"

She laughed merrily.

"Ah then! What a sad waste of my cousin's perspicacity!"

Philip shook his head at her.

"Not necessarily. If Iñigo does establish an equal claim with you to the Mendoza estates, a part of that claim might stand, I think, no matter how well Magdalena does her duty. As you will not lose everything by the birth of a brother, it appears to me that Iñigo, once roused, will stick to his claim on your claim——"

"So I am threatened with ruin whatever happens!" She threw up her hands in mock horror—for she did not really believe in these threats to her established splendour, and also she was not mercenary or easily alarmed about material things. "Here I sit ruined and Your Majesty's mysterious command to me is to go to Madrid at once, and ruin myself entirely!"

"Not quite that. I desire you to do what Ruy would think necessary in the situation as it is."

Ana's one eye looked straight into the king's grave face. Her voice betrayed no humour and no reserves of meaning when she spoke.

"In the situation as I think it may be, Philip—I know very well what Ruy would insist on."

Philip raised his brows. He seemed suspicious, as if he felt truth probing a little under their serenity.

"Yes, Ana?"

"He would insist on locking me up, in the hour of battle! He always said it was the only thing to do—don't you remember?" She leant her head against the tall back of her chair and laughed in reminiscence. " 'I like my quarrels moderated,' he would say, 'so we'll just keep Ana out of it!' "

Philip felt a pang of irritation.

"He knew you."

"No, Philip. The point was that he knew he didn't know me."

The king smiled.

"Women like to say vainglorious things."

"No doubt. But I don't speak vaingloriously now."

Her gaze was on the fire, her profile towards Philip; but before she spoke again she cupped the fingers of her right hand over her black eye-shade, so that her face was hooded from him. He could only observe the exaggerated beauty of her fingers.

"Ruy would know that," she went on, speaking softly and slowly. "It is *true* that we didn't know each other very well— though we did get each other's meanings when we talked!"

Philip shrank, offended as perhaps she meant him to be.

"By his own wit and skill," she went on, "he evolved for himself a far better wife than I am a woman! The wife he wanted, in fact—and it wasn't me. Wasn't that clever of him, Philip? Didn't he deserve to be your Secretary of State?"

Philip did not respond to her sudden gay turn towards him, for her voice and the strain of her reminiscence offended him. He thought she showed poor taste in compelling him to eavesdrop on her enigmatic sentimentality. He had loved his servant Ruy Gomez, and could praise him richly in the right place—but the least of his love had been given to him as Ana's husband.

"I tried to reward him according to his high deserts," he said primly, "but I have always known that in arranging his marriage with you I excelled myself."

"Dear Philip! Forgive me for boring you. And be so good as to tell me why you command me to return to Madrid."

She evoked with pleasure the king's reassured response to the word "command", which, for her own part, she had enjoyed using. When, in private, she called him "Sire" and "Majesty", she knew that the irony she put into such phrases never fell quite easily on Philip's sensitive ears. He enjoyed

her feminine impudence in playing with them, enjoyed the
hint of *liaison*, but also suspected that in doing so His Most
Catholic Majesty lapsed, that the man almost winked at the
symbol. On the other hand when suddenly, with immaculate
and simple intonation, as conventionally in fact as if writing
to him, this arrogant princess professed obedience, or asked
for his commands, he was profoundly pleased. He felt more
kingly then; it was as if Ana de Mendoza's acknowledgment
reconsecrated him, from time to time, upon his throne.

She knew this foible, and liked to pander to it. The
absurdity brightened her own pride, for although, as the
greatest lady in Spain, she had an immense self-confidence,
inborn from centuries of authority, and although she therefore regarded the uneasy son of Charles V as *parvenu* in the
Peninsula, she had histrionic moods, and it pleased her
sometimes to observe how a selected word or intonation of
hers might reassure the King of Spain.

"There are a number of reasons, Ana. This probable
lawsuit is only one—but it will necessitate prolonged stays in
Madrid when it develops. The marriage arrangements of
your father——" She made an impatient movement—"it
will be necessary for us to study the legal position well, in
order that the Duke of Segorbe does not swindle your
children on behalf of his daughter——"

"But I am only forty miles from Madrid here, Philip!
Can't these things be dealt with as other business matters are?"

"No, Ana—because, as your guardian, I must give thought
and consultation to your affairs—and I dislike infrequent
conferences and hasty decisions——"

Ana smiled. If Philip truly proposed to interest himself
in whatever division of her estates lay ahead, then indeed
there would be "thought and consultation". Nevertheless
she suspected somewhat the motives underlying this anxiety.

"Naturally," she murmured, keeping her tone non-
committal.

"But there are other reasons why you must restore your associations with Madrid," he went on, rather more irritably. "I feel it my duty to keep a closer eye than I have been doing upon the education of Ruy's sons, and therefore I desire to have the children, for some parts of the year at least, where they may come under my observation. And, now that Rodrigo has been elected a page, and has duties to fulfil at Court——"

"He was happy and well looked-after when he was on duty at the Escorial in August——"

"Yes. But during a part of the winter he will have to be at Court in Madrid—and I think that he should live in your house then, Ana. He seems to be a rather vain and self-centred boy—a mother's influence——"

Ana laughed. She was not at all maternal. Towards her children she behaved as towards other acquaintances or dependants, occupying herself with those whom she liked, more or less ignoring the others. Rodrigo bored her.

"A mother's influence. Rodrigo knows nothing about that, Philip. And I promise you that boy will live as he will live!"

"As you know, I disapprove of your parental theories, Ana—that is why I must have the children nearer to me."

"I can't resist pointing out to you," she answered, "that if the gossips of Madrid heard the tone in which you say that, they'd surely revive some old stories, Philip!"

He glanced at her with sharp pleasure, which he tried to conceal.

"The gossips of Madrid! They are my final reason for wanting you to come out of hiding."

"Why—are they running short of scandal-matter?"

"On the contrary. Be serious, Ana. You are the bearer of a great family tradition, you have duties which could be called impersonal, I think. Well, one of those duties is to live in the light, as the daughter and the mother of great Spanish houses."

"I did that, and it wasn't liked."

The king chuckled.

"Neither is the other thing, dear child."

"Why—what on earth?" She was truly puzzled.

"They are saying things about you, Ana, that we cannot have said."

"For instance?"

"Well——" he laughed and looked at her with deep gentleness, to remove hurt from his words, "one story is that, since Ruy's death, you have lost your wits, that you are mad. Another is that you are a miser, and ill-treat your family and servants. Some even say—I believe—that you are dead, Ana. That I had you killed, for some strange reason." He paused and stared into the fire.

She guessed that he was thinking of Isabel of Valois, and of his dead son, Carlos.

She stretched forward and touched his hand lightly in compassion.

"Philip! Philip! Do you still care about the things they say?"

He did not answer her. His eyes had a cold, hurt look as he stared into the past—or perhaps into the future, for Ana imagined that he might well be haranguing posterity at that moment, insisting to it that he was virtuous, both as man and king.

She leant back in her chair again, and considered him. She found him interesting in this interview, as always at past meetings she had done.

Ana had never travelled outside Spain, indeed outside Castile, but from childhood and afterwards, until her husband's death, she had been accustomed to meet the most distinguished Spaniards of the time, and such celebrated foreigners as came to the Spanish Court. But very few of

these made even a passing impression, and none, unrelated
to her, was even dimly remembered once he passed. Save
this one man—Philip, the king.

She had met him first when she was a child, eleven years
old. She often rode with her father in the Retiro Wood
outside Madrid, which was then only a little town made
fashionable by the Emperor's idea that its climate was good
for his health. Philip, the prince, rode there too sometimes,
and once or twice reined in his horse to talk with the Count of
Mélito. He was accompanied, whenever she saw him, by the
same thin, dark, gracious little man, Ruy Gomez de Silva,
whom her father professed to dislike, but whom he always
greeted, the child observed, with particular cordiality.
Listening to these brief, complimentary exchanges in which,
naturally, she was not expected to participate, Ana liked to
hear the informal foreign wit break against her father's dry
Castilian ironies. It was like the play of sunny waves on a
rock, and it surprised her that anything Portuguese could be
so graceful.

But it was the prince himself who held her eyes. To the
eleven-year-old girl a man of twenty-four who was already a
father and a widower should be old, and out of any kind of
sympathetic reach, but this Philip—let them talk as they
willed of his cares and burdens—was simply a boy on a pony.
He was practically a contemporary, she decided, and were he
not heir to the throne, she could have spoken with him as
with her cousins at Guadalajara or Toledo. More happily,
perhaps, since she found him more attractive than they.

His eyes were blue, and his hair was very fair. He was the
first fair-haired person Ana had ever seen. His badly under-
hung jaw—about which, as about his father's, she had often
heard her relatives sneer—did in fact shock her at first sight
by its brutality of line; but it also gave to his face a sulkiness
and reserve with which she sympathised, and which increased
her impression, at each interview, that he and she were

young, and thus divided from the other two, who were indisputably grown up.

Philip had laughed delightedly in later years at this account of the impression he made on a little girl in the Retiro Wood in 1551. It seemed that he, for his part, had hardly been aware of her presence at those encounters; in his mind she had not been a person then, but rather a very important counter in his complicated scheme of rewards and promotions. She was matrimonially the greatest prize in Spain, and he had wanted her reserved for his faithful friend, Ruy Gomez. That had been the chief motive, he told her, of the cordial gossips with her father.

In return for this confession of Philip's, Ana did not ever tell him—lest he should use it to hurt Ruy—that when in her thirteenth year she began to pick up inaccurately some wisps of gossip floating round her father's house—about her future destiny, and the vastness of the arrangements to be made for it; when she heard the prince's name crop up again and again in dark talk of settlements; when servants winked, and dueñas and tutors gossiped unctuously of royal favour and royal presents—she decided, alone and without asking questions—that she had been chosen to be Philip's second wife. It had seemed to her a very good idea. She knew enough history and was sufficiently a bigoted Castilian to believe that nothing could better enhance Philip's moral and temporal rights in the Peninsula than marriage with a Mendoza. She also knew that, by reason of her birth, she would marry by arrangement and as family interests directed —so she thought it lucky that these interests should ally her with a fair-haired boy instead of with a staid and bearded grandee from Andalusia or Santander, such as had carried off some of her girl-cousins. And dreaming with a forthrightness always to be characteristic of her, she braced herself with inward pleasure towards the difficult proposition of being Queen of Spain. But nobody ever knew that the little girl was

both surprised and bored when she discovered that she was
only asked to be the wife of His Majesty's favourite Secretary
of State.

In June 1552 Ana celebrated her twelfth birthday. Before
Christmas of that year her mother told her of the marriage
that was being arranged for her. In April its settlements were
signed in Madrid, and a few days afterwards, in the chapel of
her father's house at Alcala de Henares, the little girl, not yet
thirteen, was married to the thirty-six-year-old Secretary of
State.

Prince Philip drove from El Pardo to be present at the
ceremony and do honour to his friend, Ruy Gomez. He told
Ana later in life that it was always his impression that he had
never seen her before that day.

The marriage contract was a mighty transaction, almost a
minor treaty. It was at once formal, shrewd and sacramental,
as every major act of a Mendoza had to be; but also it was
legendarily suggestive of worldly promise, since the bridegroom was the most gifted and honoured statesman in
Philip's train. It was heavy with endowments, scattering
money, lands and titles like roses on its two participants; it
fulfilled so many of the Prince of Mélito's petulant ambitions
that he could almost forget his son-in-law was an upstart
whose Portuguese grandfather had been a nobody in the
train of the Infanta Isabel. And its trend was so correct, in
that it set its true, enormous price on pure Castilian blood,
that the bride's father was enabled to look indulgently upon
one clause of it which, for being novel, appeared to him
faintly offensive—the clause which secured that this marriage
should not be consummated until two years after the date of
its formal enactment. A new-fangled and unnecessary idea,
Don Diego thought, as he let it pass.

But the bridegroom waited more than six years for his
consummation. At sunset on his wedding day, the wines
drunk and the Benediction sung, he bade farewell to Ana, and

departed with Philip to El Pardo, there to plunge as eagerly as ever into that cabinet-work on foreign affairs to which both gave unresting zeal. Naples, France, the Papacy, the Sultan Soliman—in talk of all these they may well have forgotten as they drove upwards through the pinewoods that the day had begun with a wedding. And soon there was all the work of arranging for Philip to marry Mary of England. The two departed in due time—to England and the Netherlands. When they returned Ana was a tall young woman in her twentieth year, who wore a diamond-shaped black patch over the cavity of her right eye; Ruy, grown somewhat grey about the temples, had won a European reputation in diplomacy and was more than ever Philip's favourite minister; and Philip himself was King of Spain, and once again a widower.

At the time of Ruy's marriage to Ana, Philip had conferred on him the principality of Eboli, with estates in the Kingdom of Naples. Ana always mocked at this Italian title. In Spain there were no princes outside the royal house, and it seemed to her ridiculous that for instance her uncle, the Duke of Infantado, should have to debate precedence with her father, whose new title of Prince of Mélito was Italian and therefore, in her view, an absurd encumbrance for a Spaniard. Shortly after his marriage Ruy had purchased the neglected estates of Pastrana from Ana's father; he established his family there and used the village experimentally for the application of his theories of agrarian and social reform. In the success of the experiment and in the increasing love for each other which he and Ana found there, they grew to love the place. And the king, pleased with all that they did for their people, created the new dukedom of Pastrana and added it to their honours. To Ana's very Spanish satisfaction. This native title conferred, she dissuaded Ruy from handing on the Neapolitan principality to his heir, coaxed him to get rid of his Italian estates, and prevailed upon him to found their house simply as the dukedom of Pastrana. Yet throughout her own life-time she had to bear as good-humouredly as she could the appellation of Princess of Eboli—a foreign vulgarity at which she never ceased to jibe.

However, Philip's showy open-handedness with honours carried brilliance and power and even gaiety with it in the early days of his reign. And Ana was designed to embellish these. So she advanced into her married life in brilliant appetite for all that it chanced to offer.

She found inspiriting company about the king.

Isabel of Valois came from Paris to marry Philip in 1560, and when Ana first surveyed her, in the Infantado palace in Guadalajara, she smiled in gay suspicion upon Ruy, who a few months before had had to leave their bridal bed to go and do Philip's wooing of this girl in France. But, "No, Ana," he told her. "It was her fat, intelligent mother I had to dally with." Isabel was fifteen then—the same age as Philip's son, Carlos, for whom indeed, while Mary Tudor lived, she had been docketed. But throughout the royal wedding ceremony, whatever cynical Castilians and watchful ambassadors may have been thinking, and however much the unhappily tempered young heir apparent may or may not have been raging in his dark heart against his father, Ana de Mendoza at least, taking her high part in all the ritual, believed quite simply that the beautiful foreign girl was lucky in the accident that gave her to the King of Spain.

Yet she had not the luck to live. And she was unlucky, unkind to Philip, Ana thought, in that she died in the same dark year with Carlos. Ruy said that 1568 made the king into an old and frightened man—and, as usual, Ruy was right. Those two young deaths and all the evil stories which arose from them had made Philip understand that even the divine right is not a sufficient armour for a king. Yet armour he must have—justification; he must not only be correct in his every action but the world must see his rectitude. And since two such premisses to peace were impossible, he grew increasingly frightened.

As Ana considered all this and related it to the expression of uneasy sullenness on the king's face now, compassion cooled in her and she recalled another observation of her husband's—that a man as diseasedly frightened as Philip and possessed of so much power could be very frightening to others.

I have never been afraid of him, she thought. He is cruel; not simply cruel as his half-barbarous old father could be, and not madly so, like Carlos. But cruel with piety, cruel in self-justification, cruel because a king must be right. I have never been afraid of all that. I have sometimes thought it graceless, sometimes stupid—and sometimes, for all I know or care, it may have been justifiable. But cruelty drops from him when he feels safe. He was never cruel to Isabel, nor is he to his other wife, who worships him. He is never cruel to his children, or to the very poor or the very weak. Or to his real friends, like Ruy. And he has never been anything but kind to me. He feels very safe with me. But if he were *not* to feel safe? And what does he really want of me now?

"Why do they think that you have had me killed, Philip?"

He came back slowly from his debate with posterity, sighed a little and then smiled at her.

"Perhaps they think I'd like an old scandal tidied up! I have such a mania for order."

"You talk as if we *had* a guilty secret!"

"Sometimes I'm a little sorry that we haven't, Ana!"

She knew now what he half-intended and half-dreaded in this appeal to her to return to Madrid and the Court. He was playing with an impulse he neither believed in nor approved of, but which would never set him entirely free—since, as he was King of Spain, it was impossible for anyone to have refused him even his rashest desire—so he must be able to prove to himself that in the end no one did. Yet he was tired, and hardly wanted the proof; would not want its com-

plications or its disillusionments. And he was virtuous now
and ruled a virtuous Court. But still—lest it should be said
that he had failed with one mere woman——

Ana laughed—in pity for his confusion of purpose,
but making it seem as if she flirted with his gallant remark.

The laugh pleased him, seduced a memory of the days of
desire.

"Perhaps they think I was afraid you'd marry again, Ana.
After all, they might say that what I could allow to Ruy
would not be tolerated in any man less dear to me."

"Then they judge you harshly, Philip, and do me too much
honour."

But he was drawing life from her again, and feeling well.

"I wonder, Ana? I am a jealous man, you know—and I
have my own ways of being faithful."

Yes, he thought, she is good to be with. She warms a
man. And, ruefully his good sense added, she feeds vanity
with more grace, more delicacy than courtiers use.

Philip was in his fiftieth year and at a point of immense
hesitation and anxiety in his reign. Spain was not merely
bankrupt as, despite her stupendous American wealth, she
had been since the death of Charles V—but at last her
bankruptcy had become Europe's open secret, and it was
impossible to foresee how the Council of Finance might re-
establish her world-credit. The Netherlands, almost saved to
peace and loyalty a year ago by the wisdom of Luis de
Requeséns, were plunged in confusion again since his sudden
death; one massacre had not solved the Protestant menace in
France, where indeed a troublesome Protestant accession to
the throne seemed unavoidable now and could only magnify
alarmingly Spain's difficulties in northern Europe; meantime
the powerful house of Guise, though friendlier to him now
than for many years and coaxing for his co-operation in the
Catholic League, had to be closely watched—for its great
pawn was the prisoner, Mary of Scotland, and any connivance

with her party in Europe might throw Elizabeth and England
into the scales with William the Silent. Philip was by no
means ready to make an enemy of England. Especially with
the Mediterranean uneasy, Venice an uncertain ally, the Turk
still restive, and the glory of Lepanto seeming far away and
indecisive.

In the Peninsula likewise. His cousin, Sebastian of
Portugal, clamouring for an insane crusade against Morocco;
the *moriscos* making trouble everywhere; the Kingdom of
Aragón for ever on the threshold of rebellion; the Church,
insinuating and arrogant; the Inquisition always liable to
make political embarrassments. The people desperately
poor; the politicians suspect, clever and self-seeking; the
nobility contemptuous, asleep. And at the Escorial, at home,
mountains of work, mountains of writing, little things and
big things for ever going wrong and needing his, but always
his, attention. Sickly children too—and now in late middle
age, after four correct marriages, the succession still im-
perilled. A plain, boring wife who had nothing to say, who
obeyed him in everything and encouraged with fanaticism his
adopted standards of high, unresting piety; a chaplain, an
encircling monastery, a fleet of corporal works of mercy to
carry him forward to salvation; and in his breast awareness
night and day of the unwinking eye of God.

Yet also, not yet dead, there was all this, for instance.
Philip looked uneasily about the beautiful room. There was
this plague of beauty and peace—there were all the un-
regenerate snares that Ana did not even trouble to suggest,
but simply stood for.

He pulled a half-dead rose from the bowl beside him.

"You should have a Titian here," he said. "I'll find you
one."

She did not answer.

"Titian has died," Philip went on. "Did you hear of his
death, Ana?"

"I believe Rodrigo spoke of it. He was extraordinarily old, wasn't he?"

"About a hundred. That is not too old. I hope I live as long."

"But, Philip—why?"

"Because I have so much to do. Oh God, so much. And many, many years will not be enough preparation for death."

His heavy chin was thrust forward. He looked grey and pinched as he stared at the fire. Ana, pitying him and also bored now, smiled a little at her ideas of a moment ago about this pious and worried elderly man. She had no observation to make about death, which she felt confident she would meet tranquilly—with or without preparation—when it came. And she disliked pietistic platitudes. So as kindly as she could she turned the talk to Philip's domestic life.

Yes, the Queen was well; he thanked her. And the little Infantas—his eyes brightened—were very sweet and good. As for the precious, desperately precious small Infante, Diego—he also was fairly well just now. And God would surely hear their prayers, and allow this little child to live?

"The Queen is a saint, Ana."

Ana inclined her head in polite assent. It occurred to her that the span of sanctity was broad, which embraced at once the fiery Mother Teresa and poor, dull Anne of Austria.

"Then things are well at El Escorial—I am glad," she said.

"Oh yes indeed—very well."

"Then why do you suddenly look so sad, my friend?"

He smiled at her kindness.

"I said I missed Ruy," he said. "I always miss him, both as friend and counsellor. But in these months——"

"We hear rumours even here of your new anxieties in the Low Countries."

He looked at her sharply, as if half-offended. Then his gaze turned back to the fire. Silence lay between them for a few seconds.

"Alva's policy was entirely wrong," he said slowly, "and Requeséns has not lived long enough to reverse it. I have need of Ruy, your husband."

Ana did not remind him that nine years ago Ruy had stormed advice at him about the Netherlands—peace, concessions, tolerance, generosity. But Philip had preferred to let the soldier, Alva, have his way. Ruy would have had no new advice now—his advocacy was always for peace and the liberal gesture.

"Rodrigo says they say in Alcala that you are sending your brother now, Don Juan of Austria. Surely that's a good idea? After all, he *is* your father's son—and the Flemings worshipped Charles."

Philip drew himself up in his chair, and she saw with amusement that she had thrust too far into Cabinet secrets.

"They gossip in that University," the king said tartly. "And I'm sorry, Ana, but I cannot talk of state affairs to a woman."

She laughed gently.

"Ruy always did," she said. "You know that."

"I suspected it, certainly. And if he did, he made a mistake."

"It never did you any harm. And I was useful to talk to, as representative of the Castilian nobility, of which neither he nor you know anything from the inside. He always said so."

"You have lost none of your audacity."

"But there's no audacity between friends, Philip, surely?"

He sighed.

"Between friends—no. I know little of friendship now. I have no time for it. And I have no friends."

"You have me."

He laughed.

"I can't afford your friendship, Ana. I am a virtuous king."

"Well, in that case I hope you have some more cheerful

companions about you usually than that gloomy Moor you've brought here with you to-day!"

"Gloomy *Moor!* Be careful, Ana! Are you speaking of Mateo Vasquez, my Secretary of State?"

"Well, Andalusian then! How shockingly he speaks!"

"He is a very learned Canon of Sevilla, and most promising in statesmanship. I cannot have you speak of him with disrespect. He is my right hand. Or is he my left? I don't know which of them I trust the more—he or Antonio Perez. You remember Perez?"

"Yes, indeed—Ruy's best pupil in politics."

"You remember when they used to say that he was really Ruy's bastard son?"

"Lord! All the things they've said, Philip! Whoever 'they' may be!"

They smiled at each other. Ana wondered if Philip was remembering, with her, the days when "they" said that her eldest son, Rodrigo, with his disconcerting golden hair, was Philip's child, and not Ruy's.

"So those are your two great men now," she went on. "A gloomy canon from Sevilla, and a pretty little worldling from somewhere in the wilds of Aragón!"

"Mock as you please, my dear. But they *are* great men. And I agree that Perez is a worldling."

"Ruy always said he'd get to the very top. But I never could see why. He seemed to me to be just a little popinjay—almost a '*mignon*'!"

"No '*mignon*', Perez! He has a wife and family, and other complications too, I hear!"

She laughed outright.

"Astonishing, what women will like! That little silly courtier-boy!"

"He's a man of forty-two, Ana—and the court courts *him*, believe me."

"Forty-two? Six years older than me?"

"Well, forty-two is young in a cabinet minister, but——"

"But in a widow who has had ten children, thirty-six is very old?"

"Let's call it maturity," the king said lightly, and they laughed together. "But I'm forty-nine now, Ana—so, believe me, thirty-six in anyone seems very young to me."

"Ever since I first saw you, when I was eleven, I've thought of you as my contemporary, Philip."

"Dear flatterer!"

"No, I don't flatter. I never learnt how to."

"That's true, I believe."

Philip threw the rose which he had been crumpling on the fire, and pulled another from the bowl.

"Then you will return to Madrid—re-open your house there, Ana? You see the various necessities——"

"Well, truly, I don't—so far. May I think it over, Philip?"

"Of course. But let me have your assent before I leave to-morrow morning, if you please."

"I'll let you have my answer——"

He turned in his chair and looked at her with gravity.

"Shall I perhaps have to *command* you, Ana?"

Before his solemnity she politely suppressed her desire to laugh outright. Was he then becoming a blind autocrat? Did he truly think he could *command* a subject in a private matter?

She avoided answering his foolish question.

"This whiff of the world, this talk with you, tempts me back, Philip," she said. "We have been dull here with our silkworms and our apple-trees."

"They are good things—but they aren't everything. Still, you must come and inspect our orchards at El Escorial."

"I'd love to. But I fear Fernando wants you to visit ours with him to-morrow morning. Would that be possible?"

Philip smiled.

"I shall make it possible. He's a sweet child. Four sons! How lucky you are!"

The fretted, anxious look of Philip the King swept over his face again.

"You are tired now," Ana said. "How very good of you to give all this time to my affairs."

"I promised Ruy to be the guardian of his house. But, believe me, it has been a deep refreshment—just to sit here and talk like this for one hour. I don't know when I've taken such a rest."

"You should do so more often."

"Then, if you think so, come to Madrid, and let me talk to you sometimes."

It was her turn to look at him gravely.

"I expect I shall," she said.

He smiled a little without looking at her. Then he laid his broken rose on the table.

"I must go back to Vasquez and his despatch-box now, I fear."

Ana rose and rang a silver handbell. One of her own manservants entered.

"His Majesty desires to return to his private apartments. Will you send his servants to him here?"

The man bowed and withdrew.

Ana crossed and stood before the fire, looking into it. Her right hand was cupped over her black eye-shade. Philip looked up at her.

"Dear *Tuerta*," he said softly.

She started a little.

"Is there no one left now to give you that nickname?" Philip asked.

"Not since mother died," she said. "But I didn't know you knew——"

"I used to hear Ruy say it——"

"Ah!"

The great walnut door opened again, and two of Philip's servants entered, accompanied by Ana's man.

The king rose from his chair.

"To work then, in God's name," he said.

"The household will have been instructed by Your Majesty's servants as to your wishes about supper," Ana said.

"Yes. Later, later. There is much to do first. But I hope that you will join me at table, Princess? You and the Duke of Pastrana?"

Ana curtsied.

"Your Majesty honours us very much. My son and I will be most happy——"

"Good, good. Till later then, Princess."

She knelt and kissed his hand.

As he crossed the room she thought that his shoulders looked old and pathetic. The servants closed the walnut door.

THE FIRST CHAPTER (SEPTEMBER 1577)

I

BERNARDINA brought wine and placed it on a stone table near the fountain. Antonio Perez rose and made room for her on the bench. It was nearly midnight, and the patio was cool and shadowy.

"The Princess regrets to have to ask you to wait a little, Don Antonio; but she has had an unexpected caller, Don Juan de Escovedo."

"Indeed? Poor Princess! A dullish visitor, I fear?"

Bernardina poured wine into two glasses.

"Yes—he seems a very serious person now. Yet he used to be gay enough—nearly as gay as you were, Don Antonio—in the Prince of Eboli's days, when you were both his protégés. Do you remember?"

"I remember." Antonio looked lazily about the wide, colonnaded patio. "What fun we used to have here then, Bernardina! What parties he gave—dear Ruy!"

"Yes, he was good at parties, Heaven rest him. But so is the Princess. We had some pleasant ones this spring, Don Antonio—even if you *were* sometimes too busy to attend them."

"My misfortune. It isn't all honey, being the king's pet boy, you know, Bernardina."

"I came to know that when you were only a page, my dear. Mother of God, the way Don Ruy had to work!"

Antonio drank his wine, and so did Bernardina.

"He set us an impossible standard. Still—it's very exciting often——"

"And you look a credit to it, if I may make so bold——"

He preened himself amusedly. He was very elegantly dressed and groomed.

"I do my best," he mocked her. "I'm glad you like me, Bernardina."

"I didn't quite say that."

"You did, you old flirt. Anyway, it's clear you like the town, and all our nonsensical goings-on——"

"Ah yes—I like Madrid. I never held with all the pious widowhood at Pastrana—Ana knew I didn't."

"Any more than you held with her mad plan to be a Carmelite nun! Do you remember that fantastic hullabaloo, my dear?"

He laughed and drank again.

Bernardina laughed too, but conspiratorially and gently.

"Dear Ana—what insanity that was! Still, I think I know what was the matter with her then——"

"What *was* the matter?"

"Never you mind, Sir Secretary of State. It's not a Cabinet matter."

"It very nearly was, at the time. The great Mother Teresa will never forgive the Princess, I'm afraid——"

Bernardina chuckled.

"You can hardly wonder. Still—don't ever mention any of that to the Princess."

"I'd hardly be likely to. But why?"

"She doesn't like to remember it—any more than she likes being one-eyed."

"Ah! that!"

"After all," said Bernardina, "we've all made fools of ourselves at one time or another—and she, well, Don Ruy's death frightened her." She sipped her wine. "It's the only time I've seen her lose her head—and I've been her *dueña* since she was eighteen."

Antonio felt vaguely bored.

"She's a very interesting lady," he said.

"She is. What's more, she's good. Ridiculously good—if you want my opinion—in a wicked world."

"Then you're a bad companion for her, I assume?" he said, automatically flirting with this lively middle-aged woman, as he did, inattentively, with anyone who seemed to expect it.

"Yes, I've always made a point of being a bad companion. Ana doesn't mind."

They both laughed.

"Still, hell to this Escovedo! He's making rather a stay, isn't he? Does he often do this?" On the second question he barely veiled his sudden politician's curiosity.

"No—this is only the second time we've seen him. Of course he paid his respects to the Princess at Pastrana in August, just after he got back from the Low Countries—out of devotion to Don Ruy. And we only came back here four days ago, as you know—so we hadn't seen him since."

"He's not much given to calling on ladies——"

"Well, that's no loss to the ladies, let me say. He's grown into a very dull old stick. What's wrong with him? I should have thought that life with Don Juan of Austria would keep *anyone* cheerful! And after all, I expect they *have* a pretty good time, in Brussels and those places? Don't they?"

Antonio laughed very much.

"Oh yes—they're having a simply wonderful time in Brussels, believe you me! The despatches from there are one long, sweet song——"

A door opened at the far end of the patio, and a shaft of light fell through from an inner corridor. Juan de Escovedo came through it, followed by a manservant of the house. As he reached the centre of the patio by the fountain, where moonlight came through from the dark blue sky of Madrid, Antonio stood up and greeted him.

"Good evening, Juan. How are you?"

Juan de Escovedo looked startled—and angry.

"You here?" he said.

"Yes, me. It was a haunt of both of us when we were younger."

"Indeed it was," said Escovedo gravely.

"I was half-expecting you at my office in the Alcazar to-day. I want a talk with you."

"Well, we could go there now—I'm free."

"Ah, but I'm not, my friend. I stop being office-boy at eleven most evenings—if I can. I'm having supper with the Princess."

"Indeed? Then I shan't detain you. Good evening, Doña Bernardina."

"Good evening to you, Don Juan."

"Good evening, Juan," Antonio said, but he received no answer. The servant led him to the outer door. Antonio Perez stood very still and watched him go.

The servant came back across the patio.

"Her Highness will receive you now, sir," he said to Antonio, who turned and bowed to the *dueña*.

"Then I shall say good-evening, Doña Bernardina, and thank you for your very agreeable company."

She lifted her silver cup and leant back in her seat as she smiled at him.

"The pleasure was mine, Mr. Secretary of State," she said lightly. As he followed the servant to the other end of the patio she watched him.

Hardly a man, you'd say, by the look of him—she reflected. But he seems very sure of himself. Well, he has good reason.

She poured herself more wine.

II

Ana de Mendoza strode up and down the large, formal reception-room in which she waited for Perez. Throughout the day she had been at once amused and on guard about this supper engagement which he had tricked from her—a shade too deftly, she surmised. But now Escovedo's enigmatic and uneasy talk had for the moment overborne flippancy, and she was troubled.

When the servant announced Antonio Perez she came towards him rapidly from the far end of the room, dismissing preoccupation from her face.

Queer to move so fast, he thought. But she has, I suppose, a curious kind of beauty.

He bowed very deeply over her outstretched hand.

"I apologise to have kept you waiting, Don Antonio. But Don Juan's visit was unforeseen—and he is a little—deliberate—of speech."

They laughed.

"Princess, I was of course impatient—but, believe me, I can be impatient very patiently."

"Which is why you are a Secretary of State?"

"No doubt. Still, we have all been openly impatient for your return from the country. Three months has seemed a long time for this house to be shut."

"Yet no doubt you all managed very well when it was shut for three years?"

"Not so well as we do now, Princess, I assure you. Truly, you are an immeasurable asset to Madrid society. Even if it were for no other reason than that it is good for the king to have so dear a friend within reach."

Perez made this speech with tact. Ana observed the well-conveyed sincerity and the careful elimination of any hint of impertinent innuendo. He spoke as one who had no axe to grind and who simply meant what he said. Involuntarily she admired the effect he got, while wondering how much it was calculated.

She had thought this man silly and pretentious when he was young and under her husband's protection. Often she had demurred from Ruy's optimistic view of him. And in the spring just gone—her first season at Court in four years—meeting him first in Philip's company, and afterwards at the houses of friends and in her own house, she still found it hard to take him seriously. Yet she knew that, under the king, he was the most important man in Spain now, and politically the most intelligent. She saw that his discreet cultivation of her friendship—its tempo increasing slightly in the last six weeks, with a chance visit to Pastrana when he was staying in the neighbourhood in August; then a note with a gift of books; later his tactful angling to be invited to supper as soon as possible after her return to Madrid; and yesterday, flowers, so friendlily labelled: "These are really from the king, from his precious Aranjuez garden. But may we not share them? He would like to know that some of them are with you"—she saw that all this was a political precaution, a career-manœuvre with its purpose still obscured perhaps even from himself. But she did not resent it; she knew this world to which she had come back, and while she remained in it she was willing to play its game. Until it bored her. It might do that at any time; but so far she was not bored with Madrid. She sometimes said to Bernardina that when she had caught up on its present-day intricacies, when she clearly saw what all these men of state, clerics and dukes and prelates, and straight adventurers like Perez, were really pursuing, when she had the threads of the contemporary situation in her hands—then she thought she would become bored at once, and would retreat again, for life, into Pastrana. And Bernardina retorted that if that was true she would make it her business to keep her puzzled.

However, she was a long way yet from having any threads in her hands; and she knew that she was far from fathoming this odd, successful man who preened himself now so amusingly before her; as far as she had been a few minutes earlier from understanding the restlessness and gloom of Juan de Escovedo. Yet she had seen these two begin their careers together, she had seen them schooled for the king's service; and now each wanted something of her—in politics.

Or imagined that in the near future he might. Well—she would play politics this evening, as she had used to in the good days with Ruy.

"We are all the king's servants," she replied now to Perez's polite speech. "But he is so inordinately busy always that he has very little place left, I think, for such a merely ornamental thing as friendship."

A servant entered and announced supper.

Antonio extended his hand for Ana's to rest on it, and they walked together to the supper-room.

"Your friendship would be indeed an ornament on anyone, Princess," he said as they went. "But the king, who has enjoyed it so long, knows it for much more than that. He has a great power of friendship, and he understands, and indeed he needs it."

Ana looked at him gratefully. She noticed that he often spoke with gravity and feeling of the king, and that pleased her. She hoped from her heart that he meant the loyalty his tone implied.

They sat face to face at table, a low silver dish of many kinds of sweet-smelling flowers between them. The room was small and darkly panelled, and lighted by candelabra. Ana did not allow the servants to stand about while they ate, but rang for them when they were needed.

"Do you mind?" she asked Antonio. "If you insist on having poor Juanito rigid at your elbow, say so and he'll do it——"

"Great Heavens, no!"

"—but I can't stand it. If you talk while they're there as if they didn't exist or had no ears that's both very rude to them —and *very* rash. If on the other hand one must discourse all through supper like an edifying *dueña*——"

"Doña Bernardina, for instance?"

"No, no—my dear and blessed Bernardina—thank Heaven *she's* not edifying!"

"I imagine not fatiguingly so." His eyes rested on the flowers, and she smiled.

"They smell deliciously—like everything from Aranjuez," she said. "It was very kind of you to share them with me."

"Why, nothing! The gardens at Pastrana can leave you in no lack of flowers. But somehow, as you say, everything from Aranjuez is particularly sweet—so I thought——"

"Thank you very much. But the king is at El Escorial still, isn't he?"

"Yes, indeed. But one of the stewards from Aranjuez was in town yesterday—and the king likes them to scatter his flowers and things among his friends—as *you* must know."

"How he loves his gardens!"

"Yes. It's curious. He's a very complicated man."

"But surely that at least is uncomplicated?"

"That's why I find it complicating."

They both laughed.

"Well, for better or worse, I think he owes it mostly to Ruy—this mania for rural experiment——"

"I think he does. I remember that we youngsters used sometimes to tell Ruy that he should really have been a farmer."

"So did I, often."

"Still, I sometimes wonder now if even Ruy understood what El Escorial was to become?"

"It is the king's darling hobby, isn't it?"

"He's absolutely *mad* about it."

"But that's good for him—makes him happy."

Antonio smiled at her.

"Yes, it makes *him* happy, Princess—and all his happy monks. But some others of his faithful servants could do with less of the simplicities of El Escorial."

Ana had heard that Perez found ways of relieving tedium in the king's mountain hermitage. The queen's ladies-in-waiting were not all as virtuous as the queen. She pretended to misunderstand him.

"But they have the to-and-fro of Secretaries of State and such great people to delight them," she said.

"Well, we do our best," he answered, smiling at her self-mockingly.

"And Rodrigo is growing into a very perfect worldling since he has attended Court up there."

"If I may say so, Princess, Rodrigo was *born* a perfect worldling."

"Yes—isn't it curious? For really neither I nor Ruy was naturally like that."

Perez knew the legend—that Rodrigo was Philip's son. But he could never feel sure that it was true. In spite of the boy's fair hair, he tended to think it as fabulous as that other—that he himself was a bastard son of this woman's husband, Ruy Gomez. Antonio doubted indeed that Ana had ever been the mistress of the king. There had been in Ruy, for all his courtier-skill, a core of self-respect and honour that should have made such a situation intolerable to him. Besides, by all the legends, the king had liked his beauties in the classical and obvious mode. One-eyed and very thin? Perez surveyed his hostess, and wondered. Well—the king's days of pleasure were over, whatever secrets they held. He was pious now. It was a pity perhaps to have become his chief confidant at such a turning point. The hard work the office exacted could have been alleviated by passages of royal laxity—and the Secretary of State would have known how to promote and protect such indulgence.

Perez laughed friendlily about Rodrigo.

"He's very young. Fifteen?" Ana nodded. "And they tell me he shows signs of being a good soldier one day."

"Yes. He's interested in military affairs."

"Has he returned to Madrid with you?"

"No. He's playing about in Andalusia still—with the Medina Sidonias."

"Ah! How is the Duchess?"

Ana's eldest child, now sixteen, was the wife of the Duke of Medina Sidonia.

"Very well, I think. She seems to be beginning to enjoy married life—at last."

The marriage had been contracted when the bride was not yet twelve.

"Well, it should be a success for them. Everyone speaks well of Medina Sidonia."

"Yes—I like him. He's a silly boy—but good-natured and affectionate." She paused and looked grave. In the spring she had agreed to a marriage contract between her third son, Diego, who was only thirteen, and Luisa de Cardenas, ten years his senior. Ana was a traditionalist, and took the practices of the Castilian aristocracy for granted. Yet sometimes in the night—disturbed, whether she recognised this or not, by her own lifelong loneliness—she worried about this marrying-off of children.

She smiled quickly, however, so as not to seem really to mean what she next said.

"We marry them too young. It's a questionable custom."

"Yet—look at you! You were married at eleven, Princess."

"Ah, but I was allowed to continue in childhood until I was nineteen. Besides, Don Antonio, there can be very few men like Ruy. I was fantastically lucky."

"I agree, indeed." But Antonio felt a sudden pang of question and sympathy towards her as he made this polite rejoinder. He wondered what this feeling meant, and it excited him. Meantime he followed her thought of Diego's contract.

"I'm sure Doña Luisa will be fortunate too, however. After all, your son is Duke of Francavilla, and a very charming boy."

Ana laughed.

"She doesn't seem to like his being thirteen," she said.

"That will be remedied. She must be patient."

"Still—I must see, I think, that they don't do that to my two babies—Fernando and the tiny Ana. I'd like *them* to go as they please."

"You're very fond of those two little ones?"

"Yes. Very fond."

"Because they're the babies, no doubt?"

"Oh no. I like them, that's all."

Antonio laughed in surprise.

"That sounds very detached—and unusual," he said.

"I am not particularly maternal," Ana answered coolly. "But Fernando has great charm for me. And Ana—oh, Ana is an angel!"

They rose from the table and went into the corridor and up a minor staircase to the Princess's private apartments. Antonio had not been accorded this privilege before, and he wondered now at the new, odd pleasure which he felt in it, and in the society of this woman whose life, after all, was over.

She's simple almost to dullness, he thought as he moved at her side up the shallow flight of steps. Talks of her children, and of the king's fads, and of the virtues of her dead husband. She isn't witty or formidable in any way, and—wisely—she doesn't play the beauty. What is it then that—by God, that almost moves me?

The candles were dim on the landing, but as the man-servant flung open double doors and light streamed over the threshold of the room they were about to enter, Ana looked at Perez and caught the appraising seriousness of his eyes as they rested on her. She was somewhat surprised by their expression. For she knew, in general terms, why this ambitious man was cultivating her, and that it was by no means for herself. Yet now she saw that at that moment he looked at her—herself; or looked at her as if in search of her.

She crossed the room ahead of him, again with long, quick steps that surprised and vaguely annoyed him.

They seated themselves in two straight-backed, silk-covered chairs near an open window. The servants trimmed the candles, placed wine on a table at Perez's side, and withdrew.

The court-yard below the balcony was very quiet, and all that was visible outside was a low, irregular line of roofs and a bright scattering of stars in the dark blue sky. The sounds of Madrid floated in; clatter of hoofs or wheels, an occasional burst of shrill singing, an occasional shout for the watchman.

Antonio looked with curiosity about the beautiful, long room. There were many pictures, of the Flemish and Italian schools, on the white-painted walls; there was a large writing-table, scattered with papers and seeming as if much used; there were some books piled about; there were flowers and tall candlesticks; there was a graceful daybed which looked as if it came from France; there were figs and apples on a silver dish. A needlework table, ruffled and untidy, stood by the Princess's chair; and a little rag-doll was lying on the floor.

Antonio considered the room as if he were learning something from it. And as he did so Ana considered him, with a more quickened interest than she was yet prepared to recognise.

She knew a great deal about this man, so now she thought she saw what he was thinking as he looked about him.

He was the illegitimate son of Gonzalo Perez and a woman called Maria Tovar. He was born in a village of Aragon, the native country of both his parents. At the time of his birth his father was a student of Holy Orders, not yet ordained. Afterwards, as a priest, he rose rapidly to political power and was a favourite Secretary of State of Charles V, who out of love for him legitimised his son Antonio by imperial diploma. When Gonzalo Perez died, Ruy Gomez became the guardian of this brilliant and promising youth, and supervised his education, first at Alcala and Salamanca and afterwards at Padua. He also trained him in statecraft; and at Ruy's death

Antonio was ready to take his place as leader of the progressive, liberal *amistad*, or party, in Philip's government.

Because of Ruy's affection for him gossips liked to say that he was his son. And because, like Ruy, he was foreign, non-Castilian, energetic and personally ambitious, he was sometimes called "The Portuguese"—as Ruy had been—in lampoons and popular jokes. Ruy had never been more than amused at this would-be jibe, regarding it as a good example of Castilian impudence and insularity; but he had long ago observed to Ana that young Perez secretly hated all such references, and that there was danger for him in his fear of being regarded as anyone's inferior.

Ana surmised that, since Antonio had to be a bastard, he would have chosen to be the son of Ruy rather than of Gonzalo Perez. Not that his true father had lacked distinction, but merely because Gonzalo's greatness had died with Charles V and was a dim story now, whereas the Prince of Eboli had been spectacularly the favourite of the reigning monarch, and one whose name was still a vivid symbol of greatness in Spanish life. Ruy's might have been the more useful paternity—and not the less so because by his marriage he had allied himself to the leaders of Castilian aristocracy.

There, Ana guessed, was the crumpled rose-leaf of Antonio Perez's success. Castile had accepted Ruy, and had even loved him. But it laughed—a vestige too drily, a little too often—at Antonio.

He made mistakes. He was too ostentatiously successful; he dressed over-well, and used—for her taste certainly—too many perfumes and cosmetics; great as was his wealth and power now, his debts were known to be large, and he was said to be venal in office; he paraded his love-affairs, and was inclined to be both charming and insolent on the wrong notes.

More than ten years ago he had married Juana de Coëllo y de Vozmediano. Marriage with this excellent and discreet girl, of impeccable family, should have been a help to him if he truly wished to conquer the amusement of Castilians, and learn to behave as they liked their great men to behave. But Juana, very gentle, fell far too much in love with her husband, and by degrees became blind to all his failings. Moreover, she was domestic and pious by temperament, and shrank from participation in his brilliant and restless public life. She was content to be his wife on his terms, and as such to serve him without question. She was preoccupied too in love and duty towards the children she bore him—one each year, unfailingly.

So he steered his course by his own charting, and although his political acumen was very nearly perfect, socially he continued to make mistakes. And Ana knew that he knew that he made them. But he was proud and impatient, and perhaps felt that he had gone too far by his natural inclinations to change his tactics now. Besides, jealousy was the chief reason why the indolent dukes and marquises of Spain laughed at him. He understood that; he could not fail to. Moreover, he knew that he was impregnably the king's man; knew that, Philip's faith once given, his support and indulgence of a friend could be illimitable; and that in fact he distrusted his weakened aristocracy and preferred to choose his statesmen from outside its ranks.

Still, since the king had almost commanded Ana de Mendoza back into society, it was natural that Perez should renew his friendship with her and her house. Not merely because she was a lifelong friend of the king, and the widow of his own generous patron. These motives were becoming and polite. But Ana knew that they cloaked another. Her name, de Mendoza, represented exactly that element of Spain which baffled him and hurt his self-esteem. But, if he could make her his friend, if he could be known to have her approval, that would be a social victory indeed, a resounding answer to the snobs who were her uncles and her cousins.

After all, she had married an *arriviste*, and been of incalculable service to his career; she could therefore possibly befriend another, were he lucky enough to please her.

In general this was the motive, Ana believed, of Perez's bid for her present friendship. There might be something more specific, more political, also. With Juan de Escovedo's conversation in her mind she believed that perhaps there was. These men had once been close friends, and she gathered that their friendship was waning now; both believed her to have influence with the king, and both took some trouble to seek her out.

She smiled a little. She wondered if Perez would show anything of his real purposes to-night.

He studied the room too attentively, she thought. He seemed as if worried by it.

Ana had never entered his own great palace, just round the corner from her house, in Plaza Santa Maria, but she knew that it was an almost comic legend of splendour. In the summer of 1576, when she was still in retirement at Pastrana, Rodrigo and his flippant young friends used to bring home crazily amusing tales of the Perez magnificence. Don Juan of Austria had been staying with the Secretary of State then as his guest, and there were many parties and receptions, and Ana had laughed at Rodrigo's reports of tables of solid, embossed silver, of gold and jewelled dinner services, of flunkeys in fantastic liveries. And even her sober and kind old neighbour at Alcala, the Marqués de los Velez, had managed to be quite amusing when he described Antonio's bedroom. His bed, it seemed, had posts carved—in silver—in the form of enormous angels with jewel-eyes and outspread wings. And there were stars and a crescent moon of jewels, and hangings of azure and cloth of gold, and perfumes burning in gold censers, on onyx pedestals. It was no wonder that this somewhat raw voluptuary did not like El Escorial, with its whitewash, truckle beds and straw-seated chairs. And now, no doubt, he was puzzled—if not disappointed—by the ordinariness of her domestic arrangements.

She looked at him gently, and reflected that she liked the light, boyish cut of his face. Not its handsomeness, which was only too obvious, but its alert suggestion behind the charm, its hint of an anxiety that might almost be taken for innocence. He's odd, she thought approvingly; he's himself. He runs quite counter to our usual male conventions. But she did not go on to reflect that this had also been true of the only two men who had ever touched her heart—the king and her husband.

She bent and picked up the little doll.

"I promised Ana that this poor girl should have new underwear," she said.

"She seems to need tidying up."

Ana sorted some pieces on the work-table.

"A *silk* petticoat, I think," she said. "After all, she *is* called Juana La Loca."

Antonio laughed very boyishly.

"After the king's grandmother? Poor girl, poor little doll!"

"Oh, Queen Juana was a wonderful woman, I think—or anyway Anichu does. Would you be so good as to move that candelabra a little nearer?"

He got up and did as he was told. He stood a moment looking down at Ana's bent dark head, and then he looked again about the room. He felt amused and rested. The king's Alcazar, its cabinet rooms and offices so packed with heavy work and shrouded national troubles, was only just across the street, but it suddenly seemed miles away.

As he went back to his chair a bell began to toll at Santa Maria de Almudena.

"How lovely it is here," he said gently. "How peaceful!"

Ana looked up from her doll and her piece of silk.

"Yes. I like this room. Won't you drink some wine?"

"Thank you—I'd love to. And you?"

She nodded and he filled two cups.

"I hope they've chilled it enough," Ana said. "It's good. We get it from Bordeaux."

"It's delicious. But I thought you scorned everything non-Spanish, Princess?"

She laughed.

"In general I pretend to. But Ruy taught me some discrimination—and I agree with him now about our *white* wines. But I love our red ones."

"So do I. Still—even those they do better in France, I fear."

"Perhaps they do. Oh, this poor, collapsing doll!"

"Shall we look for a new Mad Queen for little Ana?"

"No good. She has a passionately faithful heart."

"Ah! Do you think that a good possession, Princess?"

"I hardly know. But I understand it."

Antonio sipped his wine and watched her long hands at their work.

The convent bell dropped away into silence.

"Well," he said suddenly and lightly, "are you going to tell me what Juan de Escovedo was grumbling about?"

She looked at him, put down her sewing and sipped some wine.

"Then we are to talk politics?" she asked.

"Do you know anything about them?"

"I used to. But now I'm out of touch."

"Yet the king comes to see you here, doesn't he?"

"Yes. Usually he sits exactly where you're sitting now."

"Ah! How very much I am honoured!" In passing he wondered if Philip would whole-heartedly approve of the honour being done to him. "I wonder what he talks about to you?"

"Oh, family affairs—these settlements over my father's recent marriage, and my cousin's lawsuit, and so on. And the children and their education."

"It sounds—just a little boring."

They laughed.

"We talk about old times too, about Ruy, and—Queen Isabel. And he tells me how El Escorial is getting on. He comes here to rest, you see."

"He doesn't know how to rest."

"That's true. So sometimes his real preoccupations are hinted at too, although he hates to give anything away."

"But he does. You gather things?"

"Some things. In any case, he isn't after all my only visitor! The Cardinal—and others—sometimes call."

"Including Escovedo."

"Yes. Poor Juan. He's always been devoted to Ruy and all of us. But now he seems to be getting dissatisfied with me—I truly don't know why."

"He's getting dissatisfied with everyone—except Don Juan of Austria. It's very foolish of him."

"But he used to be exceptionally shrewd."

"That's why he was put in charge of Don Juan, who has, as you know, no sense at all. He's a romantic figurehead, and his only use to us in Flanders is that the Flemings like him for being his father's bastard with one of their own women. Escovedo's job was to impose our policy, and keep Curlyhead out of mischief."

"And why is everything going wrong—as I gather it is— in Flanders?"

"You 'gather' only too truly, Princess." Antonio stood up and paced somewhat uncertainly about the room. His face was hard and clouded. "Escovedo is the reason why everything is going wrong again in the Lowlands. That may sound absurd to you—but, believe me, it isn't. Not all the blandishments of His Holiness, nor the half-promises of Guise and the Catholic League, nor the beckonings from Mary of Scotland need stand a second's chance against one well-trained politician at Don Juan's elbow now. They are all straws in the wind against the facts. Your husband, Princess, or I, or Mateo Vasquez—any of us, who are realists, would simply have protected him, mercilessly, against his own absurdity. And Escovedo was a man like us, with our training. I'd have sworn he was equal to this job."

"And why is he failing in it?"

Perez laughed, but half-angrily.

"He is failing in it because—well, one must almost say because he has fallen in love with our Lepanto captain! He has forgotten the king. Don Juan has become his king."

Ana had not the clues to all that lay behind this outburst, but she was prepared to wait for them.

She smiled.

"Then why does he come bothering me?" she asked lightly. "Philip is my king."

Perez thought that as she said this she looked very beautiful. He paused by the table and raised his glass.

"Shall I go on being indiscreet?" he asked her.

"So far there's been no indiscretion—because I do not understand your references. For instance, what has poor Mary of Scotland to do with our mistakes in Flanders? She's still in prison, isn't she?"

"Indeed she is, thank God! And long may she stay there, and merry may she be!"

"Unchivalrous!"

"Realistic. In any case, it's much the safest place for the poor woman."

"But what is she doing in this conversation?"

"Ah, Princess—I don't think I can quite tell you that. That's a whole despatch-boxful of gossip—and very tricky."

He moved away from her, and his face grew hard and angry again. She watched him with interest. He cares about his work, she thought. Ruy would approve of this earnestness. He is not where he has got to entirely, or even much at all, for vainglory—let his enemies say what they will. The

splendours are his reward indeed, and he must have great
vitality to be able to snatch so greedily at them while giving
so much passion to his work. But the passion is there. He is
wholly in earnest for Philip and for Spain.

He turned in his walk, flung out his hands and spoke,
looking at her indeed, but still as if she were not there, or as if
he were alone.

"Parma's had to take the army back to Flanders—you know
that? Namur! And Margaret of Navarre! Curlyhead is
getting positively literary! And Antwerp now, we gather—
and despatches peppered with that dear old *cliché* 'fire and
sword'! My God—as if old Alva's blunderings had never
happened! As if we'd never heard of the Perpetual Edict!
Madam, we slaved for that, the king and I—and the Estates
were just beginning to believe in our sincerity. No thanks to
Don Juan either that we *did* get it ratified in May. And now
it's all in the dust and we're disgraced again in the Lowlands—
simply because Escovedo won't control the day-dreams of a
soldier-boy!"

"What are these day-dreams?"

"If I told you, Princess, I'd hardly expect you to believe
me."

He dropped back into his chair, and smiled at her.

"You don't remember the king's father, do you, Princess?"

"Oh yes, I do. I was seventeen when he died."

"Ah! Well, he was a very great ruler, but he certainly made
one mistake. You should never educate an illegitimate
prince as if he were legitimate. Old Charles was far too tender
towards his favourite bastard."

"Don Juan has great charm. He was a very charming little
boy."

"So he is still—a very charming little boy." They laughed,
and Perez drank more wine. "But why do I bore you like
this? Why am I treating your lovely house as if it were the
Cabinet Room?"

"I'm honoured——" Ana murmured amusedly.

"It's Escovedo's fault. Damn him, why does he have to cross my path even when I come to visit you?"

"Poor man, he seems to get on all our nerves."

"Is he on yours too? What was he scolding you about, Princess?"

Ana threaded her needle and began again on the hem of the doll's petticoat.

"A great many things," she said. "Really, if he weren't so much in earnest one would have to call him very impertinent."

"I call him that—and plenty besides."

"So I gather. But he and I aren't on those terms, perhaps——" They laughed—"And then, he *did* love Ruy."

"No more than I did. Not half as much."

Ana raised her head and looked at him. He felt a long surmise in her look, and submitted to it with a pleasure he refused to analyse. Her hands are exquisite, he thought irrelevantly, as he waited for her to speak again.

"Escovedo thinks that it is shocking of me to have forsaken my widow's solitude at Pastrana."

"Has he had the audacity to say so?" Ana nodded. "Well, he always was a rather clumsy kind of prig."

"Yes—but cunning too." Perez raised his brows in a question. "You see," Ana went on, "I think he felt it to be a duty he owed to Ruy to make that clear to me—he has come to see me twice simply to get it said. *But*, he also says that he understands that I have returned to Madrid because the king wished me to. He finds that odd and unwise in the king, he says——"

"You *let* him say these things?" Perez was laughing delightedly now.

"It amused me—and I couldn't stop him. I said nothing. But I think I vaguely saw his—his politics."

"What did you vaguely see, Princess?"

"He wants—urgently—to influence someone who may

have influence with the king. Now, though he disapproves of me at present, he knows me well from the old days, and he thinks that for Ruy's sake I might be persuaded to be of service to him. He always inclined to believe, long ago, that I was the king's mistress—and now I think he is hoping that so I am again—shocking as he finds the idea——"

Silence fell.

In the surface of his mind Antonio was smiling at Escovedo's grotesque manœuvres—but he could not trouble to smile at them outwardly. Indeed he felt his features locked in gravity, for the inner reaches of his mind were swept empty of politics now, and were filled instead with an excitement wholly personal. He recognised it, for he was practised in personal adventure; always unable to forgo its claims. And in the two hours he had been with her this woman had been gaining on his curiosity, on his desire—gently, gently, like a gentle, incoming tide; each soft ripple of surprise slipping over its forerunner irresistibly, yet without hint of force. Her hands, her voice, her dangerous simplicity, her gaunt, almost her ungainly beauty—all had been beckoning him nearer inch by inch to an adventure he dared not risk, but knew—knowing himself—he would now at all costs seek and carry through. And at last she had spoken—lightly indeed, and on a note which baffled him—of the life of her own heart, or at least of what was rumoured of that life. And as he heard her he saw that her daring joke had brought him—ruthlessly and far too soon—to the point his impulses were set upon.

"I have embarrassed you," Ana said.

He did not answer her at once. He pondered the girlish kindness of her voice as it dropped away. I shall regret what I am about to take, he thought.

He leant and took the rag doll from her hands and smiled at it.

"Juana La Loca," he said softly. He got up, still holding the doll, and walked to the window.

"It isn't easy to embarrass me, Princess." He leant against the embrasure and looked back at her and at the quiet room stretching beyond her.

"You always wear black?"

"I am a widow."

"I came here to-night feeling quite correct, quite normal. As if going to dine with the Cardinal, say—or any of the things one does any evening in Madrid. I can remember now exactly how—how usual I felt, as I talked with Doña Bernardina in the patio."

Ana smiled a little.

"You are still entirely yourself, I think."

"Yes. I don't lose myself—ever. Suddenly seeing what you have to do, suddenly being seized by a new intention — that isn't getting lost."

Ana leant back in her chair so that her face was lifted into the candle-light. It seemed exaggeratedly long and white; the black silk patch lay close and sad along her right cheekbone. Antonio appraised her calmly, shackled to his passionate intention.

"No," Ana said. "I suppose that isn't getting lost—or needn't be."

He came and stood by her chair.

"Then you understand what has happened to me? You know what I am going to ask?"

"It's I who'll ask," she said. "Make no mistake—it's I who'll do the asking."

She spoke very quietly, but in new sensitiveness he heard her words as if they were a hard, imperative call. I have no clue to her, he told himself admonitorily; I have no light. What is this coolness that I have never met before? What is this mad tranquillity?

He thought of the king, and even wondered if he was asleep then in his narrow bed at El Escorial—or praying, perhaps? Pray for me, Philip; pray for your servant. He laid the rag doll on a stool and took Ana's hand.

"Are you thinking of the king?" she asked.

"How did you know?"

"You're very near me—it seems natural to see what you think."

Antonio laughed. He had a sudden long view of what he and Ana were about to risk; he saw their future actions as from all angles at once, worldly, sensual and moral, and the vision made him laugh aloud against his own panic. "We'll have good reason to."

She looked down at their joined hands, considering them, it seemed to him, as if they were the hands of strangers. "I wonder what you really want from me," she said.

"So do I," he said. "I think I want the chance to find that out."

"You ask a lot."

"I do."

"I'm very grateful to you."

An hour ago, she thought, perhaps five minutes ago I hadn't even imagined this which I am now about to take. And I don't know that I want it. But I want to find that out.

"You say disconcerting things," said Perez.

"There's no need really to say anything."

"I agree. Still—there's something on the tip of your tongue?"

"Yes. Something unwise. It's only this. I'm nearly thirty-seven, and I'm said to have had more power in my hands sometimes than any woman in Spain. Yet this is only the second time in my life that I've decided anything for myself."

"When was the other time?"

She bit her lip, and Perez felt her hand tighten against his.

"That was a mistake," she said.

He was touched by the droop of her shoulders as she spoke. He fell on his knees before her.

He smells like a woman, she thought amusedly—like a very expensive and fastidious woman.

Yet her attention was not wholly his, for she had reminded herself of Ruy in his coffin, and of the Discalced Carmelites singing, as they had used to, in her convent at Pastrana. But that was absurd, she thought; that was beyond my strength. Coldly she shut Mother Teresa from her thought, and laid her hand upon Antonio's scented hair. I'm only seeking pleasure now, she told herself, and as she bent above her lover she smiled again—in surprise at her situation. But more than at that she smiled at her sense of inexperience.

THE SECOND CHAPTER   (DECEMBER 1577)

I

Bernardina Cavero hated riding and hated cold weather. But she liked to see life, and she agreed with Ana that it was more easily viewed from a saddle than from within a coach. Also she derived much entertainment in these days from close observation of her mistress. Ana rode a beautiful Andalucian mare, a roan, whose cavortings had no influence at all on the dueña's stolid mount, a heavy Castilian beast of great reliability.

"I don't know how you tolerate that exhausted old battle-charger," Ana said. "He must be most fatiguing. No, children! Ana, Fernando! Don't you hear me? We're going home now! Ride ahead of them, Jaime," she said to the groom at her side, "and round them up."

"Thank God!" said Bernardina. "How I loathe physical exercise."

"You'd get enormous if it wasn't for me," said Ana.

"Yes. Wouldn't that be restful?"

The two children, on small clipped mules, came cantering back with Jaime, their harness bells jingling.

"But we didn't even get as far as St. Joseph's well," Fernando grumbled.

"Next time," said Ana. The two little riders looked sweet and rosy, tight-packed in dark velvet and fur. "Poor Bernardina's nose is almost falling off with cold—look! And you know I swore to Nurse that you'd be in before the Angelus."

The party swung their horses out of the Retiro Wood and towards the half-frozen high road. They passed other riders, many of whom bowed ceremoniously to Ana, or looked admiringly at her or at the children. The trees stood stiff in winter armour; voices and hoofs rang clearly through the frosty quiet.

"It'd be lovely to go on riding here long after dark," said Ana.

"Let's do it!" said Fernando.

"God forbid!" said Bernardina.

"Alas! We can't, Fernán," his mother said. "We have to lead respectable lives."

"What's 'respectable'?" said little Ana.

"Well—you are, darling."

"It's because we know the king so well," Fernando explained to his sister. "There, Mother!" He pointed with his whip down an avenue of the wood. "There's the place where you first met the king—didn't you—when you were a little girl?"

"Yes—just along there. But he was only a prince then. And he was riding with your father."

"And you were riding with *your* father," said little Ana.

Bernardina and Ana laughed to each other, for that piece of conversation was a ritual of every return from the Retiro with these two children.

"I wonder when *you'll* meet a husband and a prince in the wood, Baby Ana?" Bernardina said.

"Any day now," said Anichu.

They rode into Madrid by the east gate, the Puerta del Sol. The open square was crowded and noisy; it was still clear day, but there were lights already in some windows, and the chestnut men were out with their braziers. Jaime and the second groom edged the party together and flanked it carefully.

"I'd love some chestnuts," said Fernando.

"Nonsense," said Bernardina. "There are loads of them at home."

"But they don't roast them so well at home—are we going by the Plaza Mayor, Mother?"

"If you like, darling."

"And just down to the Cebada Market for a minute?" said little Ana.

"Oh, that's a bit far, my pet?"

"Just to the little almond-paste woman?"

"All right, greedy—but what terrible greedies you are!"

"Anyone would think there wasn't a crumb of anything in the house," said Bernardina. "And of course it doesn't matter at all if I get a death-colic from this cold——"

"Well, let's ride faster and get warm," said Ana.

They trotted through the Plaza Mayor and by narrow, crowded streets to the gay market. The almond-paste dealer brought her trays to them, and Anichu and Fernando chose some little men and women made of nougat. The old woman kissed the children, Bernardina paid her for the sweets, and Ana smiled at her and thanked her.

"I think she's her own model for those little men and women," Ana said as they rode away.

"I expect so," Anichu said gravely, studying one of the nougat figures with care before she licked it.

In the Calle Mayor, where the great merchants had their shops, a fat man in a doorway bowed almost to the ground in salutation to the Princess.

Ana reined in her mare a little.

"Jaime, tell Don Pedro Garcia that I expect him at the palace at noon to-morrow."

Jaime rode to the kerb, and the cavalcade slowed down.

Bernardina eyed Ana gravely.

"I hear from Diego—and others," she said, "that Garcia is more unscrupulous than any jeweller in Paris—let alone in Spain."

"He *knows* about jewels," Ana said.

"They're certainly a new fad of yours, my dear."

"Oh, *I* don't care for them particularly; as you know, I never did," said Ana coolly.

Jaime returned and bowed to his mistress, and the horses fell into a trot again.

Bernardina tried not to smile too appreciatively, but she liked audacity, and she was alert to the game which, without a word said as to its rules, she and Ana had engaged upon this winter. The scandalous fact which underlay their game excited, and sometimes frightened her. She knew more about it, she hoped, than any person in Madrid besides the two whom it so passionately involved; but until Ana spoke of it to her, she knew that she must give no sign. Yet clearly Ana knew that her *dueña* knew the mad thing she was doing, and one day she would talk of it with her; for she had no other *confidante*, and their years together had surely made them trust each other?

Bernardina was not high-principled or committed to ideals of loyalty. Rather, she was a gossipy woman, discreetly loose and sympathetic to looseness. She came from the south, and mocked at the rigidities and etiquette of Castile; the religiosity in high life around the king she found ridiculous, and, without malice, but simply because her cynical and sensual nature preferred life thus, she liked to perceive betrayals, into fleshiness, into venality, into what you will of sin, among these thin-lipped aristocrats. But she knew her place and her duty; and if she was shrewd she was also kind towards her fellows in general.

To Ana, however, she had long since given affection. She was forty-eight now and in her twentieth year of service with the Princess; her husband was employed as a clerk on the Pastrana estates and as assistant tutor to Ana's sons; her only child was being trained as a bailiff at Pastrana; thus her chief interests ran through the pattern of Ana's. Ruy Gomez had been a good employer, and Ana carried on the government of his household as he had designed it; so Bernardina was content with her position in life, and naturally had grown attached to her benefactress. But more than that—she persistently found Ana enigmatic to a degree which she was too lazy to measure, but which kept in their association a touch of question and wonder that was novel for Bernardina.

Ana often maddened her; often she had felt contempt for the girlish unadventurousness with which she rode past occasions of adventure; often she had gasped in sheer, vulgar astonishment before the story-book Castilianism of Ana de Mendoza and that great lady's comical unconsciousness of her own absurdity; often she had thought that the brilliant Ruy Gomez was, domestically at least, the most complacent ass in history. Yet she loved them both increasingly with the years, and she enjoyed, maliciously and kindly, the close view of the great world which their life allowed her. And always Ana, not knowing what she did, kept the hint of question, of surmise astir. In her happiness and afterwards, at Ruy's death, in her foolishly misdirected grief, in her virtue, in her simplicity, she always seemed to Bernardina—who could hardly formulate the fancy, indeed—as if waiting, or as if unexpressed; as if there was something in her forgotten or mislaid, in the lack of which she might never be truly explained.

This hint conveyed itself to Bernardina more as a sensation than a thought—and she had found it somewhat foolish in herself, as if she were inclining to the poetic or the mock-melancholy about a life which lacked for nothing, about a woman who was only not spoilt because, in her naïve arrogance, she was beyond the power of spoilers. Yet the sensation was constant, and bred a kind of tenderness, a fixed indulgence in the *dueña*, which by now was love indeed, and so proceeded, of its nature, to loyalty. Love and loyalty unexpressed, and hardly shaped into a thought—for Bernardina was laconic, and preferred to amuse than to caress.

But now there was no occasion for mock-melancholy. Now, when it was almost too late, the scatheless and self-sufficient aristocrat had paused for a human commonplace, had allowed it to overtake her. Bernardina ought to have been pleased, and often told herself she was pleased. She preferred love-affairs to virtue; she liked intrigue and disliked austerity; she had always desired that Ana might enjoy herself on what she considered natural terms, and through the sweets of normal weakness.

Yet, if possible what had happened was *too* normal? At first Bernardina had approved cold-bloodedly—though in vast surprise—of what she perceived. The thing was begun in caprice, she would swear, and was pursued by some very private form of calculation—in cool pursuit of pleasure. Whether because pleasure was an unknown country, or having been lost must be trodden once more before the end, Bernardina could not guess. But pleasure was Ana's quarry a month or two ago. And for the man who brought it to her? Pleasure of the senses yes, and another kind of personal satisfaction too. Something to do with pride and politics and the love of danger and the need to prove his grasp on his every smallest worldly whim.

But now—the man was impassioned, infatuated. And Bernardina, who knew much about his secret life, surmised empirically from it and from the degree of his present frenzy that he would have burnt up every cinder of this desire within, at best, a year from now. Unless indeed the fabulous generosity and greatness of the lady could keep his worldliness entranced—but that would not be passion, let him simulate with all his skill.

No matter. These things were better brief and hot. Safer too. There could be no hope of secrecy. Servants were doubtless on the nod and wink already—great Heavens, what did Ana think that they were made of? But the Eboli servants liked on the whole to retain their posts, and Bernardina guessed that if an indiscretion of their mistress did not go too far or last too long, they and their talk would be manageable. And short-lived scandals seldom did much harm. If they did, where would any of us be? thought the *dueña*.

Thus she debated often nowadays, and reassured herself— and enjoyed her own common sense and its conclusions.

But a shadow moved below these, its shape evading her. A new kind of hint about her mistress teased her now, and even, in her less guarded moments, made her angry. For Ana was no longer as she had been in September and October. She was not at the beck of pleasure now. She was in love, Bernardina believed; and what so strangely mettled a creature would make of that condition the *dueña* had no means of guessing. But she was not romantic and she feared the prospect. Moreover, at present it sometimes seemed to her that whatever Ana might henceforward make of love, love already had the power almost to make her seem ridiculous.

"God bless you, Bernardina! That was a terrible sneeze!"

"Rodrigo says Bernardina's is the loudest sneeze in Madrid," said Fernando. "Did you know that, Mother?"

The Angelus, which rang at sunset in Madrid, sounded from Santa Maria Almundena.

"There, we're late," said Ana.

The entire life of the street paused at the bell, and the cavalcade with it. Everyone made the sign of the Cross and said the customary "Hail Marys" and a prayer for the faithful departed. The horses were reined in for this on the corner of Plaza Santa Maria and Calle Segovia.

Bernardina smiled as she prayed, for they were drawn up at the very porch of Antonio Perez's palace. A fine place for this family to be saying the Angelus, she thought, and glanced at Ana to see if she was smiling, but found that her face was perfectly composed.

As they rode across the Plaza, Anichu pointed back to the house they had just passed.

"Doña Juana lives there with Don Antonio," she said.

"They have a tremendous lot of children," said Fernando.

"Yes," said Anichu. "And they have one tiny, tiny one— I saw it. It's so tiny I don't think it can open its eyes yet. Why don't you have a little one like that, Mama?"

"I'm too old, Anichu. Anyway, *you* finished me. You were the last straw, my precious baby."

They rode through the gateway of the Pastrana palace, and dismounted in the court-yard.

II

Antonio Perez threw more wood on the bright fire and then bent to warm his hands. He had just left the king's workroom after a long conference, and his own office cheered him by contrast. Philip is an uncomfortable poor devil, he thought. He rang a handbell, and moved towards his writing-table.

"Bring some wine," he said to the servant, "and tell them to send me in something to eat later on. Something simple that won't delay me—a sausage or something, and some bread. And have I plenty of candles? I shall be here late to-night."

He sat down to work. Despatch-boxes were stacked on shelves by his side; the table was strewn with papers. He trimmed the candle nearest him and began to cut some quills.

The Cabinet meeting in the morning had been long and tricky; in the early afternoon he had got through much work with his secretaries; at five o'clock Philip had sent for him, and the ensuing three hours' debate meant—as did almost all private sessions with the king—secret and troublesome readjustment of many decisions painfully reached with the Cabinet.

I shall be here half the night, he reflected. Ah, but she likes the small hours; she suits me well in that. He smiled—a very brilliant, contented smile. Then he thought with pitying amusement of Mateo Vasquez, whom he had met a moment ago in the corridor—on his way in his turn to Philip's room. Vasquez, a very earnest priest, was Perez's rival in the Cabinet for Philip's confidence. Poor Mateo! If he's only *going* into conference now he'll certainly be working until breakfast-time. Good for his vow of celibacy. And now in the next three hours Philip will rescind with Mateo, or *pretend* to rescind, everything he and I have just pretended to settle. And when I send him to-night's memoranda in the morning, they'll all come back covered with marginal second thoughts—arising from talk with Mateo. But *I* won't be told that, of course. It's miraculous that we manage, between us, to keep his kingdom in motion at all!

The pens were ready. He chose one, and settled to work. In a minute he was engrossed in re-drafting a very private despatch to the new ambassador in Paris, de Vargas Mejia. He might joke about the multiplicity of his labours, but he loved the work and had a very fine grasp on Philip's peculiar and devious foreign policy. He gave it industrious attention, and never allowed his strong bent for pleasure to deflect him from the business of the State.

He worked in peace for more than an hour. He got up sometimes to search in files, or merely to pace about the room, or stand and stare into the fire. Sometimes he took a mouthful of bread from the tray they had brought him;

sometimes he chewed absent-mindedly at a chicken-leg.
Then back to his table, to a new pen and the State paper
spread before him.

When he heard the door open he did not look up at once.
None of his clerks was in the Alcázar at this hour—it could
only be a boy to attend to the fire. But he did not care to have
people fussing round, so when he came to the end of a note
he lifted his head, feeling impatient.

Juan de Escovedo was standing at the other side of the
table.

" 'Escoda' in person!" said Perez, and was pleased to see
the other start at hearing that appellation. " 'Escoda' unannounced—and indeed uninvited! How did you get
admitted to my room at this hour, may I ask?"

"Don't be silly," said Escovedo shortly. "Every servant
in the Alcázar knows *me*."

"Yes, but they know me too, and know that to disobey
my orders is a quick way to lose a good job."

"You're getting very arrogant, Antonio."

"Am I?" He paused to pour some wine. "Perhaps I am.
Will you drink?"

Escovedo shook his head. He stood rigidly, his dark, long
face unrelaxed and solemn. Perez eyed him with calculation
and dislike. He was a most unwelcome visitor, all the more
unwelcome because he was in these months a very great
weight on the mind of the Secretary of State. But now he was
here, might it not be useful to Philip to make one clear, firm
appeal to whatever was left of political judgment in this man?

As he pondered this and his possible approach to any such
appeal, he carefully folded and covered all the papers on the
desk, and closed the lids of despatch-boxes.

Escovedo almost smiled as he watched him.

"No need for that, Antonio. I haven't your skill in reading
other people's letters."

"I believe not. Still, I take no risks, 'Escoda'. You don't

like my making free with your new Papal pet-name? Ah well, you see the fact that I can, is proof that Pope Gregory and his ambassador aren't as tidy with their desks as I am with mine——"

"We all know your methods——"

"Yes, I'm thorough. I get to know everything. But you ought to have remembered that sooner, Juan."

Escovedo drew himself up to a still greater rigidity, and spoke with fanatical and solemn disgust.

"You have become an entirely corrupt and dishonourable man, Antonio Perez."

Perez leant back in his chair and smiled.

"For one who, during at least two years, has plotted in consistent dishonour against his king, who made him whatever he is, and to whom he owes everything, that's an audacious and comic pronouncement."

Escovedo waved the comment off.

"I've come to talk to you of private matters."

"I don't give a curse what you've come to talk about. You've no business coming here at all at this hour, and without appointment. But now that you are here, you'll talk about whatever I choose. And first, will you be so good as to sit down?"

Escovedo shook his head.

"No? Then I'll stand up. No need to get a stiff neck from looking at you." He rose, walked to the fire and threw a log on it. When he turned his face again to Escovedo its expression had altered. He looked boyish and serious.

"Juan," he said, "we used to be friends. And we learnt our profession together, from the best of all masters." Escovedo drew in a sharp breath, as if in pain, but Antonio went on talking. "Before I go into any of the politics of this mess you're making, therefore, I'm going to give you some strictly personal instructions—and they are exactly what he, Ruy Gomez, would give you——"

"Will you in God's name keep *that* name off your lips?"

"Don't be such a fool! Listen to me, Juan. Before God I ask you to listen now—for *your own sake*. There are three things that you *must* do: (*a*) Write no more of those insane letters to the king; (*b*) resign at once from the service of Don Juan; (*c*) retire to the country, and live a private life for at least five years. Will you—for *your own sake*, man!—undertake to do those three simple things, and do them at once?"

"Please save your breath. I repeat that I have not come here to discuss my political work with you."

"Your political work! Oh God!" Antonio moved uneasily about the room, then came back and faced Escovedo again. "Then you persist? You commit yourself to a planned course of—treason?"

Treason was a dangerous word at Philip's Court. Sinister memories and rumours drooped about it. Therefore Antonio used it now deliberately. It produced an effect.

"Treason? To differ from *your* party in the Cabinet as to policy in the Netherlands isn't treason, Perez. I serve Spain as I was commissioned to; in promoting the legitimate and valiant projects of Don Juan of Austria."

"Legitimate projects of a bastard!"

"You are a bastard, Perez."

"Yes—but a commoner. So I can't howl for the canopy and insignia of a legitimate prince of Spain—like your precious Don Juan! And by the way, he can have his canopy and insignia—though without a vestige of title to them—any time he likes, if he'll just have the grace to try to please his long-suffering brother in one or two matters of State. Philip is nothing if not indulgent to his relatives! But to come back to the point—we were talking of treason, Juan——"

"You were."

"Yes—I was. Now look here—you know, because I've told you so plainly again and again, and so has the king, more circuitously—you know that here in this Alcázar we know all your plots and European negotiatings probably as soon as you know them yourselves. I'm not going to go on about 'treason' now, because it's merely childish to pretend that Don Juan's dreams aren't just a flaming challenge to the king. I merely used the word so that you may know that it's being used here about your activities—and so warned, you can proceed as you like. But I propose to talk policy for a minute——" Escovedo moved impatiently—"and you're going to listen.

"Firstly: we are having peace in the Netherlands. You've smashed that up for us this summer, but, believe me, we are getting it back. Thanks to Juan's recent nonsensical 'victories', we may indeed have to send Parma back with some troops to police the place awhile, as you seem to have it in wonderful confusion. But as you know, a commission is on its way to Brussels now, to re-establish the Perpetual Edict at all costs. And the Estates are going to be asked to choose a new governor—you know all that?—instead of our precious Juan. They are to have anyone they like—probably one of their beloved Archdukes from the Holy Roman—there's Matthais or Ferdinand—oh, they're to have their pick. And our armies are coming home, and there is to be peace."

Escovedo smiled quietly.

"Juan knows the armies—you don't."

"You say a thing like that, and then object to the word 'treason'! By God, man, you must trust insanely to our old affection! Meantime, no matter who knows the armies, Philip pays them, and he will pay them no longer. So much, then, for the Netherlands, and your disastrous efforts there.

"Now, the next thing: we are having no chivalrous volunteering into France, if you please, and absolutely *no* tomfool offers of Spanish troops to the Duke of Guise! Will you once more and firmly instruct Don Juan as to that! Why, Guise hasn't even asked for his assistance—and he's far too wily to risk exasperating Philip at this juncture.

We are keeping out of France's private affairs—understand?"

"A holy war is the affair of any Christian!"

"A holy war?" Antonio laughed. "Oh Juan, what's happened to your old acumen? What has Curlyhead *done* to you? But 'holy war' leads me neatly up to our last and strongest prohibition. Listen, my friend. Don Juan's invasion of England will not take place. That, as you know, was settled years ago. The king *did* consider it at one time, uncertainly and in my opinion *madly*. But he won't have it now at any price, is that clear? And he's very angry at this new and much extended revival of the plan. Oh yes! We know all about the new offers! The Pope's blessing and the Pope's money and the Pope's men! We know that our Charmer is to set free Mary of Scotland and marry her and become King of Scotland. We know that he is to sunder all England and restore it to the Faith; and capture Elizabeth, of course, and give *her* a turn in Sheffield Castle. A 'holy war', indeed. Upon my oath, Juan, it's the most wonderful daydream that has *ever* come to my attention. It's so wonderful because it doesn't bear the remotest relation to existent political facts, or trends, in England or Scotland or any part of Northern Europe. It really is the perfect dream. For one thing—it would enchant the Netherlands, because at its first move it would drive Elizabeth and all England straight into the outstretched arms of the Prince of Orange. France would be ravished with joy at what she would rightly foresee as the end of Spain; the Holy Roman Empire would be magnificently amused. And Elizabeth—before you imprisoned her —well, Elizabeth would just defeat you, Juan."

"You are absurd and cynical," said Escovedo. "Worst of all, as Spain's Minister of State, you are shockingly indifferent to her spiritual responsibility in Europe. But if you *will* discuss what you clearly refuse to examine impartially——"

"I've been examining it for the last two years! You've forced me to. You've wasted more of our time here, and caused Philip more anxiety than any other one problem in external affairs. The king has been extraordinarily patient. He loves Juan, and he has wanted to give him his head, and let him test his own ambitions and find his place in government. But no one could have foreseen this development of blind, supernatural vanity, or—worse still—the power of that vanity to unhinge the judgment of a trained man of politics like you. However, I have warned you, for the last time. And if these lunatic plottings go an inch further I take no responsibility for your fate, or Don Juan's. Philip is extremely embittered against you—far more so than he will let you see just yet. But you know his methods in anger. I don't have to tell *you* anything about the complicated character of the king."

"You talk as if you owned the king," said Escovedo. "But I am openly here in Madrid as Don Juan's emissary to him. I am here to argue with him the advisability for Spain of certain actions we propose in Northern Europe. I see Philip fairly often, as you know, and I am in correspondence with him. I know his character well, and I know therefore that he is probably at present more strongly opposed to my propositions than he lets me see. I even accept your view that he is very angry with us just now, and that therefore my career, and Don Juan's, and even our lives, may be in danger."

When Escovedo said that the two men looked at each other steadily.

"Go on," said Perez.

"But it is my duty to plead this cause, and to pit my conviction against yours. Philip is, after all, a man of deep religious faith—that is where your influence ceases to count, and mine begins. I may not influence him directly, but I can find those who can. Naturally, since we are neither of us 'treasonous', Don Juan and I realise that we can only undertake what we see to do when Philip grants us his blessing, or at least his tolerance. But if he does, he will live to rejoice in the event, and we shall be content to lay all the honour before His Majesty. But he has a clear duty now to the Eternal Faith—and Don Juan is God's instrument, waiting to his hand."

Antonio Perez looked about the room as if totally at a loss for means of expression. Slowly he poured more wine and sipped it slowly.

"Eloquent and idealistic," he said after a pause. "But unluckily I have done more deciphering than you know. I didn't sketch out the whole of Don Juan's dream to you just now. There is an epilogue. When Juan is King of Scotland and England, and Elizabeth is in the Tower, he plans to have more to do than be embraced by the Pope and enjoy the celebrated pleasures of Mary's bed. There is a codicil— something about bringing all your new great armies and fleets from the north to Santander, and undertaking to rescue Spain from the inertia and cynicism of her present ruler. That has all been noted down in my private archives, Juan."

Escovedo flung his arms apart.

"And it isn't true!" he cried. "It's been flung in my face before, that vile and senseless tale! There is *no* plot against the king, never has been, never will be!"

"I've seen it in writing."

"Not in mine—or his! Oh, Don Juan gets angry some- times! Who wouldn't, with the king's eternal evasions and delays! And I've heard him lose his temper very indiscreetly, and say senseless things, of being the better ruler for Spain, and of invading, and so on. But those were only the briefest and silliest moments of exasperation. Even so, I have reproved him for them—and I have feared that they were overheard."

"Such things creep into ambassadors' reports, and into despatches you know nothing of, 'Escoda'."

"And if they do, *you* should know how to value them. You are cynical and corrupt and opportunist now, as we all know

—and you are Philip's most corroding influence, from which it has become imperative to rouse and rescue him. Him and Spain. But you *are* astute—and you cannot fool yourself about my loyalty to the person of the king. You cannot, Perez!"

"In my work I never calculate on persons, as apart from what I see them do. A person more or less is of no account in state affairs—it is what he promotes and what he does that I have to reckon with. I see your recent actions and your future intentions, and I hold them to be invidious. So I am not interested in emotional recollections of the kind of person you are, or seemed to be. I only work on what I see you doing. And I intend to put an end to what you are doing now—because that is my duty. You're a brave man, and I used to think you intelligent, and I used to like you. But your present performances in statecraft are a danger to Spain—and so they will be stopped. I am not sentimental, Juan."

"No, you are *not* sentimental. And that brings me to *my* business here."

"You have no business here that isn't now concluded. I have given you my last instruction. Henceforward you know what is required of you—and you have been warned of the king's extreme displeasure. So good night. I'm very busy."

Perez walked back to his table and sat down.

Escovedo did not move.

"I shall say what I came here to say," he said. Perez did not look up from his work. "I have discovered that you are the lover of the Princess of Eboli."

Perez looked up now, in well-calculated amazement.

"You have what?"

"You heard me."

"Indeed I did." Antonio lay back in his chair and laughed. "I heard you, you scurrilous old woman you!" He paused. "I have been a Secretary of State for eleven years now. For ten of those years I have been a satisfactorily married man—I have eight dear children, Juan. Yet in that period I have been 'discovered' to be the lover of at least eleven ladies of the nobility, most of them—so far as I know—almost as high-bred and of as impeccable virtue as the great lady you have just named, you ass. Yet they still hold their heads up in society, and so do I and my wife and family—and I am more than ever a Secretary of State."

"I have always known those stories to be true of you——"

"Indeed? That's rather generous of you, Juan! But you attribute powers to me—of every kind—which truly I don't possess. And now will you please be a good fellow and clear off to a more suitable place with your kitchen-boy's tattle?"

"You are not going to have your bluff called, I see. But that doesn't alter anything. I know that what I have said is true—and for Ruy Gomez's sake, for his honour and his children, I protest with my whole soul against such a dis-graceful situation—oh God!" he moved at last, pacing a short distance across the room. "Oh God! He was our friend and father, Antonio! He worshipped and cherished her! I was executor of his will, as you know, and he entrusted many of her and her children's affairs to me! I knew his heart in these private things. And so did you! Ah Christ, Antonio, so did you!" He paused, but Perez continued to stare at him in cool amazement. "And now—this hideous, backstairs dishonour in his house and bed!"

"'Backstairs dishonour' is good! The lady you are traducing so effectively is an honour whom many greater men than you and I would have climbed any old stairs to reach. We've known that always, Juan. We used to debate their chances—including the king's, do you re-member?—here in this very Alcázar, when we worked together down the corridor, in the secretaries' room. With Ruy alive to be dishonoured. But you were young then, and even a touch humorous."

"Ruy was alive then, and could be trusted to manage his own wife."

"Agreed. But say this notion of yours were true—say, for the fun of the thing, that the Princess of Eboli *were* having a love-affair with, well, *you*, or me, or the French Ambassador—what of it?"

"She is having a love-affair as you call it! And not with me, and not with the French Ambassador! And I tell you it is intolerable."

"Why? Because it's not with you?"

Escovedo brushed the flippancy aside as if it were a gnat.

"Do you really require to know why? She's elderly——"

"About eight years younger than you and I, if I remember rightly——"

"She's ugly——"

"*Belle laide*," said Antonio. "Magnificently beautiful, I've always thought. But then my taste in women is extraordinarily good. I take what I can get, I grant you—but all the same, I know what I like." He laughed and stood up again. "All right, old friend, you've broken up my night's work to tell me that Her Highness of Eboli is elderly and ugly, and is therefore to be held in abhorrence for consoling her miserable life with a love-affair. If the only way of getting you to go home now is to say that you're right about all this, naturally I say it. You're perfectly right, Escovedo, and your zeal for chastity is consoling. And now—please may I get on with my work?"

"I would have done anything at any time for Ruy Gomez. He knew that. And just because he's gone I will not see his name dishonoured in intrigue, I tell you, his children rendered absurd and their fortunes squandered on a venal, climbing jackanapes whose fame and destiny were made by him!"

"Very good. Go to it—since you so conceive your duty."

There was a pause in which the two looked at each other. Antonio's face was cold and neutral; Escovedo's mottled with anger. Yet when he spoke again his voice was so steady that it might have been Perez's.

"It may be necessary for me to tell the king about it," he said.

Perez seemed to weigh this remark judicially before he answered.

"Indulging you in your hypothesis, which you haven't even *tried* to prove to me——"

"I don't have to, to you!"

"Indulging you, I say—may I remind you that Philip is still a bit in love with Ana de Mendoza? On his own peculiar terms, I grant you, but still, I'd say he's in love. Apart from that, he's very, very fond of her."

"All the more reason why he should see her as she is."

"Maybe. Only, he doesn't like bringers of bad news. Oh Escovedo, you fool—are you in love with death?"

"It comes to every man."

"No. Some men run to find it. And believe me, if just now you add to your errors with Don Juan the madness of making this grave accusation against someone so dear to the king—if you do that, you are finished."

"What matter? I shall have saved Ruy Gomez's honour."

"But he came from Portugal! He was a man of sense. He didn't have this Castilian disease about honour! Moreover, how will you have 'saved' it? By starting up an enormous and laughable scandal about his wife and family? Ah, poor Ruy! How he'd shudder at your crassness!"

"Or at your cynicism."

"Oh yes—at that too. He used to warn me against it—but one can only be oneself in the end. You, however, are being somewhat excessively yourself of late. But don't you see? If you do tell Philip what you suspect about the Princess, it will take him years, very possibly, to decide whether or not to believe you. Meantime he will torture himself, and take vengeance for his discomfort on you. It is even probable that he will have you despatched—you know how easily he does these things—before he makes up his mind to ask you for proof. But say he *does* ask you for proofs——"

"I have them."

"Aye! Against the massed oaths, threats and testimonies of all the Mendozas of Spain and all their vassals and cousins and chaplains and servants; against the iron ring of loyalty and if necessary perjury which Ruy Gomez's household could instantly form about his widow; against Madrid's immediate sympathy with any woman so preposterously singled out for censorship; above all, against Philip's vain and megalomaniac desire to have you vigorously disproved—for if he doesn't love Ana, believe me, he loves the legend of their love, he loves the gossip and the echo of it, and its reminder of gayer days, he loves to think, perhaps, that only their shared love of Ruy prevented him and Ana from giving really flagrant scandal long ago; also he loves to think that whatever he prizes no man touches save with his royal permission. He gave her to Ruy—so that was all right. But he's not giving her away again, whether or not he wants her—so you see, against all that, above all against Philip's colossal vanity, you'd bring your proofs—a bought footman or sewing maid or pantry-boy—servants too young and raw to know that you don't sell the great for a few ducats, and that if you do, that finishes you for employment by any majordomo in Spanish society henceforward. No, no—I don't care what you think you know against Ana de Mendoza—as I once loved you, I implore you now for your own sake to forget it. Don Juan of Austria has led you quite far enough into the displeasure of the king—much too far for my liking, I promise you. In sanity's name forgo this other dreadful whim. It's unbecoming anyway. It's back door stuff—and very, very shocking from you."

Escovedo smiled a little.

"That's a good speech—in difficult circumstances, Antonio. You certainly are a trained diplomatist."

"Yes. So well trained that I see diplomacy behind all this gloomy and 'honourable' fuss of yours to-night. I see your game, in fact. But you'll lose it, every way. You're on the wrong tack. Consider well, however, what I've just said. He's a brave man indeed who tampers with Philip's personal illusions."

"I have usually been as brave as the average."

"Then let that suffice. I for one like your being alive, 'Escoda'."

"Thank you. Good night."

"Good night."

After Escovedo left him, Antonio sat still at his desk for some minutes, with his eyes half-closed. When midnight rang from the chapel across the court-yard he opened his eyes and began to unfold the papers he had covered during the interview. Alert and composed, he set to work again.

III

Ana heard his quiet footsteps in the long sitting-room. The door which led from there to her bedroom was half-open.

"You may come in," she said.

Antonio entered the bedroom and crossed to her bed. He carried a tray with wine and glasses, and smiled from it to her.

"Do you mind if I drink?"

"Do I ever?"

He set down the tray and sat on the edge of the bed.

Two candles were burning in a branch-candlestick beside her. She lay low on her pillow; her hair fell cloudily away from her high forehead; the black silk patch, narrow and tragic, fitted closely along her right cheek-bone. She stretched her beautiful hand to him and he took it in his.

"You're very thin, Ana, too thin. You seem almost as if you're not there at all when you lie flat like that."

"I wasn't expecting you to-night."

"I won't stay long. But I find it almost impossible now to pass your gate. I'm bound to you." He relinquished her hand and poured himself some wine. "Are you bound to me?"

"Yes. But I can pass your gate."

He smiled.

"Well—you have to, after all."

"I think that wouldn't matter if I couldn't."

"You mean you'd go in—to Juana's house?"

"I'd have to, if I couldn't pass it."

They laughed together.

"Thank God then that you can pass it," said Antonio.

"Yes. Because I'm troublesome, really."

He mused over her, sipping wine.

"That's true, I'm certain. And yet—you've never given anyone the least bit of trouble."

She made no answer. He looked at her and guessed that she was thinking of Mother Teresa de Jesús, and the Discalced Carmelites at Pastrana.

"But no one could know you at all well," he went on, ignoring her thought, "without apprehending that. The sense of threat in you."

She laughed.

"I'm no judge, as you know," she said, "but I think you must be a superlatively good lover."

"Actually, I am," he said gaily. "But why mention it now?"

"Because you come here, weary from your old Pope and Netherlands and Bey of Algiers, at two in the morning and you sit down and start talking, as if there was nothing else in the world, about *me*."

"Silly one, ah silly, inexperienced Ana, that's why I come to you! Because you always play that trick on me, and yet never, never let me see how it's done."

"I have no tricks—truly," she said. "What's troubling you, Anton?"

"Nothing now. Your watchman welcomed me in as kindly as usual just now. I passed that young footman you like, Estéban, in the patio; and in the corridor outside your rooms one of your maids bowed to me. Is it—is it all right for you, Ana?"

"No, it's all wrong. I don't need my chaplain to tell me that. But it isn't the servants' business. It's mine. It's also yours—and your wife's. No one else's."

"You cheat—that isn't what I meant."

"But alas, it's all I mean. I wish I were sophisticated like other ladies. What do they do to help you over this worry about the watchman and so on?"

"Ah! They get up to all sorts of plans and dodges—most fatiguing!"

"That's what I thought—fatiguing. And in spite of them my *dueña* always knows everything that everyone in Madrid is doing."

"I expect so. Does she know what you are doing?"

"Bernardina knows what happens in Madrid. But she doesn't always know why things happen. However, she can be surprised without fussing. She has good sense."

Antonio leant his back against a post at the foot of the bed and looked towards her with an expression of puzzled pleasure in his eyes.

"There ought to be more light," he said. "You look a bit too tragic just now—yes, even when you smile. Shall I give you some wine?" She shook her head. He refilled his own glass, and leant back again to the silk-curtained post. "There's a foreign painter in Toledo, a Greek called Theotocopuli——"

"The king was talking to me about him the other day——"

"Oh?"

"He's considering some canvases from him for El Escorial——"

"What good luck for the foreigner!"

"But Philip isn't at all sure that he likes his work."

"Neither am I, indeed. Very hysterical, saints and ecstasies. I was in his studio not long ago, with the Archbishop. By the way, did I tell you that that good friend of yours is getting his red hat? I'm glad—aren't you? But about this Greek, Theotocopuli—the point is that a lot of his praying boys and uplifted Annunciations and things remind me of *you*. In fact, I think that perhaps he ought to paint you. However, you'll have to grow a bit saintly first—at present he's not interested in worldliness."

"I'm not either, very much."

"Ana! You are the very epitome of it!"

"Perhaps that's why it doesn't interest me."

"But aren't you interested in yourself?"

"Immensely. That's why you're here. That's why I'm your lover."

"Ah! An experiment?"

To answer that as her answer came would be pompous and egotistical. So she laughed at herself instead. "Don't be hurt—you make me talk selfishly, you are so gracious. But you know, now, that I'm in love."

She said that and knew that it was true, true in the way she had surmised it might be before she made the experiment of taking him. Yet, pronounced, the sentence always struck her as over-blown, and she always felt her soul cock an eyebrow at it. For it sounded as if it were important, as if it proved something and justified the utterer. Whereas all it did was put her in her place, among sinners.

That was well enough. She was a sinner indeed, and at present shamelessly content to discover that she could in fact pursue the fabled pleasures of sexual intercourse to that point of irrational, participatory understanding and hunger which she had awaited legitimately in marriage, but which somehow there had just evaded her. Yet it was ironic to come to it illicitly at last, and find it accompanied by no more than a conventional, almost a comedy, sense of sin. It was ironic to feel like a loose woman. The fault—or the joke, rather, of that, since she would not censure him—was in Antonio's character. She suspected now that long ago when Philip, in the full flush of his sensual arrogance and restlessness, had attracted her so strongly, she had not become his mistress simply because he could not forgo the final obligation of his personal morality. An adultery here or there was nothing to Philip the king when he was young; but the sin against Ruy Gomez was outside his courage. She would never know if it had been outside hers, because Philip, for all his love-making, had never confronted her with the final decision. Theologians would say that the present sin against Juana de Coëllo, Antonio's wife, was exactly what hers and Philip's would have been against Ruy. But neither she nor Philip would agree with the theologians; for Antonio Perez was naturally amoral, and had never, even as he uttered them, regarded his marriage-vows as more than a formality. Juana and his children would always have his duty, his kindness and his care; and she, Ana enchantingly as he loved her now, was simply another delightful and necessary loose woman. After all, Ana thought amusedly, one cannot break the sixth Commandment alone—and Antonio had never accepted its existence. So, when she said—just privately to her lover, for their joint pleasure and because it was true—that she was in love, she felt nevertheless that she was making heavy weather.

Not that she would eschew or deprecate storminess; indeed when she was young she had never dreamt that she would spend her life becalmed. She had been a spoilt and arrogant child of many tempests. She touched her black silk eye-shade now, and pressed her finger-tips against her empty eye-socket. That absurd disaster, that duel with the silly boy from Granada, her father's page—what *was* his name?—had been the first real check to her spontaneousness. The first and perhaps for ever the most effective. In her lifetime she had not become resigned—though no one had ever heard her say so, not Ruy and not her mother—to being one-eyed, *tuerta*. She was not vain in the coquettish sense, but from babyhood had taken satisfaction in the rightness, by her own standards, of her own appearance. Beauty, good aspect, in things and people, moved her very quickly; she was attracted or repelled decisively by physical attributes. So when— having challenged and punished an Andalusian jibe at Castile's claim of premiership among the kingdoms of Spain —she found herself disfigured, made grotesque for ever, the shock to her self-confidence was so profound that she understood that if she was to live with it at all it must be on terms of apparently blank dismissal. Nobody must regret or condone a misfortune which only she could measure. She wrote herself, fifteen-year-old child-wife, to tell her elderly husband in the Lowlands what had befallen her, and she was grateful to him for the unperturbed tenderness with which he replied to her letter. Thereafter, as he learnt very deftly, save sometimes to call her *Tuerta*, and once or twice to joke about her soldierly sacrifice to Castile's honour, Ruy had to leave her disfigurement entirely in her keeping, and guess or not how little or much it troubled her. Sometimes she thought that she was faithful to him and good and tame and lived as he desired her to live merely because she had lost one eye; and sometimes she thought that he also thought so. But nothing of this was said, and they grew happy together, and she wore her diamond patch with a nonchalance which the world admired.

Antonio leant along and took her hand and kissed it.

"What are you thinking about now?"

"A quarrel I was in when I was a little girl."

"I thought so," he said delicately, and she looked at him with caution. Often she suspected that his intuitions were very accurate. Yet he never betrayed more than a glint of those she did not choose to have him uncover.

She marvelled at the delicacy of feeling to be found in men, and wondered if perhaps she perceived it only because the very few she knew were overtrained in courtiership and diplomacy.

"Ah! I nearly forgot," she said, and laughed somewhat shyly as she pulled a small leather box from under her pillow and gave it to him. "See if you like it, Antón."

Giving him presents was a great delight and yet made her nervous, for he had a zest for baubles and adornments which she did not share, and so she was always afraid of mischoosing and disappointing him. In defence, she bought extravagantly and from the most fashionable dealers—but she liked, as far as possible, to like what she gave him. So, as her taste was as restrained as his was florid, every present was a hazard.

"Another present?" His eyes gleamed. "Oh but you mustn't, Ana! Is this for Christmas?"

"No, no. This is just for now."

It was a bracelet, heavy, lissom, set with large, clear topazes. It had a heart-shaped clasp of diamonds.

"You wear these things, my Frenchified *mignon*."

"Indeed I do—or shall! Oh Ana! It's disgracefully beautiful!"

"Is it? As you know, I'm never sure——"

He laughed.

"How I'm debasing you! How much I'm teaching you! And everything wrong!"

"Put it on."

"Shall I?" He clipped it round his wrist and flourished it about delightedly. "Oh, but it's lovely! Shocking, shocking, Ana!"

"It was made in Paris—but the topazes came from our own empire——"

"Spoils of the Conquistadores!"

"Yes. It seems right that our Secretary of State should have some."

"You most indulgent, wicked Ana!"

He laughed and kissed her. And she felt inevitable delight rising in them both, and she welcomed it and was glad. Yet her spirit was saying to her simultaneously that even sensuality and sin, when they were reluctantly and late allowed, should have more to expose than that one was as natural a sinner as the next woman, a vulgar, satisfactory and satisfied mistress. The spirit was saying still that the private life, however deprecatingly one chose to view it, must surely be about something more than the commonplace of any street or bed. There still must be a reason, Ana thought, for being oneself, and this is not it. Suffering perhaps, or conflict or faith or an argument or a test of some kind.

THE THIRD CHAPTER   (FEBRUARY 1578)

The Eboli children had not been in Madrid for Carnival since the year of their father's death, 1573.

"So we are not being let off the tiniest detail of pleasure-seeking," Ana told the old Marqués de Los Velez. "Bernardina and I are distracted with all their fusses and preparations."

The long, quiet sitting-room proclaimed the holiday. Masks and paper favours lay about; sugared fruits and marzipan tumbled out of boxes and little gilt baskets; and there was a wig of curly black hair—a man's wig—on a stand on Ana's writing-table.

De Los Velez pointed amusedly at this.

"But surely, Ana, you know that even *you* daren't impersonate a male character? It's against the law, dear child."

"Oh, that's not for me. Rodrigo is going to the Venetian Ambassador's masquerade to-morrow as his ancestor Santillana."

"Ah! The poet!"

"Yes. And of course Rodrigo's fair head mustn't be dyed —he's much too fond of it. So this wig has been very expensively made from study of the portrait of Santillana, at Infantado's house in Guadalajara."

"No trouble too great if Rodrigo is to look his best, eh? But what's the wig doing here, my dear?"

"Oh, I'm to see him try it on, and suggest the general make-up of his face. You see, he thinks his mother is so old that she must somehow even remember what her great-great-grandfather looked like!"

The old Marqués laughed.

"And instead of growing old to please your son, you grow young. Suddenly very markedly young. Why, Ana?"

Having left a Cabinet meeting in the Alcázar, the Marqués had called on Ana by the king's instruction to tell her that Philip would visit her informally later in the evening. Also to take his own leave of her, as he was withdrawing to his country place near Alcala de Henares for Lent. At Pastrana Ana was his near neighbour and they had many associations in common; he had served with Ruy Gomez in the Cabinet, and always stood for Gomez's policy of liberation and progress. He was fond of Ruy's wife and children.

"You're tired," Ana said.

"Yes. I'm growing too old for the king's delaying tactics. I would have liked to see a *few* decisions taken for Spain before I died."

They laughed.

"But what's this talk of dying? Are Cabinet meetings like some slow form of death, then?"

"Yes, my dear—creeping paralysis. Still, Vasquez and Perez are really energetic men, and I think that in spite of Philip they get a few things done. But the king has come back from El Pardo in a peculiarly cautious frame of mind."

"The boar-hunting should have livened him up—it always used to."

"My dear, he doesn't hunt nowadays. Even at El Pardo of all places he *prays* all the time, poor fellow! And to-morrow, he tells me, he's off to El Escorial to tackle the Forty Days in good earnest with his monks! Ah, poor Spain!"

"Poor Philip, too. He's a good king—at least, he's an extraordinarily dutiful one. Perhaps if the queen were a little more amusing——"

"I'd go further—I'd say if perhaps she were a great deal more amusing, and perhaps the least little bit attractive—still," he laughed and ran his veined old hand over his face, "that mightn't alter Cabinet methods, Ana dear."

"No. I think all this that you're talking about is *our* fault, you know—the fault of our class, I mean. I used to grumble to Ruy about that—that none of my relatives or any of the landowners ever know the least thing now about the government of Spain. He didn't think that mattered—he didn't like my class."

"He might agree with you more now—in any case, he would deplore Philip's fixed obsession with European politics and total inertia before our economic plight. We're bankrupt on paper, and Philip is always raging for money; and you've only to drive through this town or a league out into the country to see that we're bankrupt in fact—the people are starving, and nothing is being done for them. Yet we have greater possessions than any country on earth. Our empire is a sheer mystery of wealth. Some merchant ships, some system of transport, some attention to import and export, some expenditure on harbours and agriculture and roads—Oh well, I'm an old man, but younger than I will not see these simple things done for Spain, my dear!"

"Philip would attend to those things—they're the sort of things he cares about, believe me!—but he simply hasn't time. He has a million times too much to do. And it is the laziness and cowardice of all our class that make it impossible for him to get things done——"

"He doesn't want us, Ana! He simply has to rule alone——"

"But he shouldn't be allowed to! *We* own Spain; why does *he* rule it?"

"His father fooled us into letting him, and now we don't care——"

"I do—when it occurs to me."

"Exactly—when it does. And anyway you're only one, and a helpless widow-creature——"

"We've lost a principle somewhere——" Ana said.

"And a lot besides. Ah well, what talk for the eve of Carnival and with my lovely Ana! I'll be glad of my own house to-night, and the sound of the sheep coughing in the orchard."

"You're going to-night?"

"Yes—to avoid to-morrow's uproar. We'll get home for supper."

"You can give my love to the road."

"I will. You'll be at Pastrana for Easter, of course?"

"Indeed we shall. We'll have our customary feasts together, won't we?"

"To be sure, dear child. Ah, here's Rodrigo—and full of gossip, I expect, just as I have to go!"

Rodrigo Gomez y de Mendoza, Duke of Pastrana, bowed very correctly to the Marqués. He was a springy boy of sixteen, with fair hair turning now a little to brown, and with light, well-cut features. The gossips who made Philip his father were unobservant, for his fairness had none of the pallor of the king's, and the contours of his face were trim, sharp and small as had been those of Ruy Gomez.

"Telling Mother Cabinet secrets, sir? You sat all day, I believe?"

"We did indeed, my boy, and I feel unrefreshed. Tell me some town salacity, to make me laugh."

"I'd tell you plenty if Mother weren't here! May I have some wine with you?" He poured himself a drink. "Ah, there's my wig! Oh—here's a piece of news that may well blow into a scandal, and it's not salacious either, Mother—on the face of it!"

"More's the pity," said de Los Velez. "Still, let's have it. Mustn't be out of things!"

"You know Don Juan de Escovedo has been ill? Not that that matters, God knows! He's an awful bore, isn't he, Mother? But the point is—Pepe Salazar has just been telling me—that poisoning is suspected. Deliberate poisoning, I mean. I shouldn't be at all surprised. Would you, Mother? I wonder if he'll die?"

"I don't suppose so," said the Marqués lightly. "He's far too much of a worry to us all just now."

"But that's just why I think he may die, sir! He's making political enemies all the time, Pepe says. After all, this might well be one of the king's neat ideas——"

"Rodrigo——" Ana began.

But de Los Velez rose, interrupting her.

"Young man, you are so young and such a fool still that I can't be bothered to snub you as I should," he said coolly. "But don't forget yourself so idiotically again in my hearing or your Mother's." He pulled the boy's ear somewhat cruelly, and Rodrigo winced away, more from the indignity than the pain. The Marqués had not looked at Ana throughout the passage of speech about Escovedo, nor she at him. "Come now, young fool, try on this wig for me before I go. I'd like to see if you *can* look anything like a great Mendoza, when you try."

Rodrigo, who regarded de Los Velez as a *démodé* old fool and had deliberately tried his treasonous gossip on him so as to see him get excited, and also in order to annoy his mother who, he knew, adored the king—was very willing now to posture in the new wig and be admired.

"It's quite well made," he said, as he pulled it on in front of a mirror. "Ought to be, at the price. Look, Mother—how does it seem?"

"Exactly as I remember dear old great-great-grandpapa, darling! A plain old man he was!"

"I'll have to make up very sallow, alas! Oh, all you green-faced Mendozas! What an ancestry!"

"What an ancestry, indeed!" said the Marqués. "Merely the history of Spain. You're not big enough, Rodrigo——"

"Oh, it's only a masquerade—that won't matter," said Ana.

Rodrigo paid no attention. He was studying himself gravely in the glass.

"Black hair—there's something to be said for it, don't you think, Mother? I've been reading the old Marqués de Santillana—must be up to my part a bit. Do you know he was rather a good poet, sir?"

"Yes—I've read him. He's one of our glories, Rodrigo."

"He introduced the sonnet-form from Italy. That was creditable of him, I must say. I do admire Italy, and Italian ideas."

The door at the end of the long room opened and, briefly announced, the king entered.

Ana swept down the room to him, laughing as she went. But she dropped on her knee with a very correct grace as she kissed his hand.

"Your Majesty is most welcome."

"Thank you, Princess. I am earlier than I intended. I found myself suddenly free of work for half an hour—and as to-night is laden, I thought I'd come to you now."

"At any time this house and all it holds are yours, Your Majesty." Then, becoming informal again, she indicated the untidy room and Rodrigo trying to adjust his own hair with one hand and replace the wig on its stand with the other. "You must forgive us, sir. It is Carnival, and we are re-hearsing our disguises."

"So I see," said the king, taking in the whole scene friendlily and with precision. "Sit down again, old friend," he said kindly to de Los Velez. "I've given you a hard enough day; I should have known better than to interrupt your interlude of refreshment here."

De Los Velez bowed.

"Indeed no, sir. I am most happy, most happy," he murmured graciously, though in fact he was bored, and would have preferred to finish his glass of wine in peace with his "dear child", Ana.

Rodrigo, trying to forget his tousled head, made a beautiful courtier's bow, and spoke his duty.

"Thank you, boy," said Philip. He always looked indulgently on Rodrigo, Ana noticed, although the latter was not of a type normally to attract his interest. She sometimes suspected that the legend of the boy's royal paternity, amusing and half-pleasing Philip, tempted him sometimes to seem to promote it. "We have missed you from among the pages this winter, Rodrigo. However, we realise that you must study too. You'll be rejoining the Court for a part of the summer, I assume?"

"Yes, sir, indeed. I look forward to being at the Court for some weeks, before I go on military exercises."

"Ah, of course! You are to be a soldier, they tell me."

Rodrigo bowed assent. "With your cavalry, sir."

"And meantime, what do they teach you at your University?"

"Philosophy, of sorts, Your Majesty. I study French and Italian too—and I read much military history."

"Ah! He's learned, Ana, I fear. Formidably learned. How much philosophy have you, to counter his?"

"None, sir. I've never needed any. My life has lain in happy places."

The king smiled at her, seeing a compliment in what she said, and already feeling rested by the sense of her friendliness.

He sat now in a tall chair near a window, and looked about him at his ease.

"Do they behave themselves at Alcala, Los Velez, these young students?"

"Oh, not uniformly well, sir," said the Marqués lightly. "I hear grumbles from the *alcalde*. But there's nothing exactly criminal against Rodrigo at the moment. And now, if Your Majesty will permit me, and you too, my dear Princess, I shall take my leave. I have my journey to the country this evening——"

"Yes, indeed," said the king, and Ana rang a handbell. "Good gardens those of yours, my friend, but not as fertile as Pastrana."

"Ah well, Ruy Gomez was the best husbandman I ever knew—save one, Your Majesty. You certainly set us all a great example with your magnificent gardens."

He bowed low in farewell over the king's hand.

"A garden is the most grateful of earthly possessions, dear friend," Philip said. "It is very consoling sometimes."

"That is so—and I wish you all its comforts, sir, in the coming weeks at El Escorial."

"Thank you, Marqués."

The manservant was waiting, and with smiles to Ana and Rodrigo de Los Velez left the room.

Rodrigo thought the king a prig and a bore, but he appreciated passionately all that he stood for, and delighted in the familiarity with which the ruler of Spain honoured his mother's house. Ana sometimes reflected with amusement that although—short of being a reigning monarch—Rodrigo could hardly throughout all Europe hold higher rank than his birth gave him, yet the boy manifested all the signs of a social climber. Where does he hope to climb to? she often wondered—and found his snobbish antics comical. At this moment, though the actual intercourse would bore him, with its pieties and its avoidance of gossip and malice, Rodrigo would like, Ana knew, to stay and entertain Philip, so as to enjoy his own effect upon the latter, and also for the satisfaction it always so curiously gave him to be able to say that he had sat at ease for a while in a private drawing-room with the king. But he was already too good a courtier to indulge this inclination now. He knew that it was unwise, when the king came to his mother in this room, to make a third too long. He knew all the old Court gossip about them, though he did not quite know what to make of it; but he did know that they were intimate friends, and that it was not discreet to get in their way when the king came visiting Ana.

So he bent again over Philip's hand.

"Your Majesty will wish me to leave you now. This has been a very great honour and happiness. Adios, sir."

"Adios, Rodrigo."

As the boy crossed the room he picked up the wig on its stand.

"I'll take this, Mother. It's a bit incongruous here," and he laughed and bowed himself away.

"He's a pleasing boy, Ana—but he'll never be the man his father was." Philip permitted himself to smile with faint mischief as he said that.

"He has charm, I suppose," Ana replied, "but certainly he's no Ruy Gomez. I sometimes think he'd have exasperated Ruy very much—and that wasn't an easy thing to do."

"Does he exasperate you?"

"He comes near it. I dislike all this mincing social nonsense. Oh, but I'm glad to see you, after so long. May I sit?"

He laughed contentedly.

"Nonsensical woman!" She sat down opposite him. "Yes, it has been a long time, I'm sorry to say—not since just after Christmas."

Ana had taken her family to Pastrana for the Feast of the Kings which they always celebrated there, and did not return to Madrid until Candlemas. By then the king and Court were at El Pardo. So that this glimpsing visit, as he passed through on his way to El Escorial, was important to Philip. Always now when he was at the Alcázar he came to see her, without ceremony, whenever he allowed himself an hour to spare from work. Sometimes he came unannounced, sometimes he sent a servant to say that he might call—but he never named a time. Clearly he regarded her as very much his own possession, over there so conveniently across the street.

His assumption meant that, when the Court was in Madrid, Ana and Antonio Perez had to move delicately within the king's hours, which could be gambled on as being normally between noon and midnight. For herself, now that Ruy was dead, Ana acknowledged no man's lordship over her days or her actions, and Philip might enter her drawing-room when he chose, and like or not whom he found there, as he chose. As to her right to do as she pleased in her own house she no more regarded Philip's judgment than that of the youngest washer-up in her kitchen.

But, she understood that Antonio Perez's career could be ended, in fact, by Philip's least whim of jealousy or irritation against him. And she knew that his career was what Antonio really cared about on earth, and on the whole thought this a proper state of mind for a man of brains. She believed that any threat through her to his ambition would deprive her of his present love; and she was in love with him and desired him to love her as long as might be possible. So, against her nature, she was cautious when Philip was in Madrid.

Now however she smiled, leaning towards her desk to push further out of sight a note which she had received that afternoon.

"It looks as if I shall be working until dawn, if Majesty is to eat his Mardi Gras supper at Escorial to-morrow. Especially as I want to avoid having to go up there just yet myself. So put out your candles when you will, and go to sleep. Meantime, there may be a free moment when this Cabinet breaks up, and if there is I'll cross the street for a seasonable exchange with Fernán and Anichu. I have, as a matter of fact, a Carnival present for you also—but I don't suppose you'll like it. Anyway, I'll not give it to you this afternoon—that wouldn't be at all correct. I hope I shall manage to see you before the night's labours descend. You are my refreshment. A."

There might well be an encounter—as there had been once or twice before. But a call by a politician on a great lady was no more than correct—especially at this hour of the evening. And Antonio, secretly furious at the *contretemps*, would carry it off with grace.

Philip took a sugared grape and ate it.

"I told my people to send your children a Carnival cake from me, Ana. I said it was to be a very pretty one."

"Ah! How thoughtful of you! They'll be enchanted."

"Not that I imagine they're going to be short of cakes!"

"Great Heavens, no! What a greedy festival it is! But a cake from the king! My family simply revel in these special marks of your friendship, Philip. I'm afraid they'll boast about it all over Madrid!"

"Good children." He smiled. "How wise I was, you see, to make you bring them back to Madrid."

"Well, certainly they think so!"

"And they're right. It's good for them to mix with their contemporaries, and get to understand gradually what Spain really is and how we govern. And of course it's very important that I should be able to keep my eye on them, as Ruy desired."

He leant back in his chair and closed his eyes.

"Did you rest, at El Pardo?"

"No. I don't rest."

"That is unwise of you; it is even undutiful."

He smiled a little at the censure, and opened his eyes, which were strained and red-rimmed.

"It might be more undutiful of me," he said, "to seek the rest I could enjoy."

She allowed herself to look baffled; his reference might, after all, be to death or abdication.

"I could rest here, Ana," he said self-pityingly. "You rest me, always."

"I'm glad," she answered, and strove to keep the mood of her speech at once truly affectionate yet innocent of provocation. "But there is so little that I can do for you—it is so seldom——"

What he needed from her now he took, for all her care; the hint of a temptation between them to which *he* would never permit them to yield. And Ana, watching him take his own cue, reflected with amusement—in love with another man though she honestly was—that Philip's game was indeed founded on fact. For it remained true that he attracted and touched her—and she thought that that was all he meant, did he but know it, when he said she rested him. His sensitive nerves felt a particular quality in her liking for him. That is restful to all of us, Ana thought, thinking of herself; and whether we are lovers or not—and Philip no longer is anyone's—can seduce us into fantasies.

"It should be never," he said gravely, believing himself master of a great desire. "Dear Ana, we must thank God that we grow old. You are somewhat younger than me, of course, but a woman ages early."

She laughed at that a little.

"Dear friend, do you know that you always pay court to me—may I call it that?—in such terms as make it seem that you are profoundly thankful to have escaped me!"

"Perhaps indeed I am. For say we had been lovers once, is it conceivable that we would sit together now, as we do, in such total trust and friendship?"

The innocence of this speech made Ana wince. Yet she told herself that her passions were her own dominion, and that the makers of naïve claims punished only themselves, if anyone.

"Can't lovers be friends?" she parried.

"What do you know of lovers?" he asked, indulgently. "And now your day is gone, and it's my fault that you have escaped all the sins your beauty entitled you to. But I was right, believe me. And you have far fewer penances to do now in your old age than I, alas! But there was one sin at least I didn't commit—I didn't rob Ruy of what I gave him."

"Between you and Ruy I was well taken care of," Ana said softly.

"I think you were," said Philip, feeling no mockery. "And I continue the work—though it's easy now."

"That's as well, seeing how incredibly busy you have become in these years, my dear friend."

"They reproach me," he said suddenly. "Oh yes, I know they do, for my method of government. But there is now no other way. There are intricacies and subtleties to be balanced in Europe now which of their nature must not be openly explained to any Cabinet. I alone can judge the full case, Ana, in all our foreign problems. Simply because I alone feel Spain's duty and destiny, and only I can be trusted with it. One man can be counted safe thus far, and another to another point—but they are only politicians—and I know therefore that they cannot judge for Spain——"

He was off on a frequent theme—self-justification. It was her belief that he was too proud to talk in this vein to anyone but her, and that therefore these wild and vaguely directed speeches for the defence which it was his pleasure to deliver to her did him more good and meant more than was apparent. They never contained any factual information; he never stated a worry, or named a significant name; he merely condescended to fret and argue with himself in her presence, and she knew that this was a relaxation normally impossible to his conceit in the presence of another.

It's like being married to him—a little, she thought.

She wondered if Juan de Escovedo was on his mind, or whether, having ruthlessly directed that anxiety to its logical end, he now dismissed it, unresolved though it yet was, in favour of other troubles.

The king's conscience, though it flourished indeed and spread rankly and eccentrically through his whole life and policy, was impossible now to separate or disentangle from his over-developed consciousness of holy privilege. Ana wondered where—if anywhere—beneath all his activities of contrition, hair-splitting, penance, debate and self-consciousness, lay Philip's plain sense of right and wrong? She wondered if ever his mind lay still, still enough to accept a moment of plain guilt, or simple doubt?

Ana took for granted the political high-handedness of her time. She had known men murdered for the king's sake, or by the king's secret wish; had known arrests made and trials conducted for false causes, simply because what was conceived to be the national good required a neat, quick putting-away. Her husband, more humane and temperate than most men of his day, had not blenched from the treacherous despatch of de Montigny and Berghen, well-intentioned envoys from the Netherlands. Common gossip had had it, when in 1568 the madness of Philip's son, Don Carlos, made his death a necessity for Spain, that Ruy Gomez counselled and promoted his murder. Ana knew that this was not true, and that Carlos had died—hideously—from natural causes. But she also knew that Ruy believed his death to be necessary, and would have compassed it without scruple had he had to.

During the winter she had learnt and guessed enough from Antonio Perez to understand that Juan de Escovedo was now become an inconvenience of whom the king intended to rid himself. He was not to be deflected from his advocacy of Don Juan of Austria's vainglorious schemes in northern Europe; and since his was the brain behind these, and he was, so far as Philip knew, the only Spaniard in government circles who was prepared to go all lengths to serve the dreams of the bastard prince, it was simplest for Spain that he should die.

The charges which Philip's secret service had now accumulated against Escovedo amounted, Ana understood, to treason. Therefore she wondered—and said so—that the king did not take the sane way of impeaching his subject, and submitting him to trial. But Perez said that that would direct public attention to a situation which did not warrant it, and might transform Don Juan's pretensions into something like a cause. Sides might be taken, animosities engendered, many lives lost and much trouble stirred up were Escovedo to be allowed a hearing. He had been warned repeatedly; he knew the king's implacability and methods; he knew he was marked for elimination; but he was a fanatic, and he went on trying to get armies and money and some kind of brotherly blessing for his very foolish master in Brussels. So he must disappear—die from natural causes, by Philip's wish, and with no comment or publicity. He was only one man, and he schemed to destroy many. He had made a fool of himself, and when he was gone Don Juan would certainly lose heart and drop his nonsensical intriguing. Which would be the last that we would ever hear, thank God, said Perez, of that foolish Enterprise against England which had wasted so many years and brains for Spain.

Ana knew—though it was never said—that Antonio had taken complete charge for Philip of this murder-plan. This troubled her, but she was not consulted or given confidences about it; she could only marvel at the apparent serenity and enthusiasm with which he continued to live, work and enjoy himself—giving no sign of his direct preoccupation with the murder of a man he had grown up with and whose friend he had been. But she had marvelled at similar examples of male detachment before—in her husband and in Philip. That passion for affairs, for government, which was so strong in the three men, must contain, she thought, the secret of how callousness can live day by day in apparent harmony with qualities humane, touching and charming which were paramount, with characteristic variations, in all three.

When she persisted sometimes in arguing the greater wisdom for Philip to have Escovedo arrested and tried, Antonio repeatedly laughed her off. "Impeachments are tricky things; might even rouse the nobility out of its long sleep——"

"That's what I mean. That would be a good thing."

"Nonsense, we've our hands quite full enough as it is! No, no. One little death—it's very easy, and we all have to die." He paused and smiled at her. "I won't mind—and *you* shouldn't—when poor Juan is under the ground. He continues to make a terrible nuisance of himself about my private life!"

"I know. But, thank Heaven, he seems to have despaired of reforming me. He doesn't call on me any more, at least."

"Oh, don't flatter yourself he's not attending to your business still, because, believe me, he is!"

"I wonder why he has taken up this—well, this extraordinarily impertinent position?"

"I've considered that, and I think that it's primarily just devotion to Ruy. You see, he *does* think it shocking of you to dishonour a great man's memory, and his children, by an intrigue with a cheap, married adventurer; he also thinks it shocking of you to spend Ruy's substance, and your children's, on that venal creature—and in both of these points, he's perfectly right——"

"I spend my own substance. The children are extremely rich—loaded with estates that I have nothing to do with——"

"I know. Still you *are* madly generous——"

"So are you."

"No, I'm not, Ana. I'm always in debt and on the make. I'm very dishonest, as you know."

"I find you honest."

"You're not a judge—you don't notice about money and things. I do, all the time."

"Well, I'm glad someone does. It makes things sound a little orderly."

He laughed at her.

"But, to get back to Escovedo. I think his indignation against us is quite sincere and natural—though I agree that it's most damnably impertinent, as expressed. But I think increasing bitterness now makes him see his scandalous secret as a powerful political weapon."

"Ah! That was what I feared from the beginning."

"You 'feared'? Is there then something that you fear, Ana?"

"Nothing, for myself. After all, what could there be? Who owns me? What crimes do I commit? But for you—yes. The king's first minister has everything to fear."

"Not really—no need for melodrama. You see, the king's first minister usually understands the king. And with Philip that's all you need. He's brainy but he's slow; I'm brainy too, and I'm quick. Now, look—Escovedo actually has a heart of gold. He respects old friendship and old times——"

"How can you say these things of him and yet seem to support Philip's intention?"

"Because I have intelligence. Because I *am* therefore first minister; because I never, never hoodwink myself. Men aren't killed because they are monsters, Ana; many most enchanting people have to be removed—and we all have to die. Well, as I was saying, Escovedo has a heart of gold. That's what has in fact betrayed his brains and training in the matter of Don Juan. Well, being what he is, he truly does not want to be informer on Ruy Gomez's *post-mortem* humiliation. He would very much rather it was never known of that great man that his widow insulted him with amorous adventures. Also, he remembers good fun with me when we were pages and under-secretaries together; he remembers good turns I did him, and that he always thought there was some good in me. He'd rather not ruin me. And there I understand him perfectly, because I would much rather not ruin him. Though I think him as great a bore as he thinks me a cad. Quits so far—but I shall win, and on the political issue. I wouldn't kill a man, or have him killed—I *think*—because he was a personal irritation. That's a dangerous tendency—leaving morality aside. But, when the king insists on the removal, for his high reasons, of someone who is also privately on my nerves—then I do find it easy to see the king's point!"

"Could Escovedo 'ruin' you, as you say?"

"I wonder! He could make a situation in which I would not have my bearings. But you, of course, might be able to give them to me? We've never talked about this—and we needn't now, of course. But—how much is Philip in love with you?"

"At present he is in love with our virtue—and with the dream of desperate temptations overcome long ago."

"What do you mean by all that?"

She paused.

"Well—all it amounts to is that we were never lovers, Philip and I."

"Ah!"

"Do you believe me?"

"Yes. I believe you, Ana." He asked no other question then about her relationship with the king, but returned, reflectively, to the theme of Escovedo. "His disgust with the private life of the Secretary of State is now becoming a part of Juan's political passion, I think. It may seem to him that if he can disillusion Philip about his right-hand man, and incidentally about so old a friend as you, that he will thereby gain his personal trust, and persuade the king away from corrupt advisers, and back to the field of Spain's traditional honour. He would argue from the particular to the general, and force himself into my shoes. And not for selfish reasons, mind you! Plain altruism—duty to Spain. But of course he doesn't know anything about how Philip's mind works. He doesn't know the king's dangerous way of turning against the bringers of bad news. Above all, he doesn't know that he's not going to live much longer."

The greater part of this conversation had taken place round about the New Year. That was six weeks ago. Since then it was clear that Perez had made fresh overtures to Escovedo, as if in endeavour to bring him at last to terms in the government of Don Juan. He had him to conferences at the palace; Ana saw them riding together once in the Retiro; and three or four nights ago Antonio had had the other to dinner at his house.

Now Escovedo was ill, and if, as Rodrigo said, he was poisoned, it was likely that he swallowed the poison at Perez's dinner-table. The end of the affair was in sight, might even already be here—and Antonio was in charge of it, and betraying no unusual emotion. From the manner and speech of the Marqués de Los Velez when Rodrigo uttered his careless gossip, it was evident that the old statesman was somewhat in the king's confidence as to Escovedo's fate; but not entirely, Ana surmised. No one, not even Perez, was ever entirely in possession of Philip's intentions. Perez's great strength, like Ruy's, was that he never forgot that, or forgot to reckon with its dangers.

Ana contemplated Philip now with some anxiety. He must know that Escovedo was ill; if the poisoning story was true, he knew of it. One of his subjects, a man of honour who had served him well and was still in his service, was being meanly murdered by his wish.

It occurred to her with sudden vividness that if anything went wrong, if there was investigation or outcry after Escovedo's death, it could be very, very serious for Philip. Theologians argued the divine right of kings, and a prince's claims of life and death over his subjects—and nervous old men like Diego de Chaves, Philip's confessor, could twist morality to any shape to suit their master. But no intelligent person gave the hoary idea more than a tolerant courtesy-shrug now, and Ana was sure that Philip himself did not believe it, though he would never appear to discard any conception which increased a ruler's power.

Because the people of Spain were not informed of events until they were well over and their motives blurred, and because of the lethargy now seeped through the aristocracy which, until bullied into sleep by Charles V, had been a ruling class—Philip had indeed carried off some dangerous crimes against human rights, and managed by keeping calm to steer safely past their consequences. But those actions had always been perilous, and there was no reason why the luck of his absolutism should hold.

The sudden death, here in Madrid, of a very well-known Spaniard renowned for his service with the beloved and romantic Don Juan, was bound to receive attention. If there was an inquiry—and many people would be found who, for reasons motived by principle, by family, or by private spleen, could press for one—Philip would be in a dangerous pre-dicament. Antonio Perez would also be in peril. But he would have Philip in his hand—the king, the trump card.

The plot was bad and criminal indeed. Yet Ana almost smiled now as she considered its melodramatic elements. What adventurers and dreamers, at once what savages and babes men can be! Was anything on earth furthered by their elaborate processes of cunning and criminality? Would the world ever be run by anything better than personal passion, and the scoring off each other of amoral schoolboys?

Meantime here was this man of fifty-one, highly trained king of the greatest dominions on earth, this good man Philip whom she knew and loved, plotting plain murder and protesting in perfect sincerity that only he "can judge for

Spain". And on the face of it he's right in that, she thought. In any case Spain has only him, and he cares. And it must be admitted that he looks at this minute like a man with an active conscience. Which is more than one might ever say for Antonio.

"... They are politicians, you see ... I only ..."

This was still his broad theme, while she pondered the fixed issue of Escovedo. He would pause now and expect her soft intervention. As always when he rested himself by muttering at her and giving nothing away, tags of counsel such as a wise or witty woman might give a man floated into her mind. But she was no adviser, and no wit. Buried in her was her own personal reserve of understanding of right and wrong and human action, but she knew this to be so very much, so idiosyncratically, her own that she could never extricate any of it. Its form, in her shy manipulation, would never apply to another's need—and in any case she detested the idea of giving counsel. What Philip came to her for, what he found in her nowadays she honestly did not know. She knew, with enduring surprise, what Antonio found—sheer sexual delight and peace. Arguing from that, but modestly and uncertainly, she guessed that perhaps—Philip being more imaginative than Perez, more poetic and delicate in reaction than any man she knew—he found, irrespective of what she said or did, an edge, a store of pleasure all his own, a symbol for memories, an echo, a perfume from what had never been. She thought that it hardly mattered really what she said or did in Philip's presence—so long as she didn't offend him. Her existence and the sight of her promoted some favourite fantasy which he would never be so simple as to explain.

In effect she was right. She was all that he allowed himself now of common vanity; she was all that was left of the days of pride of life; and he was very fond of her, and very glad to have her to himself on these easy, middle-aged terms which asked no guilt of him. It pleased him too that she was a widow and well past her prime, much as it had always pleased him that she was one-eyed. For he thought it eccentric in himself to be able to admire so much a woman thus afflicted; and that had always made him feel safe about her. But the surface of his consciousness did not reveal these reassurances to him. At the top of his mind she was safe and restful not because she was ageing, disfigured and too unusual-looking to appeal generally, but because she was the admired and chosen intimate of the king—towards whom therefore no other man would be so foolish as to presume.

"Spain is grateful to you, Philip," she said dutifully when he paused. "But we'd rather you didn't age yourself prematurely in our service."

He stretched for her hand and spread it out on his, admiring it.

"There are many people who *don't* think you beautiful, Ana," he said. "But your hands—well, they are just child's play."

"I suppose so. Myself, I prefer some of my more eccentric features——"

"I hope partly because I admire them?"

"That's one good reason. I've always been very proud of your admiration," she said.

"You say I age. But that's a good thing; it's necessary; I welcome it."

"I don't see why."

"One can't be a king and a man—not such a king as I have to be; not now, not in Spain." He bent his head over her hand, leant his forehead against it. "If I could take you with me to-morrow," he said softly. "Up there at El Escorial I sometimes feel like a very young man, Ana. And then I think of you." He dropped her hand. "If there were time for pleasure!"

She smiled at him.

"There's evidently time to dream of it," she said.

"Yes, barely that. And that is best, dear Ana. You and I are old now, and it is our duty not to make ourselves ridiculous."

She laughed outright, for the word "ridiculous" brought many private and wild images into her mind.

"Dear Philip, dear mentor," she said. "How firmly you guide me in virtue!"

"I have to. I always have a feeling of anxiety about you and me."

"Perhaps that's my revenge on you for being my first love——"

"Perhaps indeed," he said delightedly. "A long and true revenge." He ate another candied fruit. "Where are the children?"

"Fernán and Ana may be dashing in here any minute—they won't know you're with me. And they'll be enchanted if they meet you! Poor little Diego is spending Carnival with the Cardinas family and his very grown-up bride."

"It is a good match, Ana."

"She's rather cruel with him, I think—and he's only just fourteen. We all miss him."

"I'm sure you do. Still, you've done wisely."

"Young Ruy is out with his tutor somewhere. He promises to be learned. And Rodrigo you've just seen. They grow up and go their ways. I hear that our little Duchess of Medina-Sidonia has quite taken to matrimony now, and leads society in the south."

"That's as it should be. I have my eye on her husband for future offices. He's a promising young fellow."

"Would you say 'promising'? He's extremely good-natured and pleasant—but I always find him a little stupid."

"He may appear stupid, socially—but in public affairs I think he is observant and serious."

"Well, he and Madalena seem enchanted with each other anyway—which is a little surprising when you reflect what a bore Madalena is."

MADRID AND PASTRANA · 111

"Now, Ana, you know I hate you to talk in that cruel way about your own children."

"I suppose it *is* cruel? I wouldn't do it to the outside world, Philip."

"I should hope not! It's very shocking—and a foolish affectation, my dear!"

"Oh no, it's not an affectation. Ah! I think I hear the children! Do you mind their coming in?"

"I'll be delighted," Philip said, as a door opened and Ana and Fernando came in, followed by Antonio Perez.

The children were in their riding coats; Fernando carried a painted toy windmill with bright sails, and Ana had a wooden donkey, saddled in scarlet cloth.

They hurried to the king, and dropped on their knees to take his hand.

"Your Majesty," they said gravely, and then rose.

"Actually," said Fernando, "we knew you were here. Estéban told us in the *patio*."

"I suppose we shouldn't have come up without permission," Anichu said.

Antonio Perez, having bowed his duty, joined in now.

"I was consulted, sir, downstairs, on the point of etiquette, and as your Secretary of State I risked advising that we all come up." He turned to Ana, and bowed low. "I called, Princess, to leave these Carnival offerings——" he pointed to the toys the children clutched—"when I met the recipients coming in from a ride. So I ventured to come upstairs, to wish you also a very happy Carnival."

"I am glad you did, Don Antonio."

"Yes. Well met indeed. You're on your way to the Alcázar?" Perez bowed. "We'll be along together in a moment. Those are very fine presents you've been given, children. Have you had my cake yet?"

"Your cake, sir?" said Fernando politely.

"I told them to send you a Carnival cake. I said it was to be a very pretty one."

"Oh!" breathed Fernando. "I'm sure it will be beautiful, Your Majesty."

"I wonder *how* it will be decorated?" said little Ana.

Everyone laughed.

"When we've eaten it, sir," said the Princess, "Anichu will herself write to you, in all our names, to thank you."

"Oh!" said Anichu.

"I shall look forward to that letter," Philip said.

"I have just this moment called at the house of Juan de Escovedo, sir," said Antonio. Philip looked at him with mild interest. "I don't know if you've heard, but he hasn't been well and I was a little anxious about him. Also, I wanted to send some personal news of him in the Brussels despatch."

"Well—and how is he? Will your news be good?"

"Quite good. He's in bed still—I sat with him a while. But he hopes to be up to-morrow, and in any case whatever it was—some stomach trouble—seems to be under control now."

"I'm glad," said Philip coldly. "I had not heard that he was ill."

Antonio laughed.

"I thought you might have missed his daily letters and memoranda, sir. But they'll soon be starting again, you'll be glad to hear!"

Philip smiled.

"I haven't been reading his memoranda lately. I think I know their contents by heart. Still, I'm glad he is no longer ill. My brother will be glad to have good news of him."

Ana watched this conversation; neither speaker gave any sign of its being more than casual exchange, yet she knew that Antonio had engaged in it because of some whim of bravado before her, and that Philip in his slower way had enjoyed its cold insolence.

"How *is* Don Juan of Austria, Your Majesty?" Ana said. Philip shrugged.

"Depressed, Princess, and petulant. He likes his own way, and a great deal of money. We don't give him either—do we, Perez?"

"No, sir; we do not."

Fernando was looking sadly at a basket of sweets on Ana's table, and then, for guidance, to his mother.

"Would it be a very great breach of etiquette, Your Majesty," she said, "if Fernán were to eat a candied fruit?"

"Not if he gives me one first, Princess."

Blushing and delighted the little boy brought the basket to the king. Philip chose a piece of marzipan.

"Anichu next, I think," he said, and the baby Ana came and chose a sweet, still holding her donkey. "Who's to ride this donkey?" Philip asked her.

"It's for Juana La Loca, Your Majesty."

"That poor old doll!" The king laughed and looked about the room for her. "But she's past donkey-riding, surely?"

"She's certainly in very poor health," the Princess said.

"Mother Teresa—you know, sir, the great Mother Teresa? —well, she rides donkeys everywhere," said Anichu.

"And Bernardina says that she's often very sick," said Fernando.

"She is, indeed," said Philip.

"But she doesn't allow herself a saddle, Anichu," said Antonio. "Do you think Juana La Loca will be so self-indulgent as to use this saddle?"

"Well, she's very thin—as thin as Mother, really," said Anichu. "I think she'd better have the saddle."

Antonio smiled. Philip stroked the little girl's head. "No, Fernán," he said. "Take that basket away from me now—or I shall have stomach trouble."

"Like Don Juan de Escovedo," said Fernando.

"Exactly. Ah, my dear friend," he said to Ana, "how you

seduce us! How I should like to spend Carnival here—with Anichu and Fernán and Juana La Loca!"

"How deeply welcome you would be, Your Majesty."

"I believe that, Princess—and thank you. But come on, Perez! What is the spell of indolence this lady casts? Beware of it, my friend," he said, rising. "You have no time for such delights, and neither, alas, have I."

"You warn me kindly, sir. I shall beware, believe me."

"Good-bye, Princess," said Philip. "Thank you for a happy hour. I have few."

Ana knelt and kissed his hand. So did the children.

"God bless you all," Philip said as they rose, "and I wish you a happy Carnival, and a holy Lent."

"And we wish you, sir, great peace and pleasure at El Escorial."

Philip inclined his head. Antonio Perez bowed polite farewell over Ana's hand. Smiling again at the children the two men crossed the room and were gone without ceremony.

THE FOURTH CHAPTER   (EASTER MONDAY 1578)

Ana got up and left the supper-table when the meal was only half-way through. The children and their guests and tutors were very gay and hardly noticed her movement. It was an informal family meal after a long day of village festival. Only Anichu, sleepy on her high chair, protested as she passed.

"But you're asleep, my baby," Ana said and kissed her hair. "Bernardina, have her taken to bed—it's after midnight."

"I'll take her myself. I'm tired of all this din," said Bernardina, and picked up the little girl and carried her off.

Ana went into the garden, and climbed its long shelves. She liked its furthest level, where, from a broad and quiet terrace withdrawn and raised above her house and the town,

she could look out in many directions over the gentle lands of
Pastrana and smell and enjoy their fertile peace.

This last night of March, starry and clear, seemed like a
night of late April. Many of the fruit-trees were in blossom;
the midnight light touched throngs of ghostly flower-faces,
and the air carried a confusion of sweet perfumes.

Ana paced her favourite quiet plateau and scanned the view
below her as if she sought something new from its familiarity.
The village pressed about the dark mass of her house;
dwellings, barns, schools and storehouses all sheltering
prosperously still under the beneficence of their dead duke.
Ruy's bones lay there in the *Colegiata* church, with the bones
of four of their ten children—where her bones too would lie.
It is much to have buried, she thought, the bones of a
husband and four children. While life still burns hard in the
breast, to have already ended so much means that I am old,
however I forget it. It means that I have been old for these
five years, since all those bones of mine rejoined each other
then—to wait for me.

Further off than the *Colegiata* shone the roofs of the
Franciscan monastery and convent. Ana was the patroness of
these two religious houses and so had much business and
many friendly contacts with their inmates, yet, secretly, she
never thought of them or entered their precincts without
wincing in discomfort.

When Ruy founded his dukedom and set to the work of
developing the life of Pastrana, its monastery and convent
had stood empty for some years, so he offered them, with
endowments and generous patronage, to the new Reformed,
or Discalced, Carmelites.

The gesture was wide in implication. It associated the
progressive wing of Philip's government with the new cause
of the rebel Mother Teresa who was then—as she was still—
sweeping about Spain in search of foundations where she
might exemplify with her followers, as a movement of

Counter-Reformation, the ideals of the early Christian Church. Support and friendship from Ruy Gomez were, when they came, a great political boon for Mother Teresa, and the new Carmelites established themselves happily at Pastrana.

Ana was not religious-minded, or ever disposed to examine or undergo the real rigours of spiritual progress. It was as natural to her to be a Castilian Christian as it was to have nails at her finger-ends, or an appetite for dinner. She believed, perfectly simply, the essential tenets of her faith, and was careless as to details. She said her prayers with undimmed belief and, until she had fallen through Antonio Perez into what she frankly named to herself as a mortal sin of the flesh, she had kept the major rules of Catholic life. There had been passages of dream and temptation when she was young and Philip and his desire attracted her; but otherwise she had been good, and unassailed. Now that she was by her own acknowledgment living a life of sin she did not cheat; feeling unrepentant, she did not feign repentance, and had to forgo reception of the sacraments. Very often and very honestly now she looked in dismay at this *impasse* of her soul. But it had to stand. She saw no way of clearance save to give up her pleasure in Antonio Perez. Living in mortal sin now, she knew that what she was doing did not merit eternal hell in the eyes of any human judge, and wondered—as often more detachedly she had—how theologians dared make categorical pronouncements. But she was no mystic, had no private ease of communication with God, and had to be content to take her chance, a sinner, before the tribunals of eternity. If the rules were in fact as the self-confident preachers shouted them—so be it.

But all of this had nothing to do with her discomfort before the religious houses in her village—or so she thought.

She had been pleased to have the new Carmelite foundations under her husband's wing. Less aware than Ruy of Mother

Teresa's national importance, and less attached than he was to her complex personality, character in action did nevertheless interest her, and she felt with sincerity that Mother Teresa was indeed living as the best kind of Spaniard should—and that she was a great individual and a great Castilian. And the foundations settled down, and prospered.

What happened afterwards was a large embarrassment arising from a very small and private cause.

When Ruy died, Ana, who had ended by surrendering all her will and all her forgotten, buried self to his quiet, insistent domination, became invested with panic. A sense of total incompetence, of being a cripple, swept upon her. She felt, angrily and somewhat madly in her grief, that her keeper had died either much too late or far too soon. She felt a great sense of waste in her long subjugation, and that all her life had been like an athlete's training for a course never to be run. In a chill of isolation, sick against Ruy for his bungling of everything in leaving her to have to be herself when she had been so carefully made over to be wholly his, she walked away from the whole future. She decided—in pure hysteria— to be a nun. She presented herself—scarcely remembering to ask permission of the Prioress—as a postulant of the Discalced Carmelites in Pastrana.

Had she ever been able—indulged great lady from birth— to accept the rules of a religious house, this was not the time, when she was ill, deranged, and derangedly set on doing what was unnatural.

The episode was foolish and humiliating. It was the one attempt she had ever made to express a violence from within herself, and it failed pitifully. Ana quarrelled with the Prioress, distressed the community, and caused consternation to her mother and her friends. Mother Teresa refused her the Carmelite habit, and ordered her monks and nuns to leave Pastrana. Ana withdrew to her own home, and began her widowhood in suitable seclusion. And those in Madrid who had heard of the brief *fracas* laughed and told each other that Ruy's death had unhinged her. Later, Franciscans came to teach and pray in her convents, and the life of the village went on, and the Princess's brief folly was forgotten.

By all but the Princess. The memory of it was an unclosed wound in her vanity, and it ate against courage. Before Ruy had come to her she had lost her eye; immediately he left her she acted as a madwoman; and whilst he was there, gentle, considerate, devoted, she had never been able to be anything but exactly his, as he made her. She was, it seemed, mutilated, *tuerta*—depleted in some sense she would never discover by the perfect taking over and direction of her life.

But her attempt to be a nun hurt more than her vanity. In quarrelling with Mother Teresa, in injuring the cause of reform, Ana knew she had offended against a principle important to herself; against courage and against life in action; against the best of Castile. There was no redress against that; but the oftener she considered it the more it hurt her instincts and her spirit.

It was an old pain now, and—as has been said—she often winced at it. It was like her blind eye, and both were sharp sentries over her general, surprised sense of never having managed to be herself throughout her singularly successful life. Both, she half-guessed, were answerable for the hour, the unforeseen moment in which, visited by a physical desire so precise as to be cold and shocking, she had made herself mistress of Antonio Perez. But there at least, and at last, they had not been sterile; there feeling had flowered in her, feeling entirely her own, defended and cultivated by no one. There— and let the theologians rave—she had found in pleasure that which might conceivably be allowed to be love.

But now she was unhappy. Her unhappiness was ten days old. It dated from a night three days before she left Madrid for the Holy Week ceremonies at Pastrana. Never, she thought, had she been so glad to return to the innocence and rural modesty of Pastrana. Yet now the place hurt her night and day through these very qualities she loved in it.

She looked eastwards now, towards where Alcala de Henares lay.

She and her children had spent yesterday, Easter Sunday, there—as by tradition they always did—as guests of the Marqués de Los Velez. Antonio Perez was spending Easter with the Marqués, whose neighbourliness to Pastrana, combined with his worldly suavity and indulgent love for Ana, was very useful to the lovers. The day had been brilliant and everyone light-hearted and easy, the children exacting all the sanctified customs of this outing. There was a bullfight in the town—not a very good one, but correct and exciting. Later there were feasts and fireworks.

Antonio, not having seen Ana for a week, was shamelessly enchanted with her again, and would not leave her side. He wore her Easter present, a collar of heavy, close-set rubies; he was gay and boyish, very much on holiday. But withal, she thought, secretly anxious lest she might not catch his mood. He was sensitive, she conceded—for she could feign, she hoped, but she could not feel light-hearted.

When her family were being piled into carriages for the drive home, Antonio—his mood changed now—begged her very gently to let him ride over to Pastrana to her after midnight. And for the first time in her love for him—which probably meant the first time in her life—she hesitated, worried, and declined her lover's request.

This distressed him. It touched her that, arrogant as his nature was, it did not make him cold or angry. Simply, he was distressed. He explained to her that he would have to be back at the Alcázar by Tuesday afternoon, and that on the following night, this night, Monday, his despatches would be coming from Madrid; that the courier might be late, and that he would have to await his arrival lest there was news requiring an immediate answer; that, in short, Monday night was not easy, and might be impossible.

Ana did not answer as, to her pained astonishment, the greater part of her cried out—that that would be well, and she would be glad if he did not come. She did not answer so, because she found him always very dear to her senses and she remembered what it was like to be with him in love. She loved him still, in the plain way of sensualism—and more than that, out of the gratitude, friendliness and mutual knowledge born in sensual pleasure. But her spirit had newly received a crazy shock. She knew, from the far depths of his eyes, that he was anxious about that—but he did not measure it rightly. There was no reason why he should ever do so. He thought—sympathising passionately, she knew— that the shock, the outrage was, as it must appear to anyone, to her *amour-propre*, to the sense of decency, to all the inherited rules and codes that govern civilised life. She did not discard or belittle these—and she was grateful to him for the passion with which he had reacted against their recent outraging by a madman. But she could never explain to him that her trouble was quite other—that she too was mad, perhaps, had been driven mad by the mad gesture of Juan de Escovedo, and had fantastically thereby come to share his view of herself and of her lover.

No, was all she had said to his anxiety. Cowardly and cold. No, he must not ride to Pastrana to-night. Then to-morrow night, Monday? But his despatches—he wouldn't be able to? Oh yes he might, very late. He might have things to tell her. And he *had* to be in Madrid on Tuesday, so Heaven knew when he'd see her again.

So she had driven home last night, leaving him uneasy. She felt wearily aware of her unbecoming, girlish awkwardness. She had no finesse, no style with which to meet the moods of love.

But was this a mood? She suspected that she had no style for moods because she had no moods.

Bernardina came up to her high terrace, carrying a silk cloak. "There may be frost," she said. "No need to take a chill. You're in bad enough form as it is."

Ana thanked her and put on the cloak.

"But why do you say I'm in bad form?"

Bernardina, who knew—as indeed was her duty—everything that happened to Ana, knew therefore of the shocking episode of ten nights ago in her bedroom in Madrid. It still made her sweat to consider it, and she knew that as long as she lived she would not forgive herself that such an unbelievable thing had taken place when she held any responsibility. Diego, the butler, and she had not been ashamed to weep for Ana's humiliation when they talked it out together, in hushed tones and behind locked doors. They were aghast, and would not have been surprised at instant dismissal from the Princess's service.

But nothing was said, nothing at all. Uninstructed, Diego changed the locks on all the doors, and posted night-watchmen to side-doors which had hitherto been little used and left to chance. The servants were sharply instructed—without explanation—as to admittance or non-admittance of visitors. Diego did not know what they knew or guessed of his reasons for this fuss, and in his anger and distress he hardly cared.

The Princess said nothing, and presently left Madrid with the children, as had been arranged. Only Bernardina, who knew her well, saw that she had changed overnight. Heaven knew she didn't blame her!

Still—it would be better if she spoke of the affair—to someone, once, and then no more. And this question seemed almost like a lead. Bernardina, gathering up all her affection and remorse, followed it.

"Because I'd expect you to be, even if I didn't see that you are. Ana—I shall never forgive myself—as long as I live." She raised her hand. "No, don't interrupt me.

Listen, it's better for you to let me talk—this once. That'll take some of the unnaturalness out of it."

Ana looked about the quiet landscape as if searching for something.

"It wasn't unnatural—that isn't the word," she said. "It was—like a vision of judgment, or like seeing yourself in hell."

Bernardina was very much startled.

"My dear, my dear," she said, and tears came into her voice. "Don't talk in that queer way—as if you were sleepwalking. It's over now, and it's as if it never happened——"

Bernardina's room in the Madrid house was very near to Ana's. On nights when Antonio Perez stayed very late and when she knew that he was in Ana's bedroom, Bernardina slept lightly or hardly at all. There was always a faint uneasiness—a young servant might make a mistake and go to the Princess's room, or one of the children might want her. Bernardina kept watch. Usually she heard Antonio tiptoe away in the dawn, and then she composed herself and slept soundly into the late morning.

One night, ten nights ago, dozing at about half-past three, she half-heard a man's step in the corridor. It's early for him to go, she thought sleepily; and then, it's a heavy step for him, and it's going towards her room, not from it. She became full-awake. Some idiot manservant parading where he had no business, she thought, and left her bed to look along the corridor. She was in time to glimpse a male shoulder and leg, in court dress, against the lights of Ana's room before the door closed on them. Ah, he was just wandering about, she thought—and then it struck her that the figure she had seen was larger and taller than Antonio Perez. She stood, frozen in speculation. And after some seconds of great stillness she heard a man's voice raised in Ana's room. Clear, hard and accusatory it rang—no voice of a lover in the night, no echo of Antonio Perez. It spoke again—having had no answer that Bernardina could catch. She could not hear the angry words, but only that they were indeed angry. She knew the voice, yet in agitation could not name it. She kept still in a curtained alcove, not knowing how to judge or what to do. There was silence again—no answer to the hard, male scold. And then the door of Ana's room opened, and Juan de Escovedo came out. There were candles in the corridor and they lighted his face with precision. He walked, not troubling to tread lightly, past where Bernardina stood in the alcove. She followed him down a small staircase and saw him let himself out of the house at a side-door where there was no watchman, and which was never used. He unlocked this door with a key he produced from his belt. She heard him lock it again on the other side and walk away. She did not sleep when she returned to her room. She paced about, sick with pity and anxiety. Before five o'clock rang at Santa Maria Almudena she heard Antonio Perez tiptoe away as usual, going by the stairs he always used.

That was all. That was all she knew, and however one regarded the happening it was loathsome. She did not know how to help Ana—yet she felt impelled to try.

She took her arm and drew her close to her.

"You'll forget it all, I promise you, *chiquita!* Just stay here at Pastrana for a while and rest, and let the whole thing blow away out of your dear head! Nobody knows a whiff about it —except me. I swear to you! But what everyone does know is that that poor individual is mad. We've all known that for months! He's been piling up trouble for himself with the king and everyone all the winter. But now! Oh well, there was someone else concerned in this who'll know how to make him answer for it, never you fear! You leave it all to him, my pet——"

Ana always walked too fast for Bernardina, but the latter did not notice this now and ran along, holding her arm and coaxing her. And in fact Ana felt some of the comfort the other wished towards her. It was a relief to hear this practical, kind voice lapping round the region of her shock; in some sense it distracted her from its hidden centre, made her view the event for a moment as others might, as an extraordinary piece of scandal. So that she suddenly felt a vast desire to laugh, to laugh outrageously and long—and she thought of how gloriously and salaciously this dear loyal Bernardina would in fact have laughed had the identical tale been brought to her about any other woman in Madrid save this one. She thought of the details that would have been dug from the story then, and of how crudely and unkindly they would have relished these, and added to them, together. Poor Bernardina, this time there could be no realism, no elaboration.

Yet blazingly true and crude the moment had been. So crude and true that it became of necessity, by its pure strength, a vision of sin and judgment. What would the jolly Bernardina have made of the actuality? Ana wondered. Juan de Escovedo, his dark face seared and tortured, his hands and shoulders shaking, his voice tearing like a file over iron words of rage; and she and her lover at bay in the wide, illumined bed; prone, abandoned, weary with voluptuousness, taken ludicrously in sin, unable to speak, unable to move because of the pitiful farce of nakedness in such a bitter hour. What would Bernardina make of the heaped-up minutiæ of that cartoon?

For her own part, Ana knew that it was either agonisingly funny, or serious in the mad sense in which Escovedo saw it. Indeed, it was both—and nothing in between. So therefore it might be easiest now to laugh, and make Bernardina laugh. For the other vision must remain her own. No one would ever understand her if she said—what was the simple truth— that her dignity, as they might call it or her *amour-propre* or any of those customary abstractions which constitute a lady, that none of these had taken any harm that she could re- cognise, and that in fact all that mattered to her outside the plain farce of that moment in her bedroom was that during it she saw that for her Escovedo was right. He was mad, and he was right.

This discovery made a problem for her which was entirely her own, and composed her present unhappiness. But the insult she had undergone was irrelevant—and she had no way of making that clear, so would not try to. All that was left was to salute the farce, and try to reassure Bernardina somewhat by that means.

She laid a hand on Bernardina's kind one that pressed upon her arm.

"Ah, you dear, true one," she said. "You mustn't worry. I'll forget it. It'll blow away! Everything does."

"That's right, *chiquita*. That's my own good girl——"

"You know," said Ana, steeling herself, "you know it's *you* I'm sorry for——"

"Me?"

"Yes, you. Oh Bernardina, how you must be ill with wanting to laugh! Yes, laugh——"

"At what, may I ask?"

"Dear saint, at the wildest piece of bedroom farce that can ever have taken place in Madrid!" As Ana spoke she laughed outright, enjoying herself. "Poor Berni! was there ever such bad luck?"

"No," said Bernardina firmly, for she felt at sea with this mood and did not think it healthy. "I admit freely that I'd laugh my guts out if it happened to someone else. But the fun of a thing depends on whom it happens to, *chiquita*! And there's something about you that *isn't* funny. No, you won't get *me* laughing over this affair. *I* feel like murder. That's what I feel like."

"Indeed, Bernardina?" said Antonio Perez's voice on the steps below them. "Then perhaps you *are* the murderer?"

The two women turned to him.

"What murderer?" said Bernardina.

He came to them and taking Ana's arm smiled at her

somewhat anxiously. When he spoke his voice was serious.

"I come with strange news," he said. "At sunset to-day in the Calle Santa Maria in Madrid Juan de Escovedo was assaulted and stabbed. Three men are being looked for. My despatch says that Escovedo is dead."

The three stood very quietly. Bernardina loosed Ana's arm and moved a step away.

"Praise God," she said coolly. "A man of Spain usually knows what has to be done."

She went down the steps then and towards the house. As she went she felt a brutal, happy impulse to laugh, and did laugh aloud, but checked herself at once, and hoped that the two she had left did not hear her.

Antonio did hear, and smiled. But Ana, in his arms, was sobbing. He felt her body wrench and shake against him. He had never known her to cry, but after the tension of recent days and as a reaction to the violent news he brought, he thought it was a natural thing. He stroked her hair and comforted her.

THE FIRST CHAPTER   (MAY AND JUNE 1578)

I

ANA stayed at Pastrana throughout spring and summer. She sent the children to Madrid for April and May, escorted by tutors and governesses, and the whole party captained by Bernardina.

The king was disappointed. In his brief visits to Madrid he counted now upon her awaiting him at his pleasure in the long, quiet room across the street from the Alcázar. He wrote peremptorily to her to express his annoyance. But she stayed in Pastrana.

While Bernardina and the children were away she made a kind of peace with herself.

The death, by murder, of Juan de Escovedo, falling pat upon her terrible encounter with him, had driven her into a region of pain and debate for which her simplicity provided no compass. That the murder had been ordained and directed by the man who had shared her last intolerable glimpse of Escovedo and had felt responsible for her having to endure it —this was indeed a dark and unmanageable threat within her particular confusion. Yet, Spaniard, she could relegate it to a place below the plane of action. The murder had long been commanded by the king, and had already been attempted— twice, Antonio said—before the terrible private injury was offered.

She accepted the plain sense of that; she knew it was true. Yet this did not affect the visionary panic, the superstitious woe in which she felt the blow upon herself of Escovedo's death. For all she knew, men's little plans, and indeed the fore and aft of days in their designs, might even be small pieces, chessmen, in God's fingers. A sin and a soul, however small and silly both, might conceivably be at once foreseen and important in Heaven—more important than Philip's policy in the Lowlands. She laughed at her attempt to grasp God's timing of this possible intervention—laughed at her own revealed pomposity. Yet she knew what she meant—that a blade of grass might, just conceivably, by Heaven's values, be worth a planetary explosion.

She did not formulate her hysterical apprehension—indeed, she found courage to laugh at it when it came up near words and thereby suggested megalomania. But her soul was bowed, nevertheless. So it had been from the night when Escovedo stood over her bed and shouted at her. So now it was, when he lay so soon in his grave, sent there by Philip and her lover. She had not resented his admonition then, when he lived; she had only felt its truth. Now more than ever she felt that.

So through the gleaming, sweet weather she rode about the mulberry farms and the orchards, and let their tranquillity assuage her. This eastward extremity of Castile, with Aragon just over its shoulder, was not the very Spain of her heart; she understood better and admired more the land about Toledo, and the great *mesa* from Salamanca to Medina and Segovia; the people here too—Catalans and Aragonese having mixed their useful, stimulating blood with that of her own slower and more formal people, and the cross having been calculatedly bettered by Ruy, the good husbandman, by his plantation of *moriscos*, the mulberry farmers and silk-makers he wanted—the people, as she had often said to Ruy, were only by elastic courtesy Castilian. Whereat he used to laugh and gently deny the need for courtesy.

"It isn't a bar sinister *not* to have been born on a granite crag and spent ten generations starving there, Ana," he used to say. "It isn't an affliction *not* to have a brain made of granite. And I'm a foreigner too, you see, and I get on well with my fellow-mongrels. It's just that I like to see things *done*, whenever possible."

He had taken pleasure in her inbred intransigence, without ever yielding an inch to it in the conduct of life. She, however, had been perfectly gracious to his utilitarian philosophy, and obedient to it during his life and, as far as she could without his direction, after his death; while retaining her right to make the archaic, conservative observations which were native to her and which, she knew, brightened his enjoyment of her society. But she had found peace with him in his tranquil, well-governed lands, and since their early days of settlement there it had never occurred to her to desire to live elsewhere. Even in the frenzy of helplessness which had overtaken her at his death, her only idea of refuge had been the convent at Pastrana. Turned away from there in disgrace and anger, she had not even thought to seek another cloister. She had returned to her home and gathered about her the healing obscurity of the village she knew.

And now humiliated and guilty again, feeling sore and sordid, she was glad of Pastrana and desired to stay there.

I am marked for the grotesque, she told herself, as she had before, in the relentless night. And, alone, she would take off her black diamond patch. She would stare then in the mirror at her hungry, long face, so halved and split into blankness, and at the closed and dark-stained empty socket of her eye. And she would think of Escovedo in his grave, and of the cold beastliness of calculated love-pleasure, and the absurdity of sexual delight. And she would pace her room and long for the cocks to crow in daylight.

But by degrees daylight won her over somewhat. Observing, at first with resentment and forlornly, how the external process of days and pieces of work went on, how complicated all this was and how it depended upon the self-control and attention of men who were, it must be assumed, much else in their own hearts than the performers of their visible duties, she began to find patience with herself.

She watched the movements of the sky and the changes in fields; she saw how, by bell and light, men moved from work to food and from food to rest. Passion, after all, love-making, cheating and the counting of money; prayer, fear of death, the desire to know God and to have children—all these things, perilous with traps for the hasty, lay privately within the gentle, obvious surface, for every actor on that surface. If they did not the routine would have no meaning; and perhaps it derived its apparent grace, and its heavenly grace too, from the fact of underpinning dangers, private shames and snares. Sin, after all, was a commonplace; and perhaps others too felt sometimes that the most idiotic part of sin is our failure to understand our own motives within it. But a part of self-disgust must be, she thought, that we bear it alone; we have to learn to live with it in silence, and simultaneously go on being the people our fellows know and work with.

She fretted thus, riding and walking about Pastrana or looking at the open faces of villagers who smiled good-day. She looked at the lovely, changeful sky attentively, and towards the pure, high Guadarramas, and at the budding roses that Ruy had planted. And often she knelt in the *Colegiata* church beside Ruy's tomb, and wondered what he thought of her crude, blundering sins and of her love for Perez; and begged him to help her if he could, and to find mercy for her.

News came often from Madrid; from many people, but most welcomed from Bernardina and from Antonio. She had asked Antonio not to visit her for a time and he obeyed, though protesting gallantly against the ban. But she knew from his letters that he was overworked and unusually anxious and that secret journeys to the country would have been an excessive addition to his present cares.

The chief news, which came before April was half-done, did not surprise her. The family of Escovedo had not taken his murder as an act of God; and neither had Madrid society in general. Arrests and the procedure of justice were looked for, and as weeks passed and nothing happened, began to be demanded with free comment.

Antonio reported flippantly that when his wife Juana had called, in courtesy, to condole with Escovedo's widow, the latter had raised a dramatic wail upon her entrance, threatening vengeance upon unnamed enemies. Other ladies of Madrid had witnessed the curious little scene, and Juana was much surprised by it, Antonio said. "However," he went on, "the family are taking their grievance to the right quarter. My learned colleague, Mateo Vasquez—you remember him? The Andalusian cleric, my *vis-à-vis*, who controls that half of the royal mind which is not *my* territory—well, he is a family friend of the Escovedos, and so has very properly undertaken to lay a petition from them before the king, so that justice may be speeded. Speed is not, of course, what you get from taking petitions to Philip, but the Escovedos don't know that yet. And the good Vasquez is at El Escorial now, and no doubt will do his utmost. Meantime here in the town the unhappy affair is quite a topic . . ."

Ana pondered this news more gravely than she was intended to. She knew that it was thrown off carefully, as if merely to show her how the wind blew, and otherwise to indicate how pathetically blind was the appeal through Vasquez to Philip. Vasquez himself was acting with perfect correctness in undertaking the petition, and had of course no more idea than Escovedo's young son of the grim comedy of going to that tribunal.

Ana knew that Perez felt safe. Philip was bound to him by friendship and gratitude; bound even closer by shared and dangerous secrets of high politics with which Perez could do him grave harm; bound above all in this instance by his own guilt. Escovedo was killed by his royal instruction. This statement must never be made in any Spanish court of justice.

Even if it could not be proved—but Perez had the instruction in Philip's own writing—it must not be said. It would endanger the king and his whole policy, past and future, to a degree Philip dared not try to measure. So, clearly, Perez felt safe, and could not help relishing somewhat brutally the farce of Vasquez laying the grievance of the victim's family in all good faith before the victim's murderer. Yet she pondered the news more gravely and more often than Antonio would have thought necessary.

Bernardina wrote often—of the children and the house and shoppings she had been instructed to do, and of Madrid as she found it. She, not having the Secretary of State's powers of sealed safe conduct for letters, was very careful in her news-giving. " . . . to tell the truth, we are all a bit dull without you, *chiquita*. Even the children admit that, though we do our best with all the parties and sociabilities. And such a lot of clothes we are having made—we'll come back to you like a lot of dandies from the court of that fancy King Henry in France! Many people call on us, and all are disappointed that you stay in the country. But never mind them—you are right. And I hope you are resting and sleeping well—and drinking red wine at night, as I told you. La doña Beatriz de Frias sends you her very particular love. The Escovedo family is all in town, but naturally in deep mourning, so we do not meet them. But they say they are in a great clamour to have the murderers caught—which is very natural. It's said they are appealing to the king. But Diego tells me that so far as he can make out the police are doing nothing at all—and he thinks that it's certain that whoever did it has got out of Spain long ago. I expect so. I am having your bedroom stripped, and the pictures and ornaments removed, as you told me to. That room you want for a bedroom now is small, *chiquita*, and rather far from your other rooms. However, I'll see about hangings and all you said, and send you patterns soon. Anichu and I were looking for something in your sitting-room this morning and she said to me: 'I don't like the Long Room to-day. But I think it's lovely when Mother's here.' She's right—it's a dead hole without you. Fernán and Anichu are writing to you. Ruy tells me he wrote yesterday. We don't forget you . . ."

II

At the end of May the Marqués de Los Velez drove over from Alcala to see her. He had been in Madrid and at El Escorial for some weeks on government affairs, so Ana had not spoken with him since Easter Sunday.

His eyes looked worried, she thought, and he seemed somewhat guarded in his brightness. It was late afternoon when he came and he was tired. He said the drive was tiring. They sat in her drawing-room above the front court-yard, and the servants brought a *merienda* of bread and various cold dishes; Ana poured wine and pressed him to eat.

She knew he wanted to talk about Antonio, did not know how best to begin, yet would not be at ease until he had found an opening. So, after he had eaten and drunk a mouthful, she spoke plainly.

"Is there any danger for Antonio in this Escovedo situation?" she asked.

He looked at her gratefully.

"I'm not sure," he said. "I can't see any positive danger, yet it is true that the king is acting curiously. What do you know of recent news? What does Antonio tell you?"

"Nothing real, at present. His letters are gay and evasive, and as if he were very busy. Which indeed I am sure he is. And you see, I haven't seen him since—since the night of Escovedo's death."

"Ah!" De Los Velez looked at her, then took some bread and fish and chewed slowly.

He knew that Ana was the mistress of Antonio Perez, and

that she knew he knew that; he knew the shared culpability of
the king and Perez in Escovedo's death, and that Ana also
knew that; he knew that the dead man had lectured and
interfered inexcusably in her illicit love-affair. Antonio had
told him of that and of his rage against Escovedo because of
his fanatical preachings. He had *not* told of the awful climax
of those preachings; Ana knew that no one living would ever
hear of that from Antonio's lips or hers. Still, the old
Marqués knew in general the personal as well as the political
shadows that hung across the grave of Escovedo.

He believed that when moving among possible dangers it
was better even for trusted friends to make few, very few,
plain assertions. If one has never heard a statement made, or
oneself made it, then one can so swear, if need be. Thus he
had never said, or heard anyone—not Ana, not Perez—say
that the two were lovers; and he guessed, and rightly, that
Perez had never, to Ana, verbally or in writing admitted his
actual direction of the murder of Escovedo. Yet these things
were known to those concerned and could be presumed
upon, within the right formulæ, in the conversation of two or
three close friends.

De Los Velez sought now, as he ate, for an idiom of plain
statement which should be neither offensive nor dangerous.
He lifted his glass.

"Let us drink to Philip together," he said with a malicious
small laugh. "Do you feel loyal to him?"

Ana raised her glass at once.

"Always," she said. "Much more loyal than he needs or
guesses."

They drank, and smiled at each other as they set down their
glasses.

"Yes, indeed," said de Los Velez. "If only the man
would understand our loyalty, how simple it is, how willing!
If only he didn't have to make a sort of witch's brew every
now and then of the feelings of his faithful servants. My

Heavens! Look what we do for him! Look what Perez does,
and risks! Yet——"

"Yet, what? What's brewing now?"

"I wish I knew." He paused. "Perez clearly hasn't told
you this—and perhaps that only means that he thinks no
more of it than of any other antic of the king. Or perhaps
he'll be very angry with me if I tell you. Still, I believe you
ought to know. Maybe you'll reassure me?"

"What is it?"

"You know that Mateo Vasquez has taken charge—quite
kindly and rightly—of the petition of the Escovedo family
concerning the—assassination of their father? Now Vasquez
has no access to the Netherlands files in foreign affairs, and by
Philip's deviousness has had no idea at all of the king's
exasperation against Juan de Escovedo. No idea at all in fact
of the truth in the affair he is championing. But the
Escovedos—and their advisers, many of them people in high
office and well known to you, people who know their way in
our politics and who, whether or not they have axes to grind,
know better than to make idiotic assertions in a case like this
—well, these people have assured Mateo Vasquez that
Escovedo was murdered by Antonio Perez." He paused, and
Ana did not move or interrupt. "They assert, Ana, that the
murder was in expiation of a private grievance; that Escovedo
knew of an illicit love-affair of Perez's, and was threatening
to expose this secret to the king."

He waited and looked at her. Her answer surprised him.

"Escovedo did know," she said. "And he did threaten to
reveal what he knew to the king. But that is accidental. The
king ordained his death, and the king was obeyed."

"Yes, that is so. Well now. Vasquez wrote a despatch for
the king on the death of Escovedo. In it he stated plainly this
accusation. He said that Escovedo's family knew that Perez
had had him murdered, because of a woman. He said that
Perez feared exposure because this woman was well known,

and her honour was in his hands. He presented his despatch
to the king."

Ana smiled a little.

"But how do *you* know this?" she asked.

De Los Velez laughed outright.

"There's the question of someone who knows Philip!" he
cried delightedly. But instantly he grew grave again, and
poured more wine and drank some before he went on. "I
know the contents of that despatch," he said, "because
Philip did what I regard as a quite inexplicable thing with it.
After keeping it to himself for some days, he showed it to
Perez—and to me—and asked us how he should answer it."

"But—surely, to show it to Perez was very injudicious?"

"Outrageously—as a child could tell him. Yet Philip did
it premeditatedly. And if he has a fault—and, Lord, he has
many!—it is excess of judiciousness. So, you see, I can't make
it out."

"What does Antonio think?"

"He hasn't told you any of this?"

"No."

"Oh! Then I wonder what that means? Well, firstly he
was somewhat struck by the boldness of the accusation, and
by Vasquez's audacity in presenting it. After all, Perez *is* the
favourite minister and much longer in the king's close service
than Vasquez is. Besides, he wields a general influence
Vasquez will never command. So the despatch struck him as
courageous, and *naïve*. But I think he thought that the king's
showing it to him was a measure of its *naïveté*."

"And so it might be," Ana said. "After all, it shows
Philip's own dismissal of it—well he might dismiss it too,
seeing all *he* knows about Escovedo! And it shows his trust in
Antonio."

"Maybe. I think Antonio thinks that such an apparent
indiscretion from the king means that he's weary of Vasquez,
on the way to getting rid of him. I don't think it means that.

But I haven't told you the *close* of the story, child—which is that Perez, by Philip's request, drafted his reply to Vasquez's despatch. That, I think, is positively funny."

"So funny," said Ana, "that I believe Antonio must be right."

De Los Velez shook his head.

"There's no real sign of it," he said. "Vasquez is too valuable—indeed, Philip's trouble is that both these Secretaries are at present irreplaceable. He has trained them to be perfectly complementary in foreign affairs, and he simply doesn't want to be inconvenienced by the loss of either. I've watched Vasquez in committee, my dear, and I often have to read his memoranda and debate his ideas. He is quite first-class—and in addition a blameless character, and a demon for work."

"So is Antonio," said Ana. "A demon for work, I mean."

They both laughed.

"Yes, I didn't think you meant a blameless character."

"I have always thought Vasquez an unpleasant sort of bore."

"Oh, he's priggish and graceless—and to the world he's just a dull, good cleric. He seems to have no personal tastes or ambitions, and no vices. He takes no bribes in office, and he steals no wives from ageing noblemen. He doesn't notice whether the pages at Court are pretty or not. You can't catch him out, and he has no enemies."

"All of which adds up, sadly enough, to having no friends," said Ana.

De Los Velez laughed appreciatively.

"That's true, indeed—in your and my interpretation of the word 'friends'. I admit that I, for instance, would take elaborate trouble at any time to escape the *ennui* of ten unnecessary minutes of the company of Vasquez—whereas his *vis-à-vis*, that scamp Antonio, may have at will my time, my house, my purse, anything of mine indeed, except perhaps my daughters—if he had ever sought them, and *if*—a long if!—I could have argued them away from his charm!"

The Marqués was growing cheerful. He had cleared a dish of anchovies and eaten a great deal of spiced sausage and smoked ham. He was fishing apricots out of syrup now and eating them whole.

"Delicious, Ana. What *is* your secret of preserving? I simply can't get them done like this by my people."

But Ana's mind was on Antonio and the king.

"What has this contrast of types to do with the Escovedo petition?" she asked.

"Nothing—just yet. But, should the present situation ever come to an open issue between the two Secretaries, don't be surprised if the man of a thousand friends and with all possible power and influence should lose his game to the man who merely has no enemies."

Ana rose and paced across the room to the great window. De Los Velez watched her kindly.

"Why should it come to an open issue between them?" Ana asked.

"It needn't, of course. But Philip's curious tactics may force it that way. He's likely to be in a bad fix himself if the Madrid gossip and outcry for the Escovedo murderers do not subside—and he sees that, and he's playing for time, as usual. Oddly enough, he seems to think that he'd gain something—or that's my guess—by setting Perez and Vasquez at each other's throats. A herring across the trail, I suppose—but honestly, I cannot see his game. Simply I think it conceals danger—for Perez."

"I can't see the danger. Philip is the guilty man, and he knows that."

"My dear—the divine right!"

They both laughed, but Ana not very happily.

"But are Antonio and Vasquez at each other's throats then?" she asked.

"Antonio is certainly in a very dangerous rage against Mateo, who, not knowing that the king has betrayed his private despatch into the hands of the man he accused in it, is touchingly bewildered! And, after all, he is only doing his duty, and will continue to do it. It is perfectly within his function to bring appeals against injustice to the attention of the king. Perez meantime has—just a little—lost his head."

Ana came back from the window slowly.

"How tall you are!" De Los Velez said. "Too tall, really."

"In what way has he lost his head?"

"Oh, he's taken to insulting Vasquez in and out of season—across the Cabinet table, and at public gatherings, and everywhere. Makes a great farce of his adoption of the Escovedo cause, and in general treats him disgracefully. A very foolish policy."

"Maybe." She paused. "You haven't told me what Philip's reply was to Vasquez's despatch. What did Antonio draft for him?"

"Oh, that was quite cunning, very neat. To the effect—I can't remember it precisely now—that Vasquez was on the wrong tack, that Philip had better information, but was awaiting a certain line of evidence before proceeding to justice; that the crime had nothing whatever to do with any woman, but that its perpetrator had a far graver reason for it; and he begged Vasquez to give no further credence to the very rash guesses and accusations of the Escovedos and their friends. That kind of thing. So far as we can make out it has quieted Vasquez down."

"Well then?"

"Oh, but only temporarily! The Escovedo party is still after him, and of course it's clear to him that a course of action must be taken when an innocent citizen is murdered. Besides, he's certain he's right about Perez, and under the stress of Perez's recent outrageous treatment of him he has begun to say what he thinks—in sheer self-defence—to this one and that one. He'll come back to the attack. And meantime it's clear that Perez isn't going to tolerate him much longer as a colleague. Which is very easy to understand. And oh, my dear, the gossip that's flying already, and the side-taking and the surmising! It's really becoming quite a bore in Madrid, this topic. You're very well out of it."

Ana sat silent awhile. A servant came in and removed the tray of food; then he returned and lighted candles.

"No, don't draw the curtains," Ana said, and he went out.

"I meant to get up and look at that picture over there before the light went," said de Los Velez. "It's a new one, isn't it?"

Ana looked with pleasure towards the small canvas he indicated.

"Yes, it's only been here a few days. You must look at it before you go. It's a Mantegna. Antonio found it somehow —through some dealer."

"It looks a beauty from here."

"Yes. It's lovely."

Ana let her eyes rest on the picture, and thought, with anxiety on many planes, of the man who had given it to her. Just when he is about to lose what he valued most between us, the surface of her mind was saying sadly, he begins to know me. This picture, for instance—but her attention was not really on it, or on the giving of presents between lovers. She was perplexed by the talk and news de Los Velez had brought; vaguely, unwillingly she felt herself trying to peer ahead and measure Philip's slow ruthlessness against Antonio's present power over him.

"Don't, Ana," the Marqués said. "Don't look like that, my dear! I've made you sad with my wretched Court gossip. Which is probably all it is—no more than gossip! In any case, what's a mere domestic side-show like this to Antonio, who spends his whole life sharpening his wits on the vast intrigues of France and Italy? He's got his hands on all the strings, my dear. He'll see the whole thing through and over without losing any sleep. In any case, what *can* Philip do, except protect him from his slanderers?"

Ana smiled a very faint question on the word "slanderers".

"It's a cold and brutal situation," she said. "Thinking of it makes one shiver a little for everyone. The poor Escovedos!"

"Well, yes, the poor Escovedos," said de Los Velez coolly. "But they're all of a sudden of major importance in Madrid—which is a novelty for them, and I don't think they are exactly disliking it."

"That's hard-hearted of you."

"I agree. I've been living too long among courtiers. Still, even I can spare some pity for poor Vasquez now. To have made Antonio his enemy—and then to have to work so close to him, day in day out!" He laughed.

"I expect Philip is already regretting that mistake of the despatch," said Ana.

"Oddly enough, I don't think so. I get the impression that he sowed this discord quite deliberately. But I wonder if he can tell what the harvest will be?"

"How does he seem, Philip?"

"Exactly as usual. Busy, tired, friendly. Immensely pleased with the new *Infante*, of course. Enormous relief to everyone that the creature was born alive and is so far staying alive!"

"Is it a healthy child?"

"Oh, no. It looks a little horror, I think."

"Poor Philip!"

"But he's ravished with it, Ana. Greatly puffed up. Full of work too, and rather boringly interested in all his building and planting up there. Impossible to assess, in fact. But I've an idea—now here is my last comment, I promise, on all this dreary news, and I only make it because I think it may be important—I've an idea that he does suspect that Perez has somehow got a woman mixed up, quite accidentally, in the

Escovedo matter. I think he'd like to verify that suspicion, and get the woman's name. So far no name has been given."

His eyes had an anxious look again.

Ana leant forward and touched his sleeve lightly, as if in reassurance.

"Thank you," she said. "I know you wanted to get that said. And there's nothing to be afraid of in it. Our private lives don't belong to the king."

"Spoken like a Mendoza," de Los Velez said, but he did not look entirely reassured. "And let's hope you don't have to test your theory about private lives."

"There isn't any way of testing it," she said amusedly. "One doesn't submit private life to public tests."

"My dear, dear Ana! Shall I have to start praying for you, you innocent? Give me a little more wine, child. It's dark now, and my coachman will be wanting to start for home."

III

Bernardina and the children returned to Pastrana early in June.

The weather unfolded into slumbrous heat. But there was water in the streams from the Guadarramas, and the gardens and farms flowered; the trees were heavily leafed for shade. The children played with their village friends. Life was timed by the *Colegiata* bell, and Madrid was far away.

Bernardina indeed spilt out her load of gossip bit by bit, and in it naturally much hearsay of the Escovedo scandal—but none of this seemed more than gossip or to carry facts as far as the Marqués had brought them.

Antonio's letters came; presents too, and luxuries from Madrid, constant tokens of his thought of her. But she did not invite him yet to visit her, and he made only joking protests against this. " . . . De Los Velez tells me that he told you of my feud with Vasquez," he wrote once. "Well!

you will understand that I have cause! The ass is quiet at present, though I hear extraordinary tales of his subterranean inquiries against me. And his clients are *not* quiet! However, that part is the king's trouble, not mine. All I need watch for are my colleague's allegations against me. I am having no more of them. Sooner or later, the king will have to choose between us, or face an enquiry. So, naturally, I'm not worrying. In any case, I'm kept at work like seven mules. And when I come out of that side-gate of the Alcázar at all hours of the night I look up in vain to the windows of the Long Room. No light ever, no one there. But to-night I drive up to El Escorial, God help me! Several days of conference, and you know how I hate the place. However, the king is being agreeable, and even considerate, at present. And Madrid isn't alluring. It wasn't so dead somehow when at least your house was open and I sometimes saw the children cantering about. But now—well, I get so bored that I almost hate you, and think of throwing stones at your detestable blank windows. Still, I *shall* see you again. You haven't vanished off the earth, have you? And when I do, how is it to be, Princess? . . ."

Summer moved on; the Escovedo stalemate slid to the background of thought; even Bernardina seemed to have forgotten it, and Antonio dropped the ominous name from his letters. Ana's days were filled, as by fixed country habit; mornings of estate and family management, either at her desk or riding about the land with bailiffs or tenants, or in conference sometimes with silk merchants from Zaragoza or Madrid; afternoons, too hot for movement, of sewing or letter-writing or indolence in her drawing-room, or with the children in the watered patio; evening rides and picnics with the children; songs in the garden with them, under the moon, and to Bernardina's guitar; and early to bed—or so Anichu protestingly called it at midnight—with music still straying up from here and there about the village street.

A suitable, conforming life, such as Philip would approve, she thought; the life, in fact, that Ruy had fixed for her and that she knew by heart.

It gave her time to think. But she did not think, or thought less and less as the days passed, of politics or of the crimes of Philip and Perez and the possible clash which these were likely now to cause between the two men's temperaments. Somehow day by day her mind withdrew from all that story, shrugging it off fatalistically until it might become necessary to consider it again.

She thought of her passion for Perez, and sought to discover whether she repented of it truly now, or whether the strange shock she had undergone—of sympathy with Escovedo's scorn and acceptance of his verdict—had been no more than hysterical, an hysterical escape perhaps from an outrage which should have been, on the face of it, unbearable.

She feared to turn sanctimonious, and therefore false, against herself; more than that, she feared to fall into the trap of seeming to judge Antonio, instead of leaving that to him. She had a horror of all such impertinence, and so should have felt, as Perez did, sheer, unadulterated loathing of their insane judge, Escovedo. But she could not. The very madness of his last gesture of condemnation attracted and held her attention, as all his former boring sermons had only made her laugh impatiently at his bad manners. There had been no question of manners at the last. It was fanaticism, right or wrong.

She missed Antonio very much in these days. He had carried her a long way in pleasure; had taught her, late, the whole art in great and little of reciprocal love. Very gratefully she had learnt to count on her delight; and now her nerves were restless; the quivering daylight, the dark-blue nights, all stars, hurt her as before she had not understood them to do.

"We're just two dull and bored old countrywomen, Bernardina, you and I," she said one evening in the garden.

"Speak for yourself," said Bernardina. "I've a perfectly good husband here at hand, may I remind you?"

Ana laughed.

"Perhaps it's well to remind me," she said. Bernardina was not faithful to her Espinosa.

"You're getting racy in your style," she said amusedly. "A year or so ago if I had said we were two dull old country-women, you'd have wondered what on earth I was sighing for. Oh, you've learnt a lot in one winter in Madrid, *chiquita.*"

"I wonder. I wonder if what I really learnt was that it's best to stay here, and be dull."

"You're sad to-day. You have a little headache. It'll pass."

Ana looked up towards the Guadarramas and thought of Antonio far away at the western end of them, with Philip in his monastery. Monasteries, convents; Philip with his monks and prayers and ceremonious barricadings against sin—but the natural answer to love and its perplexities is not in these. And Antonio in any case sought no answer, knew no perplexities. He was so much without sense of guilt in his exploitation of the senses as to be innocent. She liked this blazing pagan innocence which at once made him almost a foreigner in her eyes and a young, understandable boy.

She shrank from offending against that sweeping ease of his sensuality, that refusal of fuss, that attention to generosity and simplicity which gave style to his love-making and had been of immeasurable help to her uncertainties in the first days of their union. Was she now, because of a resolution in her breast which he could never have patience with, to hurt and strike at that in him which had meant most to her when passion was unclouded? Was she now, having taken all he gave, to be contrite at his expense, and torment him with prayers and explanations which could only appear to him stupid, medieval, hysterical, and a dull disfigurement of her?

She shrank—even if the salvation of her soul hung on it—

from thrusting her alien remorse upon his soul. She despised
the unfairness, and the interference with him, of a repentance
which was only hers. She had grown fond of Antonio Perez,
and so she wished neither to hurt him nor, by gracelessness,
to lose his dear regard. And easily now she might do both.
She found herself wishing that his love had tired, as she had
thought it might, in the spring just past.

One evening Anichu walked down the village with her on
an errand to a woman who was weaving silk for the dining-
room chairs.

They came back past the Franciscan convent as some of the
young nuns, returning from work at the school, were passing
in at the gate. They smiled and bowed to Ana, and one of
them kissed Anichu.

The little girl beamed at them. She knew all their names
and told them to Ana.

"I like our having Franciscans here, you know," she told
her mother as they went on. "They're every bit as good as
Carmelites, aren't they?"

"I'm sure they are, sweetheart. Certainly they are very
good, nice nuns."

"Of course, I agree with Fernán that it's a pity you
quarrelled with Mother Teresa."

Ana was startled. She did not know that her children knew
so much about her.

"Yes, it was a pity. I'm sorry I did."

"But then of course *you* couldn't ever have been a nun!
Really you couldn't! Didn't you know that?"

"Not for certain, until I tried."

"If I'd been bigger, I wouldn't have let you," Anichu
said.

Ana smiled down at the little girl.

"Well, I've got you now to take care of me," she said.
"Let's go in and say a prayer."

They went together out of the sun into the dark *Colegiata*

church. Ana lifted Anichu up to the holy water font, and
they splashed each other's foreheads and made the sign of the
Cross. Then they went and knelt side by side on the flag-
stones near Ruy Gomez's tomb.

THE SECOND CHAPTER   (OCTOBER 1578)

It was mid-October when Antonio came to Pastrana.
Officially his visit was to the Marqués de Los Velez, for two
days' rest and hunting at Alcala de Henares. But on the
evening of the first day he drove eastward, to have supper
with Ana.

He came into her drawing-room eagerly, almost running to
her and to the fire. He kissed her hands and gave a little
shiver as he smiled at her and then at the warm, illumined
room.

"Lovely," he said. "Lovely to be with you again—*and* to
be indoors!" He dropped on his knees to get near the fire.
"Forgive me if I warm my hands a minute. I love this room.
And how well you shut away the howling night! Not a
sound of it through your great walls!"

"Is it very wild now?"

"Horrible. I'm glad I didn't ride. I thought of doing so,
as really I need exercise. But to tell you the truth, I was too
tired."

Ana had never before heard him say that he was tired, but
now indeed he looked it.

"What can we do for you, to rest you?"

"Let me stay here on the floor by your fire—and come and
sit near me, where I can see you. Ah yes—just there." He
leant his back against a chair across the hearth from Ana.
"I'll tell you later how you're looking," he said gently, "what
it's like to see you again."

She smiled at the characteristic, flattering ease. He might

never tell her, as he said, how she was looking, yet if he liked he would charge every other phrase he spoke with implication of her beauty.

"I wish only to obey you," she said, "but don't you think I ought to offer you something to eat or drink?"

"Nothing. You're not to move. Oh, Ana! This is rest."

"I've never heard you talk of rest before."

His face was level with the fire and at this moment turned towards it, so she could note in this exaggerating light how deep-driven were its lines of weariness. But he laughed as he turned back to her.

"I'm getting old, girl—that's all it is. Do you know that I actually dozed off and on during the drive from Alcala! Now I'm not a dozer, am I? And on my way to *you*—and after so long!"

Ana smiled.

"It's a warning."

"I'm not taking any warnings," he said, stretching himself again contentedly towards the fire. She felt a light question in his words, and let them fall into quiet.

"That was sad news from the Lowlands," she said. "Poor Don Juan of Austria. He was young to die."

"Yes. He seems to have been ill all the summer. His last letters to Philip were sad affairs."

"And Escovedo needn't have died."

He flicked a hint of hard amusement from his eyes before he answered.

"Well, no," he said. "Not for Philip's reasons."

"How did Don Juan die?"

"The pest. His wretched army has been dying of it like flies for weeks. Ah, the confusions of that whole campaign!"

"Yet he might have succeeded with the Flemings? After all, he was one of them."

"Yes. And curiously enough great numbers of them adored him to the end. But he detested them—he had none of his father's feeling for them. His letters were extraordinarily abusive and impatient."

"He was attractive."

"I never cared for him. But I have little use for these charming soldierly fools."

"How like Ruy that sounds!"

"Well, I am Ruy's pupil."

Ana was thinking of the early days of her marriage when Isabel of Valois was Queen, and when the two brilliant boys, Don Juan of Austria and Alexander Farnese, were the chosen companions of Philip's son, Don Carlos. Carlos was indeed already indicating then the ill-health that was to end in misery; but no one foresaw that, and the boy had an eccentric promise and originality which fed Philip's heart and, together with his pride in his beautiful new wife, made him happy, and adventurous. The court was young in character then, and owed to Isabel its light, exotic grace; Ruy was its shrewd and tactful controller; and the boys, the three royal sprigs, with their rivalries, follies and achievements, encircled the more sophisticated antics of their elders in the aura of their innocent, endearing promise.

Carlos had died, neither innocent nor endearing; and now Don Juan was coming home for burial.

"He died on the first of October, didn't he?"

Antonio nodded. "He always said October was his lucky month, since Lepanto."

"Lepanto itself was unlucky, if you ask me," said Antonio. "What are you thinking about?"

"The past—the days of Isabel. Do you remember that time?"

"Very well. I came back from Italy before the French marriage, and became Ruy's overworked assistant secretary."

"Yes. I remember. You were a vain and dandified creature."

"I still am."

"You are. Where is Alexander Farnese now?"

"The Duke of Parma? In Brussels, I hope. We're handing him the lovely tangle of the Netherlands."

"Well, *he* didn't grow up into a 'charming, soldierly fool'."

"No. He has brains. We must wait and hope. His mother didn't do so badly there, you know. At least, by comparison with what followed! Oh Christ, Ana! Don't start me off on the follies of our foreign policy! God knows I didn't come to you for that!"

Ana came to the fire to put more wood on it. Antonio scrambled to his knees to help her. They knelt side by side adjusting the heavy logs, and he watched her face attentively as the warm light caught and dramatised it. It was her left profile that he saw, and he marked how almost too delicate the fine skin seemed as it lay so spare over her narrow cheekbone; he noted the blue-brown shadow beneath and above her hollowed eye, but how golden and true the eye shone into the exacting firelight, and that her lashes were as ever, shining and childlike. It was indeed a sorrowful thing, he thought, for *her* to have lost an eye. At very close range the details of her beauty, its secret, unproclaimed treasures of delicacy, of accidental girlishness, continued, however often noted, to surprise him, to take his fastidiousness again and again by storm. Often in a side-glance, in a moment of slackness or of what he had thought to be complete inattention from her, he would be brought up sharp on an entirely unforeseen pang of appreciation of her; the edge of her eyebrow, the too-well sculptured bone of her wrist, the light, slim run of sinew from her ear to her throat—such things in her could, he found, besiege his unwary attention, and suddenly suggest themselves to him as containing all beauty. It is by these, he sometimes said to himself, by these inconsequences that I'll remember her for ever.

She leant forward, dropping pine-cones here and there among the logs of the fire. He sat on his haunches and let her do the work.

"You're unlucky," he said. "Your beauty is of a kind that only a lover or a baby can get near enough to see."

Ana rose from the hearth, and ran her hand quickly across his forehead as she did so.

"I wonder what I'm going to do without you," she said.

He sprang to his feet.

"Ah! So that is it?"

"Wait. We must talk."

"Indeed, indeed we must. Oh Ana, I've been frightened of this."

He looked about the room and back to her, and she was distressed to notice that indeed his eyes did look frightened. He moved to a table where there was food and wine, and turned to her as if in apology before he poured himself a drink.

"May I, please?" She smiled. "Oh Ana, you drink too! Drink with me! Let's drink to my power over you, that it may not fail us! Come!"

He moved towards her with two glasses full of red wine. As Ana stretched her hand to take one the great door at the far end of the room opened and her eldest son, Rodrigo, came in.

It was not correct of him to come to her drawing-room uninvited while she entertained a guest, and indeed Ana had thought that he was still at a house-party with his cousins at Guadalajara. However, she smiled at him without concern. He seemed at his ease, and was dressed in indoor clothes, so he must have got back to Pastrana a little before or after Antonio's arrival. He bowed gracefully to his mother and her guest. Ana thought there was a fraction less humour than usual in Antonio's acknowledgment of the boy. As a rule Rodrigo amused him wildly, but she supposed that the inopportuneness of this entrance was exasperating to a man already tired and overstrung. He was in no mood for courtly chatter. Well, they'd get rid of the child in a minute or two.

"I interrupt your little festivity—forgive me!" he said.

Ana raised her brows. This was insolent talk, but as she had never played a maternal role with Rodrigo she could not bring herself to call him to order now. Besides, she was more puzzled than annoyed by his tone. A courtier always, he was always excessively polite to men of power, and regarded Antonio Perez as second only to the king in Spain, and perhaps in some ways more powerful than the king. Ana had heard him make an aristocrat's mild jibes sometimes at Perez's upstart grandeur, but never in any hearing that might endanger their repetition to the Secretary of State; and always, face to face with Perez, he was—as he hoped—charm incarnate; always he seemed delighted to be in the company of this great man, and to do his best to please and entertain him. Therefore this impertinent opening gambit puzzled Ana so much that she thought she had perhaps misheard it.

Perez looked coldly at the boy.

"Yes, you do interrupt us," he said. "Why?"

Ana smiled, more bewildered than ever. It was uncharacteristic of Antonio to waste contempt on trivial people or trivial irritations. Poor little Rodrigo, she thought amusedly, and set herself to watch a scene to which she had no key.

"Because I had not heard that Your Excellency was expected, and indeed my cousin, the Duke of Infantado, told me this morning—I've been staying with him at Guadalajara —that you were due at de Los Velez's place these days, he believed, for some hunting." Ah, thought Ana with a cold shock of surprise—then that's why he came back so soon. He's here to spy on me. My children grow up indeed. Perhaps they even grow dangerous—to my friends. "But when I got here, just after dark," Rodrigo went on suavely, "I saw some men in your livery in the yard. So much smarter than ours, I couldn't be mistaken! So, as soon as I'd changed, I just came along here, to make sure. As Your

Excellency's visit was unlooked for, I take it it is—un-official?"

When this speech, so deftly embroidered with impertinence, ceased, Ana and Antonio, standing some distance from each other and without catching each other's eyes, simultaneously laughed. Two clear, grown-up and spontaneous laughs that ceased with civilised precision before the amusement they held was quite fully expressed. Each realised with pleasure, watching Rodrigo's face and refraining from looking at each other, that they could hardly have done better. There was no denying the natural enjoyment of those two laughs—and they saw Rodrigo wince and begin to look careful. Ana continued to keep her eyes on her son. She was still unable to interpret what was happening.

"How do you mean, unofficial?" Antonio asked in a bored, unanswering tone. He walked towards the fire, taking his wineglass with him. "One doesn't cart one's despatch-boxes about to supper-parties in country houses."

"No, naturally," said Rodrigo, very much a man of the world. "What I meant was that apparently at the Alcázar you are understood to be at the house of the Marqués de Los Velez."

"That is so—that's where I'm staying. May we continue our conversation now, Princess? I'm tired, and not willing to waste time on interruptions."

"I know that," Ana said, "I'm sorry. I invited Don Antonio to visit *me* to-night, Rodrigo. Had I wished you to join us in this room I would have had word sent to you. And you know that it was not correct of you to come to me here uninvited when I have a guest." She was about to add a mere word of dismissal, but suddenly—from where she hardly knew—from Antonio's eye towards which she hardly looked, or along some current of their sympathy—she apprehended, for the very first time in this scene, some real danger to Antonio, some far-concealed threat from his own wide, adult world, just hinted at, foreshadowed in caricature perhaps, by this impertinent boy, her son. So, instead of dismissing him outright, defensively for Antonio she eased her cold contempt and smiled as if indulging a juvenile mistake. "But now you're here, let us overlook that—and perhaps you'll drink a glass of wine with my guest before you leave us?"

"No, thank you, Mother." Rodrigo bowed, then drew himself up and spoke solemnly. "I came here, in fact, to utter a protest. You have not spared our honour in the past— the family should, I suppose, be used to you. Indeed, myself, I have grown up without protest under the shadow of your rumoured royal gallantry. But now Madrid is ringing with another scandal—this time a criminal one. His Excellency may indeed think the world well lost—and indeed I believe for him it *is* lost!—that is his affair, though very odd. But we, the Mendozas, have had enough of *your* legend, Mother. You are old now, you see, and a little ridiculous. And in any case your children set their name above your pitiful pleasures. So I must ask you to dismiss a guest whom I had hoped I might not again have to encounter in my house."

Ana, long trained out of anger, and totally unused to conflict with her children, heard this speech with astonishment which took her so far into surmise that she did not even consider at first that it must be answered. Indeed, though she heard it all and held its implications close, for later analysis, chiefly she attended now to this irrelevance: that though she disliked Rodrigo while he spoke, as she always mercilessly tended to dislike him, and though she thought some of his phrasing—all allowances made—objectionable, yet she saw unblinkingly the justice and right convention of his case. And she watched him with pity, and wondered what it would be expedient, for everyone's sake, including Antonio's, for her to say when he ceased speaking.

But Antonio forestalled her.

He came forward from his place by the fire, holding up a hand to her for silence, when Rodrigo's speech was done.

"Listen, Rodrigo," he said, "if it's a habit of yours to abuse your mother to her face as if she were a street whore who had overcharged you by a *real*, then let me instruct you to keep that habit to where it belongs—your private life. Because by the rules of Spanish honour—which it's time you learnt, isn't it?—any man, catching you at it, is entitled to run you through the body, as a national duty. Now, you have allowed me, for instance, to eavesdrop on one of your moments of ignobility. That's the sort of thing you mustn't do, if you want to live. Because——" Antonio's manner of speech was uniformly cold and advisory; there was no hurry and no variation of tone—"because if I call you out for this performance—and I only hesitate because you're such a baby-boy; ah yes, you are also the first-born of my friends Ruy Gomez and Ana de Mendoza—but if I do call you out, you will die within one minute of the crossing of our swords. You're a promising blade, but you know that my swordsmanship is quite simply out of your reach."

"I await your seconds, Your Excellency. Good night, Mother."

"No, I haven't finished," said Antonio. "All that was only about manners, which is the general reason why I may kill you before your seventeenth birthday. But I want to say this about the gossip you spat out so unbecomingly. I am His Majesty's Secretary of State, and it is my boring duty to know everything about such major political scandals as this with which you say Madrid is ringing. Madrid is not ringing with it—clearly you haven't been there lately. Neither has that example of provincialism, the Duke of Infantado. If either of you was just a bit in touch with events you'd know that a slightly alarmed hush has fallen in Madrid about the Escovedo petition—and that the very good reason for this discretion is that the President of Castile—Don Antonio de Pazos, whose eminence and power I need hardly stress, I think?—has examined the case which was to be offered to the High Court of Justice. His ultimate counsel to the unhappy Escovedos was clear-cut, and is known to most people of importance now. Not of course to sporting Dukes like you and Infantado. However, it behoves you if you want to save your neck and get on in life, either to keep up to date with our scandals, or if you can't do that, keep out of them. And, in conclusion, Rodrigo—I was a witness to-night of your offence of *lèse-majesté*. You're not too young to go to prison for that. So you see, I can do as I please with you—and that's all for now. Consider whether or not you've made a fool of yourself."

Antonio jerked his head in dismissal, and then turned to the table where the food was and helped himself to a handful of prawns.

Ana looked in pity at her son. It was clear that he had lost his bearings; needed time to think.

"You must go now, Rodrigo," she said gently.

"I go with alacrity," he said. "Poor Mother, what a fool you are! Good night."

"Good night, Rodrigo."

He bowed to her and left the room.

"It was a silly bluff," Antonio said. "But it did scare the little ass, I hope."

Ana was pacing the length of the room.

"Oh that!" she said, dismissing the details of the episode with a flick of her hand. "You managed him very well. And saved *me* the dilemma of answering his moral strictures! Which I couldn't very well have done, could I?" She paused in her striding in the middle of the room. Antonio noticed a faint flush rising in her cheeks—she looked excited and young. He came to her with her glass of wine.

"We were going to drink—do you remember?—to my power over you, Ana."

She took the wineglass without paying attention to it or to what he said.

"What's been going on in Madrid that I don't know about, Antonio? What does it mean, what does it come from, this amazing behaviour of Rodrigo?"

He paused before he answered her.

"Actually," he said, "I think it means a very great deal. In itself it's nothing—but it's a straw in the wind. A rather strong wind, I'd say. It surprises me a great deal more than Rodrigo guessed, I hope. There's much to be deduced from it that I hadn't known." His eyes narrowed and he spoke slowly, carelessly; it seemed that his thought was far ahead of his words, moving rapidly through obstructions and long-shot surmises. "Come, drink," he said, changing his manner. "And if you won't take that other toast, drink, girl, to my power and omniscience as Secretary of State! Ah, what a bluff it is! What a boring game we play who work with the king!"

"You are troubled. What is it? Are you in danger?"

"Troubled—no. But in danger, possibly yes. I think that we are both in danger, Ana."

"I, in danger?" She laughed incredulously. "That really couldn't be so."

He sat down near the fire.

"Perhaps you're not. Perhaps I'm thinking too fast. I often do. Coming here to-night I was in two minds as to how much to tell you—but now I see I'd better talk. Since your own son is running about to spread the news—you may need the facts at any time."

Ana came and stood beside him. She took his hand and held it lightly between both of hers. She felt very much in love with him.

"Then we were both in two minds about what we had to say to-night? That isn't like us. I suppose it means that changes are coming?"

"No. Things are happening to us from outside, happening fast and treacherously, I think—and we have to be ready for them. But nothing changes between us. I belong to you, just as I have done since that night when you seduced me so coldly. And you belong to me."

"Yes. I belong to you—in the way in which you mean it. Though not perhaps demonstrably now."

He sprang up with a sharp, protesting laugh at her odd word, "demonstrably", and took her hard and close into his arms.

"'Not demonstrably'? Ah, girl, do you want me to demonstrate this instant what I mean by your belonging to me?"

"You needn't. I belong to you far more to-night than I did on that night when I seduced you. Though that was heavenly, Antón."

"Not the best though, was it? Not the best of all?"

"No, not the best. Oh, I am grateful to you! Grateful for ever."

"That's what I mean by my power over you, Princess——"

She kissed his forehead and then moved away from him, out of his arms.

"There are other powers," she said. "Philip's power over you; Escovedo's over me."

"Escovedo's?"

She rang a silver bell.

"Wait," she said. "That must wait. There's a lot to be said to-night."

A servant entered.

"Ask Doña Bernardina to be so good as to come to me for a moment, please."

The man withdrew.

"I think I'll drink this wine now," Ana said.

"Do, I beg you. I'm tired of offering it and seeing it pushed aside. Bernardina—she is devoted, isn't she? You trust her?"

"Yes. I wouldn't expect her to face the three tortures of the Holy Office for me—why should I? But she has a good, true heart."

"She knows your secrets?"

"I assume she does. We don't discuss our private lives, but we know some things about each other."

"Ah, reciprocal blackmail!"

"Yes. Are you hungry?"

"I believe I am."

"We'll have supper early."

Bernardina came in and Antonio greeted her.

"We're very glad to see you here again, Don Antonio," she said. "It's been a long absence."

"Much too long, my friend. I'm happy to be in the Princess's house again."

"It's safer than some places, I should think, *señor*."

"It is indeed," he said, amused by her coolness.

"Listen, Bernardina," said Ana. "Supper has been ordered, of course, for Don Antonio and me? But will you tell them that we want it now, and in this room? Tell them not to fuss, and that if some things aren't ready, to give us whatever they have. That will do, won't it?" she asked Antonio.

He nodded. He was considering Bernardina and wanted to sound her friendship. Ana might need the devotion of her household soon, but would never think of playing for it.

"Oh, anything will do," he said. "I'm very hungry. Won't you drink a glass of wine with us, Doña Bernardina?"

"Do, Berni. I'll have some more please, Antón."

Pouring out the wine he smiled at Ana's casual informality. Calling him Antón before her *dueña*! Certainly she was no intriguer. He must remember that.

"Thank you," said Bernardina. "I'll just drink your health, and then fly off and tell them to hurry supper."

"Yes—do please ask them not to lay a state banquet for the

Secretary of State," Ana said. "Just let them bring a few things on trays."

"I'll do my best—but you know Diego doesn't like your slipshod notions. You're looking tired, Don Antonio. Are you overworked?"

"Naturally. You aren't, I hope?"

"Oh, she makes me earn my keep."

"She's a lazy Andalusian," said Ana. "Oh, Berni—and this is for everyone, please, including my son Rodrigo—I am supping *alone* with Don Antonio, and I do not desire to receive anyone else to-night. Make that clear, will you?"

Antonio was surprised by this stressed instruction.

"Indeed I will, *chiquita*," said Bernardina. "I beg your pardon humbly that Rodrigo came bothering you—but I didn't even know he was back from Guadalajara."

"Oh, you couldn't have stopped him. He was determined to see Don Antonio."

"So I gathered," said Bernardina grimly. "I've been giving him a piece of my mind just now. He's getting a little above himself, is Master Rod!"

"I got that impression," Antonio said, and he and Bernardina laughed together.

The *dueña* set down her emptied glass.

"You'll have supper in a very few minutes," she said. "And I promise you'll be left in peace, *chiquita*."

When she was gone Antonio looked inquiringly at Ana.

"Since we've been lovers," he said, "I've never heard you tell a lie to protect your secret, but neither have I ever—until now—heard you say anything to seem to advertise it. Why were you so emphatic about everyone knowing that you desire to be alone with me?"

"For Rodrigo's benefit—and I think Bernardina understood me. Do you mind?"

He laughed and shook his head.

"Go on. Explain."

"It's easy. If Rodrigo and the world in general are going
to talk as apparently they're talking, then it has to be made
crystal-clear to them that you are my very dear, particular
friend——"

He laughed delightedly.

"Perverse and mad! Oh, Ana!"

"Not mad at all. I have a plan. And besides, you *are* my
very, very dear, and if the wind is blowing cold for you at
present, I'd like it known that you will always shelter here."

He stared at her.

"I believe you *have* a plan!" he said.

"But that's what I've just said," she answered innocently.
"Of course, you have to tell me yet what in fact is happening,
but still, in a general way I have a plan."

"Having a plan suits you," he said. "You look wonderfully excited."

"I am wonderfully excited."

"What is your plan?"

Servants flung open the great door and began to carry in a
laden supper-table.

"To put away that very dull Pantoja de la Cruz," said Ana,
waving towards a picture. "I want a clear space round the
Mantegna."

"Yes—you should do that. But what will the donor of
Pantoja say?"

"I doubt if he'll ever be here again to see. Doesn't the
Mantegna look lovely?"

Antonio walked over to the small picture and studied it.
The servants set chairs ready to the supper-table, trimmed the
fire, gathered up used wineglasses and withdrew.

"Come and eat, Antón."

They sat down to supper.

"And the plan? Come on, I'm dying to hear it!"

She laughed somewhat shyly.

"Oh, I don't know what *you* call a plan," she said. "But

I have, all of a sudden, a general idea of attack."

"Attack on what?"

"*You* have to tell me that."

"It must be a splendid plan," he said, laughing at her, feeling amused and happy now as he had not felt for months. "Outline it—come on!"

"I will when I've eaten a little more," she said, for a footman came in as she spoke, to change their plates.

"Ever since my birth," she began when they were alone again, "I've been hearing that I am probably the most powerfully placed female in Spain. When I was a child I thought that that solemn fact meant something. I thought I was a pawn—a very important pawn—in the hands of our nobility!"

"How old were you when you were thinking these high politics?"

"Six, seven, eight."

"Does Anichu think in that powerful, masculine way?"

"I've no idea. But she seems a gentle character—more modest than me."

"*Your* modesty is heart-breaking, I think."

"If I have any modesty, life imposed it, Antón. Very rightly. But I was a self-important child—like Rodrigo."

"You were never the least bit like Rodrigo. He's a changeling."

"Well anyway, I just quite simply thought that I was a very important pawn in Spanish affairs!"

"Sweet child sitting among her dolls!" said Antonio. "And you were right. The Mendozas justified your faith, and sold you high."

"Not high enough, I thought at the time. I was taken aback by my marriage. I had thought that they were marrying me to the king."

"You terrible little girl," he said. "How old were you when they signed you up?"

"Eleven. I don't think I was pure politician. I had seen Philip often when I was small—and he was romantic-looking. Somehow he seemed a boy to me, even when he was twenty-four and a widower. And Ruy of course was an aged, aged man of thirty-six. I think it was Philip's fair hair had made him seem so contemporary. And then, he *was* the only fair-haired man in Spain!"

"Did you tell Ruy of your matrimonial disappointment?"

"Oh yes; he loved the story."

"No, don't ring. I'll put the plates over here. Let's just eat fruit and things now, shall we?"

She nodded.

"Philip likes that story too," she said.

"Ah! He knows it?"

"Yes, indeed. I told him—when I was older."

"When he was in love with you?"

"Yes. I told him he had mistimed—that he had been my *first* love."

"He'd like that. Does he ever remind you of it?"

"Yes. Sometimes he surprises me by jokes about it."

"Surprises you? But don't you know the length of his memory, the depth of his vanity?"

"I don't think he's much vainer than other men?"

"Perhaps not. But he has the power other men have not—to sanctify vanity, and if necessary to avenge its wounds."

"Maybe. But this about my childish fancy for him is just an old family joke, Antón——"

"But he *was* in love with you when you were grown up?"

"Yes. Yes and no. I think perhaps I was more in love than he."

"Really in love with him, Ana?"

"Attracted, restless—oh, I liked him very much. But he had given me to Ruy, and he knew that my husband had come to set store by his marriage and was determined to keep me faithful. So—give him his due—he couldn't make up his mind to the sin against his beloved Ruy. And anyway I don't honestly think he wanted me enough. He had Isabel then, and he was fairly happy——"

"So there were endless love-scenes, and again and again he tantalised you both for proof of his seductiveness——"

"You seem to know him. You talk like a woman——"

"Politics or a love-affair—oh yes, I know Philip. And so I think—from all you tell me—that you *are* in danger now."

"And I think not. That's why I've told you all this. It's part of the plan."

He laughed gently.

"If it is it's a dangerous plan."

"Plans have to be. After all, you only make plans in danger."

"Nonsense, Ana. Plans are made so that danger need not arise."

"But how do you make them then?"

"You're talking like Anichu. Lunatic, tell me the plan. Afterwards I'll tell you what to plan about."

"Perhaps it isn't much of a plan," she said nervously. "It's merely that I'm going back to Madrid. I'm going to be there, at hand, as long as you're in trouble—for all to see."

"Ana!" he said, and his eyes blazed on her. "Oh, Ana, I have nothing against that—speaking generally. But go on. I'm waiting for the *idea*."

She bent over a dish of fruit.

"I hate pomegranates," she said. "Don't you? All that spitting."

"But you don't have to spit."

"I can see no other way. These are the last figs—let's eat them."

"First or last, let's eat them."

"The idea is this. Your security is being threatened by Mateo Vasquez?"

Antonio looked at her questioningly before he answered.

"He is the instrument of the Escovedos," he said.

"Hardly. The Escovedos have a tragic grievance, but what possible reason have they to assume that you are their target?"

"They'd know about our political differences. And he probably talked at home of his disapproval of my private life. He may even have said that he and I had quarrelled about that."

"Even so—how could the poor Escovedos *dare*, all by themselves, to bring a major charge against *you*—on that much evidence?"

"Extraordinarily rash of them, I agree. Oh, certainly they are encouraged—perhaps they're just being used——"

"By Vasquez?"

"And some of his friends."

"He has friends? Who are they?"

"Oh, nobody you'd know."

Ana smiled. "Yes, but tell me."

"There's a man—Augustin Alvárez de Toledo—he's in the Treasury. And he's got a brother, a very brainy priest——"

"I've never heard of either of them."

"Well, you will hear. They are great supporters of Vasquez—live in the same house with him, I think."

"That must be charming for them."

"Then there's a man called Milio—half-Italian, and wealthy. Calls himself Dr. Milio, and frequents the aristocracy. He seems to have some hidden axes to grind. He's at present very much Vasquez's partisan. But really he's some kind of protégé of the Duke of Alba. Still, except that he would not interfere *against* any plan to ruin me, I'm certain that old egotist isn't bothering himself with courtiers' plots. Simply, his name may be used by Milio, to encourage the timid in this present affair. But mentioning Alba brings us back to that straw in the wind of a few minutes ago— Rodrigo's behaviour."

"Does Alba come into that?" Ana asked in surprise.

"I think he does. You know Rodrigo is growing up very anti-liberal?"

"Yes. He talks surprisingly about his father's mistakes. And I've heard him express disapproval of the continuing dominance of the liberal *amistad* in the Cabinet. But Rodrigo's politics, after all!"

"Oh, they may make you smile—but they're forming all the same in that pretty head. He's a reactionary, and an admirer of the soldier's way in government. Hence he admires Alba, and favours Alba's party."

"But Rodrigo's just going to be a cavalryman——"

"He's beginning to see that it would be nice to be a cavalryman with political power—as Alba has been. And he may seem silly to you, but out in the world he is the Duke of Pastrana, and could therefore count in affairs later on—if he wished to."

"I still don't see why that very remote idea should make him suddenly drop all restraint and good manners at the sight of you. He's usually only too polite to the important."

Antonio smiled.

"That's it, that's the point. Rodrigo always knows his gesture. There's going to be a gathering of the eagles against me, Ana. They think it's time."

Ana stood up.

"Not all the eagles," she said.

Centuries of assurance, Antonio thought, lay within the amused and casual phrase.

Ana rang her silver bell, and servants came to remove her supper-table. While they were setting things in order she paced up and down the room.

She wore a black dress, as always, and very few jewels. Antonio thought it a pity she was committed, as a widow, to perpetual black, for it did not in his opinion truly accord with her very black hair and Castilian pallor. Sometimes he pleaded with her for more jewellery, more ornament to challenge her distinction; but clearly she did not see any need of them. She was incorrigibly austere, and he suspected that she took far more pleasure than she recognised from her own eccentric native elegance. He pondered on how strongly it had grown on him in a few months of intimacy—his pleasure in her physical qualities. When he was a young man and she was Ruy's young bride he had simply thought her odd-looking, always too thin and in everything exaggerated; and had dismissed Ruy's delighted devotion to her as the slightly senile gratitude to a girl of an ageing man.

He smiled. Gratitude indeed it might well be, for he knew now how she bound a man by gratitude—gratitude for a way in love which was in the possession of no other woman he had known, and which indeed contradicted love's tradition. Simplicity, unpretentiousness, a tolerance which was even exasperating; lack of the impulse to change, influence or directly assist her lover; lack of claim; inability to become domesticated or proprietary in love; inability to fuss or be a bore. And supporting these negatives some complementaries more positive—reluctance to discuss herself; refusal of those intimacies which should not be given and which are the gift of a careless sensuality; caution and delicacy before that of a man's life which is not hers. Yes, gratitude might well be the word for what Ruy Gomez felt about her. It was a roomy word; it suited what she gave.

As she paced about she pressed her hand against her eye-shade. Antonio noticed that she did that when disturbed or excited. He wondered if the destroyed eye hurt her then.

When they were young and indeed always until he was her lover he had thought this disfigurement most terrible, and it had made him uncomfortable to think of any husband having to bear with it. Now, watching her tenderly and wondering if the socket ached, it struck him that if an archangel appeared in the room and undertook to touch Ana's right eye and restore it, he would probably beg her to refuse the miracle. This selfish idea made him smile, and he wished he could tell it to her. It was the sort of thing she appreciated. But one must not speak to her of her blind eye.

"What are you smiling at?" she asked him.

The servants were going now, closing the door.

"At your talk of eagles," he said. "You're not a bit like an eagle, thank God. You're just a greyhound—with all a greyhound's defects of character."

Preoccupied, she waved that off.

"I don't see what the reactionary party, and that master-mind Rodrigo, have to do with your affair. Vasquez, after all, is a liberal like you."

"Oh, it's only that they're thinking of *using* him and the Escovedo affair. They don't like him, but they could never get both of us wrenched away from Philip, and I am much the more obnoxious. I am after all the leader of the party, and by nature a dangerous man. And far too successful. Vasquez's politics may at present be wrongly tinged, but he's the pious, good kind and they know they could manage him. Anyway one of us controlling Philip is better than two—and I'm the one they fear. So they're interested in this Escovedo threat—and see that, carefully managed, it may ruin me."

"I see. They're innocent really, aren't they? And Rodrigo's moral indignation against *me*—where does that come in?"

"Rodrigo has been hearing the news, and has made up his mind. It is going to be made perfectly clear to the next group in power that he, his house and name are violently antagonistic to the fallen favourite. And that is the crux of the whole matter which—if you'll ever let me get a word in edgeways—I'll explain to you."

"I'll let you. Rodrigo must deal according to his disposition with the honour of his house. But I'm selfish, and take an interest in my own honour, which I can only manage in my own way. Now—do you want to hear my plan?"

"Haven't I heard it?"

"Not really. Here it is. Your danger comes from this cleric, Mateo Vasquez, and some people you mentioned whom I've never heard of?" Antonio laughed at her. "Well, as I've said, I'm tired of hearing all my life that I'm a person of power and privilege. At last I see advantage in the legend. You have these enemies, Antón. And you have two friends."

He looked puzzled.

"Two friends?"

"You have me."

"Yes, I have you. Who is my second friend?"

She stared at him.

"The king! The king, who asked you to embrace for him the danger you are now in; the king, who is in that danger with you. The king and you, who are in this trouble together, are at this moment—let Rodrigo squeal as he likes—the two most powerful men in Spain. And I am, they tell me, the most powerful woman. And I am the friend of both of you. Indeed, after Anichu, you are the two creatures who interest me most on earth."

"I see. So?"

"So—I'm going to Madrid. I'm going to see everybody, including Philip, naturally. I'm going to stay there and give scandal and make a fuss—and see what happens. That's all."

He came and took her hands and kissed them, laughing and moved.

"No rings? Oh Ana, where's my emerald?"

"I didn't feel inclined for it. Tell me, isn't it a reasonable plan?"

"It's utter nonsense. Oh, come to Madrid, girl! Come indeed! The place is a plague-spot without you. And your plan, Ana, your silly, silly plan will make a good last act—if you insist on it! But, it won't get either of us out of the scrape we're in."

She laughed, drawing her hands away from him.

"Come, sit down. Tell me about this scrape."

He took the invitation slowly.

"Well, you've heard things, haven't you? De Los Velez told you——"

"Oh yes! Bernardina gets the stories too. She drops hints. That you are involved with a woman—somebody of very great importance! And that Escovedo was killed because he wanted to interfere in your liaison. Dear old de Los Velez warned me very gently that Philip might be curious about that. Bernardina thinks so too, I think. I agree that he might. And say he were? Oh, they have short memories about the ineptitudes of gossip, or perhaps you haven't been the passive subject of those ineptitudes—as I have been."

"Go on. Say your say."

"I think I've said most of it before. All it comes to is that as long as I can remember the populace has tended to tell itself that I lead a life of crime. I won't bore you with all the fables you know—why, they couldn't even bury that poor child Don Carlos without saying that he was my lover, and therefore was killed in criminal concert by Philip and Ruy, who were in the habit of sharing me. From then on they've said everything they liked about me—including that I'm raving mad. I know why. It's because I was born in a vulnerable, high place—and because I'm—well—odd-looking. There was a time when these waves of malicious popular amusement against me used to worry Ruy—and Philip—but I never could see why. Fussy little men in the street I told them they were—and I was right. Gossip is natural. If you choose to live by your own light you must take it—and so long as you don't try to answer it, it won't as much as bruise you. Look at me. Have you ever known a time when I wasn't slandered in Madrid?"

"No—honestly I haven't."

"Yet here I am and no bones broken—and no ill-feeling

between me and my habitual detractors. So now—let them
begin again. I can ride these little dust-storms, and so can
you. We'll ride together if you like, Antón—that's the *plan!*
—to enrich their trivial entertainment. And if they tell
Philip the whole truth about us—well, why on earth should
he *not* hear it? If it annoys him, I shall be flattered, and
touched. But beyond the prick to his already half-dead
vanity, it isn't his affair—our being lovers. For the rest of
the story—he knows why Escovedo died."

Antonio poked the fire, and made no answer.

"So why look solemn about our 'scrape', as you call it?
True or false, it is only another will-o'-the-wisp. Or are *you*
a fussy little man in the street, like Ruy and Philip? I believe
you are. It's curious you should all three be like that—and my
three favourite men."

"Philip. He does hold his place in everything you say,
doesn't he? It's odd. Ruy was your husband; I am your
lover. But Philip—why must he be always so close around?"

"Because I've always been fond of him, and I have a
narrow and faithful heart."

Antonio felt suddenly desperately weary.

What relation could there ever be between the loose-
riding, human reasonableness of this woman and the close
intrigues of the Secretaries' Rooms in the Alcázar? He had
drawn her into a situation in which she would be of paramount importance and entirely at sea. He was tired of
turning it over in his own mind, well-trained to its kind of
intimacy. Must he really try to explain it now, to someone
who would be honestly unable to apprehend its values, and
who even if she did perceive them would be their victim
without fuss, if necessary—but never their subscriber? He
beat about his mind for a short cut through all that should be
said.

"It's annoying," he said gently, "your affection for
Philip."

"Is it?" She paused. "It's a strange thing to say, I know—but, I trust him."

Antonio smiled a little. Here was the short cut.

"If you're right, Ana—I mean, if in the next few months he honours your trust in him—then there's nothing to worry about. I, on the other hand, *don't* trust him. And if I'm right, well, it'll be impossible to see ahead, for better or worse."

"Explain."

Antonio straightened in his chair and drank some wine.

"I agree with you about gossip. I'm not a fussy little man in the street—can't afford to be, as I don't live like those gentry. I've always let gossip have its blow-around—and like you, though less deservedly, I'm alive to tell the tale, and no bones broken. So I'm not here to bother you with gossip. This is the true position, underneath the gossip. The Escovedo family isn't gossiping. And it's had enough of Vasquez's little petitions to the king. It's employing good lawyers now, and has captured one or two pieces of evidence on which it is certainly reasonable to found a case. So now a full brief has been drafted which they desire to present at the High Court of Justice. Vasquez informed the king recently that this *dossier* was ready—thinking no doubt that Philip would be pleased by such a show of energy! What Philip said to Mateo we shall never know, of course. But what I do know is that in fact the news frightened Majesty very much. After consultations of an incredible circuitousness—with me, with the Cardinal, with de Los Velez, with God knows who else—he instructed Vasquez to have the Escovedos submit their lawyers' draft to the private study of Antonio de Pazos, the President of Castile. You gathered that from what I said to Rodrigo?"

"Yes. What then?"

"De Pazos was shaken by what he read. The Escovedos charge me outright with the murder of Juan de Escovedo—and they charge you, naming you explicitly, with full complicity in the murder. Our reason is given, and the evidence of some witnesses is given; one or two servants—no one from your household, but some names from mine, and from the Alcázar. People I've used for errands, or who may have watched my homing steps at night."

They smiled at each other. Ana lifted her thin shoulders in expression of amusement.

"There always are these people," she said. "After all, we know that. But truly—must one go to the top of the Credos Mountains to meet a lover?"

"Uncomfortable. But please don't be frivolous. There is the evidence of a locksmith, who made a key for a little-used side-door of the Eboli palace in the Calle Santa Maria Almudena."

Ana looked at him and laughed, almost giggled like a little girl.

"So that episode's in?"

Antonio was puzzled.

"I gather it's indicated. De Pazos was—delicate in reporting it to me. Why do you laugh now? I've never mentioned that dreadful night to you because—well, because, obviously it must have been an unbearable shock——" he was still puzzled and diffident.

"Yes, it was a shock," she said, and now her face was grave and non-committal. "But not in the way you mean. It was a private shock."

He waited, not understanding, and expecting her to say more.

"Go on, Antón. We are both charged with the murder of Escovedo, because he threatened to expose our relationship?"

"Yes. There are subsidiary charges—arising from the lawyers' explanation of Escovedo's disapproval of us. His anger was not merely against our lack of sexual virtue in itself, but as an executor of Ruy Gomez's will he desired to protect Ruy Gomez's children from my venality. So, the

brief charges me with living on you, with having you pay
money-lenders for me, etc.—and accuses you of squandering
on me in lasciviousness what belongs to your children. That
is the accusation—expertly set out, de Pazos says."

"It is untrue in every word."

"Not quite in every word, Ana. You have paid debts for
me; you do spend money madly on me."

"I don't spend the children's money. No, it's untrue."

"De Pazos assured the lawyers of that, warned them they
were on a wrong tack and dangerous ground, and counselled
them strongly to withdraw a brief which would only
grievously damage their clients' case. This advice does
appear to have unnerved them, and for the moment there is
silence."

"Yet the Escovedos have a serious plaint against the civil
authority."

"Exactly. They intend to have it heard. And Vasquez,
now in full charge, is convinced of our guilt, and delighted
with this new worry that has fallen on him. That brief isn't
burnt."

"Very well then. When it is proffered again, let it be heard.
Tell Philip so."

He laughed; then stood up and moved about the room.

"Tell Philip so! You are superb. Heaven knows where
you'll land us all in this affair!"

She looked at him with sympathy. It was very well for her,
she told herself, to look ahead with calm. She was innocent
of the crimes with which she was charged, and for the
scandal of trial hardly cared a *real*. If the world must gloat
over the commonplace of a woman's having an illicit lover—
that could be understood and must be borne, if it came, for
the brief time the public interest lasted. She would bear it
and welcome, if she had to. She knew where true humiliation
lay—and that too she could bear without words said. But
the world, from which she had no need to ask anything, could

therefore deny her nothing that she coveted. Unfairly, it had given her all it had to give before her birth, and she had never had to make demands on it. Even did it remove all earthly power and pomp from her now, that would not matter, she knew. She had no more use for them than to enjoy their ease as they passed—but she could do without ease. Having no demands to make on life, she could face its outcries unperturbed.

But Antonio was—as Ruy had been—the servant of success. He had competed for prizes, and now he held them. Possession and responsibility *were* what he was, and in risking these he risked the forty-six full years of his life—risked everything, for himself and for his wife and children. And he, with Philip, was guilty of the death of Escovedo.

"I won't land you anywhere dangerous, if I can help it. I promise," she said gently.

"I know. And I agree with you when you say let the case be heard. You know what the risks are for me. Still, now things have gone like this, I think it would be best to have the case heard, and tell the truth."

"I'm glad. Then what we have to do is brace ourselves for a coming ordeal, you and I and Philip."

"No, Ana. Philip won't brace himself—and unless he does, you and I can't."

"But if it's coming, he must."

"He won't let it come. I see his terrible dilemma. He can't stand up in court and admit to the murder of Juan de Escovedo."

"If it's proved he'll have to. And it won't be half as bad for him as for any ordinary citizen. For one thing, they can hardly execute the king. And for another every theologian in the country will be willing to swear on oath to the divine right and the grave national necessity——"

"No—Philip will never face that. Whatever else happens about Escovedo that will not take place. Philip simply hasn't got the decisiveness for it—and, to give him his due, he is privately far too sceptical of the divine right to commit himself to it on a clear issue. No, if it came to an open trial his plight would be worse than mine—and he knows that. I, after all, could be shown as the audacious statesman doing the king's bidding and chancing everything in his service——"

"Which is what you are, and did."

"Yes—come to think of it," said Antonio, on a sudden laugh. "But it won't work out that way."

"How will it work out?"

"I don't know. No one knows. Vasquez intends it to ruin me. The Escovedos—naturally—intend to have justice. And Philip hopes for the best. Time may resolve all, as he says. Time and he—you know his style when he's cornered."

"Yes, I know him. But I know him in ways you don't. I shall talk to him, Antón."

He looked at her at first as if amazed at what she had said; but then his expression altered to surmise. He was sitting on the edge of a table where there was a tray of wine-bottles and glasses. He turned to these now, as if to avoid her and get time to think, and poured wine into a glass. He sipped some wine, and looked about the room.

"Hitherto," he said, speaking slowly, "no one in all these plottings and gossips has mentioned your name to the king. We all know that. It seems that even the sexless and innocent Vasquez has had an intuition of caution about that part of the story. A woman—as instigator—has been mentioned, and Philip has shown, oddly, some animosity about her. Oddly, I say, since he knows the true story of the death of Escovedo. But he's looking for bluff, and points of delay—so he wants to know all the twists. De Los Velez has thought that *you* have crossed Philip's mind as the possible woman—and that has made him nervous for you. But I don't think you have. He regards me as a shocking dog, and liable to have slept with every woman in sight. But I don't think he associates me at all with—well, with his preserves."

"Why have people been afraid to name me?"

"They know that you, your husband's memory, and all that concerns you are very dear to Philip—whatever the terms of that dearness. They know the risk they take in hurting him about you—they can't be sure how thin the ice may be. Even when bad news is true, you know, Philip has a way of turning against those who bring it to him. We are all aware of that—and wary. But now—time passes, and supported by lawyers, briefs and witnesses—likewise consumed by a sense of duty and the desire to be quit of me—*now* I think Mateo Vasquez will tell the king the contents of the Escovedo brief. De Pazos and Los Velez think so too. So does your good friend the Cardinal." He looked at her, sipped more wine, and smiled. "If you *are* going to Madrid, Ana, if you are putting your plan into execution, remember that by now Philip knows that we are lovers."

"It's as well."

"I disagree. But then you trust him."

Ana thought she saw now as much as anyone yet could of the misty contours of Perez's trouble.

Philip could not face an open inquiry into the death of Escovedo, yet so long as he was defending himself from the consequences of his crime he would also loyally defend his servant who had taken the whole risk of carrying through the murder he had commanded. *But*—if a man of brains, say Vasquez, could gradually work him round to believing that he had been duped, or half-duped, by that servant—if he could be veered into suspicion that Escovedo's death was in fact desired by that servant for private reasons, and that his, the king's, wish had been used as a mere safety-device, then, pressed into panic by a demand for justice which everyone acknowledged to be the Escovedos' due, Philip might indeed take refuge in his suspicion—let it rise against

Perez, and even destroy him, while it saved his master.

Philip was capable of that. Against it stood two arguments: the one, that Perez, de Pazos and de Los Velez knew from the king's own lips that he had commanded Escovedo's death; so, Ana believed, did the Cardinal Quiroga, and the royal Chaplain, Chaves. And Perez had Philip's instruction thereto in the king's inimitable handwriting. So that a trial, unless it was faced honourably, would be both dangerous and disgraceful for the king. The second argument was that Perez was at present irreplaceable in his work, holding in his hands all the threads of relationship with Italy, France, the Pope and the Lowlands, and at a time when it was essential for the king to be free to direct his mind on Portugal and the campaign for the imminent succession. Philip would go to many lengths of trouble and deviation rather than lose at present a very sure and reliable First Secretary.

But—a dark and formless *but*—were he to be personally hurt, were his incalculable habits of self-consolation and of dream-life to be offended by this episode, were the news that *she* was Perez's mistress to sting him into secret pain and shock—then, she admitted, there was no mapping of a course. Philip would still have to protect Perez from the ordeal of an Escovedo trial—because he must; he would still have to hedge, and placate Mateo Vasquez, and search dishonestly for lies and delays and—even in despair—for some unlucky scapegoat. And he would have to behave well to Perez meantime, if the complicated work of the Foreign Office was to proceed in safety. But behind all that fixed screen—she admitted there was no guessing how Philip's inner storm, driven by vanity and exasperation, might not blow. He could be indeed as merciless and treacherous as he could be faithful. And Ruy, from the grave, could give her the long measure of his fidelity. So she understood well enough where Perez stood now, and why he looked ahead uneasily.

Yet she saw light. For she did not believe, as these men did, in the monstrousness of Philip's vanity. She did not think that his now lazy, friendly feeling for her would lead him into real dishonesty or real cruelty. It wasn't worth all that. It had outgrown its days of danger and vengefulness; it was too tired for such companions. She thought that, given all the other difficulties which Escovedo's death had heaped on him, he could be brought to compromise with a mere jab at his male vanity—could even be made to acknowledge it, and laugh. Delicate work—but worth an attempt. And if he couldn't—conceited donkey—what then? What could he do, in his dilemma? Were free Castilians to ask his permission before going to bed with this one or that?

Yes, there was plenty of light. Spain was a country of free people. And if it actually came to victimisation of Antonio because of Philip's conceit, she would enjoy asking the king how he dared intrude himself thus upon another's privacy.

"I think I know now most of what you know and think so far about the situation?" Antonio nodded. "Thank you, Antón. And don't look sad. We won't talk any more about it now—there's no need to. We'll be talking of it all the winter in Madrid!"

"In Madrid? You're really coming back there, madwoman?" He laughed delightedly. "Then I'm not sad. Or need I be? Need I, Ana?"

He came to the fireplace and stood in front of her chair, looking down at her.

"It's been a long abstention, girl. And I know it wasn't accidental. I know you wanted me to stay away. Six months and two weeks since I've seen you; nearly seven months since I've made love to you. I think, or rather I thought, I know why."

He waited for her to speak but she did not. She was looking into the fire; her beautiful hands were folded together in her lap.

"I don't want to talk about that last time," he went on. "When I do think of it it simply makes me want to have Escovedo back to kill again, and again, and again——"

"Ah, no," Ana said. "That's not it."

"Forgive me. All I mean is that I understood—I thought— the disgust, the need to rest from it all, the distaste—that's all I can say. But that—the whole thing—must pass, must get a bit forgotten, surely?"

"I don't think so," she said gently.

"Ah! Then I was right to feel—frightened when I first came here to-night? When you said that about doing without me, you meant something?"

Ana turned her face to him, and it was haggard and very white.

"Juan de Escovedo," said Perez, "have you done this to me too?"

Ana hesitated. Anxiously now she wished for speech, speech about herself, speech that might storm out selfishly, carelessly, if it had to—driven on the gusts of indecision that blew about her brain. But she simply did not know how to make such assault on another creature, and now it was too late to learn. Juan de Escovedo haunts me, she desired to say. I have forgiven all the outrage and the madness, I think I have even forgotten our plain human discomfort, yours and mine. Indeed—and don't be hurt, she would say—some- times I can laugh quite coarsely and calmly at the thought of our predicament that night. All that external thing doesn't matter. It's a humiliation which anyone might undergo, and be said to deserve. What I remember is how my thought fitted with his while he shouted, and how precisely I under- stood him. He was simply telling me what my spirit knew quite well—that love and pleasure on our terms, Antonio, are an evil thing. For me he's right—he only said what I agree with. My soul has no place in your arms. That is a dreadful, pompous thing to say, it's the word of an egotist, and I abhor the sound of it. But I don't know any nearer way to say it. Could you help me? Could you tell me what to do—for I still love you, I still want you——

But she could never speak aloud like that, or claim attention from another for mere states of mind. And as to this man, her lover, she knew that whatever he could give her and however acutely he searched, as he always did, to be in sympathy with her, he could not—of his very nature—accord with her in the inner ranges of her spirit. For there, guarded by her worldliness and by her will to feel, enjoy and behave according to her natural law, she was credulous and simple. There she was pure, and sought a purpose in herself which should not merely eschew but might even contradict self-gratification. Towards this purpose she had once made one mad, selfish rush, and made a fool of herself. Thereafter it was more than ever to be dismissed, and she grew shy almost to insanity of her idea that life was not about the self. And she escaped from it easily into normal social practices, and so by them back to her natural curiosities and desires. But Escovedo the madman, dead now, killed by the man who had released her into perfect sensual freedom, who had borne her most happily out of reach of that small, lost self that used to cry out for a purifying explanation of itself—Escovedo had renewed the cry, and driven her back to that place of perplexity where she was simple and credulous and knew she had a soul which she must save.

Her hands fell apart and she stared up almost stupidly into Antonio's face.

He's tired, she thought. He's worried to death; he's even within measure of disaster. I've brought him into real danger. When all was well with him I took with both hands all I wanted, and cared very little about my soul or his. Now, now when the world I enjoy and know so well, the world he works so hard for is gathering up excuses to destroy him—is now my time to harass him with convent

metaphysics, and the entirely private, small question of my
soul?

"Absurd, preposterous," she said.

"What is, Ana?"

"Did I speak?"

"Rather loudly, for you."

She laughed, and reached up to his hands. "How unattractive of me! Come here! Come down."

He fell on his knees; his face was radiant.

"But——?"

"Oh yes, there are buts! When you aren't here there's a
whole theological school of them!"

"And when I'm here?"

She bent nearer to his lifted face, loving it suddenly again
with some of the sharp pleasure of their winter nights
together in Madrid. Grateful to him for this pang, guilty,
disturbed, she searched for an answer that would please him.

"When you're here? Ah, my poor theology! Have you
then a little forgotten your power over me, Antón?"

To her surprise he did not laugh. He stayed quite still at
her feet, looking at her. And in astonishment she saw what
she had never seen before—she saw tears flood his eyes and
pour along his cheeks. Then he bent forward and buried his
face against her.

She held him, and kissed his perfumed hair. She smiled.
She had forgotten his sandalwood perfume. It's been a long
time, she thought.

Is my poor scruple greater than what I give this man and
take from him? Am I to set my little private sense of sin
above his claim on me and his unhappiness? Am I cheating
because I want him, and have grown tired of the unimportant
fuss of my immortal soul? Am I pretending to be generous
simply to escape again into his power? Well, he has power
—and I, it seems, have none. Answer my questions,
Escovedo.

When Antonio left her in the early morning she went downstairs with him to the stables to rouse his men.

He protested at this, but only with delight.

"It's part of the plan," she said. "You'll see. And I hope Rodrigo hears us, and is at his window."

"You're an irresponsible parent."

"I have my own precise ideas of honour—but I fear Rodrigo doesn't understand them."

They walked about the court-yard, waiting for his carriage. The world was still and cool; a cock crowed far away, and a bell rang from the Franciscan convent.

"You and I are used to convent bells," Antonio said, remembering the chimes of Santa Maria Almudena in Madrid.

Ana shivered a little and drew her cloak about her.

"You're cold? You're troubled?"

"I'm neither, as you ought to know. Ah, here they come!"

The carriage clattered through into the court.

"God bless you. I'll be in Madrid almost as soon as you."

"I wish we could stay here," Antonio said.

He got into the carriage.

"Give my love to Philip," Ana said mischievously as the door closed on him.

When he had driven away she walked through the gateway and stood in the empty square of the little town; she watched a last star fade, and the thin frost melt along the roofs. Down the street a door was banged, and a man's voice sprang up, singing. Across the square the bent old sacristan unlocked the door of the *Colegiata* church.

At last she could hear no sound at all of carriage wheels on the Alcala road.

She crossed the square and entered the *Colegiata*, to wait for early Mass. She was the first worshipper. She went and sat on a bench near her husband's tomb.

THE THIRD CHAPTER   (APRIL 1579)

I

Ana had said to Antonio that they would likely spend the whole winter in Madrid talking about the Escovedo issue. But she was wrong.

The topic faded, surprisingly; not merely from the attention of casual gossips but even out of the horizon of those whom it concerned. It seemed that the President of Castile had indeed impressed the unhappy plaintiffs with his advice. And as the world in general turned its curiosity and chatter elsewhere, the Marqués de Los Velez and Antonio, true to their diplomatic training, discouraged even the most private references to what was best left sleeping.

Ana, wondering somewhat, followed their lead, and let the whole unanswered question float out of sight. But not out of memory. From Antonio's few, quick references—always savage—to Vasquez, from the old Marqués's exaggerated discretion, and from her own observations she knew that the problem was not dead, and that Philip would yet have to solve it—at someone's expense.

Twice between All Saints' and Christmas he was at the Alcázar, yet did not cross the street to call on her.

"Then he's been told that you killed Juan de Escovedo for my sake?" she asked Antonio.

"He *must* have been. But do you know, Ana—*nobody* can find that out! The man's extraordinary. I'm with him, as you know, for hours and days together, and so is Vasquez. And he knows that I know what Vasquez has done to my repute and goes on doing, *and* he knows the truth about this situation which Vasquez had got all wrong. But whereas earlier in the summer he was a shade overplaying friendship with me—which made me very jumpy and annoyed—now he is exactly as we've always been. Perfectly natural and calm and kind, making me work like an Indian, trusting me with all kinds of dangerous information and views, and never once referring to anything outside what comes before us officially. Except to joke me vaguely, as he's always done, about my extravagance, and about women, and so on. And to make his usual kind enquiries now and then for Juana and the children. I must say I admire him—tortoise though he is, he's subtle. He can keep anyone guessing—even me—when he likes."

Antonio might advise, but Ana was hurt and surprised. Philip should come to see her. If he was angry with her he should come and say so. They were intimate enough for that, and he had a right to jealousy, if he liked to be so silly. But he had no right to cut their friendship because she had a lover.

At Christmas he sent presents and greetings to the children, and nothing to her. She let Fernando and Anichu write their own thank-you letters. She did not write. She waited and surmised. She was somewhat shaken by how much the king's silence hurt her.

But she was kept busy that winter in frivolous ways, and she took refuge—by fits and starts, and from more than her guesses about Philip—in the light preoccupations of town life.

Madrid, which as a child she had known as a small and arbitrarily chosen pleasure resort of the old king, Charles, was now growing fast, and seemed indisputably henceforward the capital of the kingdom. Philip encouraged the town in this conceit of itself, as it was conveniently near his two favourite retreats, El Pardo and the new, beloved Escorial. So now the Alcázar was the centre of government, and the ambassadors had their official establishments in Madrid. And naturally all the seekers after office, or trade, or news, or blackmail crowded in where these great ones were—so a capital city seemed established.

It was an odd accident. That Castile and the centre should
rule the rest was obvious, but then Toledo, with its great
cathedral, its long history, its beauty and a real river, the
Tagus, might have been the obvious repository of the future;
or even little Avila, with its walls, its nine towers and its
pure Castilian style. But no. This dry, new place, watered
only by a trickle and having no character other than that its
climate was treacherously warm and that an ageing, can-
tankerous king had thought he felt well when he was there—
this upstart place was apparently to rule, capriciously, the
kingdoms of Spain.

It was amusing. All the great who formerly had been
content to have their houses in the towns of their titles or
estates, were now uneasily looking for establishments in
Madrid—at least, the young, the pleasure-loving and the
ambitious branches of the great families were doing so. Ana
who, because of Ruy's constant business at the Alcázar, had
long possessed her Madrid palace, felt—somewhat to her
disgust—that she was a pioneer of the new, ugly town and its
ugly gospel of centralisation.

However, her children were all, according to their ages, in
the thick of its lively growth, taking their part in building its
conventions, snobberies and rituals. And they knew everyone, were related to all the eminent, and were assiduously
flattered, spoilt and cheated by swarms of place-seekers and
money-makers. They enjoyed themselves, and filled Ana's
house with their young friends, and her time with frivolous
duties on their behalf.

As a widow and unprotected she was herself barred—to
her great relief—from all full-dress ceremonies of Madrid
society. She could neither be invited to banquets and
dancing parties nor could she invite her acquaintances to any
such formal pleasures. But her house was open, informally,
and most of the aristocracy and diplomatic corps knew better
than to omit to call on a senior Mendoza who was also the

widow of the Prince of Eboli. During the winter she entertained to supper, singly or in small groups, most of the important men, Spanish or foreign, then in Madrid. Sometimes Antonio brought them; sometimes she had the Cardinal to meet them; sometimes they brought their wives.

"But it's a funny thing," she said to Antonio, "there seem to be no significant women in the world."

He whistled.

"Margaret of Navarre, Elizabeth of England, Mother Teresa, the Princess of Eboli——"

"None in Madrid then——"

"The Princess of Eboli."

"God help women!"

"He doesn't, Ana. That isn't his idea."

Margaret of Valois is a poet and a notoriety, she thought; Elizabeth has England to rule; Mother Teresa is trying to reform the Church. But I have nothing to do. I never have had anything to do except behave nicely and enjoy my easy lot. It's silly, she thought—as often before through her adult life. She did not sigh in these moods for poverty, so as to have to wash her children's faces and cook their dinner. She supposed that she could have done those things if necessary, but the humble ideal had never attracted her. Still conscience, or rather personality more than conscience, fidgeted spasmodically in her under a sense of her own pointlessness. When she was having Ruy's babies—ten in thirteen years— she had felt that in the world's terms at least, if not in her own, she was being useful; and her dislike of the maternal function and its processes had increased her reassurance. Because at least she could say that Ruy, who loved his large family so much, had never heard a word of complaint or self-pity from her throughout the years during which she was adding to it for him. It was no more than her duty, as well she knew; but she gratified some private need in herself by doing it gaily and as if she liked it. Yet Heaven did not allow her a complete gratification, because her health was good and child-bearing had been easy, and had left her when it ceased almost as well as in her first bridal days, before she conceived Rodrigo.

But Anichu was rising six now, and Ruy was more than five years dead—and for long the old placatory saw, that she was doing her duty in that state of life to which it had pleased God to call her, had seemed boring and untrue. She supervised the affairs of Pastrana; but the farms, orchards and silkworks had all been so ordered by Ruy that she knew that the foremen and bailiffs, respectful and affectionate, yet regarded her authority as purely formal; and she noticed with amusement that already they paid far more heed to Rodrigo's occasional very businesslike interventions than to any suggestion of hers. She did not mind this. So long as the prosperity of the place continued, for everyone's sake and in Ruy's memory, she was content. She was not looking for great labours, or to shine in any unusual light, but simply felt a recurrent private need to feel, rather than accept, her own contact with life—to feel somehow persuaded about herself.

When she had talked a little sometimes to Ruy of this restlessness, this sense of disappointment that everything came to her and that she had always to be passive and pleased, he did not laugh or dismiss her nonsense. On the contrary, he was wise and kind, though he liked to tease her about this mood which he called "looking for a fight". "But I'm a pacifist, Ana; you live with a man of peace." She came to notice, with private amusement, that always for many days after such conversations Ruy made love to her with great increase of amorousness and assiduity. And she thought she saw his idea, and that it was good. But it did not actually bear—how could he know?—on the state of mind she had sought to examine with him.

It had been out of one of these moods of search for a personal position that she had been moved to the sudden and for her startling action of taking Antonio Perez for her lover. It was at least, as she had said to him that night, a decision of her own.

It had justified her—on one level at least, by bringing her at once into close sensual acceptance of joy. Joy which was at first so disturbing and formless, so dazzlingly luminous over the twenty-four hours of the day, as to seem silly and to be honestly enough describable, in public places, as about nothing. But her senses, though taken by storm in middle life, were not so imprecise as her heart. They had won her at last, and they made her pay. There were days in the beginning when she went hungry for Antonio Perez as a tramp for food. There were nights when she waited for him, lying in her bed and listening to the bells of Almudena, and thought of him at his desk across the street, deep in work, fully at peace with it and richly, blessedly forgetful of her—thought of him and of whether or not she might see him before dawn with an urgency which astonished her, and which sometimes seemed controllable only barely on the safe side of an act of outright folly—such as getting up and crossing to the Alcázar gate and trying to see him.

But it was this very wretchedness of joy and the press of danger, of near-lunacy, in it, that in fact made her so contentedly acceptant, and so well able to be cool and ruthless with her unhoodwinked conscience. So be it, she could say then to that monitor—I am living in sin. But I've found something that has been missing always, and that may indeed be just as important as what your voice tells me of. And I don't feel this sense of sin you warned about. No doubt I shall, but meantime—this is a battle, with rules, exactions and trials you concealed from me; this love, this sin has a morality of its own that I find I understand. I see my plight and I acknowledge still your old imperatives. But I can't obey them now—I must take a chance. This other is an imperative too—and what I like is that it seems to be my own, and not just the hearsay word of Heaven.

So she took her chance. And conscience, long-trained, did not give in and fought her every inch of the way. A ding-dong battle, but with her new-found paganism always the winner—a paganism which was learning to smile a little, in hardened amusement, at the egotism of chastity. But she knew she was too vulnerable to pursue that defence, and shelved it—marvelling only at how unsinning and un-sinned against she felt in her life of sin.

But in the ordinary human journey none of these skirmish-victories is final. So Ana found out, without overmuch surprise. Yet when Escovedo came and discovered her in her pleasure, she *was* surprised, in spite of all her own debates, to see how coldly she did in fact agree with the doctrine out of which his madness spoke. She saw with him that self-denial was a better thing, or a thing more to her taste, than self-expression; and that self-expression through the senses solely, and as practised in sterility and with accomplishment as by Antonio and her, was in itself entirely bad. She could plead very well against that judgment, and indeed again and again had buried it out of her own reach. But she knew it lived and stood—and she heard it from Escovedo with an assent which was almost solemn. For she felt while he shouted that whereas he might not be saving her soul for her, he was certainly expressing her own unadmitted judgment on this delight, sexual love.

That much was clear to her that night.

And now that she had returned, for complicated reasons, to the pleasure he had driven her from, she knew that his message stayed, as the voice of herself, and that love was henceforward what traditionally she understood it to be—a Christian passion.

So henceforward she was Antonio's lover on new and shifting terms—because of this and because of that, because he needed her, because there were moods when she couldn't do without him, because friends were failing him, because she loved him—for every stormy reason of a heart that has grown truly warm towards another; but not any longer now because she was simply in love.

The trouble of this changed temperature ran through all the movement of her life in Madrid that winter. But superficially she was gay and indiscreet. And if anyone was so uninformed as to wonder where the allegiance of the Princess of Eboli lay in the now accepted feud between the king's two chief ministers she left him in no doubt; she was Antonio Perez's friend and patroness for all to see, and at every mention of Mateo Vasquez she made it her affair to jibe, and even very dangerously, no matter who listened. When Antonio protested against this—though only with half a will, because he loved her championship—she laughed at him. It was part of the plan, she said, and she desired Mateo Vasquez to be in no doubt of what she thought of him. "Besides, you yourself say the most terrifying things about him, to all comers."

"Oh, I! That's different."

"I agree it's different."

One bright afternoon in late March she and Bernardina, returning from a ride, had to rein in their horses at a corner of the Calle Carmen, to let some market traffic cross the Puerta del Sol. As they waited she observed a tall, dark cleric on foot very near her, and bowing to her with a great show of respect and anxiety. It was Mateo Vasquez. She was astonished, and disgusted. She stared at him, her face full of recognition but implacably refusing his salute. Still motionless and close beside him, she turned to Bernardina and said in a tone as clear as ice:

"This is Mateo Vasquez trying to bow to me. What can he possibly mean?"

The tall priest shrank back instantly into the crowd, and vanished. Ana and her companion rode on.

Bernardina admired audacity, but she thought that gesture unnecessary, and she said so.

But Ana seemed pleased with herself.

"Let's hope that *now* he knows that you don't bow to the ground before those whom you're seeking to destroy! We'll teach him a little etiquette, Bernardina!"

"He looked terrified when you spoke."

"I noticed that. Poor cringing wretch."

II

Three weeks later, on an evening of April, she sat with the Cardinal in the Long Room. Antonio Perez was to join them for supper. Ana had taken the children to Pastrana for Holy Week and Easter, and had just returned to Madrid.

During March there had been stirrings in the affair Escovedo, and Ana had received some unlikely callers. And the Cardinal had views and gossip for her.

The windows of the Long Room were open and the noises of the town floated up happily; the evening was clear, and westward from where they sat they could see the shining peaks of the Gredos, immaculate against the pure sky. There were violets and early roses from Pastrana in the room.

"Well, for a woman in somewhat questionable case, I must say, Ana, that you look very splendid."

Gaspar de Quiroga, Archbishop of Toledo and now a Cardinal, was a distinguished and worthy churchman. His friendship with Ana and her husband was of old standing; and in recent years he had also become interested in Perez, and even attached to him. Antonio frequently went to stay at the archiepiscopal palace in Toledo. The friendship between these two men was odd—the venal, self-seeking politician and the detached and virtuous priest—but it was also disinterested. They quite simply liked each other.

"But *am* I in questionable case?"

He smiled at her.

"Actually, that's what no one knows. But still—we all feel that you are."

"I think you are all, in the goodness of your hearts being a little *too* intuitional! Philip knows—to his cost—why Escovedo died. And for the rest of this scandal, may I say, dear friend, that what I do with my—heart is no affair for the *Alcalde*?"

"You may, Ana. And I agree with you."

He had been standing in the window. He moved about the room now as one quite at home. He picked up a book that lay on the writing-table.

" '*Histoire Des Amants Fortunés*'. Ah, a first edition! Mine is called '*The Heptameron*'."

"Yes—I'd never read it, and Antonio found this 1558 copy for me."

"You find the stories amusing?"

"Surprisingly so. I'm lazy about reading French—oddly enough I read Latin more easily. But I find this a surprising, witty, *natural* sort of book."

"Yes, they're graceful, well-set stories. I confess I prefer them to Boccaccio. She's a woman I'd like to have talked with. She attracts me more than the great-niece, the present Margaret of Navarre."

"But *this* Margaret of Navarre is said to be so beautiful that she takes the breath away."

"So I hear." He put the book down. "I only said that the Heptameron lady attracts me more."

Ana laughed.

"You don't mean much when you say that you're 'attracted'."

"No, thank God. A dead authoress suits me well. I was born austere."

"You're a holy man."

He shook his head.

"Indeed I'm not, you foolish child. I wish I were."

"Yes—you're a holy man. So why do you continue to come to my house, and be my friend—and Antonio's? Aren't you afraid that by doing so you scandalise the little ones?"

"Yes, sometimes I worry about that. Antonio leads a bad life, and my friendship for him may indeed be misunderstood, and disturb the innocent. And you? Well——"

He looked at her in gentle surmise.

"What do you think of me?"

"I have great affection for you—which probably corrupts my thought, or rather my refusal to think. I say to myself, Ana, quite simply that I am *not* your confessor. Until I am— and for ever distant be the day!—I am under no positive obligation to answer you. And you have never sought my advice, outside the confessional."

"Were I to do so?"

"I should tell you to give up your sin, or to make certain that you are never again an occasion of sin to Antonio. You know the Christian teaching. You know that fornication is a sin; adultery is another. But the first sin is enough for your properly trained mind. And as to the adultery—I would not insult either you or Antonio, to say nothing of Juana Coëllo, his wife, by saying that she is in fact an excellent wife, a wife in a million, gentle, silent, proud and true." He paused. "It is merely emotional to advert to that. If she were a drunkard, a thief and a public whore, she is his wife, and in taking you he commits adultery. But you both know that. So what would be the good of reiteration?"

"Yes, we both know that. But Antonio knows it only as a sceptic. I know it with faith."

"Ah! Then you really are a sinner—by definition. Grievous matter, perfect knowledge, full consent."

She smiled, half-troubled.

"Not *full* consent. I sometimes think that real sin is

practically impossible to the sin-conscious on that definition, because of the loophole of 'full consent'. The terms fit Antonio better than me," she ended lightly.

"No, Ana. Because he discards the first point, 'grievous matter'. His escape is that it's all about nothing."

"Yes. It isn't mine. I'm always afraid of betraying how 'grievous' the matter seems to me."

"Then, against all appearances, you are a guilty creature?"

Ana did not answer at once. A rose had fallen from a vase, and she leant forward and replaced it with its fellows. Then she turned and faced the Cardinal.

"A year ago I wasn't, I *think*," she said. "A year ago, at least, I hoped Antonio was right."

"And now?"

"Now I wish he was. But I know he isn't."

"Then you desire to repent?"

She laughed very softly.

"No. I did repent—for seven whole months, after Escovedo's death. But this is not the time. One can't be self-indulgent even about repentance, Cardinal. I have come to love Antonio, you see, and I owe him a few sins and chances. He has taken chances for me. This is not the time for private piety. Heaven must make what it likes of my confusion. That is a risk I have the right to take."

"In other words, you are seeing him through the Escovedo affair? You are just being awkwardly loyal?"

"Oh no. I love him. And if I do, it would be unnatural to stop loving him now."

"That's a curious sentence, Ana. But I take it you are telling your immortal soul to wait on the question of Antonio Perez's earthly happiness?"

"Maybe there's a grain of that in it. But you see, don't you, that if it *were* no more, I owe him much for being able to feel like that about him? And it *is* more. I don't want to do without him."

"Well said. Yet I believe that, were you in the confessional now, you would humbly admit the burden of your sin."

"I couldn't be in the confessional now, because I have no firm purpose of amendment. I wish I needn't commit sin, but that's as far as I can go."

"And still your soul is troubled—and pleasure is not enough?"

"But there is his pleasure."

"My dear—he has a wife."

Ana laughed and threw out her hands.

"There speaks the dogmatist, the innocent priest. So had I a husband, as good and dear a man as I understand Juana Coëllo is a woman. Yet I never knew until now, at the very end of my life, what union with another can be."

"Antonio can hardly be in your case. He has had so many love-affairs that the argument would be ridiculous."

"No, he isn't in my case. He is an expert in pleasure. But I'm not arguing for his conscience. I speak for myself. All I mean is that I am his present happiness, and that is—he has known how to make it—a perilous happiness for me. And he's in danger now, and being slandered about me. But he takes great pride in the situation, and also he relies very much on my love at this time. And I am not so used to the attraction and devotion of men that I can treat that lightly."

"I see. In fact, as I suspected, you are in some trouble of soul."

"If it be trouble of soul to love a man and commit sins for him, who seems by his very faults to merit love—then I'm in trouble."

"No—it isn't as tricky as that. You're just in trouble with God. His claim is eternal and overrules your foolish, earthly time-table. And you know that. Still—God forgive me!—I admire you a little. And I must say I marvel at the subtleties which you simple creatures of the flesh can weave into your animal needs."

Ana pressed her hand against her eye-shade.

"The trouble is that the needs aren't sufficiently animal," she said.

The Cardinal smiled, but she did not see the smile.

"Maybe," he said. "I don't know." He sat down and looked about the room affectionately. "Beautiful flowers. Signs that Pastrana flourishes. And how are the children?"

"Very well. Some of them will be coming in to see you in a minute. Do you mind?"

"I should be hurt if they didn't. And we'll postpone what I'm supposed to be saying to you until Antonio is here? I do hate repeating myself."

"Then you're on a mission?" Ana laughed delightedly.

"Not very earnestly, my dear—as you can guess."

"I've had some curious, unexpected callers in the last month, but *you* now! Oh, that's really amusing!"

"I think so too."

Presently the children came—young Ruy, aged twelve, small and studious and growing in feature very like the father whose name he bore; Fernando, nine now and already saying that he desired to be a Franciscan monk; and Anichu, baby six-year-old. They did not know the Cardinal as well as the king, or like him as much, and he for his part was shy with children. But Ana watched with detached amusement as the three set to their duty of entertaining the great prelate.

III

When Antonio came it had long been dark. The windows were shut, the candles lighted in the Long Room, and the children were gone to bed.

Ana, who had seen him the night before, knew at once by the peculiar brightness of his eyes that some new, disturbing factor had arisen in his affairs during the day.

At supper conversation could be neither consecutive nor

entirely free, but Ana was able—with rapid changes of theme while servants changed dishes—to amuse her guests with accounts of visits she had been receiving from the mysterious Doctor Milio, from the two brothers, Augustin Alvárez and Pedro Nuñez of Toledo, and—funniest of all, she said, that very morning from Count de Khevenhüller, the ambassador of the Empire.

"All these people come to me," she said, "pretending of course that he knows nothing about it, on behalf of this preposterous Mateo Vasquez! Can you suppose that they are sane?"

The Cardinal demurred.

"I'm not sure that you've got their credentials quite right. However—go on!"

"What did you say to de Khevenhüller, Ana?" said Antonio. "I presume his mission was the usual one?"

"Yes. These curious, busy people seem to think it of paramount importance that I—as a leader of society, bearer of a great name, etc.—should withdraw my enmity from that good man Mateo Vasquez, and even try to be his friend!"

They all laughed very much.

"What can be the matter with their wits, Cardinal? I told our poor, bewildered German this morning to take my advice and keep well back from this very local and Castilian storm. I told him that—though he might not think so—*we* all know what we are doing in it, but that *he* never could. I thanked him for his courage and kindness, and assured him—as I assure all these eccentrics—that I shall never regard as other than an enemy whoever seeks to convict Antonio Perez of the murder of Juan de Escovedo. I then asked him to be so good as to excuse me, as my dressmaker awaited me in another room."

Antonio whistled.

"Well done!" he said.

"Poor old de Khevenhüller! The ambassador of the Holy

Roman dismissed for a dressmaker!" The Cardinal chuckled in astonishment. "You're very good at insults, Ana. But it isn't really an attractive talent, you know."

"No. Ruy used to say that too. I think he went in terror of the virago in me ever getting the upper hand."

"I love viragos," said Antonio.

When they returned to the Long Room he would not sit down when Ana suggested that he might.

"No, girl," he said tenderly, as if they were alone. And by that mistake she knew he was indeed excited. "No, let me fidget. I'm going to drink a great deal of wine to-night, and you two spoil-sports must put up with it."

"Tell us why," said the Cardinal.

"Because the whole thing has broken open again. Philip is treacherous—and I have to-day written to him to ask to be relieved of office."

The Cardinal sprang to his feet.

"No, Antonio! Not that! Oh, this man Philip, this king, this cheat! *What* has he done now?"

Ana said nothing. Antonio's eyes rested on her for a second, half-absent-mindedly. When he spoke he turned to the Cardinal.

"How can I epitomise it for you? How can I cut a way through all the chaos of it, to make you see why I have resigned precisely to-day, and not yesterday and not to-morrow?"

"Well, to begin with, you must have been given a superficially correct reason for resigning office?"

"I was. But that too—like everything Philip touches—is complicated. However, here it is: as you know, the department we call the Council of Italy is my particular charge, though directed lately for general purposes by its own secretary. When Diego de Vargas died recently Philip and I discussed an overhaul of this department, where there is a great deal of waste and doubling and trebling of work. And after the usual agonies of delay and debate and pausing for prayer the king agreed with my wish to have *no* secretary appointed under me at present, and to leave it to me to train one or two of the young fellows in that office—on whom I've had my eye—to work it directly under me, with no go-between; as it used to be. I was pleased that he agreed to that. You remember, Ana? Over the whole thing he showed his old confidence in me, and seemed cheerful about the decision. I thought the episode was a good omen. Meantime, of course, the omens have *not* been good—but don't let me side-track myself. This morning, out of a blue sky, I receive a formal despatch from El Escorial, announcing the appointment as Secretary of the Council of Italy of a man called Gabriel de Zayas. To this document is added a chit from an under-secretary asking me to be so kind as to implement the appointment and instruct de Zayas as I may desire. No word from Philip—no explanation, no apology. And that is, superficially, why I resigned from the king's service at noon to-day. My letter is on the road to El Escorial now."

He turned aside and poured himself some wine.

"It's a sufficient pretext," said the Cardinal. "But, as you know, he won't accept your resignation."

"I've given him reasons why he must. I took my opportunity. This de Zayas is in himself of no import—he's just an under-secretary looking for advancement, and he's always been a hanger-on of Vasquez. Now that devil has nothing to do with Italy, but he found out this new arrangement of mine, and just decided to try his power against me on a small issue. He has won. And I'm having no more of these victories from a man who lives to destroy me. I said that. I said that I could work no longer for a king who allows my mortal enemy to supersede me in his confidence, and who moreover refuses to check or punish that enemy's active and public malignancies. I mean every word of this—and he can choose."

"What will you live on, if you do resign?" the Cardinal asked.

"Nothing. It's ruin."

"That's what I should have thought. Still, it's a good move, Antonio. It may be the one thing needed to bring this tragic farce to a clean conclusion. And believe me, you'll never be allowed to resign. Philip will fight against that with every trick he knows. Why—apart from the loss of you at a very urgent moment—he'd be at once completely in your power when you left his service."

Antonio laughed.

"Yes, I know that. And the point won't escape him. Well, let him wriggle!"

Ana sat leaning forward in her chair, her elbow on her knee and her fingers pressed against her black silk eye-patch. The two men looked at her reflectively.

"What are the omens you spoke of, Antón?" she asked, without moving or looking up.

"Oh, they accumulate. I had letters from El Pardo before Easter—you know de Santayo perhaps?" he asked the Cardinal. "Well, he's a Gentleman of the Household, and a reliable fellow. He wrote from there in March that the accusations against me and the Princess which were contained in the suppressed Escovedo brief of last autumn were now a matter of common discussion through the Court. Now he writes from El Escorial that the freedom of slander is infinitely worse, that the whole place is taking sides, and that everyone is waiting for the king to take some action. Meantime others write that Vasquez is going round like a cat with two tails, and that the king is as bland as cream, and perfectly unreadable. What do you make of all that?"

"I'd say it's not *quite* accurate," the Cardinal said. "I, as you know, had to visit El Escorial for two days in Holy Week—which is why I'm here to-night, incidentally ——"

"Yes—he's on a mission," Ana said with a little flick of a smile to Antonio. "Did you know?"

"Indeed! The two-faced wretch! Well, go on, Eminence. Tell us what you saw up yonder."

The Cardinal smiled.

"Naturally, as I have a reputation for saintliness, no one ventured to entertain me with views on the disedifying Escovedo scandal. Also perhaps because I'm said to be a friend of the two criminals. But Vasquez, to begin with, is *not* going round like a cat with two tails. On the contrary, he's in a very nervous, boring and obsequious state, and I'd say the man is ill."

Ana laughed.

"That's what his ambassadors tell me. The poor German this morning said that he lives in terror of me!"

"Oh yes," said Antonio. "I was sparing you that idiocy, Ana. But my informant says that Vasquez's new whine to everyone is that you are going mad and are a general danger! That you insult him, with obscene words, in public places, and that he knows that both of us plan to take his life!"

"Upon my word, it wouldn't be a bad idea!" said Ana.

The Cardinal lifted his hand in warning.

"Children, children, God knows who may be listening! And after all," he said gravely, "Escovedo *was* murdered."

Antonio smiled and bowed his head.

"True," said Ana. "And why doesn't the trial for murder begin? No one is running away from it."

"Except the king," said Antonio.

"Be quiet, both of you," said the Cardinal. "I was saying that Vasquez looks at present anything but well or sure of himself. And I think Philip is as much of a riddle now to him as to you, Antonio."

"How is Philip?" Ana asked.

"Wretched, I think. As usual he's overworking past belief, and is carrying his usual load of pompous frets. But this special thing is clearly an immense anxiety——"

"Ah, God! I'm tired of his anxieties!" said Antonio.

"I *made* him talk of it," said the Cardinal. "And his

position seems to be this—and in its characteristically tricky kind it's clear enough. He cannot and will not have a public trial of a Secretary of State for a political murder. That appears to be final. He cannot however have the standing Escovedo brief heard. He says that you, Antonio, have pressed for that, on the condition that the lady's name was never mentioned in court, and that all clues to her identity were rigidly disguised. Is that so?"

Ana looked at Antonio in surprise.

"Is it so, Antón?"

He laughed.

"Yes. I have asked him to have the brief heard on those terms."

Ana stretched out her hand and touched his.

"Madness!" she said gently. "And truly, you're as much of a sneak as Philip."

"I agree with Philip," the Cardinal went on, "that the case could *not* be heard that way. Philip, give him his due, won't have it because he says the accusation is flatly untrue; also because in the disproving it would inevitably merge into the political trial which he will not have; and because, however it went, it would be hopelessly damaging to you——"

"I like that," said Antonio. "I know, we all know, whom it would really damage!"

"Damaging to you," the Cardinal went on, "and very dangerous for someone whom we referred to throughout as 'that lady'." He smiled at Ana. "We were very chivalrous. No lady's name was breathed."

Ana was sitting straight in her chair. Her beautiful hands lay tense and long upon its arms.

"Philip didn't name me?" she asked the Cardinal.

"No. I don't think he does to anyone. Antonio de Pazos has told me of the *that lady* formula."

"But he knows who that lady is?" Antonio said.

"Oh yes. We are all agreed that he knows, that Vasquez

has certainly told him. But no one can get him to betray that, or to name you, Ana." The Cardinal paused. "I think that is a pregnant point," he said, "though pregnant of what I cannot say. But let me continue. Philip will have no trial—is that clear? But neither can he allow the present situation to continue for his perpetual shame and torment. Nor does he intend to lose either of his Secretaries of State."

"He's cocksure, for a man in a trap," said Antonio.

"He thinks that the unhappy Escovedos could be coaxed into pacification—I imagine by large damages, he thinks, with bribes, good positions for the children, etc.—vast pension for the widow, and so on. And some cock-and-bull lie about how dishonouring to the repute of the late Juan de Escovedo would be any true inquiry into the reason of his death."

Antonio laughed wearily.

"I gave him all that months ago," he said. "A fool could quiet the Escovedos."

"Well then, all that's left is merely to get Mateo Vasquez to drop his naïve campaign for justice. And Philip says he would; that he is frightened to death now of the enmities he has set up. Philip says he has it from Vasquez's own lips that all he wants, to bury everything, is apologies from you, Antonio, and from 'that lady' for recent offences—and some token of the friendship of you both."

There was an astonished silence.

"What do you think of that, confederates?"

Antonio turned, walked to where the wine was, and refilled his glass. He came back, drank a little and smiled at Ana.

"Speak, you," he said. "You say you're a virago. Come on—now is the time."

Ana shook her head at him and turned to the Cardinal.

"Do you mean that this is a message? That this is your mission?"

"It is. I just thought I'd deliver it," the Cardinal said.

PASTRANA AND MADRID

"It's the same as those other missions, Ana—the German's and so on. They all really came from the king, I think."

"And he thinks that we might apologise to Mateo Vasquez for having protested against his recent public crimes against us?" she asked.

"Further," said Antonio, "you believe he thinks that I am prepared to sell my whole future into perpetual blackmail to a fool? That I am prepared to work for the State in close collaboration with a man whose mean and tattling power I shall have acknowledged, and before whom I am to go in fear as long as I live?"

The Cardinal smiled.

"You have both understood me," he said. "That is the present suggestion."

"Well, if it's the only one, it just leaves us all exactly where we were," Antonio said.

"Except that now perhaps," the Cardinal suggested, "you know a little better where you are?"

"Yes," said Antonio, "that is so. Thank you for that."

"Oh, not at all," the other said amusedly. "I just thought I'd give the curious message, as I was asked to. You must forgive me. My excuse is that it throws light a little way ahead."

"It does do that," Antonio said. "So we forgive you, you arch-plotter!" He turned to Ana. "We do forgive him, don't we?"

Ana was leaning back in her chair. She looked white and weary.

"It passes understanding," she said gently. "Where is Philip? What's the matter with him?"

The Cardinal looked at her, and then spoke with hesitation.

"You are the only one who might possibly find that out," he said.

"He hasn't come to see me in six months," she said. "He hasn't written. Now you tell me that he will not name or hear my name. So how can *I* find out what's happened to him?"

"I don't know, Ana. Still, you're the only one," the Cardinal said.

THE FOURTH CHAPTER   (JUNE 1579)

The Cardinal was right. Philip refused to consider Perez's resignation from office. He held it off by every device of time-marking, cajolery and affectionate concern. Notes and long letters in the king's own hand came by courier now almost every day to Perez at the Alcázar. Wait, was his burden, and trust me. I shall return to Madrid in a very short time and arrange everything. You will see how simple it is, and how my goodwill towards you will weigh like death upon your enemies. Let me pray, let me seek counsel of the Holy Spirit. I entreat you not to worry. You have no reason ever to be other than confident. Do your work as you always do and trust me. That will be enough. Everything will be arranged as you desire. I weigh all and shall decide as God directs. Only have patience a little. You know that I am not inconstant. You can be of good heart against this passing trouble, because you have me. Time and I——

Such entreaties and exhortations, as vague as Antonio saw them to be anxious, were thick now on every paper that reached him from the king. They did not reassure him but— added to what he learnt from spies and friends of the whirl of fuss and consultation into which his gesture had thrown Philip—they made him wonder if perhaps he might not yet win, by one further effort of guile and patience.

He did not give in to the king. He continued to assert in letter after letter that as His Majesty still did not deal as was necessary with his just grievances, he had no alternative but to ask him to find his successor. Until this person was appointed he would continue in his duty as Secretary of State, save only in relation to the Council of Italy, from which he was withholding henceforward his direction. But he must beg His Majesty to look with despatch for another First Minister, as he himself would have to attend very much henceforward to his own future, and would have many personal preoccupations. This firmness of tone which he preserved unbroken, coupled with his refusal ever to reply to such sentiments as for instance that he knew the king was not inconstant, had the effect he desired of keeping Philip in an unresting state of agitation.

Perez did not under-estimate himself, but he had well-founded reasons for knowing that his departure from office in this year would be a heavy blow for Philip.

The government of Spain was now more than ever, as the king aged, a closed-in, secret procedure, wherein the real facts, the true activating policies, were known only to the monarch and to the two or three ministers whom perforce he had to trust. Charles V had taken care to vitiate the ancient liberties of Castile, of which now the Cortes and Council were only perfunctory, ceremonial bodies, without power or the desire for it. The king's Cabinet, loosely divided in two parties, progressive and reactionary, was small and for the most part uncertain or uninformed of what in fact went on behind the façade of its debates. So that Philip was, as indeed he boasted, "an absolute king". But even if he were a very much faster and more penetrative thinker than he was, he could not possibly govern in the way he chose without one or two exceptionally sure and clear-headed *aides*. And these, to be effective, needed long training in and complete assimilation to his methods and his temperament. So at their best these Secretaries of State, as they were called, were not easy to find; and once found and adapted to him, they were adhered to passionately by their master.

Until their quarrel, Vasquez and Perez had functioned

perfectly together as Philip's right-hand men. Both had been trained at the Liberal side of the Cabinet table, the side honoured by the good traditions of Gonzalo Perez and Ruy Gomez. They were equal in their love for their work and in being indefatigable and quite selfless about it; equal too in their power to seize, amass and retain facts—as in their ability to keep secrets. Both were widely educated men, both were ruthless, and both were loyal in office. Both also were self-made, and from the middle class. In all these things they were ideal to Philip's purpose; and in the strong contrast they made beyond these attributes they were hardly less to his liking. For their being temperamentally antipathetic was, for the king, a great tactical advantage, as thus they kept clear of each other outside the Cabinet Room, and enabled Philip to indulge very fully his passion for concealing the work of his left hand from his right. And in broad application to principles and politics, whereas Vasquez's steadiness, incorruptibility and quiet obstinacy were excellent things, the worldly Perez brought entirely other and more vivid attributes into play. As Vasquez did not, he knew Europe, had studied and travelled in France and Italy, spoke the languages of those countries, read their literatures and liked to associate with the diplomatic corps and with all distinguished foreign visitors to Spain. And he was quick-witted and eloquent, and always able to give—what Philip himself could not—either the forceful or the subtle answer as needed, in the Cabinet or in the Ambassadors' Room. Perez could think while he talked, in two separate streams—which neither Philip nor Vasquez could do. And the king was the first to appreciate and call upon that talent.

Now at present, as Perez knew, Philip's hands and wits were even more than usually overtaxed; home, imperial and foreign affairs were piling up towards what looked like being years of massive exaction. Were the king and Vasquez left alone with the gigantic burden of temporisation and decision, they could not but flounder, both being slow men. As it was, he regarded with glee the problem he had created by his relentless withdrawal from the Council of Italy. Milan, Naples and Sicily presented extraordinary dangers of government, and although it was customary to regard the remaining Italian princes as weak, the Pope was one of them, and he was certainly as much an Italian and a temporal power as he was Christ's Vicar. Let poor green de Zayas find that out! Let him also cut his teeth on this one's and that one's crackbrained plan against the Turk, let him find his feet with Venice, and in general see what he could do with the whole question of the Mediterranean! Antonio smiled sometimes over all that. A month or two of confusion in the Italian office would teach Philip things he might be hoping to forget.

But over the rest of the globe, the range of questions requiring constant care and argument was very formidable. Parma was at the beginning of what would assuredly be a very difficult campaign of compromise in the Lowlands. Spain's relations with England and France would hang on it— and Perez was in charge of Parma's strategy. The religious war was exhausting France, and she eyed Spain therefore with increasing suspicion; but Perez, liberal, tolerant, was *persona grata* with the house of Valois, and therefore a most useful make-weight now for Philip, whose conscience was always receiving dangerous assaults from the Guises and the Pope. And as to England—it was essential to keep Elizabeth from giving full support to William of Orange, and to that end essential to sacrifice the romantic cause of Mary Stuart and the English Catholics. The Pope nagged on at Philip about this, but Perez stood imperturbable. Mary Stuart was a French princess of the house of Guise, he insisted, and therefore for everyone's sake much better left where she was, in an English fortress. Meantime, however, English pirates and buccaneers were on the seas—a man called Francis Drake had arisen and was robbing Spain of fortunes of her home-coming wealth from the western empire. And the old admiral, de Bazan, plagued Philip, for vengeance on these pirates, to be allowed to plan an invasion of England; and the Pope plagued on about the One True Faith; and the Inquisition needed perpetual vigilance, and Mother Teresa and her rivals were on the warpath all the time. And the king intended, quite rightly, to annexe Portugal at any moment now. And Alva was stirring in his sleep, and coming back into politics with his one archaic old slogan of "fire and sword".

For three men all this was work indeed. For two of them, deprived of the one who thought quickest and who had the best manner in approach, attack or retreat, it was admittedly too much, and very dangerous.

So, viewing Europe from Philip's angle, Antonio Perez decided that he could afford to mark time in his personal quarrel, while keeping up a front of cold reluctance and detachment. For the more closely he reviewed the men and talents available to Philip for his plan the more honestly could he aver that there was no one at hand who might attempt to fill it. Only names from the past came to him—his father, Gonzalo Perez, would have done, he thought; or Ruy Gomez, the perfect statesman. Or possibly, though not so good as either of those, old Cardinal Granvelle. Granvelle, though his career in the Lowlands as chief minister to Margaret of Parma had ended badly, had undoubtedly shown statesmanship of the kind Philip liked, both there and afterwards in his government of Naples. But he was old and very much an invalid now, it was said, and lived in pious retirement in Rome. So, quite simply, there was no one to take his own place, Antonio admitted—and decided therefore to be patient while playing the effective game of rash im-patience.

Meanwhile since April the scandal of Juan de Escovedo's death, of Easter Monday of the year before, this scandal which in the winter had faded so consolingly from common view, was now, with all its offshoots of libel and lie and grotesque decoration, ablaze again somehow throughout Madrid. Everyone talked of it or became ominously, tactfully silent when it was mentioned; everyone had an opinion; everyone said it must be cleared up.

Even the great Mendoza family, spread richly and now in the main slumbrously across the Peninsula, from the Vizcaya and Montaña of its brave origins and across the great Castiles to Cadiz and to Malaga, began to stir and grumble vaguely in its sleep, as if it heard its name dishonoured on the wind. The Duke of Infantado began to fidget at the centre, at Guadalajara; the old Prince of Mélito blasphemed; Iñigo Lopez de Mendoza, claimant against the Princess of Eboli for some family successions, showed how he thought the tides were running for her by renewing his doubtful suit for the lands of Almenara; and the dutiful young Duke of Medina Sidonia, married to the Princess of Eboli's elder daughter, disengaged himself from his horse-breeding in Andalusia and came to Madrid to see what was afoot, and to use what he called his "influence" on behalf of his mother-in-law.

This action of the young duke made Ana, and more than Ana, smile.

Alonzo de Guzman, Duke of Medina Sidonia, now in his thirtieth year, was a wealthy man, and virtuous. He had made an apparent success of his marriage with Ana Madalena de Silva y de Mendoza, who, ten years his junior, was now a self-important matron and the leader of sporting circles in the south of Spain. But no one in Castile thought anything of what went on in Andalusia, and Madrid accounted it very suitable that society down there should be ruled by two such stupids as the good Alonzo and his boring wife. Lately however the king had taken up Medina Sidonia; he had made him a Councillor of Castile, to the immense amusement of Castilians; frequently he invited him to hunting parties at El

Pardo, and shrewd observers about the Court said that Philip really did seem to have a speculative eye on the young man. Now as Philip's normal method was to leave the aristocracy at peace with their foolish country pursuits, and as indeed he never troubled himself socially with anyone save to further a policy, it was necessary to assume that Medina Sidonia was regarded as potentially useful to the realm.

It was impossible not to smile and wonder at this idea. The stocky, steady young man knew nothing about anything except horses; he had neither learning nor wit; he had not trained for Spain either as soldier or sailor. He was un-adventurous, domestic, kind, and—by Castilian standards—a provincial bore. But the king continued to flatter him. Antonio Perez said that this could only have relation to, possibly, the coming campaign against Portugal; that Medina Sidonia's estates and influence bordered Portugal on the south, and that he was wealthy and loyal. Even so, the king's attentions seemed excessive.

However, they pleased Medina Sidonia—and naturally made him a little pompous. So, as he had family feeling, and oddly enough liked his casual and eccentric mother-in-law, he came bustling to Madrid in May, to use his influence for her with the king.

Ana, though grateful to him, could not take him seriously. However, she did use him as a medium, a conveyor, of her "indiscretions".

"It's *the plan*," she told Antonio. "I want all sorts of fools to spread abroad my views on this affair, and my intransigence. I have a principle, you see——"

"Mad!" said Antonio.

Ana talked with apparent freedom therefore to the anxious and attentive Medina Sidonia. She was amused to discover in these conversations that had she confessed to him on her knees, had she sworn on the Cross that she was indeed, as accused, the mistress of Antonio Perez, he would not have

believed her, but have thought it some pitiful aberration of old
age, combined with exaggerated Castilian chivalry towards a
man in trouble. For to her son-in-law, Ana discovered, she
was an unattractive, plain old woman whom no man could
possibly want now, and who must be protected for her own
sake and the sake of her great name from the consequences of
a slight tendency to craziness. He liked her because she was
kind and generous, because she was of his own class, and
because she had brought up a large family and been a good
wife; he pitied her because she was thin and ugly and had only
one eye; and he thought it disgraceful that the populace
should be allowed to gossip so loosely and absurdly about a
Mendoza, who was also a widow and old and disfigured.
He was ready to do everything in his power for her and he
had reason to believe that he had power with the king. This
point of view saved Ana trouble, amused her and made it
possible for her to talk as freely as she chose.

But her son Rodrigo took his brother-in-law seriously.
Rodrigo was now openly very angry and unhappy about his
mother's association with the Escovedo scandal.

"How could he be otherwise?" the Cardinal said to
Ana. "He is your son. It is very painful for him, all this
talk."

"I see that," Ana said.

"If you could somehow say something, do something, to
withdraw yourself from it, to seem to reprove the slanderers
—I think that would help him."

"I know. As for the slanderers—truly I can't be bothered
to seem to reprove them. But I do see the grievance of a son.
And I'm sorry." She paused. "Oh Cardinal, there are regions
of my soul I would withdraw to now, regions that matter
nothing to Rodrigo, but where I could rest, I promise you!"

"I believe that, Ana. Why don't you seek them, child?"

"This is not a time for self-indulgence."

"Repentance? Is that self-indulgence?"

"Repentance, like anything else, can be ill-timed."

"I've told you before that God's timing isn't yours."

"You're a prince of the Church, but—do I know you long enough to say that you're a shade cocksure about God?"

He laughed.

"Very likely you're right. It's because I haven't yet got over the surprise of my red hat, perhaps!"

"How gracious you are!" she said.

"Ana, you are contrite. You're tired of your sin, and God is grateful to you for that. Trust him to understand at least as well as you do your own dislike of repenting at what seems the timely moment. Repent when repentance is true, Ana— and chance the implications."

"It wouldn't be wholly true now—and I'm not tired of my sin. But I do recognise it and have to struggle with it—and that is tiring."

"Hair-splitter."

"Perhaps. Still—you see I chose this love-affair with Antonio. *I* made it happen—not he. And I have enjoyed it, and drunk life from it. It was a gift to me I won't attempt to explain to you. Now it matters to him, and his whole world is endangered for it, but he doesn't waver. He's every sort of profligate and sinner, but it never occurs to him that he and I might fail each other in this danger. Nor will we. It's just unlucky that before the danger rose I was beginning to be sorry for my mortal sins. I had refrained from sight of him for seven months and was fighting it out. And the night on which I had decided to explain my dull repentance to him was the night on which he told me of the danger threatening."

"So you resumed the relationship?"

"Yes. Rodrigo had his part in the decision."

"Indeed?"

"It's a complicated story. And don't think it's heroic. The night wasn't sacrificial, Cardinal. I simply saw that I was too much in love with him still, and had grown too near him, to resist his need. It was no moment for self-analysis, or for a splendid, renunciatory scene."

"You are very self-conscious. Very vain, perhaps. He'd have been angry and disgusted, and have left you—and that would have been that, and much better for both of you now. But you didn't want him to be angry and leave you."

"That's what I've just said. And anyway, parting or no parting, the damage was done to his career. No amount of austerity after the fact was going to be much good."

"H'm, I see," said the Cardinal. "Very human, local argument. But God is not mocked."

"I believe not. But neither is my conscience."

The Cardinal laughed.

"From what I read, that sounds very Protestant to me!"

"Heretical anyhow, I suppose. A shade Pelagian, do you think?"

"Ana, my dear, you can be surprisingly subtle, for a simple creature."

"I think a good deal lately, for a simple creature."

"Yet your thinking can lead you to please neither God nor Rodrigo?"

"My thinking tells me without any monstrous effort that I have a soul to save and that its salvation is paramount; my honour, which has nothing to do with thinking, tells me that no retreat is possible now, and that everything, including my immortal soul, must wait on honour. And pleasure and affection prompt me to follow honour." She smiled at the Cardinal, asking for mercy.

"Yet you know," he said, not returning her smile, "you once did try to be a nun, in a mad sort of way——" She winced. "No, I don't mind hurting you. You did try, and you did make a fool of yourself. And before that you lived thirty-three years continently, and without, I understand, the full refinements of the pleasures of the flesh?"

She smiled.

"Be sardonic if you like, old friend. You see, you are just a natural monk."

"And I have often thought, my dear, that you are just a natural nun."

She threw her hands apart.

"Oh silly!" she said. "Oh, go and make that claim for me this minute at the Puerta del Sol!"

"It would be a true claim—but it wouldn't improve the present situation, Ana."

"No. The only thing for the present situation—sorry though I am for Rodrigo—is to be true, and stand by it."

"It's never right to continue in sin."

"I know. I wasn't talking about *right*." She was bent forward in her chair, and her hand was pressed against her empty eye-socket. "Oh, believe me, I'm a battle-ground. And what's more, I'm haunted."

"I expect so. What sort of ghosts, Ana?"

"Only one. Juan de Escovedo."

The Cardinal drew in a sharp breath.

"Ana!" he said. "Ana, *you* had nothing to do with his destruction?"

There was real fear, real anxiety in the question.

"No," she answered. "I knew, but only by implication, that Philip desired him dead, and that he would die any day in the early part of last year. I knew—though this was never said either—that Antonio had charged himself to rid the king of Escovedo. But one night Escovedo, who was a little mad, behaved as if he were the Angel of Judgment. Antonio was present. And very promptly afterwards, without a word said, Escovedo was killed by unknown desperadoes."

"I see."

"Forgive me, but I don't think you do. I'm not haunted by his death. I'm reasonable. He was to die, and that wasn't my affair. Philip's business. But in fact, by a silly accident, he seems to me to have died a martyr. Secretly, accidentally, he died for the right—for what he and I know to be right."

"But you don't grant him what he died for?"

"No. At present I can't."

"This thing called honour?"

"Honour and love and goodwill, and seeing things through when you started them——"

"You're complicated. You're Protestant. But do try to get God's view of all this, Ana."

"To do so would be simple egotism just now, I think."

"But what about Rodrigo?"

"If I'm to be of any real value to my children, Cardinal, I can only be so by being precisely myself, however I split hairs, or bore or outrage the world. And some of my children would see that, I think, if they were old enough. But even if they didn't, I cannot give them the whole country of my conscience and its mistakes."

But no one, watching her talk to Medina Sidonia or to Rodrigo, would have thought that she was a battle-ground. For in general encounters at this time her manner was tranquil, light and worldly-wise.

"You see, Alonzo," she would say to her son-in-law, "it is necessary for the king to understand that we of the aristocracy will not approve this sneaking kind of injustice to a public servant. If no one else intends to express the opinion of honour in this case—*I* shall do so, for the Mendozas."

"I—er, I see. How exactly do you define the injustice, Doña Ana?"

"Dear boy! Listen. There are two Chief Secretaries of State. One of them slanders the other grievously, repeatedly and publicly. The slandered one protests with vigour. Yet the slanders are repeated, to the king and to everyone of note. The king takes no side, does nothing. Meantime, the actual crime which is the source of the slanders remains uninvestigated. No one is charged judicially with anything, nothing is done. The slanders spread, and grow worse.

Antonio Perez naturally insults and threatens his slanderer, and asks the king to adjudicate. Yet even then all Philip can do is ask him please to bury the hatchet, and shake hands with his enemy!"

"It is indeed preposterous."

"*Now*, as you know, Perez has resigned from office. It is his only course. But the king won't accept his resignation. All this shameless, autocratic torture of a free man, all this freezing of the usual channels to trial and justice is unnatural to Castile, and an insult to us all. As one Castilian, I refuse this impertinence from a half-foreign king. And you can tell him so. Tell him further, Alonzo, that he need not think to keep Perez because Perez depends on his salary and increments. I am wealthy, and there are houses on my estate to which Antonio Perez can retire whenever he likes, and I can compensate him in money, and for the honour of Castile, for any loss imposed on him by the king's extraordinary blankness and ingratitude. That is what I want the king to know. That I see the honour of Spain in this affair, and shall protect it to the extent of my possessions."

When Medina Sidonia talked over this ultimatum with Rodrigo the latter seemed awhile as if he might lose his reason.

"She's capable of it, Alonzo," he said, pacing about his study rapidly and with a hand pressed to his eyes, unconsciously reproducing his mother's signs of agitation. "She's totally irresponsible, you know! Indeed, ever since father's death I've often thought that she is insane!"

"Come, come," said Alonzo. "A little odd, I agree—but hardly insane, dear boy. And she *is* your mother," he added piously.

"Yes, alas! But have you ever heard such dishonest nonsense as this about protecting Spain's honour to the extent of her possessions! What possessions? Her possessions are ours!"

Alonzo understood money well, and he sympathised with Rodrigo's disgust at Ana's royal foolishness with it. But he had an orderly mind, and he liked facts stated correctly.

"No, Rodrigo. As you know I've had to deal somewhat with your family affairs—more or less in your place, as you've been a minor so far. And it is a fact that your mother is a very wealthy woman in her own right, quite apart from the trustee-ship she holds for the estates of her children. She can't touch any of those—nor indeed, I believe, would she attempt to. And may I say that you are all very wealthy people?"

"It looks as if we'll need to be—since we're taking on liability for Spain's honour!"

"What I'm explaining is that you're *not*. You're perfectly safe. As a Mendoza heiress and only child your mother has vast resources over which her dominion is absolute. It was because of her great wealth that Ruy Gomez was able to bequeath practically all his possessions to you children. He and she agreed upon that, and upon leaving her own estates inviolable and independent. I know all this for a fact, because your father explained it to me in connection with my wife's dowries."

"Still—as we are the children of a Mendoza heiress, we clearly have a right to our expectations from that? Surely we can be protected from her squandering her whole estate without thought of us?"

"I don't think you can be. She says—and rightly—that you are all excessively well provided for. All the Neapolitan and Sicilian estates and titles that your family holds now are very sound indeed, Rodrigo. I agree, *naturally*, that family money should stay in the family, and I sympathise with your expectations from your mother's estates after her death. But meantime you have no legal control over what she does in her lifetime with her own property."

"But, if she's mad?"

"She isn't mad, Rodrigo. I beg you not to be so brutally unfilial!"

"Oh, you try being her son before you preach, Alonzo! If she isn't mad, she's maybe something worse! I—I daren't tell you what I feel about her—her association with this bounder, Perez!"

Alonzo stared at him.

"But, my poor dear boy, you don't believe all that ridiculous talk, do you? About your own mother? And at her age, and—er—everything? Now, come, come, Rodrigo— you must try to be a little bit—well, realistic, my boy."

It was Rodrigo's turn to stare at the round, earnest, swarthy face of his virtuous brother-in-law. And what he read there made him laugh, in sudden weariness.

Poor, silly, provincial, he thought.

"I think you'll be a great help to us, Alonzo," he said sincerely. "It was good of you to come to Madrid. Still, I think the simplest thing for everyone now, including the king, would be if I ran my sword through Antonio Perez."

The Duke of Medina Sidonia bounced from his chair. He hated swords and quarrels.

"Oh no, dear boy, no, no! That would be *quite* uncalled-for, let me say!"

"I'm tired to death of him," Rodrigo said.

"That is no excuse for killing him," Alonzo answered primly. "Moreover he is a notoriously good swordsman."

"So he boasts. But when has he last fought seriously with the sword? He's getting old, and I am very young, and in training. I believe I could kill him easily—and more courageously than he disposed of Escovedo."

"My dear boy, I beg you, I beg you!" said Alonzo, looking cautiously all round him.

Medina Sidonia liked his wife's relations, but he regarded them as unstable. And, now more than ever after this conversation with Rodrigo, he saw their need of a steady man of affairs to guide them. So he went with a will to the business of arbitrator in the Perez scandal.

Philip was informed therefore, as Ana had desired him to be, that Perez need not fear poverty, and that her estates were at his disposition. Nobody, not shrewder wits than Medina Sidonia, not the President of Castile or the Cardinal, could read in the king's face or manner what he made of that insolent communication.

Vasquez continued to assert that he walked in mortal danger, that Perez and his friends made open declaration of their desire to murder him. He begged the king to protect his peace of mind, and to make it possible for him to do his work in tranquillity.

It was quite true that Vasquez's life was being made a torture to him. Perez saw to that.

The king reassured Vasquez in the same terms of royal affection that he used to wheedle Perez. And he wrote to Perez instructing him that this shameful persecution of Mateo Vasquez must cease. Perez replied that it would cease, that he was tired of the whole farce, that he apologised for all his own wrong-doing, and only begged to be released at once from office. That is all I ask, he wrote. In return I offer silence.

Philip made no direct reply.

But in conference one day he told the President and the Cardinal that he was thinking of suggesting to Perez that he go to Venice as ambassador for a time. The two men just managed not to smile; they advised the king against making so vain an offer.

So the suggestion never reached Antonio officially.

It was the Cardinal who told Ana about it.

"I almost told His Majesty not to be silly!" he said. "He really does have the most preposterous notions for getting himself out of trouble."

Ana said nothing.

At this time, when her true friends or people whom she regarded as intelligent spoke of the king, she did not take up the theme. In talk with Medina Sidonia, or Rodrigo, or even Bernardina, she made—deliberately—wild and arrogant comments on him, and sent him verbal messages as insolent as she could frame. She desired all these to reach and to trouble him. And once, having to write to him in reference to the lawsuit of her cousin, Iñigo Lopez de Mendoza, she took the occasion to reprove him daringly and proudly for allowing a criminal libel on her name to be made by a minister of State and to go unheeded and unpunished. Her letter was arrogant but phrased formally and as Court etiquette required. It could be read by anyone in Philip's entourage; she hoped that it was read by many.

Philip did not reply.

When the children, Fernando and Anichu, asked if the king was coming to Madrid and if they would see him then, she teased them and said he was tired of them, and had grown too fond of the new Infante to be bothered with anyone else. But they were unperturbed.

"The king loves you; I know that for a fact," Anichu told her mother. "He'll come to see us when he has time."

But although Ana said nothing real about Philip in these days, he was much and perplexedly in her mind. She did not believe that he was cold or treacherous, or at least, that he could be either of those things to her. She did not believe either that he was the moral coward he was now appearing to be. And she knew that his silence towards her, prolonged into many months, his silence, and his inability to pronounce her name even to her dearest friends, that these were signs of something other besides hardening of his heart. That Lady. She knew that it was not for nothing, not cheaply or cruelly that she became That Lady on Philip's lips.

If he went on sulking in his tent she would go and find him there, and speak to him freely, friend to friend, as she always could. And if he wanted then to lecture her, or to be jealous or impertinent about Antonio Perez, she could easily, whilst denying him his right to such intrusion, accord him it as the privilege of a very particular friend, and hear what he had to say, and even, for old affection's sake, go so far as to defend her love-affair against his busybody disapproval. But she would wait awhile for that. She wanted him to take full cognisance first of her public and unflinching allegiance to Antonio Perez, in the feud of the Secretaries of State. She wanted her broadcast challenges to reach him casually on any wind. She desired to make it crystal-clear to him, even spectacularly clear if necessary, that she for her part was afraid of nothing in this scandal. She knew that this—which was true and which he would certainly believe of her, since he knew her well—would work alike on anxiety and curiosity in him, would drive him at last from silence, force him to speak plainly with her. But she could wait for that. There was time yet. She guessed that she counted for very much in Philip's present weak and foolish policy of inaction. She had an idea that, if all other ways out of the *impasse* were to fail, Antonio Perez's whole future might turn upon the exact nature of Philip's feeling for her. As she had never been able to be sure of that, she was uneasy now, considering the charge that it might bear—and so was in no hurry to put it to the test. She would face it when the time came—and pray for wit and gentleness. Meanwhile she tried conscientiously to remember the king she knew, and to balance his reality or non-reality against the king who was now confounding and distracting his ablest counsellors.

One night Antonio came to her earlier than usual. It was high summer, but after the torrid day the Long Room, windows open to the west, and unlighted save by the starred, transparent sky, was cool and still.

When Antonio came into the room she was sitting there alone, straight-backed and quiet, by the upper window, on her

French day-bed. Her hands were joined in idleness in her lap; vestiges of light from the summer night fell about her, stressing her darkness, making her seem like a shadow.

He paused before he reached her, considering her.

"You look very holy," he said. "Are you praying?"

"No. I was thinking about Philip."

"So well you might."

He came and sat beside her on the couch, and she took his hand.

"Welcome," she said. "I'm glad to see you. But what is it? Are you over-excited about something?"

He laughed.

"How the devil do you know, Ana? Does my hand give off some disgusting, curious heat, or something? Or are you a witch? I absolutely *hate* witches."

"Then I'm not a witch. And I don't like them either. No. Just tell me what's the matter."

"In a minute."

"I suppose you want to drink a lot of wine first?"

"I wouldn't mind. But no—oh no, don't stir. This is all right. This is enough."

He stretched himself along the couch and laid his head in her lap.

"God! This is lovely!" he said.

She bent and kissed him.

"June—it's June, isn't it?" he said dreamily. "In September, on the ninth of September it will be two years. Do you realise that?"

"I do. I've been wondering already what to give you for an anniversary present. What do you want?"

"Anything. Everything. I love presents. Is my head too heavy? Am I hurting you?"

"Silly."

"You're so thin. It's awful, really. Do you remember we had a very good celebration on the last ninth of September?

You were a little drunk that night, I think."

"I was quite drunk."

"Oh girl, you were *so* amusing! I'll make you much, much drunker this time. Every anniversary I'll make you a bit drunker—until at last you're a dipsomaniac. That will be marvellous."

"Do you expect to love me for more anniversaries?"

He sighed contentedly.

"I'll tell you something. In the old palmy days I rarely reached a *first* anniversary. On the one or two occasions when I did, I was always far from willing to be there. But now, to be clearly in sight of a second, and talking like any sort of drivelling fool about the third and fourth and fifth—oh, it's inexplicable. It's terrifying. Perhaps it's just middle age. If it is, I'm astounded to find that I like it."

"We're beyond middle age. We're old. Medina Sidonia thinks I'm a decrepit old hag."

"I expect so. Do you remember, Ana, that first ninth of September—there were flowers on the table at supper that I had sent you——"

"Yes. Flowers from Aranjuez—I remember."

"Philip's flowers! Curious. I remember thinking before I sent them that they were a good excuse, being Philip's. I mean, it would have been a bit impertinent just to send you flowers of my own——"

"Nonsense, you weren't weighing up the pros and cons of me then. You were just manœuvring politically, and I was the not very alluring widow of the king's favourite minister of State."

"That's true, I suppose. It's a long time ago." He pulled her down to him. "I love you, girl."

Bent above him in embrace she leant on him, relaxed, at peace.

"Do you know that you never say it?" she said.

"Do you want me to?"

"Only when you do say it. Otherwise, I know."

He held her very close to him.

"Stay there. Keep still, Ana."

"But tell me what's the matter."

"Ah! That! Well, you'll have to sit up for that."

She sat up.

"So shall I, I think," he said, "to do justice to it."

"It's grave news?"

"It isn't news at all." He stood up. "I think I'll start drinking all that wine now."

"Can you see? Shall I ring for lights?"

"No. Of course I can see." And indeed moonlight was brilliant through the windows now. Antonio poured two glasses of white wine. "Come, drink with me, ascetic," he said. "Drink to my genius for finding out what *no* one knows." He sipped his wine. "Philip will miss that talent," he said.

"What have you found out?"

"You will remember, from Ruy's heyday and earlier, a Flemish churchman called Bishop Perrenot, afterwards Cardinal Granvelle."

"I do indeed. He was chief minister in the Lowlands under Margaret of Parma?"

"Yes. And a talented administrator. Afterwards he did well as Governor of Naples. In recent years he has been invalidish and living in retirement in Rome. He was a favourite of Philip's, do you remember? Very much trusted, and understood the king's very personal method of government."

Ana watched Antonio with interest. He was talking with precision and detachment, almost as if in the Cabinet Room.

"Yes," she said. "I recall all that about him. He was a friend of Ruy, was frequently with him."

"Exactly. That's one of his very strong points."

"I don't see what you mean."

"You will. I'm going to tell you something now that at present I believe only one man in Spain is supposed to know —and that man is the king. And I wouldn't know it, were it not for my uncanny knack of seeing how one improbable nothing leads to another—and the trouble I can take when these improbable nothings insist on engaging my attention. Well, I've had lately one of my curious intuitional attacks. I couldn't possibly explain to you the irrelevancies that led me along. But I was right."

"Stop boasting. Tell me the news."

"In my own time. Drink your wine and wait for what you'll hear." He paused and moved about the room. "Oh God! Oh God!" he said.

"What has happened?"

"When I wrote and asked to be released from office, I was bluffing of course, as you know. How could I want to resign? But I don't have to tell you. You know how I work, and how good I am at my work, and how I love it. Let's take all that as said. But I thought—let him try to work out how to let me go. He daren't. There simply isn't anyone, *anyone* to take my place. I thought: there was once my father, Gonzalo Perez; and there was Ruy Gomez, of course; and there was, possible, but not so good, Granvelle. Two of them, the good ones, are dead, I thought; and the other is a sick old man in retirement. So there's no one. Let him try to plan to do without me."

He paused again and drank. Ana did not speak.

"Well, he *has* planned. Nothing escapes him. Granvelle is coming back—on his personal and absolutely private invitation. I think he's on the sea this minute. Philip has secured my successor. The only catch is that he's old. But there are a few years in him—enough to see us through the annexation of Portugal—and by then he will have trained his successor. So I have lost, Ana. I didn't think I could lose. But I really believe I have."

"I don't see it. You are still in possession of the true story of the Escovedo death."

"Once he has found someone to do my work even that ugly fact loses its force. For now I can be assassinated, you see, like anyone else. Like Escovedo."

"You don't know at all why Granvelle is coming to Spain."

"He is coming in answer to a despatch and private appeal of the king. But I *know* what that means. I give you my oath he is coming to take my place."

"Or Vasquez's?"

"That's just possible. But his talents are more suited to my kind of work. He's a man of the world, a European. The correct complementary for Vasquez, just as I have been. You wait and see."

"Philip isn't like that."

"Philip is anything that he deems necessary."

"You know I don't agree."

He came and sat beside her.

"Oh girl, I'm tired! I've loved my life, I've loved my work for Spain."

She took him in her arms. Philip would have been moved by that cry, she thought.

THE FIFTH CHAPTER   (JULY 1579)

July was extremely hot. Ana sent the three youngest children, Ruy, Fernando and Anichu, back to Pastrana. Rodrigo came and went as he chose between Alcala, Madrid and the country houses of his friends. Ana hardly ever saw him; when they did meet he had only reproaches or bad news for her.

She and Bernardina lived almost exclusively in her private wing of the house, as if in retreat. It was too hot to ride or even drive unnecessarily by day, and casual visitors were discouraged. The few friends Ana would have been glad to

see were not at hand; the President of Castile was ill and the
Cardinal was directing an ecclesiastical conference in Toledo;
the Marqués de Los Velez wrote dejectedly from his Alcala
house. " . . . Philip goes much too far in deceit and
procrastination now. I despair of him. I feel when I talk
with him that I talk to a mask, or a ghost. I am tired, my
dear. Perhaps if one were to go abroad? I think of asking to
be made Governor of one or other of these new American
places. What do you think of that, Ana? And why don't you
come too? This silly Spain where we who used to govern are
reduced to puppetry—I'm tired of it. Meantime I fret
impatiently about this dreary Escovedo *impasse*, and I fear for
your friend. And, foolishly, irrationally, I fear for you. Let
me have a word of news. I am too old for Madrid in July.
Indeed, I can't understand why we've all been bullied like
this into accepting it as our chief city. I wish you were here,
or at Pastrana. Everything promises well for harvest . . ."

Antonio was melancholy and weary now. He had lost all
impulse in his fight against Vasquez, and had written once
again to the king, expressing this weariness, undertaking to
ignore the wrongs the other secretary had done to him, and
to subside for ever into silence, if only the king would do him
one last favour, instantly relieve him of office.

Philip did not answer. The official memoranda came to
Perez still, exactly as if there was no conflict between them.
So the latter was now making preparations to move his family
to his native kingdom of Aragon. "The ancient liberties of
Aragon will protect me there," he told Ana, "against any
pursuit of vengeance. And the border of Aragon is not very
far from Pastrana."

Ana still believed that Philip would find a better way than
this to end the confusion he had set up. But meantime she
helped Perez to take necessary decisions, paid debts for him
and did her best with love and fidelity to keep him from a too
profound dejection.

She was weary and uncertain herself now; tired of the disgraceful public embroilment with Vasquez and of the king's apparent stupidity; anxious very often to pray, but forbidden by her own spiritual honour to seek the balm of prayer; anxious indeed to be free to return in honesty and forthrightness to the questions of her own sins and the too long brushed-away desires of her soul. But she belonged to Antonio Perez in this preposterous external situation, and as long as she felt his need of her to be true and by his rules justified, he could be sure of her. Yet often now as she sat alone, outwardly quiet or busy, in the Long Room, she was visited, stormily, wildly inside her heart, with the old mad desire of six years ago to flee from everything and be a nun. She did not even wince from the absurdity, but let her spirit dwell on it indulgently—knowing that now she was in control of herself, and could only dream these things, while a paradoxical duty of sin kept her anchored to the wrongdoings of every day.

Philip was at the Alcázar in July, and sent her no message, gave no sign. Anxiously she turned over plans for visiting him there. If she did go, and she would, she hardly knew what she was going to say to him, save that she would tolerate no hypocrisy between them. But much lay for Antonio on that future conversation with the king, so she pondered it uneasily and often as the hot days passed.

And one evening as she sat by a window of the Long Room and thought of him, Philip came to her, unannounced.

She came across the room to him quickly. She fell on her knees, as usual, as she kissed his hand. And when she rose and looked into his weary face there was such pleasure and gratitude in hers that the king forgot himself and his knotty troubles for a minute and smiled at her as he had always liked to do throughout the years.

"Oh! This is good of you!" she said, without any etiquette of 'Majesty' or 'sire'. "Oh Philip! I've wanted to see you! Sit down. How tired you look!"

He had a small sealed packet in his hand.

"I came with this," he said. But he did not explain what the packet contained, or set it down.

He stood and looked about the room as if memorising it, or checking memory. And Ana had the impression that he was undergoing some great stress of feeling and wished for a while to avoid looking at her face. But she was so glad to see him, and so confident that his gesture in coming meant friendliness and boded well for Antonio that she decided to have no care for procedure, to let the king take his own way with what had to be said, and trust to their old sincerity and affection—Philip's for her as much as hers for him—to steer them into safety and understanding.

It was dangerous, this impulse she always had to like and find the best of him in Philip. And never more dangerous than now—if for no other reason than that somehow she always communicated to him this sense of her great liking. It had ever been a mighty charm in her for Philip, that in her presence vanity and all its unresting, self-conscious attendants could lay down arms and go to sleep. Her affection once given, a fellow-creature was safe with her. There was no sharpness in her then, no mockery or self-parade, no impulse to alter or outwit or dazzle. She could be cruel and careless to those she either did not know or did not like. She was consistently, if passively, cruel to Rodrigo; she was cruel in her casual contempt for her old father; she was notoriously cruel in her every public utterance about Antonio's enemy, Mateo Vasquez. But her affection once engaged, goodwill dominated it. So those whom she loved could rest in her, as nowhere else, from the persecutions of their egoism. She was in fact not merely passively but actively non-cruel in affection. And it was the *activity* of this principle which differentiated it from mildness; made it an intelligent and potent force, almost a peculiarity—and by no means just a condition of slumbering gentleness.

It was this active principle of goodwill in feeling, which could face conflict with other strong principles of her nature, that had made it possible for her to stay at home with Ruy for all their years, and be content and make him happy. Because he had been so lucky as to reach to the centre of her affection; and thereafter she would never be able to persuade herself that her own needs or moods were more important than his. There was no theatre and no virtue in this for her; it was her fate, because it was the way her nature worked. So it was with Antonio Perez. He could be every sort of schemer, egoist and cheat; he could commit crimes and take very long chances on honesty and even on good manners. But he had warmed her heart, he had won her goodwill, and so he was safe.

But to Philip love of any kind had never brought, could never bring, the ease it brought to Ana. For her—and she was not stupid, and had encountered and wrestled with many complications of feeling—but for her mainly love simplified life. There it was and in the midst of much nonsense one saw it to be real, and one could therefore weigh and measure it. It simplified by its positiveness, and because she, of her nature, could not haggle.

But Philip could haggle until time stood still. His curse was that he was a natural haggler. Indeed, because he and Ana were opposites in this they suited each other well. For throughout the years of his uneasy desire of her he had had, he thought, as King of Spain, to fuss and haggle all the way; and she, unacquainted with the methods of hagglers, hardly noticed what he did. For her their situation had been simple. They had a persistent attraction for each other—she never saw him in her early years without wondering what it would be like to be his mistress—but they both loved Ruy, and Ruy and his happiness were worth a great deal to anyone who loved him. So the sinful decision was not taken, though Ana in her honesty could never assure herself that had Philip been truly urgent she would have resisted him.

Yet when she was a widow he left her unmolested. He was ageing then, and crazy to save his immortal soul and have an heir, and be a virtuous king. He was haggling fiercely with heaven in these latter years, and his waning, tired desire for her was now become one of heaven's easier taxations. Ana understood this, and so did not share the vague fears of Antonio and de Los Velez that her having taken a lover would disturb him in some degree which might make his future conduct towards her incalculable. She outraged no claim of his in loving another man, and her private life was her own. And she knew him as reasonable, considerate, gentle, faithful. She knew him, through many years, as a man who could not resist any direct appeal of poverty or of little children, or of the holy, or the mad, or the sick. She knew him as a man of constant and gentle charities, and as one who was naturally attracted to painters and gardeners and scholars and monks. She knew that he liked simplicity and quietude, and cared, after holiness, for those earthly activities which can be called true and eternal. She knew him also in his plight as a politician, and as a ruler who believed himself marked by Heaven, and she knew many of the sins which he had justified within that conception of himself. But she would have said through thick and thin that, guilty, conceited creature as he was, fanatic, bully, megalomaniac—she still knew him better than his shrewdest judges, because she knew him another way; knew him in little, knew him at home as it were, knew him at rest.

This was her secret argument, and it was well-founded and in that sense true. But it did not compass the whole of Philip —and because in her innocence and mercy she thought it did, it was dangerous for her.

Because affection meant in her goodwill and a consequent dismissal of cruelty, she inclined to think that that was what affection was, the world over. That for another it might be, or have to be, power, absolutism, self-assurance, and indeed an appetite more subtle, greedy and constant, more jealous and unkind than any sensual lust, was a guess outside her compass. So Philip might, if she hurt him, be stiff, offended, difficult, sly and all the boring, slow delaying things that he could too often be. But yet affection—which was goodwill—would prevail between them, if it lived. And by his coming to her, by the way he looked about the room now, she knew that affection lived, and had brought him here. So having welcomed him with natural gladness, she was suddenly peaceful, and content to let him speak, and even be as silly and irritating as he liked.

The more fool she.

Much was indeed in the balance when Philip came into the room. But had she met him in some alien way, had she played cold or haughty, or even virago-ish with him, or in any way been false or new or disconcerting, it might have been far better. What in any case was unlucky—though neither she nor Philip could possibly feel it then—was that she gave him in their first minute together after so long the old, precious feeling of peace, of having come to where there was rest and faith. For Philip, the absolute king, the lonely, wretched, vain and hungry man, it was insufferable to feel and take this peace, this illusion, from a woman who was the declared and shameless mistress of a subject.

But Ana, clear-cut and generous, having never refused Philip anything he asked or ever suffered real unkindness from him, welcomed him back to the Long Room now with an open and uplifted heart.

"I hadn't thought to see this room again," he said.

"That is a dreadful thing to say. What do you mean by it?"

"Oh, Ana!" He moved slowly to what had been his usual chair by the lower window, and sat down. "How are the children?" he said.

"They're very well. Rodrigo comes and goes. He's very

much a man of the world now, and I hardly see him. I sent the others back to Pastrana last week. It was so hot, and they were getting far too frivolous. But they'll be wretchedly disappointed at missing you."

"They've wanted to see me?"

"But, Philip—of course! They love you. We all love you, in this family."

He bit his lip and looked uneasy.

"It hasn't seemed like that," he said.

"So you appear to have thought. I'm waiting for you to tell me why?" she said simply.

He looked at her as if genuinely surprised.

"You're very cool," he said. "You're really very, very audacious. I suppose I must blame myself. I suppose I've encouraged you——"

"Blame yourself!" she interrupted him. "Encouraged me? But Philip, my dear friend, what do you mean? I've only asked you to tell me why we've been estranged?"

"Ana! Please!"

He laid his little sealed packet on the table near him, and then laid his hand upon it as if in close protection. She noticed how thickened and stiff his hand was. She noticed too, now that he sat in the hard, dramatic light from the west, that his face was green-white and older than she had remembered it, and that his eyes were weary and red-rimmed. His once fair hair was neutral-coloured now, half-grey, half-dun. But she liked it still, and liked the paleness of his weary eyes. She always liked to look at him; his washed-awayness, his curious foreign pallor appealed to her.

"Yes, Philip. Go on!"

"I fear I must," he said piously. "You have disgraced yourself, Ana. You have dishonoured Ruy's memory and your children's name."

She smiled a little. This was the sort of nonsense that she well knew he could talk. It did not perturb her.

"I could pretend to be mystified," she said. "But I don't want to tease you." He looked amazed at this gambit, but she went ahead without waiting for his protest. "*I* have done no harm to Ruy's memory or my children's name. That part of me which belongs to what I associate with those phrases of yours still belongs to them. *But*, my private life *is* truly private. There have been, Philip, as long as I can remember, thoughts and even acts in that private life which, presented to the world, would seem to injure this or that. That is so, I should think, for everyone from cradle to grave. But I do not present my private life to the world. Which is not the same thing as saying that I sacrifice it to the world. I own it, Philip. If I do wrong in it, that wrong is between me and Heaven. But here below, so long as I don't try to change it into public life, I insist that *I* own it. Not Ruy's memory, and not my children's name. These are clouds I can't really see at all—I only bring them in because you did. But my private life is all that I own, and I insist on managing it myself, under God."

To Philip, the absolute king, no one had spoken like this in his lifetime. If he censured, or hinted censure as now he had, to any subject, that subject either took his censure silently or with a great flourish of submission. He had never had occasion seriously to censure Ana de Mendoza, but his habit of total authority had probably made him imagine that she too, being his subject, would be solemn and helpless under his displeasure. So the friendly coolness of her counter-censure struck him as might some astonishing foreign custom, or even a speech in an unknown language. Yet a part of him heard what she said with approval, and with envy.

"I repeat," he said coldly, "that you have disgraced yourself. This public scandal is an outrage against everything you stand for."

"I agree. And I have protested against it, and shall continue to protest. It was not *I* who made this public scandal."

He moved uneasily in his chair. Through all the honesty of her speech and in spite of her dismissal from it of forms of ceremony and care for his royal dignity, he felt the charm and kindness of her flowing towards him as it always did. He was a suspicious man and in middle life was growing pathologically so, yet now he had the restful feeling—very novel to him —that anything might be said or suffered in this room in perfect safety. He could fight here, if he liked, for the obscured meaning of his own conduct, and whatever might be exposed in such a struggle, however he might be humiliated, he would be safe.

"Ana," he said, and she did not miss a new note in his voice as he went on, a note almost of pleading, and certainly of tentative honesty. "Ana, the man who informed me and some other people about your immorality, is an honourable public servant, and had to do his duty."

She smiled.

"I know that. It began that way. But since then he has widened the scope of his duty. The whole town knows things about me now, Philip, including that I connived at the murder of Escovedo, which are quite simply untrue. This is a curious outcome of the high dutifulness of a public servant."

"It was self-defence. You have driven him far—you and another."

"Why will you have the thing upside-down? Why must you make the victim into the criminal?"

"You are all criminals now, in this public feud and cross-feud that is turning my very Council Room into something like a thieves' kitchen. I intend to put a stop to the ridiculous thing. I have work of enormous scope to do, and so have these two men, my servants, and I am tired of this disturbance of their and my efficiency."

"Everyone is tired of it, Philip. You know that. End it."

He smiled wearily at the simple advice.

"I have been trying to. Mateo Vasquez is now quite

willing to drop the whole charge," he said carefully, and watching Ana.

She laughed.

"That's very kind of him," she said. "Considering how very little trouble he has given everybody for the past nine months. But what about the poor Escovedos? It's *their* charge surely, a little bit?"

Philip frowned.

"The Escovedos will be managed. The real trouble has been Vasquez, as you know. But he has been so terrorised by—by the other Secretary of State and his partisans—that he is willing now to bury the whole argument for ever."

Ana was laughing softly in a continuous light accompaniment to Philip's careful dull words.

"I see. Oh Philip my dear, are *you* here too on that really silliest of missions?"

He looked startled.

"Silliest of missions?"

"Yes. Because if so don't please let's wade through it again! I've lost count of the people who have come to this house and told me—in the last five months—that Don Mateo is willing now to forgive himself for all his recent sins of slander and criminal libel, and that all he needs to be quite comfortable is apologies from me and from Antonio Perez for having been the awkward cause of all his crass mistakes. Just that, a public apology, a civil bow, and a promise to withdraw our threats against his life. I have repeatedly told his very odd ambassadors that never having threatened his silly life I can't withdraw a threat. And that the rest of his proposal is just plain lunacy, bearing no relation at all to life." She saw his face growing rigid with anxiety against this flow of impudence, so she rose and came near him, her hands out almost to take his, as she went on speaking. "So please, Philip, please as I love you, spare me the bitter joke of pretending, you too, that *anyone*—let alone I—owes anything but everlasting scorn to this poor Mateo Vasquez!"

She took his hands and dropped on her knees beside him, laughing and gracious. He looked in perplexity into her face and felt in spite of himself great gratitude for the warmth, vitality and trustfulness of her approach to him—after politicians, after prelates, after courtiers.

"I was not going to suggest this pacification as anything but the most cynical trick in the world," he said simply. "I don't think I could say this to anyone else, Ana—but as you know the Escovedo trouble has been mishandled. It went wrong, and is now out of hand. So we are in a fix." He looked at her, doubtful perhaps of himself for talking to her of a State affair at all, and moreover with this new, confiding freedom. She stayed on her knees by him, her hands on his, and simply waited for him to finish what he had to say. "In a fix," he repeated, still marvelling that he could say "we are" to her in such loose and almost confessional application. "So there is nothing left but to patch up a bad affair, and hope for silence and time. And the only way to do that is to pacify Mateo Vasquez. Naturally, I see your point as to the ethical absurdity. But no one could literally ask you for any apologies. Some formula is all he wants, so that he can bury the hatchet without too much loss of face—and with a sense of future safety. And so I thought that you *might*, in the painful circumstances and for—well, for many people's sakes, manage to be cynical about it, and look for a formula——"

He was so grave, and this honest speech was so complete a sacrifice of his public self, and therefore such an effort for him and so deep, so moving a tribute to her, that she could not laugh again, deliciously amusing though she found the passage about "the formula".

"I believe," Philip went on carefully, "I believe that if you could somehow, however formally, arrange to satisfy him that your enmity is no longer directed on him, he might somewhat waive similar exactions from—others. For I understand that he thinks that you exercise influence over his worst enemy—and therefore——"

Silence fell. The king had said something that was very difficult for him. It was indeed hard to believe that he had said it. We must indeed, thought Ana, be "in a fix". This is pitiful. And he is the King of Spain.

She released his hands gently. Then she rose and moved away from him. There was no use in being contemptuous or humorous now. The thing was to be literal and simple, and keep him from becoming again too soon his histrionic conception of himself.

"I'm sorry, Philip," she said gently. "It wouldn't do. It would dishonour everyone."

"I've told you it's a resort of cynicism only."

"I know." She paced along the room, backwards and forwards. "It's not cynical enough, I think. No, I'm sorry."

He watched her in silence for a few seconds, drumming his fingers nervously on the little sealed packet that lay near him.

"If I were to command you to do it, Ana?" he said at last.

She paused in her striding, and came and stood before him.

"You know that I have always been as childishly and fanatically your subject as Fernán or Anichu. You know that in everything of me that your office commands I am absolutely yours. But if you *were* to forget how to be a king, my dear—which you never could!—but if you were to command me to do this outlandishly silly thing, you know perfectly well that I'd refuse."

The conversational tone, the ease and affection she kept in this speech gave it a formidable quality. It was the quietest possible kind of comment on his wretched politician's troubles; it was suave and sweet defiance—but he knew it for what it was.

He looked away from her, looked towards the distant peaks of the Gredos.

"Then we remain in our fix," he said.

"Yet there is one clear way out. There always has been."

He looked at her almost hopefully.

"And what is that?"

"But, Philip, you know. You've always known."

"I wish I had. What is this clear way out?"

She came to the window and stood there with her back to him, looking towards her golden, fair Castile. But her thought was not on landscape. Ruy, her husband, came into her mind, and she appealed to him. Help me, she said. Give me courage now and help me to help him.

She turned and leant against the window-frame.

"Philip," she said, "Philip, my dear—as I love you, listen to me. Have the Escovedo charge heard in its proper court of justice."

He looked at her as if he had not taken in exactly what she said.

"Don't pretend to be outraged," she went on. "You know it's what must be done."

"It's what will never be done," he said harshly. And then he grew mysterious and royal. "This is, at its base, a grave affair of State. I must beg you not to plunge into it out of your depth."

"I'm not out of my depth. I know all about it," she said. "Antonio has asked you again and again to have the case heard, hasn't he?"

He looked at her without friendliness now. He loathed the free reference to Perez, and loathed answering her question. But he answered it.

"Yes, he has made that request."

"He's a good judge of lines of action."

"This instance doesn't prove him so."

She smiled. She was about to say that at least it proved he had the courage requisite to a normal man. But she decided that "for everyone's sake", as Philip would have her say, she had better let Perez be for a moment, and wheedle the king back to his fluttering mood of honesty. There was hope in that—for Perez.

"Philip, I beg you—have it heard. No, listen to me, have the brief as it stands presented. All that is untrue in it will be very easily disproved. My complicity, for instance, in the death of Juan de Escovedo. And all the minor charges brought in to prove motive—Antonio's venality, his desire to get control of my money, his fear that Escovedo could expose all that. It is every word untrue, and can be swept away in a sentence or two by any reasonable lawyer."

"Be silent, Ana, or I shall leave you."

"No—you won't do that. You know I am your friend, and you must listen to me, this once. Antonio will plead guilty to the central charge. You know he's ready to, and only waits for your permission. He will of course say why he had Juan killed. After that the rest is easy—the case will become a long argument between judges and theologians about the divine right. And very likely they may even condemn Antonio to death. But you will naturally intervene with your royal prerogative—and after a lot of fuss and pamphleteering, the air will be clear. And, as Ruy would, we'll all have learnt something, and will begin again. He never would tell me what he really meant by his 'begin again'."

She had rattled on, to help him, to give him time to see the common sense of her argument, and in general to throw out ropes and bridges. For she was startled by the staring helplessness in his tired, pale eyes, and wanted him to pull himself together. She did not like to see this abject, silly panic in his face.

Yet it did not leave it.

"What *is* it, Philip?" she said, changing tone. "Why can't you face this simple action? What are you afraid of in it?"

He rose from his chair and strode away from her across the room.

"Be silent, Ana. You are allowed great liberties. But even you must not ask me if I am afraid."

"I am compelled to," she said coolly. "And yet I cannot think you are. For say—and I suppose it's preposterous, but I don't really know the terms of your sovereignty—but say, for the fun of the thing, that a Madrid court of justice could find you, the king, guilty of murder, and say you were condemned to death——" he shook his head, almost amused at her—"I simply don't believe you'd be afraid of that. What's death? It comes once, and it comes to everyone. It's an end, a bad moment, and nothing to be what one calls afraid of. You aren't afraid of death."

"I am. I'm terrified of death, Ana. But not of dying, the physical process. Not of being condemned to it. That isn't why I refuse to have the Escovedo case examined in a public court."

"I knew it wasn't. You're afraid of moral judgments."

He wheeled about to search her face. This was an accurate observation. It took him sharply by surprise.

"I know that," she went on, "but I find it odd, in this situation. After all, you can support—I don't know how well —but still you manage to support in your own soul, and reflected in the souls of a few friends, the moral burden of your right or wrong in disposing of the life of Escovedo. Why then can't you face the breathing and blowing of the larger world on that dilemma? It might do good; it might define your powers. Certainly in any case Spain has the right to know, if she asks, why her public men are liable to disappear sometimes. And you love Spain and serve her night and day; and if you do make mistakes in that service, Spain will forgive you if you appeal to her."

"I will *not* appeal. I do not make mistakes."

"Nonsense," said Ana. "Don't be foreign, don't be German. Go to our common courts and let us hear why Escovedo died."

"I am not German," he said coldly.

"I suppose not. But what are you? Where did you get your fair head? Oh, don't try to look dignified again. You've done it far too often this evening. You know your fairness is enchanting. It must be sad for you to see it fading now."

"You are preposterous," he said, defending himself half-foolishly from the pleasure he took in all this casual impudence she flung at him.

"Half Portuguese," she said, "half Flemish, half Holy Roman——"

"Well, I can't be made up of three halves," he said angrily, "and anyway, Juana La Loca was my grandmother."

"Ah! I'd forgotten. Of course. That's a saving grace. That must be why I like you so much, Philip."

She smiled at him and stretched out a hand, and he came to her slowly, and took it.

"Listen," she said, "listen to me, a Castilian. Let your people have this story—and then, let them argue. They'll argue for ever, and they'll never decide on your conduct, but they'll understand readily—here in Castile—that your point of view is very, very important. Because every man's point of view is—in Castile. Govern us *our* way, Philip—and you have resolved your fix."

He drew back from her.

"It seems to me that *you* are very cynical."

"That's subtle. Does it mean something?"

"'Govern us our way', you say. But I have *studied* to govern *my* way. And government is intricate and grave. It cannot be submitted to the vulgar flash-opinions of Madrid. I govern with my eyes on the real world, Ana, where they must be—Spain has a world-mission. Her king cannot submit his failures, his mistakes, to the judgment of the gypsies and thieves of the Plaza de Cebada. You seem to see Spain provincially, as something small and simple that you ridiculous Castilians have in charge. But I *know* what Spain is. And before the world and Heaven I represent that Spain I know. If, in my frailty, I have made an error for the sake of Spain, I am content to ask Heaven to judge me—but *not* the riff-raff of Madrid. Wrongly or rightly, I do not rule this nation in the light of their anarchical vulgarity, but before posterity, and Europe's destiny. And so I cannot, cannot be subject to Castile's small moral judgments. You called them moral judgments. I would not so honour them."

He was now in such a fine heat of imperial and esoteric righteousness that Ana decided that all was lost, that she had somehow thrown away a chance and done more harm than good. So she answered him straight out of her thought, without troubling at all to choose her words or deflect his anger.

"Nevertheless," she said, "you are finally subject to 'Castile's small moral judgments'. And you fear them. It is because you fear them that you have built up with so much caution this system of secret government, which now may break open in disgrace any moment, if you persist in hiding your actions from your people. No, let me finish, Philip. I love you too much not to have the privilege of saying to you sometimes what I think. This long speech you've just made—about posterity and Europe's destiny, and our local anarchical vulgarity—it seems to me to contain the truth of your error in government."

Error in government. Philip was so much astounded to find himself standing still and *listening* while a woman spoke such words to him, that when she paused for his answer he could not find one. The moment was isolated in experience, and found him unready. So Ana, surprised by his silence, went on.

"If Ruy had been listening," she said.

"Ruy?" the king asked almost eagerly, forgetting his plight of indignity because of his constant, pathetic wish as he grew older to know what Ruy might think of this or that.

"Oh, I may sentimentalise about Ruy's days—Spain wasn't perfectly directed then either. Still, I think Ruy would have been shocked by what you said just now. He'd have thought that you've got into bad habits, Philip. But, in my view anyhow, you give everything away when you jibe at the gypsies and thieves of the Cebada, and deny their right to their moral judgments. That is the end of all moral right in you, if you mean it. It's the end of princeliness, and of understanding of your place in Spain."

"I didn't know you were a thinker, Ana."

"If I am, then there are others. Many of your best friends 'think' as I do. Oh Philip, come back from inside that curious web you're weaving at El Escorial! Come back into the streets where we all are! Come back to govern us so that we can see what you're doing! Take this chance, make an instance of it. Make this gesture of having a fair trial and facing the consequences! And begin again in everything from this one awkward point. Summon the Cortés, summon the Council of Castile. Let us feel the *movement* of government in Spain again; let us throw in our responsibility with yours, and lend you those moral judgments that you fear! Oh Philip, see this! Do it! I've never seen it so simply myself before, though I've often felt it, often thought of it. But now it's clear. It can all arise from this one small entanglement. Have the trial. Make this honest gesture, which will take everyone by surprise—and see what happens! Will you do it, Philip?"

As Ana spoke, the simplicity of the solution she offered the king became enchanting to her, good in itself, and offering, by chance, an entirely new hope to Spain, a cleared horizon. She felt very happy, and almost envied Philip the opportunity he had to seize. But she reminded herself that she would have her share in it. The Escovedo trial would not be pleasant for her either; she was not urging on others an ordeal which would leave her scatheless. And she would be glad of her punishment—and think it less than she deserved, on the

whole, perhaps—if it brought about between Spain and the
king that renewal of co-operation, that revival of mutual trust
which was so desperately to be desired.

She had surprised him beyond anger, beyond the inept
refuge of imperial commands to be silent. She had surprised
a whole region of his anxieties as king. Her assertion that he
feared the moral judgments of his people; her appeal for what
she called movement in government and letting his subjects
add their responsibility to his; her casual inference that others
besides her among his friends observed his methods with
anxiety, observed and discussed them—all this was apt,
audacious and paralysing. And at its centre was her simple,
obvious answer to the festering Escovedo problem.

The whole thing lay before him now in the silent room,
monumental and awkward.

Ana waited, contemplating what she had said. When
Philip entered the room she had not known that she was going
to say to him all that now was said. Often in their more
recent days of friendship, since her return to Madrid, she had
pondered his secretive way of government with dislike, had
even spoken to him lightly sometimes of it, and had thought
that some day she would argue it frankly with him, however
angry he became. And since the Escovedo brief had come
into existence in the autumn she had unswervingly advocated
that it be heard in the plain way of justice. Philip had known
that such was her wish, because through the Cardinal and de
Pazos as well as through Perez she had sent him this advice.
And always she had intended to repeat it to him, face to face,
when he should give her the opportunity. But it was only
whilst arguing with him now, and seeing the pitiful in-
decisiveness to which one single question could reduce the
ruler of Spain, that she felt the connection between the
Escovedo ordeal and the future of his relation to his people.
She had suddenly seen that he could make it his gateway back
to them.

Delight in this idea as it revealed itself had made her, she feared, incoherent, emotional and perhaps more forceful than was wise. But that could not be helped, and she knew that she meant from her heart and chiefly, in that heart, for Spain and Philip, what she had said.

But she had shot her bolt now, and could only wait.

Philip moved, with his slow, stiff gait, to his chair by the window. When he was seated and Ana could see his face again she could not read it. It was closed and weary, sealed off from expression like a death-mask. She did not wonder that his ministers so often cursed and fretted under his yoke. He could indeed be enigmatic and exhausting.

But when he lifted his eyes to her, as she stood, tall and grave, in the centre of the room, their blueness held a curious deep light.

"There's statesmanship in what you said," he said slowly.

Is it possible that I'm going to win? Ana thought. But she tried to betray no ripple of this thought.

"You would have made a good queen for Spain, maybe," Philip said.

To please him and thereby, she hoped, to help him into replying naturally to her appeal, she took this up, although it was a deviation, and therefore dangerous from one who so perpetually made use of deviousness.

"I thought that once, Philip—a long time ago."

He looked about the room, yielding himself a little, as often before, to its peace, its good effect on him. It occurred to him that if he could in fact stay here, stay here a long time protected by her presence and her restful courage, that so he might untie the Escovedo knot, and others too, by her direction; might begin again, as she suggested, to rule the people in the streets, as one of them who walked the streets in their company. If a man could have peace sometimes, and be sure he was loved. In this room he had sometimes almost begged her that, ageing and faded and belated as he was, she

would take him, and in mercy give him some of that peace
that flowed from wherever she lived. He had almost begged
her—he, the King of Spain, who would not have her when he
could.

But other thoughts pressed on him too, thoughts of a kind
which all through this winter had so much sickened his *amour-
propre* that he had had to train himself into a kind of false
refusal, half-denial of them. Thoughts of the love and licence
taken here by another man, a commoner; thoughts of the fool
he had made of himself in coming here as to a refuge that was
his own; thoughts of a day of Carnival, eighteen months ago,
when he had sat here in blind man's innocence between the
two, thinking himself almost her lover then, almost her
tempter, giving them reason to laugh at him together afterwards, in their cunningly stolen delight. Two friends of his,
and one his all-but mistress, and both of them knowing him
their king, their ruler. In this room, this room he had used to
dream about. The thoughts which all the winter he could not
take, and had to take, and again had to deny, swept over him
now in one strong, bitter tide.

He pressed his hands against his face, and groaned aloud.

"Philip! Philip!" Ana cried in innocent alarm, thinking
him ill, and striding to his side.

"It isn't to be borne!" he said. "Go away! It isn't to be
borne!"

"What isn't to be borne?"

He stopped groaning, and dropped his hands from his face.

"Ana," he said, "you have made me suffer. You have
made me suffer as no man should suffer."

Ana could hardly repress a smile. And it even occurred to
her to say that it seemed as if his own self-pity made him suffer
as no man should suffer. Instead she went simply to the point.

"You mean—it has disappointed you to learn that—I have
a lover?"

He looked at her as if he thought her a little mad.

"You choose words cunningly," he said. "Disappointed? I have not known how to speak to you! I have been shocked; I have been grieved."

"I understand that, Philip. It's not edifying. It sometimes shocks and grieves me too."

"It has undermined everything," he said. "It has poisoned all our years of—of love."

She let the word "love" go by, half-amused and half-exasperated by his use of it.

"It is *true*?" he said suddenly, on a sharp, hard note.

"Yes," she said, "it's true."

"It's still true?"

"Yes," she said, somewhat surprised.

"But, you *could* give him up?" he went on harshly.

"I don't know exactly what you mean, Philip. Or really by what right you ask me these things. Still——" she shrugged, "naturally, I *could* give him up. And naturally in any case, one of us will tire, or die, before the other."

She withdrew to the window, offended by the peevish catechising.

"I came here this afternoon to give you these," he said.

She turned back. He was holding in both hands his little sealed packet, and eyeing it as if it could wound or poison him.

"And what *are* these, Philip?"

"They are some letters of yours—to Antonio Perez."

She stood and looked at him in cold amazement.

"Where did you get them?"

"Mateo Vasquez conceived it his duty to secure them for me, so that I should have to believe what I was unable to believe."

Ana leant back against the window-pane, and pressed her right hand against her injured eye. She looked so strangely frail and white that for a moment Philip thought she might be going to faint.

"Oh, no, not that!" she said softly. "You haven't done that, Philip! Mateo Vasquez—yes—of course! But you! Oh Philip!"

She could not look at him. She stayed as she was, leaning against the window-pane.

"I have the right——" Philip began.

"You haven't a vestige of right," she said wearily, "to steal and read another person's letters."

"As head of the State——"

"Oh, don't! Be quiet!" Suddenly she was standing straight, and her voice was vibrant. "Who talks of 'rights' and 'heads of States'? It's *feeling* you offend against! The feeling I have always clung to between you and me, the certainty of something true that I could always reach in you— the kind of *goodwill* there's always been between us!" She paused, and became weary again. "But now? Oh, clumsy, clumsy ass!"

"Yes, I'm clumsy," Philip said, and his voice shook a little. "But let me speak, will you? I did not steal any letters, or ask to have them stolen, or think of such a thing. Mateo Vasquez's secret zeal drove him to the measure, unprompted. When he gave me the letters and told me what they were, I instructed him to leave them with me. He has heard and seen no more of them."

Ana was sickened, and could hardly bear to listen to this explanation. Yet she did listen because the slight shake in Philip's voice pleaded with her against her disgust, and so did his fingers, tapping on the sealed packet.

"I was shocked at his bringing them—but of course he couldn't know what he was doing, and in particular to me," Philip went on. "I was shocked at having letters from you— to another man, in my hands. I locked them away and decided not to read them. But I knew I wanted to read them. Indeed I think in a part of me I was determined to. I took them out often and held them in my hands, and tried to read them. But—Ana—I couldn't. I don't quite know why. I think I was just afraid of the pain, of the awful pain they'd be to me."

He looked up at her at last; his eyes were swimming with tears, and tears ran along his cheeks.

"So take them, will you?" he said, and held the packet towards her.

Ana came and dropped on her knees, as if receiving him ceremonially, when she took the small parcel.

She kissed his hand.

"Thank you," she said, "and forgive me."

He laid his hand on her head.

"That's a lot to ask," he said.

She rose. She was too tired to take up his implication; also too sorry for him in his weariness. Enough had been said for now. The ice of the winter was broken, and she would see him again. She felt satisfied and hopeful.

Philip brushed the tears from his cheeks.

"I am privileged," Ana said gently. "To have seen the king in tears."

"Your privilege is even greater," he answered. "Because I shed few, and many of them are for you."

"Ah, Philip!"

"But now I believe I should be in the Ambassadors' Room at the Alcázar. I don't think anyone knows that I am here."

"Well, they will soon, because I shall boast about it. And since you've come back you'll come again?"

He looked about the room.

"I don't know. I have loved it very much, coming here—in the past."

"We don't change here, Philip."

He rose, and she rang a silver bell.

Servants came at once and set the doors open for the king.

Ana dropped on her knees again and kissed hands ceremonially.

"Good-bye, Princess," Philip said, and then he turned and left the room.

THE SIXTH CHAPTER   (28TH JULY 1579)

Days passed, torrid and quiet.

Philip did not come again, but Ana learnt from Antonio that he had gone to Aranjuez for a week, and would return to Madrid before the end of the month.

Antonio was reassured somewhat, as Ana had hoped he would be, by her account of the king's visit to her. The news of it surprised him greatly, and set him to fresh reflection on Philip's possible processes.

"But I gather that, on his side, the interview was at once emotional and non-committal?"

"It was emotional on both sides—and I was not in the least non-committal!"

"Oh girl, I wish I'd been a mouse under your chair! But it's Philip's feelings that make him dangerous. In politics and in things in general I've observed again and again that while you can keep him more or less cold on a problem, he will reason exceptionally well and justly, and will be sane and long-sighted, and even honest and consistent, in handling it. But let feeling blow up, let him suspect that his own person, his prestige, his inner self is related to the matter—and then the intricacies begin. Then you really have to bear in mind that you don't know him at all, that you move through virgin forest!" He laughed. "And the trouble is that so does Philip! If he'd only find out—just for his own private guidance, what he's got in his forest, and what he wants to find there!" He paced about the room. "No, Ana—*your* being in this scandal has made an emotional storm of it for Philip— and when that happens to him I for one have no clue. Still, I do think it's a good sign that he was enterprising enough to come and talk to you."

"It's a good sign that he brought me my letters."

"H'm. Maybe. But that, and his not having read them, betray emotion, much emotion. However, we'll see. And he is at present being quite endearingly fatherly and conciliatory with me. Still says that I am safe in his hands, and he will settle all my grievances for me according to God's will."

Ana smiled.

"You don't trust him when he drags in God's will, do you?"

"Well, do you?"

"No. I don't like it much."

"And I now know for certain that old Cardinal Granvelle has landed at Cartagena. He is bound to be summoned to the Alcázar during this month."

"I see nothing for you to fear in the return of that old man. After all, if Philip is going to conduct the Portuguese annexation himself, he probably just wants a respectable old regent to leave in Madrid."

"Yes, that's very possible. Meantime he works me to death, and flatly refuses to arrange for my withdrawal. But I'm getting my family and possessions into Aragon next month. I can argue quite easily from there—and more safely."

Ana talked of all this with no one else. Madrid was still empty of her real friends, and she began to desire Pastrana.

"I think," she said to Bernardina, "that when the king comes back from Aranjuez I'll ask if I may see him again—I want to see him—and when I've done so we'll go to Pastrana. I'd like to get there before the first of August."

So Bernardina set going their preparations for return to the country.

"There's a great deal of talk about His Majesty renewing his visits to you," she told Ana.

"Indeed? And what do they say?"

"Oh, this and that. Plenty they shouldn't, you can be

sure—but they don't try much of that on me, naturally. Some
say it's a good thing. Some say it's a scandal—with all the
other talk that's been going, you know."

Ana laughed.

"Tell them from me, Bernardina, that it's always a good
thing for friends to be friends."

Bernardina looked at her quizzically.

"They'd agree with you," she said, "and so do I. Only it's
well to know where you are with that word 'friends'."

Madrid wearied Ana now. She sewed, wrote letters to the
children, attended to business affairs; she read; she gossiped
with Bernardina. And in the dusk when it was cool, missing
the fields of Pastrana and missing her horse-rides, she forced
the lazy *dueña* to walk with her about the streets—sometimes
towards the Retiro Wood, sometimes to San Isidor, or by the
path of the little Manzanares.

She went to Mass on Sundays and feast-days at Santa Maria
Almudena or in her own chapel; she attended Vespers too
sometimes, and she read her prayer-book dutifully. But she
did not go to Confession, and so could not receive Holy
Communion. And this half-and-half state of soul, this living
in sin while refusing to be outcast as a sinner, dragged at her
conscience.

So she thought with particular longing of Pastrana. Away
from Antonio there, safe from her inability to haggle with
him in his time of trouble, away from the attractive tenacity of
his passion and the temptation he still was to her, un-
distracted by each separate surrender, she could much better
face the whole field of her mortal sin, and try to arrive at that
decision of repentance and abstention which was as honestly
necessary to one part of her spirit as it was daily refuted by the
rest.

She did not forget her last encounter with Juan de
Escovedo. Antonio thought with contentment that it was
emotionally forgotten, and remembered only in an occasional

surface-thought of disquiet against a bad moment of mischance. And they never spoke of it. She slept now in a different bedroom in her house in Madrid. And he suspected that when she had made that change, her intention had been that he would never visit her there. But he made no comment, asked no question. And she was grateful to him for that, and despised herself for having been so melodramatic as to change her room and yet so weak as not to complete the curve of her melodrama. Yet often she lay awake in the new bed to which Juan de Escovedo had driven her, and confronted him with free and honest thought. I understood what you said, she said to him. I had agreed with you and forgiven you before you began. Because I have your touch of madness, or exaggeration. I agree with madness and exaggeration. I could have been a fanatic, but they married me young to a sceptic. And I've never escaped from the education he gave me. Yet I know, with my first intimations, that you are right. For me you are right. That was really your offence against me —your being right. Only I wouldn't have killed you for it, believe me. But the killing is between you and him—and you were going to die anyway, because the king wished you to die. Don't haunt me, you don't have to. I remember—and in fact I don't really think I needed your warning. I understood it too well—I could have taken the words out of your mouth. All I object to is your simplification. Because it isn't just the thing you called it. It's that—and it's more, and less. Still, I saw your point. Believe me, believe me, you needn't have died for that.

But Antonio continued to be her lover. And she continued to find pleasure in this; yet continued now to desire Pastrana and its solitude; and to pray, and to wish she could pray from a repentant heart. When he goes to Aragon, she told herself uneasily, when he goes to Aragon it will all end. Yet he must not go to Aragon, for going there was the end of his life and career, and would be a bitter injustice to him from the king he had served only too meticulously. Wait, wait, she said half-ashamedly to her uneasy soul. We must save him first, or at least be true to him when others are failing. Later we will argue about my salvation.

On an evening very near the end of July she walked far and, as Bernardina thought, foolishly through the south end of the town. It was a night of great beauty, with even a little movement of breeze from the west. Ana strolled through the crowds with pleasure. The Plaza de Moros and de Cebada were rowdy at night, and Bernardina grumbled against the danger she said they were in, and against the madness of being seen, the Princess of Eboli, in this quarter after sunset. Ana felt no danger among her own people, and laughed at the fussy Andalusian. She could not say that they would go unrecognised, as she supposed that she was the only woman in Madrid who wore a black eye-patch, but Bernardina must not make this point. So they went as Ana willed, skirting even the Rag Market, and going down to the Toledo road, where gypsies camped and sang all night.

Ana listened and looked about her. Madrid might be new and an unnecessary kind of accident, but it was growing out of the very heart of Spain, so it would be possible to give it some affection. How lively and real we are, she thought, outside of our solemn royal monasteries and stuffy ducal palaces. Oh, Philip, take my advice! Come back and rule us by the ordinary terms of life.

The singing of the gypsies pleased her.

"Anichu would like to hear that boy," she said.

"My goodness, don't be silly," said Bernardina. "Don't you know the *flamencos* are at it all night in the square in Pastrana at this time of year?"

"That's true. I remember. I must answer Anichu's letter to-night."

"Well, come on home then, in God's name, and do that," said Bernardina, turning implacably northward.

Ana followed her, laughing.

"I don't know why you pretend to like town life, Berni," she said. "Whenever I treat you to it—real town life, like this —you're in a perfect twitter until you're back indoors with everything bolted up."

"I like town life in respectable streets and when I can see what I'm stepping on," said Bernardina..

"Well, never mind, you'll soon be as safe as safe in Pastrana. The king is back from Aranjuez, came back yesterday. I'll write to-morrow and ask if I may see him, and say that I want to go to Pastrana on the first. Where are we now?"

"To-day is the twenty-eighth," said Bernardina.

"That leaves three days. I think I'll tell Anichu she can expect us on the first. Must we really go in so soon, Bernardina?"

But Bernardina, who dragged and dawdled on their outward walks, always led the way home and took the shortest cuts. She was almost trotting now along the Calle de Segovia. As they passed the corner of the Plaza del Cordón Ana looked up at Antonio's great palace. How he would hate to lose it, she thought—and after all, how much it means that he wrung it and all it stands for out of his own sheer brains and zest. The building looked dark and as if locked up, which was absurd, she thought idly. She was not seeing Antonio to-night. He had arranged to leave the Alcázar early and devote a whole evening to the ordering and packing of his own private papers. He was still determined to withdraw to Aragon at once when Granvelle came to Madrid.

She smiled towards his house, and thought of him affectionately—busy within it now, concentrated, by no means thinking of her. He would be amused to-morrow to hear that she had been prowling by his gate not long before midnight.

"Come on," said Bernardina. "This, if I may say so, is no place for you to loiter."

"Well, you chose the route, not I."

When she was back in the Long Room, she found a letter there from him.

"I wish I could have found even three minutes in which to see you to-day. To-morrow night is very far away. I feel a kind of pressure in the air, an anxiety. I suppose it is this decision I am taking about Aragon that makes me hyper-emotional. Silly. Because I really believe that the king regards me as essential to him now, and by doing this I shall force his hand. And anyhow secure safety for Juana and the children. Still, I do feel overwrought. I think, in a way, the king's visit to you has frightened me. I can't explain that—and it probably means nothing. Since his return from Aranjuez, where he tells me the roses are like a miracle of Our Lady, and his new fig-trees bending with promise, he is even more kind than he was ten days ago. We have said nothing in these two days—I don't like to nag!—about my imminent withdrawal from his service. But his whole manner is, I know, calculated to woo me back to patience. To-day he made some general joke about trusting him. 'You must, you see,' he said. 'Whom else can you trust?' Later, when I was leaving his room just now, he did something quite extra-ordinary. He spoke of you! Oh, not with reference to my quarrel with him, and not at all indiscreetly! But, he actually pronounced your name! He said he assumed that the Princess of Eboli was still in Madrid, and did I know when she thought of moving to Pastrana? I replied that his assumption was correct, and that I believed the Princess would leave for the country on 1st August. That was all. But it means a lot—his naming you to me. I wonder, in fact, *what* it means? In the time I've taken to write all this I could have been across the street to take one look at you, and back again. And that would have been a lifetime better than what I've done. Well, good evening, Princess—and take care of yourself until our next, faraway meeting.

"A."

Ana folded the letter and laid it aside to read again. She too was feeling some pressure in her heart to-night. So she was grateful for the letter and for the freshness of its feeling. Always, she thought, her hand on the folded sheet, always he can reach me with this *life* he's got, this power to make you feel what he is feeling without ever a protestation——

"Let's have supper here, Bernardina, you and I. Don't have servants and fuss. You just bring some things, will you?"

Bernardina smiled. She liked very much having supper alone with Ana and casually, and Ana constantly suggested it.

"While it's coming, I'll write a letter to Anichu," Ana said.

In spite of all the lighted candles, she would not have curtains drawn. Moths beat about the room, and Bernardina said that they'd have bats in their hair any minute. But Ana waved her off, and turned to her desk to find Anichu's last letter.

" . . . we spent yesterday afternoon with Sister José watching her do the bees. Fernán was a bit afraid of them, he said. Sister José is my favourite Franciscan. To-day at catechism Juliana—you know, Juliana from the shoe-making shop, not Dr. Juan's Juliana—couldn't even answer about the Unity and Trinity. And she's *seven*. Don Diego says that I can make my First Confession before Advent. Did the king say he would come to Pastrana, or what? It's a long time since we met him. Fernando and I remember when he came before. That was the first time I saw him, Fernando says. Ruy does Greek all the time. He talked Greek at supper last night. I didn't like it much. Is Bernardina very well? I hope she is. I hope you are very well. When will you be coming home? I dust your drawing-room sometimes with Paca. When I have time. Come home soon. I'll write to the king soon, I think—if you say I am to. Fernán says he will too. This is a long letter, but I must do my geography now.

"Your loving daughter,
"ANICHU."

Ana sharpened a quill.

"Anichu, my pet,

"That's a very fine, long letter, and this won't be half as good, because it isn't worth while writing much, since I'll be home nearly as soon as you get it. I'll be home in about three days, *chiquita*. Tell all the others. I don't want you to make your First Confession yet, if you'll forgive me for interfering. Wait until you are six at least. I'll talk to Don Diego and you about it when I see you. Write to the king if you want to, pet. He'll be delighted. Oh, here's Bernardina with supper— I'm sure she sends you a kiss. I'll finish this after supper, my little daughter . . ."

Bernardina laid her tray on a table by the upper window.

"Come now," she said, "I'm hungry. All this tramping about the slums!"

Ana went to the supper-table and they began to eat. Bernardina poured out wine.

"This is beautifully cold," said Ana, sipping it.

"Did you send my love to Anichu?"

"Yes. I haven't finished the letter yet. I've told her though—and I know it will break her heart—that I don't want her to make her First Confession yet."

"Of course not. That old Diego! What nonsense!"

"Anichu's First Confession!" said Ana gently. "Poor little sins. Dear good little child."

"You make a terrible pet of her, don't you?" said Bernardina.

"I don't see how one could fail to. She's pure gold, it seems to me."

"Yes, she's a nice little child."

One o'clock rang from Santa Maria Almudena. They ate a good supper, talking or not as they felt inclined.

"I'll be glad to get back to Pastrana," Ana said.

Suddenly there was a noise of heavy feet in the corridor, and of voices raised, as if in argument.

The two looked at each other in surmise.

"Some of the footmen must be drunk," Ana said.

The door at the further end of the room was opened with noisy force even as she spoke. She saw two of her servants being pushed aside on the landing, as three armed men thrust themselves into the room.

They paused on the threshold.

Ana looked past them to the anxious servants outside.

"It's all right, Estéban," she said. "Would you just please close the door?"

The door was closed.

Ana recognised the leader of the three soldiers. He was Don Rodrigo Manuel, Captain of the King's Guard. He was a friend of Mateo Vasquez, and during the spring had come to her house as one of the latter's absurd ambassadors, asking for her friendship. She assumed that this was another such *démarche*, only more idiotically initiated.

She rose from the supper-table, but signed to Bernardina to stay seated.

"Continue to eat, Bernardina. This need not disturb *you*."

Bernardina was looking very much disturbed, but she obeyed Ana's wish that she should stay where she was.

Don Rodrigo and his men saluted Ana politely.

"This is a surprising entrance, Don Rodrigo," she said. "Only a little more surprising and ill-timed than your last. You come on your old errand, I suppose? But why do you come armed and with such a clatter to my quiet house?"

Don Rodrigo bowed again.

"I beg Your Highness's pardon for the disturbance, but your servants, not unnaturally, questioned my right to intrude upon you unannounced. Yet it is my duty to do so."

"Your duty?

It was Bernardina who spoke. By the pompous, embarrassed and excessively military aspect of the three men, and from her knowledge of common gossip she had read far more quickly into the purpose of this visit than ever would the innocent and arrogant Ana. And in the word "duty" she saw—in a sudden light that seemed to wither her heart—its end.

Don Rodrigo looked towards her. She had come to stand beside Ana. He bowed, but with less ceremony this time.

"Yes, madam, my duty."

Ana laughed.

"This is a new, funny way!" she said. "How can my dislike of Don Mateo Vasquez influence your *duty*, Don Rodrigo?"

"Your Highness, I do not come from Don Mateo Vasquez. I come as Captain of the King's Guard. I come on His Majesty's commission, to secure your person, awaiting His Majesty's pleasure."

Ana looked at him as if at first she still found his presence amusing. But almost instantly her face became grave and non-committal. If there was surprise, if there was shock in her for what he said, Bernardina, who was watching her in a painful closeness of attention, could not see either. Simply it seemed to her that Ana's face passed from amusement in one flicker to neutrality. And, masked thus, that face turned from the Captain of the Guard to her.

"I did hear correctly, Bernardina?" Her voice was still amused, unlike her face. "Then the next thing, I suppose, is to ask for the King's Warrant?"

Don Rodrigo stepped forward and with another bow presented a rolled parchment.

Ana took it and looked at it. She did not even unroll it.

"The King's Warrant," she said softly.

Don Rodrigo took it back and unrolled it. He pointed to its opening lines where she and Bernardina both saw her name, and then to the last paragraph, and the king's signature.

"From Philip to me," Ana said.

Silence fell over the room.

"Well, Bernardina, you're a practical person," Ana said. "When this happens, what do you do?"

Bernardina lost control of herself.

She snatched the parchment and flung it across the room.

"We protest!" she cried. "We raise the town! We send at once for the *Alcalde!*"

Ana looked at her admiringly.

"A very good idea," she said. "How do we send for him?"

Don Rodrigo smiled, and one of his adjutants picked up the parchment.

"You do nothing of the sort, madam," he said to Bernardina. "You prepare a small bag of necessities for this lady, and with as little delay as possible she leaves this house in my charge."

"For where?" Ana asked, still half-dreamily.

"My instructions are to convey you to-night to the Torre de Pinto."

"Where is the Torre de Pinto?"

"It is some fourteen miles from Madrid, Your Highness— on the road to Aranjuez."

On the road to Aranjuez. But Philip had just come back from there. She knew the road to Aranjuez. In the days when Isabel was queen they had often driven it together. Isabel had loved Aranjuez, and so had Philip too—planting his English elms, his English roses. She remembered the waterfall at Aranjuez, and Isabel's baby daughter playing among the fountains.

"I ought to know it," she said. "I know that road. But why am I being taken there?" she asked in wonder.

"Why indeed?" Bernardina questioned much more forcefully. "What is this farce, this foolery?"

Don Rodrigo unrolled his parchment again and brought it to Ana. Holding it so that she and Bernardina could see it also, he read aloud a turgid piece of prose. Because Ana de Mendoza y de Cerda—and all her titles were given—was at

present incapable of governing her own estates and was
thereby in the course of doing great wrong to her children,
because moreover she was in danger of becoming an inciter
to public disorder and was a threat to the general peace, and
finally for her own good and safety it was necessary to
remove her to a confined place to await the king's pleasure,
and such alteration in the conduct of her affairs as would
ensure the best interests of her family and of herself.

The sentences were long and vague. No charge was made;
the whole was windy, inefficient and without any base or hold
in common law. Ana listened with amazement and felt sorry
for the well-trained officer who had to read aloud such
nonsense to justify summary action. But Philip's signature
and seal were in their proper places. And the warrant had
been issued from the Alcázar, and was dated 28th July, 1579.

To-day, Ana thought, looking at the word "Philip".
To-day. The day on which he was able to pronounce my
name to Antonio. She turned towards her desk where
Antonio's letter was lying. Philip had made a joke about
trusting him to-day. "You must, you see. Whom else can
you trust?" And Antonio's house had looked dark and as if
locked up when she passed it an hour ago. So he won't get to
Aragon, she thought.

"Thank you," she said to the still reading Don Rodrigo.
"That will do. I understand it. And I apologise for having
compelled a man who knows the laws of Spain to read such
stuff aloud in the name of those laws."

Bernardina snatched the document and spread it on a table
to read it herself.

"There's no charge in this," she said. "You can't arrest
people without a charge!"

"This isn't exactly an arrest," Don Rodrigo said awkwardly.
"It is a measure of safety, directed chiefly towards the
Princess's own eventual benefit."

Ana smiled.

"Have you made another arrest to-night, Don Rodrigo?"
He looked at her cautiously.

"No, Your Highness, I have not."

"No? But there are other officers of the Alcázar who could be sent on such a mission as this?"

"Your Highness, I regret that it is outside my duty to answer irrelevant questions."

Bernardina pushed the warrant away.

"There isn't a word of a charge in it," she said. "You can't arrest her on it. I'm going downstairs to Diego, and we'll send for the *Alcalde* and his men!"

She moved briskly towards the door, but one of the young soldiers stepped in front of her. Don Rodrigo almost laughed.

"Do you really think we conduct affairs as amateurishly as that, Madam?" he asked. "All your servants are under strong guard downstairs, and no one can at present leave this house under any pretext whatever. We are here on the king's business. I beg you to be serious."

"We'll try," Ana said. "But you make it difficult. Bernardina, come here—sit down a minute." She drew her down beside her on to a couch. "It looks to me as if, for the moment, I must submit to this extraordinary farce. After all, I can't have everyone in the house put to the sword over it. But I shall not *stay*, I assure you, in this—where am I going, Don Rodrigo?"

"To the Torre de Pinto, Your Highness."

"Ah, Torre de Pinto. Ridiculous place it sounds. Philip can't do this to people—and he'll find that out. So don't worry now, like a good Berni. Go and pack things for me, will you?"

Bernardina looked mulish still, but after a minute she got up.

"I suppose that's the only thing," she said. "Though it's enough to make you choke! My God, I'd like to have the choking of you three!" she said firmly.

The soldiers remained impassive.

"You wouldn't be any good at it, Berni," said Ana. "Go and pack now, will you?"

"I'll pack. But it'll take a little time," she said threateningly. "I'm packing for both of us."

"My instructions relate only to the Princess of Eboli," said Don Rodrigo.

"I won't tell you, in the Princess's presence, what to do with your instructions," said Bernardina. "I'm only telling you that I'm coming with her to this Torre de Chinche!"

"And I am telling you, Madam, that you cannot."

"Berni, don't! What's the good? For the moment we're in their hands. But it won't be for long. I promise. And meantime, you'll be needed here. Your being here will be a tremendous weight off my mind."

"But you can't go off with them like this—alone?"

"Suitable female attendance will be provided for the Princess at Pinto," said Don Rodrigo.

"Oh, lovely female attendance, to be sure!" said Bernardina. "But in the meantime what's to stop these ruffians torturing—or murdering—you?"

"You mustn't call them names, Berni. And, say they do murder me, it'll be easier if I know *you* are still alive—because of Fernán and Anichu, you know."

Bernardina looked at her wildly for a second.

"Ah, those two! Ah yes!" And then she flung herself on her knees before Ana and threw her arms about her and sobbed and cried. "But I *can't* let you go like this, into the dark, into the night! There must be something I could do, and it's my duty to do it! Oh my dear, my *chiquita*, don't go with them! Refuse their nonsensical piece of paper! You're a Mendoza, you're the greatest lady in Spain! You have all those dukes and people on your side! Tell these fools to go home, Ana! Tell them to keep their noses out of what they could never understand!"

She raved, but on a theme of courage and coherency. Ana listened with respect. "I wish I could do what you say," she said. "I think it's right and it appeals to me. But all those dukes and people are at this moment scattered over Spain and fast asleep in bed, I imagine. Even my son Rodrigo is in Santander to-night. And if they were all in Madrid and wide awake, how could we get to them, Berni? No, for the moment we must do as Don Rodrigo requires, my dear. So help me now, will you? Stop crying—there, my good Berni, there! You're calmer now."

Bernardina rose, sniffing and red-eyed, but in command of herself.

"If it wasn't for the children I'd never agree to this—but we must be careful for them, I suppose. I'll go and pack for you, *chiquita*," she said, and her voice shook again on the last word..

One of the soldiers opened the door for her.

"Escort the lady to the Princess's dressing-room," Don Rodrigo said to him. "Stay with her, and see that my orders are obeyed. We take only a minimum of personal requirements."

Bernardina glared.

"Be as quick as you can, Berni," Ana said. "I shall be lonely sitting here, waiting to go."

Bernardina hurried from the room, and Ana, watching her, guessed with pity that she was crying again.

She turned to her desk.

"I may sort some letters?" she asked the captain.

He looked uncertain.

"Well, I suppose so. I have no definite instruction."

"Thank you. Would you and your lieutenant care for a glass of wine? And do sit down, won't you?" She pointed to the tray of flagons and glasses.

The men looked awkwardly grateful.

Ana turned away from them, and sat down at her desk.

She would not be able to finish her letter to Anichu. She glanced at it, afraid of it now. She could never write in that letter that she had just been arrested as a common malefactor —by the king, Anichu's dear king that she was going to write to. She picked up the sheet she had been writing, to tear it up, but she laid it back again. The baby might be glad to have it, Bernardina might give it to her, after she had explained why it was not finished. And how was that to be explained?

Ana opened a heavy inlaid box, brass-bound and with a lock and key. There were a few old half-forgotten treasures in it. She began to add to these now, carelessly, dreamily. Anichu's letter, Ruy's seal ring, a miniature portrait of her mother. Antonio's letter of that day. She looked indifferently about the desk—I suppose I might take this; I wonder if I'd miss that. Oh, better put a few things in for company, I suppose. The Torre de Pinto. It really does seem that I'm going to prison. The Arevalos used to have a shooting place at Pinto, I think. Going to prison, Antón. Are you gone too?

She leant on her elbow, pressing her fingers along her eye-shade. She sat very still and listened to the sounds of the night. She reflected that if this that appeared to be happening was happening, if in fact she was being arrested by a tyrant on no charge at all, then anything might follow. I may not come back; I may not sit here again; death may be near me; near him. For him, it can't be possible; he couldn't die yet.

The sweet, over-ripe smell of the roses on her desk made her feel tired. She heard the cautious movements of her guards as they tried to be very quiet with their glasses and their clanking gear; she heard the contented, familiar noises of Madrid, clearest of them—as it always is in the small hours— the voice of a young man singing. She thought of the children at Pastrana, asleep. Asleep. Oh Anichu, oh little child!

I'd better take some quills and ink and things, I suppose.

Or will Bernardina think of them, or will they be provided? She smiled at the absurdity of being provided for, altogether at the comic impossibility of being in prison. Oh don't bother with this silly packing. Let's see what it's like when I get there. It's quite a new experience. Philip, Philip, what is it? What have I done? What are you doing?

She stared into the darkness of a blind eye and a closed one. Smelling the roses, hearing still the sounds of her own free life, she looked into incalculable, future darkness. She was not afraid, but only sad, exhaustingly sad. Names and shadows swam in the sadness. Philip, she said, Antón, Fernán, Anichu. She felt sad, and stupefied, and a fool. I suppose I must go with these soldiers, for now? I suppose it's the only thing to do.

I'd better put this prayer-book in the box. I wish I could pray. I will, later on; I'll try to then. I'll pray for the children. Love your enemy, she thought, as she put some more things in her box. Love your enemy, do good to him that hates you.

She laughed gently.

"Yes, Your Highness?" said Don Rodrigo.

She hardly heard him, did not answer. She was thinking with amusement that she had always loved this enemy, and this very night did not see how to hate him.

"Torre de Pinto? Will it take us long?"

"We have good horses, Princess. We should be there by day-break."

Santa Maria Almudena rang out two o'clock. Ana snuffed a guttering candle. Often that two o'clock chime had rung before he came to her, from the Alcázar across the street.

She stood up straight, and locked her brass-bound box.

"Let us be going," she said sharply. "Let us be gone, in God's name."

Bernardina came in, the soldier still escorting her. She came to Ana, carrying a long black cloak on her arm. She

looked calm and weary now, as if resolute to cause her
mistress as little more distress as possible in this extraordinary hour. Ana's heart was wrung by this look of
desperate composure.

"They've taken your luggage down, *chiquita*. I tried to
think of everything you might need. But I couldn't find a
maid, or any of our people. The house is packed with
soldiery " she said contemptuously.

"Thank you, Berni. Remember, I leave it all in your
charge, until I come back. And you must tell the children, tell
Anichu——"

"I'll tell them," Bernardina said.

"If Your Highness will now be so good as to say good-bye
to this lady——" Don Rodrigo interposed.

"I'm coming downstairs with you," Bernardina said.

"No, Madam, that is not desirable. Will Your Highness be
so good as to come now?"

"I'm coming down——"

"No, Berni—leave it. I'd, I'd rather leave you here."

Ana looked longingly once about the room as she took her
cloak and threw it across her shoulders. Then she turned and
took Bernardina in her arms.

"Until a little while," she said. "Tell them I love them,
Berni. Tell Anichu I'll be back."

Then she turned to the soldiers.

"Will one of you carry this box for me?" she asked. "I am
ready now."

Escorted by Don Rodrigo and followed by another soldier
she left the Long Room. She did not look back at Bernardina,
whose former escort stayed with her.

She was led in what seemed to her the wrong direction
down the corridor, and towards a staircase she never used.

"This is not the way," she said.

"We are using this staircase and a side-entrance, Princess,"
the captain answered.

"But—I wish to see my butler, Diego, and others of the household. Where are they?"

"Under guard in the patio until we have left, Your Highness."

"Then let us go through the patio and say good-bye to them!"

"It is not desirable. We go this way, Your Highness."

Ana looked at him in astonishment. But then she thought —this is what it is, this is being in prison. How extraordinary! How long could one live like this? And she shrugged and went down the unfamiliar staircase. As she went it occurred to her that it must be the one by which Juan de Escovedo had made his mad entrance eighteen months ago.

"You seem amused, Princess?" Don Rodrigo said suspiciously.

"Yes. I was thinking of an odd occurrence."

They came to a doorway Ana hardly knew about. A soldier standing by opened it, and Ana saw the street without, and carriages and soldiers waiting for her. All was brilliantly lit by the high-riding moon. She paused on this threshold of her house that she had never crossed before, and looked with love about the little street. The church of Santa Maria Almudena lay at the other side, its porch a little to the south of where she stood. She had often prayed in that church, and its bells had hour by hour admonished her. She would have liked to pray there now.

The street seemed quiet.

"If Your Highness will be so good as to enter this carriage?"

Ana got into the carriage.

While they adjusted luggage and locked doors she looked out of the window, towards the porch of Maria Almudena. Someone moved in it sharply, drew back into it as if afraid he had been seen. But the moonlight was strong, and Ana knew the fair-grey head it fell upon. Philip was watching her go, from the porch of the church across the street. She saw his face as if he spoke to her in the Long Room.

She leant back into the darkness, so as not to see him again. Love your enemy, she felt herself saying, but she was crying as she said it; she shook with sobs.

The guarded carriages drove away southward.

PART THREE: *PASTRANA*

THE FIRST CHAPTER   (MARCH 1581)

I

WHEN Ana came home to Pastrana after twenty months
in prisons she came in a litter, and they carried her
across the court-yard and up the great staircase to her own
apartments. They laid her on a couch in the gold-and-white
drawing-room and she looked about her in weary, wondering
delight.

"Well, if I die now, Berni, that'll be all right. It will be
good to die here."

Bernardina, bending over her to adjust pillows and
coverlets, took her thin hand and kissed it lightly.

"You're not going to die, *chiquita*. You're home, and
you're getting well."

It was true that she was not going to die. In January she
had reached the point of death in her prison at San Torcaz,
and permission had then been obtained from the king for her
return to Pastrana, but only now in March was she thought
strong enough for the short journey. But she had all her life
been unacquainted with ill-health, and even under the crude
hardships of the Torre de Pinto had remained so well that she
had no way of judging gradations of illness. When she was at
brush with death she was mostly either in delirium or coma,
and remembered nothing of the crisis; now, getting better,
she found that to move a hand sometimes exhausted her,
or to look a minute at ordinary daylight, or to try to follow
a speaker through one short sentence. To her this seemed
a condition of dying—she did not see what else it could
be, for assuredly it was not life. However they told her
that she would not die, but was making a good recovery.

And she thanked them, and lay and waited.

And now they had brought her home.

She could not at present remember very clearly why she had been away so long. Nearly two years, they said. She knew she had been in prison, in two prisons; she knew the king had quarrelled with her. But she was too tired to ask anyone to remind her of what had happened. Still, it was surprising to be back in Pastrana. She wondered why that had been allowed.

She tried again to look about the room. The great window on to the court-yard was fully open; the noises of the village day came up, and sunlight poured across the floor.

"The sun. My own window," she said.

"Is the light hurting you, *chiquita*? Shall we turn the couch away from it?"

"No, please, no!"

She lay still. She could smell violets very near her; she could smell applewood burning, and could hear the crackle of pine-cones among the apple-logs. That was Ruy, that dull Dutch portrait on the wall quite near her. You were much nicer-looking than that, she said. Much more yourself. Well, I've come home, Ruy.

"Berni?"

"Yes, chatterbox?"

"The children? Fernán and Anichu?"

"Of course—but not yet, my lamb. You must rest here first after the journey, and have your milk and a little sleep. Then you'll be able to let us move you into your bedroom— and then, when you're safe in bed, you'll see them for a tiny visit."

"No. That's a bad plan."

"So *you* may think, but it's the plan, my dearie, and you've got to face it."

"No, Berni. Not in my bedroom. I want them here—I don't want any milk."

Bernardina knelt down beside her and felt her pulse. Her hands were dry and hot.

"Listen, Ana," she said, "you're talking too much. You haven't talked as much as this in an hour, during the last two months—let alone ten minutes. The doctors knew that coming home would excite you a bit, and they begged me to protect you against that. Are you listening?——"

Ana wasn't listening. She was remembering that when Anichu was allowed to come and stay with her for a little time at San Torcaz, the child told her how she used to sit in this room at Pastrana and pretend that she was there. I sit there by myself, she had said, after I've dusted it with Paca, and I have the window wide open and all the sun in, because that's how it always is when you're there. And so I pretend you're there. Ana could not find the words for this for Bernardina.

"There, there, *chiquita*—of course they can come to you here! Don't cry, don't cry. I promise you. Only first a little drink of something, lamb—and then we'll see."

Bernardina rose, and moved about the room gently adjusting things. "Josepha is bringing something warm for you to sip," she said.

"I brought it," said a small, gentle voice. "I told Josepha I'd better bring it."

Ana moved her head and smiled as if she dreamt.

Anichu stood by her couch, small and grave in her stiff silk dress. She placed a little tray carefully on a near-by table.

"Well, what next?" said Bernardina softly.

"Anichu!"

Ana stretched her arm and took the little child into its curve. Anichu swept herself in against her.

"Oh, you're home!"

"Yes, I'm home. How are you? How's Fernán?"

"We're well. But you're sick. You're very sick, are you?"

"No, not very. I'm nearly well."

Ana lay in peace, her arm about the child. Anichu leant back in the embrace and looked at her mother with attention.

"You *sound* nearly the same," she said. "But you feel very thin." She touched Ana's face and neck carefully. "I saw them carrying you in," she said. "We weren't supposed to— they said it might frighten us. But I hid in a place I know, and I saw."

"And were you frightened?"

"Yes. That's why I came now. I had to see if you were still the same. You are, I think—really."

"I'm quite the same."

Ana was beginning to feel real. Along Anichu's beloved steady voice the thread of life, of memory was spinning back.

"I'm sorry you were frightened."

"Oh, it's all right now."

"Yes. People get ill, and they get better."

"But why can't you walk?"

"I will, in a few days. We'll go for a walk, Anichu."

"Oh! Like before?"

"Like before."

"Only further ones now. Because I'm seven. I go much further now."

Bernardina intervened.

"Now truly, children, that's enough."

"Not enough," said Ana.

"You must rest, *chiquita*."

"Anichu brought my milk. I must drink it."

"Oh yes, I forgot," Anichu said, and got up and went to her tray.

Bernardina lifted Ana against pillows, and helped Anichu to feed her from a silver cup. Ana leant on her pillows and drank as they bade her, and looked at the sunlit window and at her little daughter. More and more memories came back and into place. The complicated story of all the imprisoned months before her illness began to emerge from its recent cover of darkness. So that she wondered very much, the facts re-assembling, why indeed she was here, at home. Her glance fell on the small Mantegna, caught now in full sunlight, noble, sculptural. I wonder how it is with him? I have lost touch. I wonder why I am at home. Is he at home?

"No more; no more, my baby. It was lovely."

She pressed back into her pillows. Life, her life, her world was rushing into her heart again—Pastrana, Anichu, Bernardina—and this room, its symbols, its memories, its admonitions. She was not dying, no indeed. She had returned to where she lived.

"No more."

"She's falling asleep," said Bernardina softly.

"I'll sit and look at her," whispered Anichu.

"No, *chiquita*, she must really rest."

"Stay with me, Anichu. I'm not asleep."

Anichu touched her hand.

"I'll be here—on this stool. I'll stay with you."

Ana's hand groped out and found the child's face. Bernardina moved on tiptoe between her mistress's rooms. Silence of noonday lay over Pastrana, and sunlight poured on Anichu as she sat on a footstool by Ana's couch.

II

Ana grew better rapidly at home. Within four or five days of her return she was able to walk almost unaided from her bedroom to the drawing-room; she ate solid food again, and was eager for more and more conversation, with her children and with Bernardina. There was much that she wanted to know. Many of her questions Bernardina could not answer; some of them she evaded.

Bernardina had borne a part in the troubles of the past twenty months. Two weeks after Ana's arrest and removal to the Torre de Pinto she also had been arrested, without

charge, and was confined in the same cramped and filthy little
prison. She was told by the officer who arrested her that she
was held by the king to be an instigator of restlessness and
disorder in the Princess of Eboli.

Grieved though Ana was that her *dueña* should also be
victimised for her unnamed offence against the king, and
furious and intractable as was Bernardina under such injustice, the two, so long used to being together, were surprised
and delighted to have the alleviation of each other's company
now, and they contrived often to draw comedy and even wild
farce from some of the least bearable parts of their plight.

Contrasted though they were in their ways of confronting
this plight, they made between them, by the force of their
personalities and the impregnability of their friendship, a
severe and constant problem for their guards.

The Torre de Pinto was a small square keep, built of stone.
It consisted of three square rooms one above the other, and
joined by a stone staircase which passed through all three. Its
windows were slits, one set high in each wall, and without
glass or shutter. The guards lived and slept in the top room
and the bottom; Ana and Bernardina occupied the middle
room. They had two truckle-beds, a table, two stools, a stone
basin and pitcher and an iron bucket. Food was brought up
from the lower guard-room. The decencies had to be looked
after as might be; there were no screens or doors to cut the
stairway off from the rooms. Neither prisoner was ever
allowed to leave the middle room. The "female attendance"
which the king provided was a gypsy girl who lived in a hut
somewhere near, and slept most nights with the guards.
"And thank God she does," said Bernardina. "It's the one
useful thing she does for us." But in fact Bernardina, as Ana
told her, was in no danger of rape. Don Rodrigo Manuel
knew who his chief prisoner was, and went in some fear of
her. Apparently it was the king's wish that she should suffer
considerable discomfort, so as to break her spirit; but the

Captain of the Guard guessed what the Mendozas would do to any man who went beyond his duty in this fortress; and instructed his company accordingly. And even as to the discomforts he was not brutal, but in such a place it was impossible for two female prisoners to live other than wretchedly.

Neither woman had ever dreamt of living as in that room they had to live, nor had paused to think of the details of such discomfort and degradation. Bernardina, in her early fifties now and always comfort-loving, raged and railed therefore in protest, and made the guards' lives miserable with demands and quarrels and abuse; but she became very expert also at imposing as much order and decency as she could upon the icy-cold room and its wretched equipment, for it was by now second nature to her to protect Ana's material needs and she was domesticated and deft about a house. Her coming therefore was a vast relief to Ana who knew no more than any other great lady how to empty slops or wash an under-shirt, and whom the later arrival found sitting, patiently enough but surprisedly, in a state of outright neglect. The gypsy girl was kind and the soldiers too; but they hardly understood Ana's speech, and had no idea at all of what might or might not seem filth to her. And Don Rodrigo, the captain, did not live at Pinto, but only came on visits of inspection. Bernardina bridged this confusion, and forcibly, after she had rallied from her first shock. But her best efforts could only mean relatively less misery for two who had long taken for granted the highest attainable standard of living.

Ana cared far less than Bernardina about their physical privations. Although she was grateful to the other for her resolute attempt to keep them clean and supported her faithfully in her battles with the guard, she found all that irrelevant; useful as an amusement and for keeping Ber-nardina occupied and so less miserable than she might have been. But for her, Ana, if Philip had shut her up in the lovely

little summer-palace of Aranjuez the farce and the wound
would both have been what they weie now.

So while Bernardina reacted against their plight by
wrangling with the guards and the gypsy girl and by talking
treason loudly and clearly, Ana treated her sojourn in the
dilapidated little keep as a fantastical episode, which almost
she had nothing to do with; almost as a bad play which she
had to sit through. And her manner with Don Rodrigo and
the guards, always polite, might be compared to that with
which we convey to actors that we do not hold them responsible for the insane conceptions of the author of their
play.

During her seven months in this prison she was allowed
only such invigilated correspondence with the world as made
it quite useless. She might write to her children and to
certain persons in charge of her estates—and to no one else.
And these letters must be handed to Don Rodrigo, unsealed,
and she need never be told how he disposed of them. The
same rule governed the letters she received. And she was
allowed no visitors. So she sat and waited, and marvelled at
her own helplessness, and wondered if all her friends and
relations in the world outside were being helpless too, and if
she might in fact be left to die in Pinto.

She came nowhere near dying. She endured the terrible
winter in that damp, draughty and hearthless tower far better
than did Bernardina, whom indeed she had to nurse through
the worst of it, helped by the guards and the gypsy girl. But
except for January, when Bernardina's cough and ague made
her anxious, she cared little for their physical misery. Her
imagination was struck by Philip's mad gesture against her—
and she even took exhilaration from it sometimes, from the
effort of standing against it; so that she had bouts of high
spirits which astonished her as well as Bernardina and the
guards.

Sometimes as she sang and laughed with Bernardina, and

recalled old scandals and old jokes, and listened with amusement to the other's silly, naughty stories of her girlhood in Sevilla and her first love-adventures, sometimes as they laughed in their beds at night until the guards below or above growled at them to let them sleep in God's name—she thought of Philip's face as she had last seen it, pale and exaggerated in the moonlight, solemn, cold, hooded by the dark porch of Maria Almudena. And she wondered then how much this mad-seeming laughter, this almost schoolgirl peace, would baffle him, if he could hear it. And bitterly, sadly she wished he could.

But all she could do was wait, and help Bernardina to keep things tidy, and laugh with her like mad in the name of sanity, and write lovingly—though unable to explain where she was or why—to Fernán and Anichu; and read their baffled, loving, worried letters when they came.

After her illness in January Bernardina developed some enterprise about trying to get the gypsy girl to smuggle out letters. They tried it twice, and twice they were caught, and all three punished—the girl by a beating, they by being deprived of supper, and by having their writing materials taken away for a week. Ana found it exquisitely amusing—being punished. But it was clear that the girl was too stupid to be of any use as a smuggler—so the two waited for another idea.

Before it came they were separated.

Don Rodrigo, frightened by Bernardina's illness, advised the king against keeping the prisoners in Pinto to endure the rigours of March in mid-Castile. Also, he may have suggested that the *dueña* was more dangerous as a prison-companion for the Princess than at large in the world. One February morning therefore the two were ordered to pack; Bernardina was told that she was no longer to be held at the king's pleasure, but that a condition of her liberty was that she did not return to Pastrana, or to the Eboli Palace in Madrid. The Princess was informed that she was being moved to a small house at San Torcaz, by Alcala de Henares, not far from Pastrana.

The news surprised the two, and except in that it was to separate them—they were now close and devoted confederates—it seemed good. While they packed they formed a plan to get over Bernardina's problem of where to live. Ana had a house in Alcala which was seldom used—Rodrigo lived in it when attending university lectures—and it was arranged that Bernardina should go there, keep a close eye on San Torcaz, and work out a plan of communication.

So they left Pinto, and parted.

San Torcaz was a better place than Pinto. It was a house, and Ana was allowed a few servants, and to walk in a restricted small garden. Also, after some months, her children were permitted to visit her there.

Rodrigo came first. Ana was surprised by her pleasure in seeing him again, and touched to see that he too was moved. He gave her news. The nobility was actively concerned about the outrage the king had committed against her. Medina Sidonia and he himself never ceased to protest and petition His Majesty. Infantado, de la Ferrara and Alonzo de Leyva thought that a league should be formed, to challenge and defeat the king on this action. Meantime, the king's closest counsellor, the President of Council, and the Cardinal and others, continued to insist that Philip either release her or bring her to trial for whatever was her crime. Indeed, the king was having no peace, because her enemies as much as her friends were pressing now that she be tried for her offences. Meantime Philip was busy. The old King of Portugal was dead, and Alva was advancing the armies over the border to take possession; Philip intended to go to Lisbon too and establish a Court there. He, Rodrigo, was going at once with Alva, with his cavalry regiment. He was very much excited by this, and Ana was pleased to see that he was eager to be a good soldier.

"And where is Antonio?"

"Perez? Oh—he's been a kind of cat-and-mouse prisoner since—since you were taken. But much better treated, of course! He always gets on velvet everywhere. He was first shut up in the house of the Court *Alcalde*—quite luxuriously. Then he got ill, and his friends worked up an agitation, and he was allowed back to his own house. He's a house-prisoner there now, I believe—and he's always agitating for this and that. We're not bothering about *him*, Mother."

"I dare say not. But I am. He is in this trouble with the king because of me."

"Oh, it's not all that. He's been corrupt in office too. There's to be an inquiry into such corrupt practices now—just to catch him, I think—as there seems no other way. It's a good get-out for Philip."

"I see. And his offices?"

"Old Granvelle has his chief job—First Secretary of State. But Perez is supposed nominally still to hold some of his other offices—Secretary of the Council and so on. Anyhow no one else has been appointed, and he still gets the salaries, they say, and does some work even, in his palace-prison. It's fantastic—but trust Perez to keep on his feet. I think Philip's afraid of him somehow. I'm not surprised either. He's a dangerous cad."

Ana smiled.

"I know your view, Rodrigo. So does Antonio. But thank you for giving me all the news. I still may write no letters to my friends, you see. I still may see no visitors except you children."

"I know. It's ludicrous, and the wildest insult—to a Mendoza, my God! Really, I think the king's half-mad. But at least this place is decent. You owe it really to little old Medina Sidonia that you were moved. He's been most awfully good pushing away at the king. Between us we'll have you free soon, Mother. Don't worry too much."

"I'm not worrying. And I'm glad you're going off to the war. You look happy."

"Yes—I like my regiment, and I want to see action. But I shall get near the king from time to time during the campaign, and I'll not let him forget that I am your son. As a matter of fact he's going to have a solemn ceremony any day now before he leaves for Portugal——"

"What is that?"

"The consecration of the Infante Diego as Prince of Asturias. I shall have to do homage then with the other Dukes, and Alonso and I think that it might be a felicitous moment to remind him of the wrong he has done you—in diplomatic language, of course."

Ana nodded.

"Maybe, Rodrigo."

She felt lonely, humiliated, ashamed of Philip. She thought of all the high and solemn ceremonies of his past, in which she and Ruy had supported him, and by their presence and their friendship added, as he always told them, to his joy and courage.

Rodrigo left the next morning, riding off to the war. Ana settled down to face the summer months. There would be the alleviation—very meagrely doled out—of brief visits from her children. And—so far as she could see into the future—there would be nothing else. The dull comfort they gave her here, with a respectable aged *dueña* and with dull decent servants, would prey on her and exhaust her, she knew, far more than ever could the dramatic madness of life at Pinto, life with Bernardina and the gypsy girl and the protesting, weary guards. There were guards here, but she never saw them, and never uttered a complaint. The solitude and isolation were vast. All that comforted her in them was that she looked out eastward towards Pastrana and could almost breathe its air; that Bernardina, watchful and loyal, was under one of those roofs of Alcala that she could see from one point of the garden; and that Fernán and Anichu would come to see her soon.

As for Rodrigo's news—she was grateful for the gestures, such as they were, of some of the young nobles who were his friends; but she knew the corrupt laziness of the existent Spanish aristocracy and counted on no league of them, no organised protest. She saw much more hope in the pressure of active men of affairs on the king—and knew that Antonio de Pazos and the Cardinal would continue through all weathers to tell him the truth. And she surmised that Antonio Perez was in serious danger, and fighting hard and cunningly on a wide, treacherous field, for his life, and for the future of his children. She knew that some day, by one device or another, when he deemed it not a mortal risk for him or her, she would hear from him again, if he lived. Meantime, she prayed for him, and guessed, far more than Rodrigo could, from Rodrigo's news how constant and unpredictable was his danger now.

She grew depressed in San Torcaz. She lost her sense of the absurdity of the situation, lost detachment. The dilemma was growing stale and silly; Philip's cruelty and egotism became more apparent than his lunacy. And her guards were efficient, it seemed—for even Bernardina managed no signal.

When the children came, in midsummer, Ruy and Fernán and Anichu, she tried to be exactly herself for them. But they were worried and asked her clear, insistent questions.

"The king is angry with you, isn't he?" said Fernán. "That's why you can't come home?"

"Yes."

"I don't see why his being angry can keep you from coming home," said Anichu.

"Neither do I, pet. Neither does any sane person."

"We always thought the king was fond of you," said Fernán.

"I thought he loved you," said Anichu.

"Oh, Mother, this is awful!" said Ruy. "Your being a prisoner! Why, it's ridiculous! What is the real reason, Mother?"

"If I knew I'd tell you, Ruy. But truly, truly I don't. I've never been given a reason."

"You can't take prisoners without a reason," said Fernán.

"I'll write to the king," said Anichu. "I still think he's sane. If he wasn't he'd have to stop being king."

When the children went away again, back to the bleak care of governesses and tutors at Pastrana, summer faded. No news came, no letters.

Ana prayed and sewed and walked in the garden. She thought about her sins, and fretted about her vain, empty life, and tried not to advance with Heaven the cause of her own repentance merely because there was nothing else to do and temptation was far away and would not come again. She prayed, for her children, for Ruy's soul, for Juan de Escovedo's. She prayed for Antonio, for his safety and ultimate peace. She prayed for Philip. But she could not pray for herself, and thought this a cheap, bad time to turn to God on her own behalf.

She watched the flowers fade; she ate less and less; she grew lonely, no messages came, nothing happened. She heard, from her *dueña*, that the Portuguese campaign was triumphant, but that the king was gravely ill in Lisbon of the plague. She heard that he recovered, but that the queen, Anne of Austria, having nursed him, had returned to Spain and died.

Still there were no messages. She looked towards Pastrana across a cold sky and saw nothing. She looked towards Alcala and its roofs were blank. And then in December she became ill, and sank with contentment into death's embrace.

But now here was the spring of another year, here were the walls of Pastrana round her, here was the sun on the floor at her feet, and the *Colegiata* bell in her ears; here were Fernán

and Anichu bringing their lessons to write at her desk—and
here was Bernardina, unexplained and peaceful. She was at
home, and getting well with every minute, and there were a
hundred questions to ask, if Bernardina would but answer
them.

III

When she had been seven days at home some of her
questions were answered. Her good son-in-law, the Duke of
Medina Sidonia, arrived at Pastrana, prepared to explain
everything to her.

He came in fact from Lisbon as the king's emissary, to
explain the terms of her restoration to her own house. As, by
loyal pertinacity, he had effected this restoration, he was
concerned for the execution of its terms.

After he had changed his clothes and eaten well he came
and sat by Ana's couch. It was a bright, cold afternoon; the
window was shut and a great fire blazed in the hearth.
Alonzo settled near it gratefully. He hated the climate of
Castile and in March held it to be extremely dangerous; but
he was a dutiful man and had willingly risked it this time for
duty. However, Ana's house was comfortable, and this room
beautifully warm.

"Your gout doesn't seem to improve, Alonzo?"

He was fatter than Ana remembered him and he walked
lamely.

"On the contrary, it has recently been much worse."

"But why is that? You don't drink too much, do you?"

"Oh no, Mother—you know I don't."

This son-in-law had the domestic trick of calling Ana
"Mother" sometimes. She disliked it very much. She
understood that it was a habit formed simply from talking
of her with Madalena and Rodrigo, and also out of easy-
going affection—but it irritated her, this cosy, dull style
of address from a fat little grown-up man.

"Alonzo, you're thirty-two and I'm forty-one—and I'm *not* your mother. Please!"

"I'm sorry—I forgot. You ladies!" He smiled at her kindly. "It's very nice to see you again after so long, and to see you *here*. And you are getting better now, aren't you?"

"Yes, I'm getting better. Being at home is a good medicine. And I believe that I owe it to you?"

"Well, yes—I think so. I'm a great deal involved with the king at present, and I don't let him forget this—this stain on his record."

"Thank you, Alonzo."

Somehow he felt nervous of opening his mission to Ana. As he came here it had seemed easy and even wonderful and he was proud of himself. But now, face to face with her, he was not quite sure of how to proceed. He thought that perhaps he'd gossip a little first, and lead in to what he had to say.

"The Portuguese campaign has been a very great success," he said. "Alva has disposed of the Pretender's forces very easily. It's a pity the king's triumph had to be overshadowed for him by Her Majesty's death."

"Yes—poor Anne of Austria. She had a dull life and a dull death."

Alonzo looked somewhat shocked.

"She was a very good woman."

"I believe so—I didn't know her well."

"Rodrigo, by the way, has distinguished himself considerably in such action as he saw. He's enjoying himself in Lisbon at the moment—and sent you his love, of course. He's very keen now to get a transfer to the Netherlands to serve with Parma—things are lively there again, and promise to be more so——"

"I'm sorry to hear that. When I last heard informed conversation—which is nearly two years ago, Alonzo!—our face was set towards *peace* in the Netherlands."

"Oh well, Granvelle's policy is strong—and I must say from all I hear it seems the only one. His Ban on William of Orange has caused quite a sensation——"

"Ah! Then the work of years is set aside?"

"No, no—why should it be? But there's a time to be liberal and a time to be strong. And Granvelle after all does *know* the Netherlands."

"I dare say," she said wearily, "I'm out of touch."

"Am I tiring you?"

"No, go on. What other news is there?"

"Well, there's this rather troublesome business of Diego."

Diego, Ana's second son, not yet sixteen, had been married for two years to Louisa de Cardenas, ten years his senior. He was very unhappy, she flaunted and despised him publicly, and now was demanding an annulment of the marriage.

"I saw Diego in Madrid yesterday. He's staying with Infantado there and seeking legal advice. I also saw Louisa. She's a dreadful, shameless creature—and seems to find her matrimonial situation quite a joke. She was very rude to me, I may say."

Ana smiled. She detested Louisa de Cardenas, but she could sympathise with her need to be rude to Alonzo if he took to advising her about her love-affairs.

"Poor young Diego! It's a dreadful thing we did to him—and Philip and his uncles truly are more to blame than I, for once."

"It's a very impossible thing, a nullity suit in the family," said Alonzo primly.

Ana laughed.

"Impossible things keep happening in this family," she said. "I hope you told Diego to come home here as soon as he can, and leave the old nullity suit to Louisa and her clerics and lawyers. It's nothing to do with him. He must come back here, away from all those awful Cardenas relations. He can study at Alcala for a few terms, and forget the whole

nightmare, poor child. I'll write to him to-night and tell him
to come home."

Alonzo looked nervous.

"I wonder if that will be—er—approved?" he murmured.

"Approved by whom?"

"Well—by the king, you know."

"Why, what's Diego got to do with the king? Or is *he*
liable to arrest now, because he has failed to make Louisa a
happy woman?"

"Nonsense! But——" Alonzo fidgeted in his chair,
"rightly or wrongly, the king takes a somewhat anxious
interest in your children's future now. You see, all this
scandal——"

"He always took an 'anxious interest'. And 'all this
scandal' is of his making, and can be unmade whenever he
chooses. No, don't fuss. I'll look after Diego. That marriage
has always been on my conscience, and I'll try to make up to
the boy now for our stupidity. He'll be happy here and at
Alcala, away from all those cheap worldlings his wife trails
after her."

"Maybe. We'll see. We'll deal with Diego later."

"*We* won't deal with him at all, my dear Alonzo. There's
no dealing to be done. He'll simply agree to let Louisa have
her nullity suit, and then come home and be young again for a
while."

Alonzo got up and began to poke the fire and adjust the
logs. He looked at Ana sideways as he did so. She was lying
back on her pillows, looking weary and emaciated. She was
so thin that her long outline was only just traceable under the
silk coverlet.

This dull man was fond of her, and had not ceased to
agitate on her behalf since her arbitrary and absurd arrest in
July 1579. But he was a manager, a compromiser. He never
even tried to understand eccentricity, either the king's or
anyone else's, and he had no sympathy at all with any kind of

passion. When he met such things in the ordinary conduct of life he contrived as well as he could to work round or under them—he never met them straight. He did not know what Ana de Mendoza's life had ever really been about, nor did he wish to know. He did not know any more than anyone else why Philip had so suddenly turned against her, and expressed his anger in so unfortunate and indefensible a fashion. All he knew was the obdurate public fact that Ana, unaccused, untried and uncondemned, was the king's prisoner. And knowing the king, he believed that the only way to remove that fact was first to accept it without argument, and then to negotiate it gently away, by compromise, by shifting of ground, by realistic acceptance of the dark ways of eccentricity and pride.

But he knew enough to know that here on the couch lay no such negotiator.

He sighed and gave the fire another poke. His gouty foot was hurting him, growing hot and heavy.

Bernardina came in by the door which led from Ana's bedroom.

"Good afternoon, Your Grace," she said, and Alonzo acknowledged her greeting, but gloomily. "I am sorry to have to interrupt you, but Her Highness is still, as you can see, an invalid, and may not be left too long unattended."

She crossed to Ana's couch, lifted her under the shoulders and shook and straightened her cushions.

"I'm all right, Berni."

"Are you sure you're able for a long conversation?"

"Yes, truly. We haven't started yet. I want to hear all His Grace's news."

"Don't you think you ought to have a drink of something, *chiquita*?"

"No, thank you. I feel splendid, really."

"You don't look it," said Bernardina. "Try not to worry her too much," she said coldly to the Duke.

He ignored the instruction, but Ana laughed.

"If he does, I'll ring for you, Berni."

"Be sure to. But seriously, if you want anything, do ring. I shall be sewing next door in your bedroom."

"I promise. Move those jonquils more into the light, will you? Ah, that's better."

Bernardina smiled at her, bowed again to Medina Sidonia and went back to Ana's bedroom. Alonzo stared after her gloomily.

"*She* has absolutely no business here," he muttered.

"What did you say, Alonzo?" Ana asked dreamily.

He came back to his chair near the couch, and she looked at his troubled face with pity.

"You come with a message from the gaoler, don't you? Well then, deliver it."

"It's complicated."

"Trust Philip! Still, we can simplify it. Tell me this to begin with—Bernardina can't. Am I home just on sick leave, or am I free?"

"You're *home* for good, as far as I know."

"Ah! Ah, thank God."

She lay back very still, her hand pressed on her eye-shade, her left eye closed.

"Then that's all right, Alonzo. I can't say much more yet, because I might cry. But—I didn't like being in prison."

He waited, gathering his words.

"You're home, certainly. And you're free, if you choose to be free."

She turned slowly to him.

"But if I'm home, here in Pastrana——"

"Listen, Mother—ah, I beg your pardon! Listen to the king's message. Now don't interrupt with any witticisms, please. Just listen. You are to live in Pastrana, as its lady and mistress, as before—free as air, on certain conditions."

"I accept none, so save your breath."

"But don't you see, you *must*."

"*Must?* There are no conditions. Either I live as a free citizen, or I am brought to trial for whatever I am believed to have done that is criminal."

"I asked you not to interrupt me. Will you let me finish what I have to say?"

"I won't interrupt you."

"You are free if (*a*) you will desist from asking foɪ the Escovedo case to be heard; (*b*) make a formal gesture of non-enmity towards Mateo Vasquez; and (*c*) undertake never again in life to see or communicate with Antonio Perez."

There was silence for a second.

Ana stretched out and patted Alonzo's knee.

"You got them said neatly," she said. "I could concede (*a*)," she went on thoughtfully. "It was always more of an opinion, a counsel of mine than a principle. If other people think it well to refuse to hear the case, I don't make an issue of it. (*b*) I refuse to consider. I shall not ever make that 'formal' gesture, and if Philip can find a criminal offence in that let him charge me before the justices and I will stand for trial. And since, you see, we break down on (*b*) there is no need to discuss (*c*)."

Alonzo gave a little groan.

"I beg you——"

"Don't. And don't be troubled. You are being so very good. But you see, I told you we'd simplify things—and we have, a bit. At least we've got this far, that I'm *not* free, after all—and this, this dear interlude was just a cruel mirage. When do I go back to San Torcaz?"

Alonzo was drying his eyes.

"Please, please! You're very difficult."

"You silly dear man! I hope Madalena is kind to you."

"Oh, keep to the point, dear lady! You don't go back to San Torcaz, ever! You stay here, bound or free. That at least we've wrung from him."

"I stay here, in this house, a *prisoner?*"

"Yes. A house-prisoner."

She looked about her, and then smiled at him.

"But who in Pastrana is going to keep *me* a prisoner? Who is going to stop me from going through my own open gate or across the village square? Who's going to prevent me from hearing Mass at the *Colegiata*, or say that Anichu and I are not to walk up to the Honey Farm or over to San Amadeo?" She laughed. "I don't think my Pastrana people will lock me up, Alonzo."

"That, alas, will be attended to—if you insist on it. Your servants will be changed. Persons will be placed here who will be guards as well as servants. The government of your household will be handed over to some stranger appointed by the king. You will never pass beyond the garden or the court-yard gate. Your letters and visitors will be subject to scrutiny, and all your affairs will be ordered for you by this appointed officer."

"I see."

"So think well, think well, I entreat you! If you do persist in flouting these silly, but simple conditions of freedom—honestly, I see little hope of your obtaining better."

"I expect you're right."

Alonzo got up and fidgeted lamely about the room.

"Is your foot hurting? Would you like some wine or something brought?"

"No, I'm all right. I have an idea—I've had it for some time, as a sort of last hope. But *please*, if you use it, don't say it was mine!"

She smiled reassurance at him.

"Why don't you fly, before the new imprisoning begins? You and the children—to France, or to some of your Italian estates, even? I think if you were out of Spain, Philip would forget and forgive everything. And there'd be time now. It will take me, it *can* take me a long time to get back to Lisbon with your answer. It will take time after that for the king to decide what to do about you and whom to send to govern you here. You could be safely out of reach long before his emissaries got back to you. I could help you—Rodrigo and I could arrange about your money and possessions and everything. And you'd be safe—safe and free, and with the children. Will you do that?"

"Forgive me again. But I won't. I can't run away from a guilt that doesn't exist. I have done no criminal wrong, and I won't be bullied out of my country by a nothing. Nor will I for such a nothing deprive the children of their natural home and friends. No, Alonzo, I'm sorry. But in this mad issue I have seen a principle, and I shall stay and hold it. Castile is crumbling under the curious, cautious tyranny of this king. I'm a Castilian. I've done nothing useful in all my life, and I've committed many sins. But by chance I can do this one small service for Castilian good sense before I die. It isn't even honour—it's only common sense. So I'll stay here—and you can tell the king that he can either also find some common sense and have me tried for my supposed offences, or he can turn Ruy Gómez's house into my prison. As he chooses. I'll be here when my new guards come. It'll be very curious— the oddest prison of the three."

"You're impossible. Think of the children!"

"I do think of them. It will be very bad indeed for them. Though they, I suppose, will be allowed to go past the gate?"

"I suppose so. They may be taken away. I really don't know."

"If they are, so be it. I would have had it otherwise, especially for those two little ones. But truly I can only serve them by my own light. And as things are, I think the best I can do is show them that I have regard for the free dignity of Castile."

"It's a point of view. But it's useless."

"Yes, I expect it's useless."

"You're tired now—very tired. I won't accept this as your final answer. I'm staying here until to-morrow——"

"No—I'm not very tired. And you've had my answer, Alonzo. It's my only one, and Philip knows it. He wastes your time and your good nature with these errands. Though of course I'm very glad to see you here."

Alonzo looked sadly about the beautiful room.

"If you persist in this, you won't be happy," he said.

She laughed at him.

"Did I say I expected to be happy?"

"Your servants will be changed, your habits will be checked——"

"Sing your dirge to Philip. I can sing my own, to my own heart."

"I know. I know." He came to his chair again and sat down wearily. "There's one other small thing that I have to say. That woman, your *dueña*——"

"Bernardina?"

"Yes. Bernardina Cavero, isn't it? She has no business here at all. The king expressly told me that she is at liberty only on the understanding that she keeps away from Pastrana and from you."

"Ah! I wondered!" Ana smiled. "Let's have her in and question her, the criminal." She rang her bell.

"Oh no, let's leave it. Another time."

"No, no—we'll talk to her now."

Bernardina came in.

"Thank you, Berni. Come over here and get into the dock. You're in some trouble with the law."

Bernardina laughed.

"Well, I'm an old lag, after all——"

The Duke of Medina Sidonia cleared his throat and looked stern. Ana's flippancy in the bosom of her family was an aristocrat's privilege, but he felt obliged to uphold the crown against the lower classes, and wished that she might try to do likewise.

"Tell her, Alonzo——"

"Doña Bernardina, I know from His Majesty that you were given your liberty in February of last year on the condition that you did not return to Pastrana or to the service of Her Highness. That condition has not been altered. I have to ask you therefore why I find you here?"

"I'm here, Your Grace, because I thought it suitable that I should be here when Her Highness came home ill and out of sorts. She's used to me. I thought I'd be good for her."

The Duke of Medina Sidonia gasped a little.

"That explains nothing."

"Oh yes, it does," said Ana. "Go on, Berni."

"I went to live in Alcala, Your Grace, when I left the Torre de Pinto. I devoted all my time to trying to get into touch with Her Highness at San Torcaz. But she was very well guarded. Nothing worked. Then I found out she was ill. I walked down every day and sked to be allowed to see her. I might as well have been talking to The Cid's mule. I nearly went mad when they kept on telling me she was dying and still wouldn't let me in. And then I heard—from one of her doctors, a very decent poor fellow in Alcala, that they were sending her home. I gathered from him that it wasn't release, but a kind of panic, and that the idea was to get her well at home and then start arguing with her again. I gather I'm right about that?" Ana nodded. "So I abandoned the assault on San Torcaz, and two days before she came back here I drove over, and settled in. I wanted to get things ready for her, exactly as she likes them. Everyone here received me with delight—naturally. They like me here, Your Grace."

"Indeed they do," said Ana.

"But the day after I arrived the *Alcalde* came to see me. He told me—what I know—that I was breaking my parole or something. And I told him to go to blazes. And he laughed, the decent man, and we had a few drinks together. And here I am."

"It's quite a serious offence," said Alonzo.

"As serious as all Her Highness's offences, I dare say," said Bernardina.

"Well, Berni, you're a law-breaker again. But conveniently enough, and no trouble to the *Alcalde*, you're in the right place. Because after all I'm *not* free, Berni. My son-in-law has just been explaining to me that this house is to be made into a gaol."

"Ah! I thought it might be so."

Medina Sidonia groaned again.

"It needn't be so! It needn't, Ana! Not if you had a vestige of common sense."

"It's because I have common sense that it must be so."

Bernardina came over to her and lifted her up on her pillows.

"You're dead tired," she said. "It's disgraceful to exhaust you like this."

"What'll you do if they lock you up again, Berni?"

"Well, if they lock me up here—and that'd be the economical thing to do after all—it could be worse. After all, we had some fun in Pinto, *chiquita*, you and I! We make good gaolbirds together!"

"Yes, we know the ropes, Berni."

"Then I take it, Doña Bernardina, that you persist in breaking the condition of your freedom?"

Bernardina smiled at him.

"Oh yes, Your Grace. I'm staying here now until they carry me out screaming."

Ana was delighted.

"Oh Berni, this is like old times! It's like being back in Pinto!"

"Well, I've been more amused in Pinto than in many places. Haven't you, *chiquita*?"

She smiled and bowed coolly to the Duke.

"If that is all——?" she said politely.

"That is all," he snapped, and she withdrew.

"I can't manage this business at all," he said when she was gone. "Is it that you're women or is it that you're mad?"

"A bit of each, Alonzo."

Ana was indeed tired now. It was almost two years since she had had so long and difficult a conversation, and she was still under the shadow of grave illness. She hoped Alonzo would leave her. She lay still and said no more—but thought with affection and contentment of Bernardina. What a stylist she is, she thought, in her plain way. How simply and breezily she takes things as they come, and follows her own honesty. Why on earth should she lose her liberty again? But why on earth should I or any honest person? It is for the answer to those questions that I must wait in prison. So be it. It is something of my own that I can do. So be it. I'll sleep now a little while, before the children come to see me.

It was dusk in the room, and the fire glowed red and hollow. The flowers, violets and jonquils, gave up their perfume richly to the warmth. Yes, she would sleep now; she was sleepy.

But Alonzo did not go away.

He sat and stared into the fire.

"Some people think," he said, "I don't know exactly why, but they do think that the only condition that matters to Philip is the third—the one you won't discuss. They say— Rodrigo for instance—that if you could tell the king that you would never see Antonio Perez again, the whole face of things would change."

"I agree with that," she said.

"Could you send him such a message?"

"If that is all he wants, let him say so in common honesty."

"And if he said so? If he asked you just that?"

"I should be obliged to tell him that he had no right to ask it—or at least to make it a condition of my free citizenship."

"But would you answer yes or no?

"I'd answer no."

"Then you *are* in love with Antonio Perez?" The Duke's voice was full of surprise.

"Why do you always miss the point, Alonzo—just when one thinks you are seeing it? My answer would have nothing to do with being in love."

Alonzo looked relieved. He *knew* he was right about that love-affair nonsense. Really, people would say anything for scandal's sake. But what was he to do, all the same? How in God's name was he to help her now?

Ana lay in the deep shadow and thought about Antonio Perez.

Hoofs clattered in the square and into the court-yard; the children were returning from their ride. Ana heard Fernando laughing—like a little chime of bells.

THE SECOND CHAPTER   (JULY 1585)

I

It seemed henceforward as if Ana's story was told. She was shut up in Pastrana and the world forgot her.

A house-governor called Pedro Palomino was installed in the ground floor, with guards and clerks and with full authority over the whole dukedom, to direct it as he saw fit—for he was also appointed governor and chief justice of her district. Sitting at his desk in her house this stranger dismissed Ana's servants, from her devoted butler Diego downwards, without informing her of such dismissals or allowing the dismissed to see her in farewell. The children's tutors and personal servants were likewise turned away; secretaries, stewards, gardeners, all who had either worked there for Ruy Gomez or were the children of his men, left

Pastrana within a month of Palomino's arrival. A number of strangers, a much smaller number than the house was used to, were appointed in their places. The estate office, which negotiated transactions with tenants, directed the flourishing silk trade of the little town and had long been the Council Chamber of all its communal enterprises and the directing centre of its prosperity, was put in charge of a civil service clerk from Madrid, who knew no one, could not remember a face or a name from one day to another, and had seen neither a silkworm nor a loom in his life. He was a man who understood all villages to be poverty-stricken and desperate places, and saw no reason why they should not, in the order of nature, continue so.

Ana lived upstairs in her own wing. Of the personal attendants she had known Bernardina and Paca, her own special housemaid, remained. Such others as she saw about her rooms were strangers. She was allowed to use a secondary staircase which led from her suite to the children's study and dining-room, and also to a garden-door. There was always a guard, night and day, by this door and staircase.

She never saw the great staircase of her house. Outside the main door of her drawing-room an iron grill was built across the landing, with a gate which was unlocked only when Palomino came to visit her. The children were free to come and go, under the eyes of the guard, between their mother's suite and their own rooms. And they could range the house, and move as they pleased outside, with only such supervision as was needed to see that they did not traffic in illicit letters or messages. Ana's own letters were controlled as they had been in Pinto, and she had no power to spend money. She might write to tradespeople for what she required; Don Pedro Palomino decided whether or not to pass her orders.

The organisation of all this was complicated, especially with children in the house, who must not be asked to live in

the atmosphere of a state prison. But no one troubled Ana
with it. It was all attended to by unseen clerks downstairs; it
was out of her hands.

Bernardina had been left to her—after one of Philip's long
and devious struggles for decision. But she stayed as a
prisoner, subject to the same restrictions as her mistress.
They two were the only prisoners; and all this new machinery
had to be set up in Pastrana, and everything on the vast
estates must suffer great inconvenience and exasperation so
that the two women might be kept under lock and key.

Bernardina's husband, Espinosa, had to leave the apartments which he and she had shared in the palace, and go to
lodge in the village. He was still employed, but in a degraded
standing, in the Estate Office—but as he was the only familiar
person left them he was a great help to the farmers and silk-
weavers as they struggled to explain their business to the
civil servant from Madrid. He was allowed to speak to his
wife for fifteen minutes every Sunday, through the new iron
grill on the landing above the great staircase. Their son had
been dismissed from his employment as bailiff of the home
farm, but work had been found for him at San Lucar by the
Duke of Medina Sidonia.

There was a strange chaplain now, and Ana and Bernardina
were allowed to pray in the Pastrana private chapel; that is,
from a tribune at the rear of it which could be entered from
Ana's suite.

So everything was provided for.

As time passed Ana's sons were less and less frequently at
home. Rodrigo was serving with Parma in the Netherlands;
Diego, tiring of Alcala University and still waiting for the
completion of his wife's nullity suit, went to Italy with a
tutor to examine into his dukedom of Francavilla; Ruy,
earnest boy, studied history and European languages in
Salamanca and spent much time with relations in Madrid and
round the Court, for he desired to go his father's way and

enter the State Secretariat; Fernando lived officially at home in the first years of Ana's imprisonment, but he intended to be a priest, a Franciscan friar, and so spent whole weeks together sometimes at the Franciscan seminary on the outskirts of Pastrana.

Only Anichu was always at home. She rode about the familiar countryside as usual, and she went on her friendly errands to people she knew in the farms, and to the nuns at her dear Franciscan Convent. But otherwise she lived a prisoner's life, contentedly, with Ana.

Very few visitors were admitted now to the white and gold drawing-room, and they only after close scrutiny were passed through the iron grill. A few harmless old local bodies were allowed, if they did not come too often—the Mother Prioress, and one or two farmers' wives, and the Duke of Medina Sidonia on the rare occasions when he could travel so far from his own estates. And the old *Alcalde*, kind and jolly man still nominally in office but greatly bothered by the interferences of the new chief justice, Palomino, made many excuses to get past the grill and have a drink and a grumble with Ana and Bernardina. Diego, her butler, never came, although he was living just beyond the village. The *Alcalde* told Ana that twice Diego had tried to come to see her, but neither time could control himself sufficiently. And within the first year of his dismissal he died.

The Marqués de Los Velez was no longer at Alcala; he had gone abroad to an American governorship. There were other neighbours of his kind who tried at first to gain admittance, were turned away as having insufficient reason, and first grumbled about this, and then forgot the prisoner.

No word ever came from Antonio Perez, so Ana knew that he was still fighting his long duel with the king. She knew that he was still in danger of his life, and that he considered her life still in danger, and that while that was so to try to communicate with her and fail would be fatal to one of them,

or both. She knew that she did not hear from him simply
because he did not want Philip to put her to death. She
supposed that she might never hear from him again.

All that she had visibly left to her therefore of her own life
was whatever her rooms and garden contained of it; and two
kind servants; and Anichu. These, and the view from her
great drawing-room window.

The balcony of this had been filled in with blocks of stone,
but she could still see her own gateway, though not much of
the court-yard. But beyond the gateway she could see the
western front of the *Colegiata* Church, and much of the open
square, and a few roofs, houses of friends and neighbours.
She could watch some of these neighbours moving about the
square in the sun, and sitting by the wine-shop, or on the
church steps, to talk. When the bell rang for Mass she could
identify the people going into the church. This came to be a
great possession, the window—for it framed life henceforward, and contained her share of the sky.

Ana had always thought, in her free past, that she led a
shockingly idle and non-contributory life. It had worried her
that she was pampered and purposeless. But now she looked
back with almost-admiration to what seemed, in retrospect,
like restless industry. She remembered the old round of her
Pastrana day; the talk of meals and guests with Diego and the
housekeeper, the business she transacted, or thought she
transacted, in her estate office, the errands and friendly visits
here and there about the village, the walks and rides with the
children, the parties arranged for them, the tutors inter-
viewed and counselled, the little local ceremonies and feasts
which she directed, the letters she wrote, the plans she made,
the advice she gave.

"Bernardina, are the State prisons full of useless drones
like me, do you think?"

"I think they break stones in some of them. Would you like
a turn of that? Shall we suggest it to old Palo, *chiquita*?"

Bernardina kept busy, because she had domestic talents, and servants were now far fewer in the house than they used to be—and she was not lowering the standard of Ana's life because of that. But Ana did not know how to polish silver or clean picture-frames, or re-cover cushions. And Bernardina would not let her try her skill at washing clothes.

"But I got quite good at that at Pinto—I liked it!"

Bernardina smiled.

"Oh yes, I did. Anyway you don't know half the filthy jobs I learnt to do at Pinto, when you were ill."

"Pinto! Those were the days! Do you remember the night old Zapo tripped on the top step, and went down backwards with the soup-pot over him?"

They laughed delightedly. Often now they caught themselves recalling Pinto as if it had been an idyllic experience.

"It isn't such fun, being a prisoner in your own house, Berni. Anyway, they're far too polite, these clerks from Madrid."

"I agree. Give me Zapo and Gypsy Rosa any time! Ah, what a slut she was, that girl!" said Bernardina appreciatively. "What a slut!"

Ana wished now, for Anichu's sake, that she had been soundly educated. When she was mistress of her own house Anichu had had—simply by convention and because she had to be chaperoned sometimes—one governess. A friendly, ageing widow who was a good horsewoman, spoke what seemed to be reasonable French, and never was unkind. But for her lessons she went to the Franciscan nuns where she had the happiness of mixing with all the other children of Pastrana, and the advantage of some good teaching.

All this was forbidden by the house-governor. The dear Viuda Maria was despatched in tears; two plain dull women were introduced to her house who undertook to teach a young lady everything she should know, and Anichu, as a daughter of the nobility, was no longer permitted to take lessons with the children of the town in the Franciscan Convent.

Ana fought against this arrangement, and the Mother Prioress fought fiercely on her side, and so did Bernardina. And Anichu fought most effectively of all by learning nothing from her two instructresses at home, and by racing off to the convent several times a day and leaving them to wonder where she was.

It was a lively battle, but it was not going to be a victory against the king's orders—and meantime Anichu was learning little of anything.

Ana burnished up her wits and tried to teach the child a few lessons. She was not a linguist, though she could smatter in French, and read Latin better than most women. But she was a naturally good arithmetician, and she was well read in the history and literature of Spain.

Anichu was enchanted to take lessons from her.

"But if you can do sums as well as this, it's absolute waste to have Doña Isabel in the house!"

"By the look of her I'd say it's waste anyway," said Ana disrespectfully—"or at any rate, it's a great increase of our trials. But perhaps that's what's intended."

The little girl chuckled.

"Anyway, I think I'll tell her I'm not doing any more arithmetic."

"Oh Anichu, I don't think you ought to say that."

"I will. After all, with you turning out to be an expert, it'd be just silly to go on with her. I suppose I'll still have to do old botany and drawing and stuff with her?"

"How does she draw?"

"Oh, I don't know. I expect it's terrible—but I'm no judge."

The lessons became a great alleviation, and interested Ana so much that she prepared them with care in advance, and became audacious and self-confident as a teacher. And friendship grew, strong and honest, between her and her little daughter, founded as it was on the deep natural sympathy that had always held them close.

One day she explained to Anichu all that she could to a child of her conflict with the king, and of his reasons for holding her a prisoner.

"I know," Anichu said. "Fernando and I have often talked it over. It's terrible—and you know we are both very fond of the king."

"So am I," said Ana.

"Yes—that's what I said to Fernando. But he and I think you're right. It may seem a bit obstinate—but really it's only just right. I don't see what else you could do."

"I'm glad you think I'm right. That's some consolation. Because it's a sad kind of life for you here now, and I sometimes think I ought to send you away——"

"Where?"

Anichu's eyes and mouth were wide open, in horror.

"To your sister's house, San Lucar, perhaps—or——"

"Oh, if you sent me away! Oh, if you did that!"

Ana gathered her up in her lap and hugged her.

"But I won't, I won't! I was only saying that if you were sad here, or thought I was wrong or anything——"

"I'm *never* sad where you are! Never! And I'd never care how wrong you were about anything!"

"Anichu, steady! Steady, pet!"

"I am steady. Only don't frighten me like that! If you knew what it was like when they took you away before, and we didn't know and they wouldn't tell us, and you'd *said* you'd come on the first of August—oh, if you knew!"

She wailed and wailed.

Ana held her in her arms.

"I knew, I knew it was like that, my baby. But I was in prison, you see—I simply couldn't do a thing—I swear I couldn't!"

Anichu stopped wailing as suddenly as she had begun.

"I know that," she said. "I'm sorry I screamed. I'll never scream again."

"Oh goodness do, if you want to!"

"I think I'd have to if—if you ever said again about, about sending me to Madalena or anywhere."

"I promise I'll never say it again, Anichu. But still, I'm glad you think I'm right about all this with the king."

"Yes, so am I glad—Fernando and I both said it would be awkward if we didn't agree with you. But we do. Still, if you were right or wrong, you'd be you just the same anyway, wouldn't you?"

"I suppose so."

"So what difference does it make then, really? I puzzle about that."

"So do I," said Ana, remembering how often she had followed that line of question about Antonio Perez, the unscrupulous wrong-doer. "But come on, child, get down off my knees. We've three more sums to do before twelve o'clock."

II

One evening of late July in 1585 a guard came to the grill outside Ana's rooms and announced to Paca that His Eminence Cardinal Quiroga, Archbishop of Toledo, was in the court-yard in parley with the governor of the house, and would shortly ascend to visit Her Highness the Princess of Eboli.

This was indeed good news and a break in loneliness. The Cardinal had only come to see Ana once before in her imprisonment, during 1581, but he wrote often, and though for her sake his letters had to be guarded in phrase he managed through them to make her understand that his concern for her was constant, that he continued to speak his mind to the king, that he sometimes saw Perez and watched as he could over him, and that one day he would visit her again, and bring her word of the world that had locked her up.

When he stood in the drawing-room and she knelt and kissed his ring she was much moved and could not speak. He murmured the Blessing softly over her bowed head and when she rose he looked first at her and then all about the room shrewdly before he spoke again.

"I've asked the gaoler if he'll be so obliging as to accommodate me for the night, Ana. I don't want to be hurried in our talk."

"And what did he say?"

It would be impossible for Palomino to refuse courtesy to the head of the Church in Spain, who was also the head of the Holy Office; yet the Cardinal was known as a frank supporter of Antonio Perez against the king, so it might be difficult for the meticulous civil servant to gauge exactly how to welcome so eminent yet dangerous a visitor to the house of Ana de Mendoza.

"He was fussed—not exactly cordial. I always thought Pastrana was a *hospitable* place, my dear?" They laughed. "However, I'm staying here to-night."

"Thank God! But I do hope they'll look after you reasonably. Isn't it strange—I haven't the faintest idea now of what goes on downstairs."

"Well, what I saw of the patio and court—it's rather like the *alcalde's* offices in any small town!"

"Oh! Oh, truly, does it look like that?"

"Yes, I'm afraid so—very much like that. I shall put it to Philip that this is a very poor way indeed of 'preserving' the family property which was so much endangered in your reign! Well come, let's sit down, let's look at you. You—you don't really look very well, my dear."

"I don't feel well. I move so slowly now, it's curious. Ever since I was ill at San Torcaz I've felt—old. I never did before."

"How old are you?"

"Forty-five. Ah, it's good of you to have come!"

"I've often tried to plan to come, as you must know. But they're working me very hard in my old age, and also things that you would want to know about have gone on being so drearily indecisive. However I had to be in Alcala this morning to confer with certain fussy ecclesiastics." He laughed. "We have our Philips and our Antonios in Christ's church too, Ana!"

"But you don't let them get to the top of the tree!"

"Oh yes we do, now and then. There's a long tragi-comedy going on just now, which was part of our business this morning." He smiled wearily. "It's about the tomb of Mother Teresa, who died as you know, and was buried at Alba de Tormes about three years ago."

"Yes, we heard that even here."

"But her native Avila couldn't have that, and recently they whisked her body off to its own place. Now Alba is appealing to Rome to have her back—and there is wild talk of miracles, and the Duke of Alba is blazing away. The young duke, thank God! It's a mercy old 'blood and iron' was gathered before this episode began. But still, we've quite the makings of a minor civil war on hand, as it is. Makes me smile, when I think of the sanity and authoritativeness of the woman they're fighting over! How easily she'd have blown their envies and jealousies to the sky! Oh well—they keep us old prelates busy."

She knew he was marking time and taking her in as he talked. She had an idea he was moved, and more saddened by sight of her than he had perhaps expected to be. He was as imaginative and kind as any man, yet she reflected that even to him the idea of six years' close confinement and deprivation of all liberties great and small, though shocking, was not in itself comprehensible—any more than it would have been to her six years ago. You have to live six such years, she thought, you have first to have accepted them from the cold and unmitigating hands of a friend you had always loved, and you have then to plod on and live them, with their dragging lifelessness, their ineptitude, their permanent mood of insult to the heart, and their blankness before the best as well as the largest of your personal attributes—you must live like that, keeping discreet and orderly in mind by means of little repetitions, invented tasks and little jokes and farces made up consciously to help out good behaviour—to be unshocked by the sum of their wear and tear.

She knew that spontaneity and health were dying in her now, that her responses were slowing down and that her mind felt dull and inelastic. She knew the efforts she made against all these deteriorations – and chiefly for Anichu's sake; but it was by measure of the effort that she understood how she was wearing out, how vitality was dying. For she, in freedom, had never known about effort in response to life.

She knew that all this inner change was in her face and movements now, and even in her voice perhaps—and she understood that they might be even crudely visible to one who had known her well in her good days, and now after this long time beheld her suddenly again.

She would have let him go on gossiping, gathering himself together—but talk of Mother Teresa still had power to make her miserable, and it was somewhat more than she could bear at this moment of joy and strain.

"Don't be sad," she said. "I'm better than I look. And I'll improve as we talk. You'll take me back to what I was!"

"Oh Ana, don't! You *are* what you were, indeed, indeed! It's only that it's a bit much, seeing you again—and we've all, all your friends, been so deadly dull without you."

"So have I been dull," she said sadly. "Have they offered you a *merienda* after your journey?"

"Yes—I'm told they are bringing some refreshment. Is the kitchen all right? Do they look after you properly?"

"Oh yes, I suppose so. Nothing is as it was, of course—but Bernardina does seem to bully some of the staff effectively."

A manservant came in with a tray of wine and cold foods, placed it by the Cardinal and withdrew.

Ana smiled.

"They're on their best behaviour," she said, looking over the food with an anxious hostess's eye. She recalled that when the house was hers she had never done that. Food was correctly offered then, it seemed, as naturally as daisies grew. It was odd to have to worry about a *merienda*-tray.

"I wonder what they'll give you for supper," she said.

"Whatever they give you, I trust."

"Oh—but I won't be allowed to have supper with you."

He stared at her.

"Either I have supper with you in this room to-night at such time as you think suitable, or I hand over that whole collection downstairs to the Holy Office, as heretics and desecrators of consecrated priests!"

They laughed.

"Oh, that'll be wonderful! Fancy having a guest to supper again—after six years! Anichu and Fernán will be ravished."

"I shall be glad to see those children."

"Bernardina will be with us too—you won't mind, will you? She always dines and sups with me."

"Of course, Ana."

The Cardinal poured some wine.

"Give me some too," said Ana.

He did so, smiling at her as she took the glass.

"Not that you need it now," he said. "You're looking wonderful suddenly."

"I told you I'd improve under your influence. Pleasure, you see—and the excitement of a supper-party!"

"Oh woman, you break my heart! Truly I didn't know I cared so much about you, you shocking, locked-up Jezebel! That's what some gentlemen in Madrid always call you now—I believe even in letters to the king!"

"Haven't they thought of anything newer? They used to call me Jezebel in Ruy's time. I know, because he told me."

The Cardinal lifted his glass.

"To Ruy's dear memory," he said.

"To Ruy."

They drank.

"I wonder what Ruy would say now of Spain's situation," the Cardinal mused. "Politics, thank God, are not my field. Yet, you know, I stare in consternation at our present paradox."

"Paradox?"

"Well, we annexed Portugal, at a loss of possibly a few hundred casualties. Our claim is doubtful, but the spoils are ours. That actually means that for all commercial purposes, Ana, we own the world. Look at the map. We now possess the two best fleets in the world. England has some good sailors, but we have two experienced and organised fleets. Pirates allowed for, we now control not only our own great western possessions, but also through Portugal the Indian Ocean. Our sailors and missionaries are everywhere. Our wealth is uncharted. This situation has been growing on us for some time, until it became fixed and inevitable. Luck caused it in the beginning, but it has been secured by the plain bravery and imaginative perseverance of our ordinary people, our sailors and soldiers and missionaries. So you'd think, wouldn't you, that there might be some sign in our national life, our home life, of this extraordinary economic strength? You'd think there might be roads and merchant ships and schools, and new houses and better shops and better wages, and more to eat and more ordinary human hope and decency? Yet there isn't. And when I talk to Philip I hear of nothing but of the inordinate expense of the Netherlands, and the mad cost of the Italian states, and this and that and this and that, as if we were beggars. And when I

look about me I see that he's right, that his people *are* beggars.
What's the matter? What is he doing? What would Ruy
say?"

"I don't know. I'm a prisoner. I see nothing. I can only
tell you that when Ruy lived and in the six years after his
death that I was in nominal charge of Pastrana, this estate and
its people were prosperous. Now it's being run by the
government, and I can tell from looking out of that window,
from walking through my own garden—even if none of the
people ever came to see me—that, for some reason which no
one can quite fix on, that is no longer true. The people here
are worried now, and beginning to get into debt. And some
of the best of them, some of the really skilled silk-workers,
moriscos from Valencia and Alicante, have already gone
away."

"Yes. I can believe it. I think the reason, both for Spain's
paradoxical plight and Pastrana's, lies in reach of our understanding. But sentiment does not sound orthodox in
economics—so we waive it. Still—Spain is mistress of the
world, Ana, and she is in hopeless decay."

"Hopeless?"

"I think hopeless. I wouldn't mind that if, say like Rome,
she had ever, her people had ever had one brief phase of
enjoying the achievement. But what annoys me is that we
have become great and are now ceasing to be great, while still
at the top of our power, in two generations. Let greatness,
anyway let absolute mastery go, by all means—if meantime
you have pulled some of its lasting advantages, its advance-
ments out of the fire for those, and their children, who
earned you that passing glory. If Spain, the people of Spain,
were to have a residue, in civic and trade development, in
training, in education, in ordinary hope and comfort, the
decline could come and welcome. But what maddens me is to
hear Philip and his sycophants exulting now over this
magnificent double empire, and then to look about the

country that gave it to them—and then to go back to the
secretariat's wails about debts and extravagances and in-
solvency. I can't see why we tolerate such crass mismanage-
ment."

"We deserve it. Don't think I talk now just as a victim of
absolutism, which I am. But when I was free, in the blind,
foolish days when I looked on, and thought that no tyrant
ever born could tyrannise over me, a Mendoza—even then I
feared Philip's tyranny for Spain. But we accepted it. We
who had the power, who owned Castile and governed it by
the free wisdom of our people, we sold ourselves to his old
father—and we have allowed him to be such a tyrant as
Charles never was. I know Philip and I—I have always
loved him, oddly enough. But he is a dangerous tyrant, and
we have been bullied, and here we are, in chaos. The decaying
mistress of the world, as you say."

"It's curious. Because there have always been men, and
men in power, to speak their minds."

"Yes, yes—there have been men, and I've known how
they've cared and worked—oh, don't sadden me too much
to-night!"

"I don't want to."

"You haven't really. Only I'm out of the habit of talking
about what matters, and it is perhaps too exhilarating." She
turned the glass in her hand and looked at the gleaming wine.
"Wine is good. I've come to understand that in prison."

"Have you become an addict, Ana?"

"Well, no. But Bernardina's always liked to drink it, and
sometimes here at night I drink with her. It makes me sleep—
it even makes me think I'm happy."

"That's a good service," the Cardinal said.

"I remember," said Ana, "that I used to smile at Antonio's
wine-drinking. He'd come from the Alcázar often, very tired;
and then he'd start talking, and he'd walk up and down the
Long Room filling and refilling his glass, talking, talking,

talking. But he never seemed to be drunk. I used to wonder at that."

"Poor fellow! How much he'd give to walk the Long Room now, and talk and talk and talk."

"Oh!" said Ana. "How is he? What is happening?"

"Much, very much is happening. But he's fairly well. Whenever I see him he sends you his—love."

Silence fell for a moment.

"Is he in prison always?"

"Yes. Ever since you were arrested he too has been under arrest. Sometimes he's seemed to be under easier terms than you. Philip makes extraordinary variations in his treatment. But all the time he has been, I think, in danger of death. He has told me that he constantly explores means of writing to you, but that he knows interception might mean your death as well as his. I think he's right about that."

"Tell me what has been done to him."

"I can't possibly tell you *all* he's been through. He's been under house-arrest, then in state prisons, then practically released to normal life, then seized again and in a dungeon, then back to house-arrest. The thing is an idiotic scandal."

"How shameless Philip can be, for a prim, respectable man!"

The Cardinal laughed delightedly.

"Exactly! That's the whole thing in a nutshell. But let's not begin on Philip's psychology, Ana! I have simpler fish to fry."

"Tell me about Antonio."

"I must cut the story to essentials. While Philip was still in Lisbon he was worked upon to settle the Antonio Perez question once and for all—and so he ordained that an investigation be held into corrupt practices among high state officials. A commission went to work—about three years ago. In the autumn of last year, on its findings, Perez was brought from one or other of his prisons to trial. He was accused of taking bribes in office, and of tampering with state papers. He declared in court that he could not defend himself against the second charge without producing private files which His Majesty might not wish exposed. This caused a halt. Our long-suffering friend Antonio Pazos—who, by the way, if this affair drags on much longer will most certainly put henbane in all our wine, poor fellow!—was sent to look at these files. His advice to Philip was for his own sake to drop that silly charge!"

Ana laughed.

"However, the bribe-taking accusation was pursued, and Perez offered no defence. He was condemned to pay a fine of 30,000 ducats—half to the Crown and half to the Mendoza estates——"

"What?"

"Yes. You are supposed to have cheated the family funds to that amount on his behalf——"

"But——"

"Oh, leave it. The arguments were nonsense, and all promoted by your vindictive cousin Almenara and his gang. But further, Perez was condemned to two years' hard labour in Segovia State Prison."

"When did this happen?"

"Last January. I was in Madrid and heard the trial and the sentence. I can safely say that, apart from my standing sympathy with Perez against the king, my sense of equity was outraged by the proceedings. Perez was only under house-arrest then and on parole until he should be moved back to prison. I went to him that evening and told him that justice and law had been flouted in his trial, and counselled him to seek sanctuary at once. Then, you see, he would be immune, in any civilised country, from the temporal power, his case would become the affair of the Holy Office and—in a word— he would be safe. He took my advice, and I went home with a quiet mind."

"Well then?"

"Ana—have you heard anything of the father of Elizabeth of England? That Henry VIII whom we all, good anti-Reformationists, comminate against in all our prayers?"

"Yes indeed, I've heard plenty about him."

"But I don't think you've heard of his breaking sanctuary—which is what the servants of His Most Catholic Majesty did that night."

"Philip did that?"

"Yes. Oh, but Philip will pay for it! The Nuncio is already under threat of dismissal for his eloquent protests, but he has Rome's support and he has mine, and the matter isn't being dropped. Meantime, however, Perez is in a filthy prison, and what's more his heroic wife and his children are in another wing of the same prison. And Juana is being put to everything but the torture to try to make her say where his private papers are. And she'll never say. And Philip the king is in Arágon, seeing how he can best set about imposing absolutism there, and improving the hour—I hear from my spies—by collecting one or two witnesses now living there who might be used in a possible trial of Antonio for the Escovedo murder. That is the news up to the present. It's not very novel—it's only ugly and cowardly and a disgrace to a king I used to admire."

"Oh God! How slow he is! How deadly! Will he never *act* in this thing? Will there never be a decision?"

"Never, I think. But any minute there'll be another change of plan, naturally. Philip, as you know, by his nature hates all Popes, and this new Pontiff just elected, Sixtus, looks like being intolerably masterful. But the temporal lord of the world is, after all, a Catholic, so he *has* to be the ally of the Papacy. And already this little affair of breaking sanctuary has received the attention of Sixtus V. I imagine that means that Perez and his family will come back from Segovia any day now, and have another spell of house-arrest. Oh the wearisomeness of it!"

The Cardinal laughed a little as he ended.

"What are you laughing at?"

"You know poor old Don Diego de Chaves, Philip's patient, honest chaplain? No man of imagination dare try to measure what *he* must have endured on this Escovedo-Perez-Eboli affair during the past six years! God help him! Well, he—who is sent everywhere at all seasons to do all Philip's dirty work with this one and that one—do you know what he is reported to have said to Juana de Coëllo herself in her prison-cell the other day?"

"Poor man! I truly can't imagine."

"He said to her that if a decision wasn't come to and action taken within the next three months, he would go into the Puerta del Sol, call a meeting, and tell the truth, on oath, to all the people, about Escovedo's death. And then, he said, he'd go home and die quietly."

"One can only sympathise."

"It's very funny though—His Majesty's distracted confessor!"

"Let's drink more wine," said Ana.

The Cardinal filled their glasses.

"You know," he said, "that all kinds of mystification and side-taking still go on among the so-called informed about this scandal of your and Perez's arrests. But I believe you accept my simple reading of it? That Philip loved and trusted Antonio and intended to see him quite safely through the Escovedo trouble, and that he has always been a bit, not entirely but a bit in love with you. Am I right so far?"

"I think so."

"Am I right in assuming that you were never Philip's mistress?"

"Yes. He never really asked me to be. He's always been, as you say, only a bit in love with me."

"Exactly. Well then he heard of your—love-affair. For

some reason hidden in his own dreams it maddened him. He
had no claim on the private life of either of you—but as your
king, on his own terms, he has power over you. Since he
learnt that you were lovers, he has not been able to be quite
quit of the thought of either or both of you. And he has got
his miserable personal emotion entangled with the Escovedo
problem—because somehow hidden in that may be, if he can
find it, the destruction of your lover. And it isn't that he's in
love with you. It's that he has long been in love with the idea
of your being in love with him."

"Yes—all that is right, I think."

"So far so good. I saw that from the beginning. And I
know too how oddly and slowly his mind works when pain
or self-defence of any kind is controlling it. But *why* those
sudden, savage arrests? I have never been able to understand
the motive for that curious, wild decisiveness."

"They were my fault, I believe. He came to see me in that
July—about a fortnight before we were arrested. I was very
happy to see him and we talked, as I thought, frankly. He
was moved and upset, and so was I. He asked me if it was
true about my relationship with Antonio and naturally I said
it was. I begged him to have the Escovedo case heard, and to
let us all take the consequences of one piece of honesty, and
he seemed as if he might consider that. He was kind and
weary, and he cried. And I thought that we had got back to
real association. I was glad of all we'd said that evening—and
I thought he'd come again. But then he sent them to arrest
me. And when I was driving away from my house in Madrid
that night, I saw him standing in the porch of Maria
Almudena, watching them take me off."

"Ah! I see."

"I think that visit to me was merely a test of himself. He
wanted to see whether or not he really felt affronted by my
having a lover who wasn't he. Somehow it seems he found
that after all he was. He tests everything, you know, before he

decides. He tested that—and decided that it was an outrage to him, as in fact he had suspected it to be! So here we are! Am I right?"

"I think so. I think that, outside of his ceaseless care for Spain, and his desperate hope to keep his one sick little son alive, his chief personal passion now is to know that some-how—without incriminating him—Antonio Perez is safely dead. And as a rider to that, to be certain that you are never again within hand's reach of Perez or any other man. And this isn't love, even at love's crudest. It's self-love, insanely indulged by a lonely and unbalanced man."

"What you say makes me wonder again what I've often wondered. Seeing how little it is—forgive me, dear ascetic—but seeing how little it need matter to a woman of brains—sexual intercourse I'm talking about—should I, for Antonio's sake and in the name of all our peace, should I have forced poor Philip into a belated love-affair that he didn't want?"

The Cardinal laughed delightedly.

"Has ever a priest been asked so amusing a question, Ana? The moral answer is of course no. But the diplomatic answer coincides, in my opinion, for once. Any kind of perjury is always to be avoided, on politic grounds. I think such a false step might only have made bad worse."

"Well then—since our imprisonment, I have frequently been told that if I would promise Philip never to see Antonio again, all would be well. My soul cannot admit his right or anyone's to ask such things of me, let alone put me in prison until I answer them to his liking. But am I being self-indulgent there? It isn't that I expect or even now especially desire to see Antonio again. It's that I cannot countenance blackmail. But should I perhaps? Should I bear that in-dignity—rather than what I do bear—in the hope of lessening Antonio's danger?"

"Again the moral answer is no. Indeed, child, this stand of yours against blackmail is one of Spain's few good deeds at present—and I for one am glad to witness it. Antonio, and good luck to him, is fighting, and not quite honestly all the time, for his life, and his family, and prestige and money, and everything he has worked for. But you, differently placed, are fighting quite simply for your idea of human conduct. If you've done wrong in the past—and you have—you are now doing something that is hard and right and cold and even disinterested. Moreover, you are acting in character."

"You haven't told me if diplomatically I am wrong."

"No, because I don't know. But anyway, it is too late for your diplomacy now; and you and Antonio have had your pleasure and your sin. If one of you can balance that feeble self-indulgence by accepting an impeccable principle, making it your fate and your penance, and even dying for it, it will have been a good deed, Ana. And I for one shall know why I have always admired you—even in your recent Jezebel days."

"I wonder. You haven't answered me."

"I can't. I can only repeat that I know that in this conflict with Philip you have been morally as right as in committing adultery with Antonio you were morally wrong."

Silence fell. Ana looked out towards the sky and the *Colegiata* tower. Night was descending. To-night would not be as lonely as evening customarily was—for the children and Bernardina would be enchanted by the novelty of a guest for supper, and the guest was worthy of his rarity. There would be wine-drinking and gossip and laughter, and the breath of the world. Indeed, a great break with loneliness, which would make her hidden heart shiver, so lonelily would the simple pleasure ring there. And meantime Antonio would pace his cell in Segovia alone, with everything he valued lost and gone.

"I gather that you think that Philip is actually now considering a trial of the Escovedo brief?"

"My answer to that can only be surmise—and it is

dangerous. But it is a fact that some new Escovedo relations have started up a new agitation, and the impossible Vasquez is again encouraging them. Now—here is my uncharitable and bitter guess—if Philip's agents can find among Perez's captured papers the fifty or sixty letters on that affair which could incriminate the king, those papers will be destroyed, and Philip will throw conscience to the winds at last and let Perez be tried—and of course condemned to death. If those papers cannot be found—and I don't believe they will be—the pressure is now so insistent in all classes for a trial of you two criminals that I think the king will *have* to risk it. He so much desires to destroy Perez that I fear it may come to that—and to corruption of the Court in favour of the king. But such a risk would take Philip a long time—and so long as you are both in gaol he won't rush it."

"It breaks my heart," said Ana.

"But I thought it would have done that long ago?"

"No. That's the curious thing. I *keep* on hoping he'll have the courage of his good feeling. I'm simple about affection, you see—and I keep on crazily hoping that before the end he'll prove to me that he is too."

"Oh Ana, he isn't and he won't prove it. In feeling, in feeling most of all he's insane."

"I've never seen it. Always he was easy to like, easy to trust. Vain and sensitive and touchy, and like a living man. That night when I saw him in the porch of Maria Almudena watching them take me away, I was shocked, and thought that he *must* be unnaturally cruel. But even so—anyone might have that sort of awful mood. Still, I've said to myself since that Philip *is* good and grateful—I *know* that. And by nature I'd say that he *couldn't* do what he's doing to Antonio, who has given him a lifetime of work and love."

"It is his nature to distort and worry nature. But he isn't a natural brute. That's why his brutalities take years, and are so hideous."

"I never knew him brutal."

"Yet in these six years he has been brutal to you."

"It's terrible to have reduced him to all these dishonours of his soul."

"That's generous—but goes too far. You have sins enough to carry, Ana—don't be officious about Philip's sins."

"Yes, I have sins enough."

"Do you repent of them?"

"I would do so more easily if the occasions of my sin were not now in so much guilt and trouble."

"That isn't your affair. You are only asked for your own soul."

"Oh you theologians! Try *living* before you counsel! Find out what it is to have sinned in twos before you start lecturing in ones!"

The Cardinal smiled.

"Your advice comes late—my hair is white, dear Ana. But God may be amused, I venture to think, by the obstacle-race you make of approach to His love."

She looked at him in honest wonder.

"But surely—for sinners—it *has* to be an obstacle-race? I mean, you can't *assume* an unimaginable thing like the love of God?"

The Cardinal pressed the fingers of his two hands together.

"That question leaps over many others," he said. "I'll examine it with you to-morrow morning, if I may. It brackets all that I really want to know about you—and so I can't have Bernardina or the children charging in on it."

"There's nothing to examine in it," said Ana, a shade wearily. "I have been six years alone now with the idea of God and the question of my own sins—and I cannot yet see how you go hat-in-hand to Him, when you know yourself."

"May I say that you are sometimes very unlike a woman, Ana? And now—you are looking perilously tired, and I must go and read my office. No, don't stir, don't move. I'll be back here in an hour—and for the rest of to-night we'll talk gossip and nonsense—and even a little bawdry, if that's what Bernardina likes."

He rose and was gone before she could decide to get up and be ceremonious. So she lay back in her chair and covered her blank right eye with her long, nervous hand. And weariness and hopeless sorrow and a sense of failure overswept her, and tears of weakness and ill-health poured down her face.

III

In the morning she walked with the Cardinal in the garden.

"You see what I mean," she said, pointing to this and that untidiness. "They're strangers to it, of course. But you did know this garden? You remember it?"

"Indeed I knew it. Many's the hour I walked it with Ruy. Don't you remember how he argued me into all kinds of expensive plants and bulbs from Holland?"

"Yes. It was his years in Holland that made a gardener of him."

"Indeed it was! I wish I had the money back that he made me spend on tulips! Tulips in Toledo!"

Ana laughed.

"We lost a few small fortunes here too on his tulip-craze. Ah, but I hate this garden now! I only walk here because I suppose I must walk somewhere in the air." She looked about her sadly at the weeds and the general tangle of neglect.

"Its condition relates to the main part of the house," the Cardinal said. "I mean, it's like a neglected park in a sordid country town. I'll describe it to Philip. Preservation of the family property indeed!"

"In a few years Pastrana will be a ruin," Ana said.

"I think so," said the Cardinal. "That's what happens when you lock up life."

"Well, Ruy is safely dead. And I'll be gone soon."

"Do you feel that you are dying?"

"It's a long time since I felt that I was living. Look at how slowly I walk."

Anichu came running up the terrace to them.

"I only wanted to tell you that I'm going down to Sister Antony for my geography lesson," she said. "Please don't tell Doña Isabel where I am if she asks, as she'll only come pestering, and they all laugh at her, and it's awkward."

"All right, pet, I won't tell."

"Then I'll say good-bye, Anichu," said the Cardinal. "I fear I shall have to be gone any minute now."

"Oh! Oh, I am sorry, Your Eminence." Anichu dropped on her knees and kissed his ring. He blessed her and she rose and bowed and ran away again down the terrace steps.

Ana looked after her.

"I constantly wonder if I ought to keep her here," she said.

"Why? Where else should she be? She looks very well."

"Still, a child shouldn't live in a prison."

"That child isn't living in prison, Ana. She's happy, she's where her heart is."

They were on the highest platform of the garden.

"Let us sit down," said Ana.

The fair-bleached land, waiting for harvest, lapped away from them eastward and westward. At their backs far off the Guadarramas rose, ridged with green-black pines; the sky was immaculate, thin, insubstantial blue, of glittering, terrible purity. Near them, below them, homely-seeming, lay the heavy quiet house of stone, with crowded about it the other roofs and towers of Pastrana.

"Does it hurt you ever," Ana asked, "to look at a scene you knew very well and consider how it will lie there happy and unchanged the day you die, and the next day, and hundreds of years after you're forgotten?"

"Yes, indeed. Our attachment to those things our senses

apprehend may be our silliest part, philosophically—but it is
also, alas, our strongest."

"Ruy used to sit on this bench very often the summer
before he died, and sometimes I came to him here and I knew
by his face that he was saying good-bye."

"You weren't in love with him?"

"No. Only because he was too old for me, I think. He
was very much worth love."

The Cardinal studied her, considering sadly that he might
never see her again, for he was old and she was losing hold on
life, though not yet old. She looked very distinguished and
ascetic, he thought, like a very good nun who has been
worked too hard. I can see why she appeals to me, he reflected, a man who has long ago mastered and forgotten all
the hungers of sex. But the strength of her appeal to Perez,
though indeed æsthetically, fastidiously one can apprehend it,
is yet a very unexpected and arresting fact.

"Your injured eye," he said gently, "has that distressed
you much in your secret life?"

She turned and looked at him in astonishment.

"I am an old man, and I may never see you again on earth.
So I say what I wish to say. I have often wondered how much
or little it has meant to you."

"I—I never speak of it."

"I know. Speak now."

"There's nothing to say now. I too am old. But I think it
decided everything in life for me."

"Hardly," said the Cardinal. "At least, by rule of thumb
one would say that it did not decide your becoming Antonio's
mistress."

Ana looked away across the fair horizon.

"Yes, that too."

"How, Ana?"

"Can't you understand? A sort of belated challenge. The
glove a panicking coward may at last decide to throw down."

"I see."

She clutched his hand, and he felt with surprise and pity that she was trembling.

"No more, no more!" she said unsteadily. "I haven't the control I used to have, I'm tired and shaky! Say no more of that!"

"I'll say no more, you foolish child. But as to the challenge —it justified itself?"

"Oh, I can't tell. How could I? But I was happy as his lover. With him I learnt and forgot many things." She had withdrawn her hand, and now was calm again and laughed a little. "Nothing is more embarrassing than an old woman talking about her love-experience," she said.

"Last night," said the Cardinal, "you asked a rather wide, loose question about the love of God. And you called it 'unimaginable'. Now I should call it 'indefinable', rather. That is—I can't tell you what it is, yet I have spent my life in dim, poor apprehension of it, in seeking symbols and reflections of it in the work and thought of man, and in my own most weak and sinful soul. And in those apprehensions— such as they are—lies all the best of me and of what life reflects to me. And in you, my dear, in your foolish, sinful life I have sometimes thought I caught reflections, intimations of what I apprehend by God's love."

"In me? Oh no—there's none of that grace in me. I have always had faith, a plain, hard, infantile faith, the unimaginative faith of all my ancestors, and I have too their plain and childish sense of right and wrong. I've been glad of that in a way—because at least for good or ill I've always known in every action where I stood and I have sinned or not with all my wits about me."

"What advantage was there in that?"

She laughed.

"Well, it keeps you from self-pity and from putting the stresses wrong; and it prevents the kind of regret that blames other people. Besides, it keeps memory clear. You'll forgive me if I say that when one has sinned—in the sensual sins, the sins of pleasure—in full private cognisance of guilt, one does not afterwards forget, as sentimentalists do, how sweet the pleasure was and how much it gave you. You buy it high, you see."

"This is a kind of epicureanism."

"Yes, you could call it that. It gives an edge to gratitude. It also makes repentance difficult."

"Why?"

"Because you know that you were as clear in your mind at the time of your sin as you are now that it was an offence against God's law, and you know that you were as sorry then as you are now to commit that offence. Yet you took your pleasure and your chance. And you can't without falsity, it seems to me, be retrospectively repentant—for that would be like trying to have it both ways."

"Oh, Ana, no! How prim you are! My child, that's where the love of God comes in."

"I dare say. I'm only saying that I find it difficult to—to assault the love of God. Because I persist in being grateful for the love of man—and the best of that that I had was forbidden fruit. But I understood what Escovedo meant——"

"What did Escovedo mean, and when?"

"Did I say that aloud? Lord, am I getting senile, do you think? Oh never mind, that's an old story."

"It haunts you a bit?"

"Yes. But all I mean is that I accept, from the teaching I never discarded, my guilt. And I have repented long ago in that clear-cut sense, and returned to the usual religious practices. And I accept these years and all this empty lone-liness and forsakenness as a part perhaps of my purgatory. But as this purgatory was forced on me, I cannot seek to derive merit from it in heaven—and in general I can't, with any honesty, turn to God, as holy people say. Because while accepting His ruling, I shall always be glad of Antonio."

"God doesn't ask the impossible of you, you conceited woman. He only asks what you are giving, your honest repentance, and acceptance of His Will as higher than your own. He doesn't ask you, while still clothed in human flesh, to see your sins through superhuman eyes."

"The trouble is that sometimes, in a calm kind of way, I think I do!"

The Cardinal laughed.

"Arrogant, self-deluding creature! Dear Ana, stop all this hair-splitting. You are lonely here and punished and weary— and all that you accept with excellent Christian fortitude, may I say. For the rest, open your heart to the sweets of Heaven, child. God isn't all made of tiny rules and calculations, and it is presumptuous of you actually to invent these games and graphs for Him. Pray, child, and love Him. It's not such a very long journey from the love of man to the love of God."

"I do pray. I pray a great deal."

"Pray more—and more freely. And since you *are* so rigidly orthodox, I take it you believe in the communion of saints?"

"Oh yes, indeed I do."

"Then *I* shall pray for *you* a very great deal henceforward, and so will many others. And our prayers will find you out here in your loneliness, and teach you how to imagine the love of God."

"Yes, pray for me. Pray for my empty heart."

"Do you pray for others?"

"For everyone imaginable. For the children, for you, for the repose of many souls. For Philip, very much. Constantly for Antonio."

"I shall tell them that—both of them."

"Do. And give Antonio my love."

A manservant came up the garden to say that His Eminence's coach was ready now.

The two rose.

"No, Ana, don't come back to the house. I'll leave you now; I'll like to remember you standing here in sunlight."

So she went on her knees and kissed his ring and he blessed her.

THE THIRD CHAPTER　　(1585-1590)

The Cardinal's prayers may have reached Ana as he said they would, for as the years deepened, as ill-health increased and the silence and neglect of the world, rising now as a great sighing forest between her and all that she had been, immured her past hope as the king's life-prisoner, she escaped further and further from the spiritual desolations which had wearied her in the first years of her entombment.

This was the more consoling and lucky as the external conditions of her life were made harder by her keeper as time went on.

Not long after the Cardinal's visit, Pastrana's house-governor was changed. Don Alonso Villasante was sent to take over the duties of Palomino. Bernardina, fat and ageing now and considered jolly and harmless by some of the guards, managed to get gossip and comment out of them sometimes, and was told that the idea of the change was reform; that the king was dissatisfied to learn that the duke-dom was losing its trade and prosperity and that the Princess's palace was slipping into disorder. Under Don Alonso there was to be efficiency and a fresh start.

But so far as Ana, Bernardina and Anichu could judge, this efficiency only meant a great multiplication of the rules governing the life of the whole parish, and a great increase of severity and callousness towards the prisoners. The material comforts which he found these enjoying were considered excessive by Don Alonso; so henceforward their food became

less attractive, requests for renewals of clothing or of household requirements of any kind were questioned and usually
refused; firewood and candles were issued on a dole and to the
accompaniment of warnings against self-indulgence. Visits
from friends in the village were cut until at last they were
totally forbidden; Ana's doctor from Alcala was hardly ever
allowed to see her; neither she nor Bernardina was permitted
to pick a flower or an apple when they walked in the garden;
and Anichu's free movements through the village and the
countryside were censured and curtailed.

They learnt too—Bernardina became almost supernaturally
successful in getting news—that in the estate office, whence
Bernardina's husband Espinosa was dismissed by the new
governor, chaos had been imposed upon chaos, and that the
old easy farming and trading methods of the prosperous days
were now lost for ever under a confusion of regulations which
no one understood. Sadly Ana heard that first this farmer
sold out and went away, and next that one, less lucky, was
sold up; silk-weavers one by one were setting off eastward to
look for work in Valencia; the craft-schools at the monastery
and convent were less and less well attended. Poverty was
coming back to Pastrana.

All this, Ana thought in wonder still, all this, affecting the
peace and work of hundreds of people, merely because a
woman he did not want took a lover who was not he.

The drawing-room grew shabby. The gold-painted
acacia-leaves, flaking off the white walls, could not be
restored, even by Bernardina's amateur hand, for the house-
governor would give her no gold paint. The silk curtains
were frayed and dusty and the dark velvet on the chairs had
faded; but the looms just beyond the gate, that had woven
these were allowed to weave no more for the Princess of
Eboli, and half of them indeed had ceased their shuttling.
No flowers came up from the garden now, no fruit lay about
in dishes, and it was many years since any new books had

reached Pastrana from Ana's bookseller in Madrid. There were at last no silks left for needlework, and the tapestry-frames stood idle.

But Anichu came and went contentedly with her lesson-books and whatever talk or news there was, graceful, sweet-faced, serious and true—every day more precious in Ana's sight. And Bernardina still laughed in the teeth of her keepers, and fished up jokes against all weathers, and bullied jugs of wine from the kitchen-men. And the window still looked out to the *Colegiata* doorway and the sky.

When Fernando was fifteen, in the winter of 1585, he went away to a Franciscan house of novices at Salamanca, and to begin his university studies there. Anichu cried very much when he left, and for long afterwards was quieter and whiter of face than seemed good for her. She herself was twelve then and growing tall, promising to be as slender as Ana and more correctly beautiful in face. Ana lay on her couch often, watching Anichu bent over her books, and marvelled at her contentment in this mad, unnatural life, and pondered anxiously her future. Her own health puzzled her. She was growing almost a rheumatic cripple; headaches were savage and frequent, and she was for ever fighting against waves of nausea and giddiness. She assumed therefore that she would not live much longer, and she deplored, somewhat remorse-fully, the passion of Anichu's devotion to her, its undeviated-ness and its great content.

"You *ought* to go to Madrid sometimes, my pet," she said once or twice. "You really ought to stay with friends and get to know your cousins again, and live like other girls."

"Don't say it. I entreat you not to say it. I don't *want* any cousins. I want to stay here, with you."

News from the world—whether true or false they could not be sure—came in sometimes to Bernardina. They heard, for instance, that Antonio Perez continued the king's prisoner; that the Escovedo murder trial was being heard, then that it was abandoned, then that it was to be heard again. Bernardina found out somehow that the Escovedo letters that the king's men had searched for so earnestly had not been found, and likely never would be found. They heard that the king was being urged again, by the Duke of Guise and the Pope, to the old mad idea of invasion of England, and that Santa Cruz, his great admiral, had gathered an Armada and was straining hard for action.

One evening of February in 1587 Bernardina came upstairs with the news that in England they had beheaded the Queen of Scots.

Ana prayed for her a minute, saying nothing. Anichu sat up, her face very white and her black eyes burning.

"How long was she in prison, Berni?"

"Oh, ages, *chiquita*—about twenty years, I'd say."

"Well, she'll have been glad of this," said Ana.

"But why?" said Anichu. "It's better to live! You know it's better to live!"

Ana saw an unpronounceable fear racing through Anichu's brain.

"Of course it is," she said. "But she wasn't lucky like me. She didn't have you and Berni with her always."

"Tyrants can go very far, can't they?" said Anichu.

"Well yes, they go far, as we know. But she was a very important queen. *Her* tyrant probably thinks it was necessary to behead her, for reasons of state. You have to have reasons of state to behead people, Anichu."

Anichu said no more, but she did not return to her book. She sat and stared into the fire.

"We'll pray for the peace of her soul, Anichu. Poor queen, poor Mary of Scotland."

In the spring of 1588 Bernardina constantly had news of coming war, of ships and alarms, of English pirates in Cadiz Bay, and of this one and that one gone to be a sailor. Once or twice there were brief letters from Rodrigo in the Netherlands,

and although he spoke of overtures of peace and of Parma's
conferences to that end, it was clear that he was excited about
some new campaign in the air, and he did not talk of coming
home just yet. But early in the spring all Spain heard of the
death of the old Admiral Santa Cruz, and Ana as well as
others who knew his warrior-spirit breathed more freely
again for the young men newly pressed into naval service,
and assured herself that now the Armada could not sail.

This relief was short-lived.

But when, a week or two after the old sailor's death,
Bernardina brought in the most curious piece of public news
that she had ever collected—grave though it might be for
Spain—it raised a wild, incredulous laugh in the Pastrana
drawing-room.

The Duke of Medina Sidonia, she told Ana and Anichu,
was to command the Great Armada and lead it against
England.

Ana was feeling ill that evening, in pain all through her
body, but this most exquisitely tragi-comic piece of news,
which she refused to accept as more than some travelling
man's fantasy, roused her to a mood of mockery that was
rejuvenating and even analgesic. She and Anichu laughed
and questioned Bernardina in a rapture of non-belief, and all
three excelled themselves in inventing dilemmas, fusses and
disasters for their important relative, when he should take his
ships to sea. They had great fun, and drank his health.

"I give you my brother-in-law, that great sailor!" said
Anichu, waving her glass above her head. They laughed until
they cried, and were merrier over this *canard* of Bernardina's
than they had been for many an evening.

That night, unable to sleep, Ana let herself wonder if such
an utterly frivolous rumour could by any disastrous chance be
true. And at the thought that it might her heart lurched in
fear for the men in the great ships at Cadiz and at Lisbon.
But she shook the nightmare away and returned to her

prayers, the many, many prayers that took her now with increasing kindness through the nights of loneliness and pain.

Spring passed; May opened and spread its beauty on Pastrana; and they learnt that the Great Armada was to sea, and commanded indeed for good or ill by their unhappy Alonso, Madalena's husband, who had never directed as much as a sardine-boat in his life, and who would be honestly terrified, Ana knew, of his appalling honour.

It sailed, and with it sailed, as occasional letters told them, many, many that they knew—cousins and friends and neighbours, and Bernardina's son, her only child, in the flagship of his new employer, the new Great Admiral.

By the end of September its tale was done—what was left of it was back in Santander, and Ana's unhappy son-in-law was hurrying south to hide himself in San Lucar from the anger of the people. Bernardina's son did not come back, and there were many others, friends of Rodrigo's, young men Ana had seen christened, who never returned from the Enterprise against England. Spain, even to two lost, forgotten women-prisoners in Pastrana, writhed in anger and grief, and Ana sometimes thought with bitter embarrassment of the February night when she had laughed so enchantedly at Bernardina's rumour and drunk the health of Medina Sidonia, "that great sailor".

During the winter Bernardina became gravely ill, with inflammation and congestion of her lungs such as she had had in Pinto. But now she was older and fatter, and the years of imprisonment had weakened her; she grieved for her lost son too, and talked to him in her delirium.

Ana, with a breaking heart—for life would now be harsh indeed without Bernardina—wrote to Philip, breaking the silence of nine years, and asked him to pardon her *dueña*, pleading her ill health, the loss of her son in the Armada, and that her ageing husband was ill too, and needed her in

Madrid. She never knew if the letter got to Philip, for she received no answer.

She moved now only by leaning on two sticks; her long, beautiful hands were distorted by swollen joints; she coughed continually, and almost everything she tried to eat except bread made her feel sick. Her hair was grey, and her face was darkened by the long deep grooves of age and pain. Sometimes, if she caught sight of herself in her long mirror, as she tried to move with her sticks across her bedroom, she was taken aback, even astonished by her own image. For well though she knew her own pain and disabilities, yet somehow she did not, could not visualise herself, Ana de Mendoza, as just a creeping ruin, an ugly, broken invalid. But that was what the mirror showed her; that was what she was.

She joked about this awful decay, half-bitterly, half-lightly, to Anichu.

"Would I have got like this in any case, do you think, Anichu? Prisoner or not, was I just bound to be an old freak like this at forty-nine?"

"Are you forty-nine?"

"Yes, indeed. But I feel a hundred."

"Somehow, I never dream you're anything like forty-nine. Oh yes, I know you can't walk very well—but that's probably because of all that ill-treatment in those awful places—and because of the way you've been cooped up here too. But—otherwise, you don't seem to me to change."

"Oh pet! Don't be so unkind! Anichu, I'm hideous now—and I wasn't, or I thought I wasn't, once."

"I always thought you very beautiful," Anichu said. "You're beautiful now. You're the sort of person—there are hardly any of them, I imagine—who is beautiful, for those who think so, once and for all."

Ana bit her lip, afraid of the weak tears that so often defeated her now.

"Child," she said gently, "I must be somehow good, to have so perfect a daughter."

Bernardina recovered in the spring, and Ana too revived, and they often made their slow way together to the topmost terrace of the now neglected garden, and sat in the sun and looked about over the dear, free stretches of Castile, and laughed at their ludicrous life, and at finding themselves turned into two feeble, plain old fogies whom the world had agreed to forget.

And sometimes there in the sun Ana thought of the Armada and of Spain and of all the disastrous mistakes of a great reign, and of the dismal failure and weakness throughout it of her own caste. And she talked in that vein to Bernardina and Anichu.

"I wish I'd been a man," she said one day.

"I wish you had," said Anichu. "You'd have been a great one."

"Some people might say, *chiquita*, and I'm one of them, that you're a great woman."

"Ah no, Berni. I've been of no use at all."

"You've set a good example," said Anichu.

"I had no choice. I mean, no choice in my heart. You can't say black is white."

"Everyone does but you, *chiquita*, when it suits them."

"Well then, it suits them. But it would never suit me. Still, being like that hasn't anything to do with being great."

"You're the only subject of Philip's who hasn't compromised with his dishonesty—in my day anyway," said Bernardina.

"Nor has Antonio Perez."

"Ah, that's different. You just stood by an idea. He's fighting for himself."

"And he's still fighting. He may win."

"I doubt it, *chiquita*," said Bernardina, looking troubled.

"But, Philip," said Ana dreamily, following another

thought, "whoever wins or doesn't win, he loses. He's losing everything, I fear. Poor Philip!"

By the autumn of 1589 the Duke of Medina Sidonia, having licked his wounds in luxury at San Lucar and been forgiven by his king for failing to do what was completely beyond his capacity, found time to worry again about family affairs. He was too out of sorts and gouty now to make a journey from Andalusia to mid-Castile, and in any case having lost heart in his battle for Ana's right to be free, saw no sense in depressing himself by the spectacle of her present life. He knew that its conditions were bad and that her health was wretched, and his heart was soft, so he had to spare it a vain ordeal. But he was concerned for the future of the child Anichu and so—his letters showed—was Rodrigo, and so were other relatives. Anichu must be fourteen now, he calculated, and would be a wealthy woman. Her mother must by all accounts die soon; Anichu's brothers were scattered, and she would need a protector and a comforter when she was left alone. It was necessary, in fact, to arrange a betrothal, possibly even a marriage for the girl.

After consultations with the king and with many Mendoza cousins including the head of the family, the Duke of Infantado, Alonso selected the young Count of Tendilla for his sister-in-law. It was a good choice, considering that so many of the young flower of Spain had recently been lost in the English Channel or on the rocks of western Ireland. The Count was a Mendoza and a cousin, young, gentle and pleasant to the eye; he had known and played with Anichu's brothers from babyhood; he was sufficiently wealthy, and his parents were good people and approved of this design for him.

So Medina Sidonia wrote of it in detail to Ana. And Ana read his letter and thought it over, and read it again, and with a little shiver of sorrow realised that she approved of it too. She remembered the boy in the old Madrid days and had liked him. And it was true that Anichu would be vulnerable and desolate indeed on a day that could not now be far removed.

She did not answer her son-in-law at once.

"Do you think of marrying ever, Anichu?"

Anichu looked very much surprised—even amused.

"No! Good heavens, no! Well, not for centuries yet, I mean."

"But what do you mean by centuries?"

"Oh—ages. When I'm a real grown-up, I suppose I'll marry. Everyone does, after all."

"In any case, I wouldn't let you marry until you are at least sixteen."

"Sixteen? But that's only two years off! I'm not going to marry in two years. In any case," she laughed, "I'll probably have to marry one of these guards or someone."

"Why, my pet? They're dreadful-looking creatures."

"Yes, I know. But it'll have to be someone who lives here, you see."

"Oh no, Anichu, what nonsense! You can't marry a man and expect him to live in a prison."

Anichu smiled.

"Then I can't marry. Because I'm never going away from here. Not while you're a prisoner. Not for fifty husbands."

"There won't be fifty of them, pet. But you'll have to go away when you marry."

"Well then, I've told you—it's quite simple. I won't marry. I prefer to stay with you."

"I see. But you won't always. A little later on you'll want to love a man. You'll want children."

"I'm not so sure. What I love is being with you."

"That's only because you think I'm wrongly treated, and you feel fanatical about my ill-usage."

"Oh yes, that too. I simply wouldn't leave you now for any reason on earth. But it's easy to say that—because I *want* to stay with you. What's put all this into your head so suddenly about marriage, of all things?"

"Well, you're growing up. And you have, as a matter of fact, a suitor, a very suitable suitor." Anichu stared at her. "Someone who desires to be betrothed to you."

"Who is it?"

"Your second cousin, Diego de Mendoza, Count of Tendilla. You remember him? He used to fence rather well, with Rodrigo."

Anichu looked thoughtful.

"Yes. I remember him. He was nice. He was very quiet, but he always looked nice."

"Well, there it is. Will you think it over?"

"No, I don't think so. I don't want to be betrothed. You wouldn't really like me to be, would you?"

Ana looked at the girl.

"I think I would. It would be a comfort. I'm old, pet, older than my age, and you know as well as I do that I'm ill. When I'm gone, you'll be very lonely——"

"When you're gone," said Anichu very steadily, "being betrothed or not to my cousin will make no difference to me at all."

"Oh yes, it will—believe me."

"Please, don't say any more of this, I beg you. I'm very grateful to my cousin, and I think I liked him when I knew him. But please excuse me from being betrothed. Let us stay here, just as we are—it isn't much to ask."

"That's true," said Ana. "Very well, I'll say no more."

And she wrote to Medina Sidonia thanking him for his project and saying that she approved of it. But she said that there could be no betrothal yet, as Anichu was still too young in spirit and asked to be excused. But that she liked her cousin and spoke kindly of him, and that if he was not impatient—and he was young enough to wait—she believed that the contract might be arranged within another twelve-month.

So it was left at the close of 1589. But Ana felt less bleak,

less guilty now when she contemplated her youngest child.
I will go, she thought, I will go soon, and she will still be very
young and susceptible to comfort, and our kind Alonso will
see that this good plan for her happiness is secured. And then
she will grow up and grow wings and be happy and normal,
and forget these years and forget her grief.

This relief to her heart was timely, for in January and
February it began to be clear that she must no longer attempt
any greater effort than the now very great one of creeping
from her bedroom to her couch in the drawing-room. She
knew now that she would never see the garden again, never
sit on its topmost terrace with the Guadarramas at her back
and the fields of Castile spread out golden in the sun. The
end was beginning. And she was powerless to spare Anichu
its sorrow. But afterwards the young life would begin. Ana
folded this assurance into her heart, and said her prayer. more
peacefully, and lay with her couch so placed that she could
always see the sky and the *Colegiata* tower. And she thought
of Ruy's tomb awaiting her beneath the tower, and reflected
peacefully on death.

THE FOURTH CHAPTER   (18TH APRIL 1590)

I

During March Ana was so ill that she was unable to leave
her bedroom, a sign in her that pain was indeed in the
ascendant over her will. But one morning towards the end
of Lent she woke and told Bernardina that she was feeling
well again. And so indeed she seemed; and she got up and
dressed herself slowly, very slowly—but still refusing help,
as all her life she had refused it.

Bernardina fretted sometimes now for Ana, about this
privacy of her dressing-room. She knew it was because of
her disfigured eye that she had all her life brushed and washed

her own hair, and she washed her face and took her bath unattended. Even at Pinto, when they had lived together in slum-proximity, Bernardina had never seen Ana's right eye without the black silk shade. But now the day was coming when those once-quick and authoritative hands would no longer be able to reach to Ana's head, or reaching there do her will. Already for many months it had hurt Bernardina to see the dressing-room door close on that weary, pain-ridden figure, and to count how long, how very long it was before it opened again. Ana, austere in personal taste and impatient of the delays and follies of elaborate adornment, had always dressed and undressed faster than any woman Bernardina had ever known or heard of. Now that was over, but by long pride and shyness of habit she still dressed and undressed alone.

However, on this April morning after a whole month in bed she seemed indeed most touchingly recuperated, and came from her dressing-room, slowly on her sticks indeed, but seeming not too much exhausted, and looking groomed and slender and even elegant in her old black silk dress. And she came back to her couch by the great window, and looked with greedy pleasure towards her view again.

"I think April is a lucky month, don't you, Anichu?"

Anichu, radiant to see her well, agreed indeed.

"This is a lucky April anyway," she said. "We must have a happy Easter."

"When is Easter?"

"On the twenty-second. Only about a fortnight off."

"Oh, goodness—nearly all of Lent is gone, and I spent it cosseting myself in bed! I must make up for lost time. I think I could crawl as far as the chapel for Mass to-morrow."

"You'll do nothing of the sort, let me tell you," said Bernardina. "That chapel is a death-trap, it's so cold and draughty."

Ana looked out at the radiant day.

"There are no draughts in weather like this," she said. "This is spring."

Every day that month she got up and came to her couch and was well, and read and did sums and puzzles with Anichu, and at supper drank wine rashly.

For Holy Week Anichu went, as she went every year, to stay at the Franciscan convent and make a retreat.

"I hate being away when you're so well," she said to Ana before she left her on Palm Sunday. "But of course it's much better than leaving you when you're ill."

"And you'll be home on Saturday—early, mind! Immediately after all those endless ceremonies. Promise!"

Anichu kissed her.

"I promise. You know I'll come flying. Keep well now—please!"

"I will. I'll always be well now, perhaps?"

"No need for 'perhaps'," said Anichu, and kissed her again and was gone.

The lovely days lengthened.

In spite of Bernardina's protests Ana did manage to edge her way across the landing to the tribune of the chapel to assist at some of the great and sorrowful rites of Holy Week. And on her couch she read the Offices of the Church and prayed and sought in recollection and silence to identify herself with the Passion of Christ. Time passed gently. There were no arguments with Don Alonso Villasante, and Ana, a prisoner now to her own health, almost forgot that she was Philip's prisoner too.

On Wednesday evening in Holy Week Bernardina came into the drawing-room as dusk was falling. Ana lay propped against pillows on her couch; her head was relaxed as if she slept, and in profile to the evening light which gleamed about her greying hair. Her hands lay still on the coverlet.

Bernardina looked at her as if in perplexity, and for a moment did not speak or move to disturb her. She looks so peaceful. She's ill and old, and it's all over. I don't think the message ought to have been sent. It's too dangerous. All very well for him, but it might mean death for her——

Ana stirred, and smiled at her.

"What are you doing, standing there staring at me, you old sneak?"

"Admiring you, my beauty. I thought we might have a drink?" She set down a tray.

"But am I allowed one at this hour?"

"Well, it's Holy Week, and we really are rather overdoing the penitential business, in my opinion. I'm exhausted."

"Poor Berni. Let's have a lot to drink."

"It's seven o'clock anyhow. *Merienda*-time in the good old days." She poured their wine, and set Ana's where it would be easiest to her stiffening hand.

Ana was watching her face, on which the evening light fell fully.

"Come on, Berni—what's happened? What are we drinking about?"

"Honestly I don't know whether to tell you or not. Still, I think you might not forgive me if I didn't. I think that, if I were you, I'd wish to be told."

Ana stared at her.

"But of course I'd wish to be told! What *is* it, Berni?"

Bernardina took a careful, steady drink, and set down her glass.

"You know old Jorge?"

Old Jorge was the retired *Alcalde* of Pastrana, and the only person from the village who nowadays managed sometimes to get further inside the house than the Estate Office. He invented pretexts in *alcalde* jargon for these entries. He was not supposed to see either of the prisoners, but one or two of the guards who liked him and liked Bernardina sometimes arranged for them to have a few words in the children's apartments or some safe place downstairs. In any case, to let him do so could not be regarded as a major crime, for he was a fat and simple old villager, not to be suspected of intrigue.

"Yes. Has he been calling?"

"I've just been talking with him in the children's study. He sent you his most devoted respects."

"And then? Go on, Berni!"

"A man passed through Pastrana to-day and called on Jorge. Jorge didn't know him and he gave no name. He said he was from Zaragoza and was on his way home."

"Ah! An Aragonese!"

"He gave this message to Jorge, which Jorge was to try to get to us. He said that Gil de Mesa wished you to know that a traveller will be making for the Aragon frontier to-night and may seek entrance here, from the top of the garden, as he passes."

"Ah!" There was silence a moment. "Thank you, Berni."

"Do you know the name, Gil de Mesa?"

"Yes. He is a friend of Antonio's."

"An escape is evidently planned for to-night. It's very daring of them—because, from what I've been hearing, it might well be expected."

"What have you been hearing?"

"Nothing much for the past two or three weeks. But then I did hear that the trial was going against Perez, that witnesses were betraying him. And that he was in rigorous solitary confinement again, in some house in Madrid. It didn't sound hopeful. But of course—by the time a rumour gets to a village——"

"When did Jorge's visitor come?"

"About four o'clock. And went on at once towards Guadalajara."

"It is about a hundred and fifty miles, isn't it, from Madrid to the frontier of Aragon?"

"About that—a little more, I think."

"An escape from a place like Madrid couldn't be started

until well after dark." Ana looked out at the twilight and its handful of stars. "With changes of horses, and good horses, I suppose a man could be near the border by daylight? That is necessary, I'm sure—to use the cover of the dark."

"Yes. In this empty countryside you could get a long way in safety in the first night. But by morning rumour will have spread and may have got ahead of you, or you might even be recognised. But I don't think, with the best horses on earth, he could be in Aragon until after midday to-morrow. It's a very dangerous scheme, for him," said Bernardina. "Because the moment he is missed they'll know there is only one road for him into safety—or possible safety."

"He shouldn't come here. It's an absurd addition to the risk."

"But we've no way of stopping him."

"No, thank God," said Ana with a smile.

"You're glad? You'll be glad to see him?"

Ana leant back into her pillows and looked out towards the sky.

"Glad?" she said dreamily. And then she laughed outright. "Berni, you're ridiculous, ridiculous!"

Bernardina felt tears sting her eyes.

"You incorrigible old rip," she said lovingly.

"Give me more wine," said Ana.

They drank, and sat in silence awhile.

"He will have planned this to the very last nicety, if I know him," she said. "He even found the means to send that message here, and took the risk."

"Remember now, he may not get this far—it's a very mad thing he's doing—if he's doing it."

"He'll get here—and get to Aragon."

"If he gets as far as here, but not to Aragon, it will probably mean death without further delay for both of you."

"And for you."

"Yes—and for me."

"He mustn't die. He doesn't want to."

"Even in Aragon they may well give him up to the king.'

"No, I think they'll stand on their ancient rights, and protect their man against the foreign king."

"Castile didn't do as much for you."

"But we Castilians sold our rights to Charles V. The Aragonese have clung to theirs. No, if he gets to Aragon he has a chance of life and freedom. Berni, did you really think you wouldn't tell me he was coming?"

"Not really, I suppose. But God in His High Heaven forgive me, *chiquita*, if it all goes wrong!"

"It won't," Ana said. "And if it does—well, it's a better ending than I'd thought of. I wonder why he's decided to do this at last?"

"He may be looking ill—or changed, you know."

"Ah, well!" Ana laughed sadly. "But why do you say it like that, Berni? Have you heard then that he's ill?"

"No, I haven't heard anything of that."

Bernardina got up and began to light candles and draw curtains.

"What time is it fully dark in Madrid, Berni?"

"Same as here. It should be full night at about eight o'clock."

"He's getting ready now."

Ana made the sign of the Cross and so did Bernardina. The latter went to the fire and piled it recklessly with wood. She was thinking of devices for getting more wood brought up, and also of how to steal candles for all the candelabra. He would be cold, maybe; and Ana would not wish him to find the room very different from his memory of it.

"If he leaves Madrid say at half-past eight, he should be here about half-past ten, Berni."

"Yes. As far as here will be the first lap. He has all his real travelling to do afterwards."

"We must get ready. We haven't got a lot of time. I'll go

and change out of this shabby dress——" She felt for her
sticks and began to raise herself from the couch. "Ah, how
he'll be shocked at me!" She stood leaning on her sticks and
looked about her. "What an odd and terrible meeting this
will be!"

"You're sure you want it?"

"Perfectly sure."

She moved as she spoke towards her bedroom door.

"It'll tire you to change your dress, *chiquita*. Won't that
one do?"

"No, I don't think so. There's an old black velvet that he
used to like——" She stopped and turned suddenly. "But,
Berni—the guards, the garden wall! How is he to get here,
ever?"

Bernardina smiled.

"I'm thinking that out," she said. "I'll manage it, *chiquita*,
if it's the last thing I do. Now away with you to your dressing-room, and I'll see to everything. And first I'll furbish up
this room a bit."

Whilst Ana was dressing she prayed for Antonio. It's good
of him to come to me, her heart was saying peacefully. Good
and true. She faced her mirror without cheating herself, and
considered what this man would see who was risking so much
to pause and salute the past, as he rode away from it for dear
life's sake. Yet he is right to do it; he is right to have courage
and come here. God, God speed him now! Oh God in Your
dear mercy protect him——

                              II

The *Colegiata* bell rang out eleven o'clock. After it had
ceased the silence all around seemed absolute. Ana strained
her ears, and tried not to, for a sound of hoofs. But better, far
better that she should not hear them, for then others also
would not hear.

He won't ride through the village. He'll turn north up the track at Holy Tree. Half a mile along there he should dismount, leave his horse with whoever's with him, and cross the Valdez orchard to the top of the garden. I'm sure he knows all that. He is so curiously observant. The wall is shallow on our side, and steep into the orchard. But Bernardina will be there; she'll know what to do. The night is clear, too clear. Oh God, have pity on him now! Grant him this one good fortune! Let him get home to Aragon! Let him be lucky just to-night, to-night and till to-morrow, Lord! Oh Lord, dear Christ, be with him!

She lay on her couch, looking like a composed and ageing invalid lady. She looked aristocratic and cold; her face was very white, her hands were still. Her only ornament was a narrow gold chain on which was slung a ring of one fine emerald set in pearls. It was the last jewel Antonio had ever given her, and she had hurt him by her disinclination to wear it. To-night she would have worn it, but her finger-joints were swollen, and it would no longer fit even her little finger. So she wore it on her breast.

She fingered it now and then, and lay still and looked about the room.

Bernardina had done well. Candles flamed in all their former places, and the fire smelt of pine-cones and apple-wood. A table was set with cold food and with silver jugs of wine. The shabbiness and sorrows of the years were visible indeed in the room, but its old elegance was astir to-night nevertheless, over-riding time and pain; and the pictures looked down as they had done in the good days—Ruy, smirking dully as he never smirked, and she herself, austere and expressionless as Sanchez Coëllo had seen her; but the lovely Giorgione too and the Clouet head and the Holbein drawing, and the noble, small Mantegna he had found for her. Once more we light you up, she said—once more, before I turn to everlasting darkness. And still she listened for the hoofs she wished no earthly ear to hear, and she stroked her emerald and prayed.

He came into the room by the door which led towards her bedroom.

He stood and they looked at each other, and for half a second she would have said it was not he. And simultaneously she thought she read the same doubt in his face.

Then he came towards her, smiling a little, and walking on tiptoe, not making a sound. He was in dark riding clothes, but wore no weapons or spurs. Nothing that clanked. His hair was grey like hers. She noticed that he held his hands somewhat awkwardly, away from himself. She stretched her own hands out, wondering if he would notice at once how they were changed.

He came and stood beside her, looking down.

She laid her hand on one of his, and noticed that it was red and hot, and that he winced. She took her hand away.

" 'The Question', the torture?"

He nodded.

"The mildest form. And I gave in. I told them I had had him killed, on the king's instruction."

"Thank God."

He dropped on his knees and laid his head against her breast. She held him and stroked his hair, wondering with sad pleasure that it too should be grey, like hers.

"You look old," she said. "Nearly as old as me."

"I'm eight years older than you, girl."

He smiled upward to her boyishly, wearily—and memories of many, many other nights when he had smiled exactly thus against her breast came back and lighted her face.

"You haven't forgotten?"

"I haven't forgotten anything, Antón."

He closed his eyes. She noticed more exactly then the aged, weary texture of his skin, a weariness grooved in below the dust and heat of to-night's hard ride.

"But you've made your soul now? You've repented and are in the state of grace?"

"Ah, yes! It's been easy. When you're ill and a prisoner, it's easy to be virtuous."

"I know. I've thought of that. I've been virtuous too."

She smiled. He lay as if he might fall asleep. His head was very heavy.

"How long can you stay?"

"Gil says not more than forty minutes. Bernardina will come and tell me."

"Did she meet you at the garden wall?"

"Yes. I saw her as I came across the orchard. It gave me a heavenly sense of long ago—to see her there, the dear good lump, just as if we were all at peace and happy and this an affair of every night. Ah! Then you have it still?"

He had the emerald in his hand.

"I'm wearing it for the last time to-night."

"The last time?"

"Yes. I want you to take it with you—you'll need money, and I have none to give you now. But I've packed together here—you see that little leather roll—I've packed all the jewels you gave me, and some others that are my own and need not descend to the children. You'll take them, and this emerald, and use them as you need them, for love of me."

"Ana—the things I gave you——"

"It's a good way for them to serve me now. No one else should have them anyway, after I'm gone. And I'll be gone soon."

He lifted his head and turned and looked at her closely.

"Are you *very* ill, Ana?"

"I don't feel very ill now, but I have done so most of the last two years. At least, I feel that I'm dying, in a dull way."

"Why? What do the doctors say? Why are you dying?"

"They don't say much. I had a fever of some kind when I was imprisoned in San Torcaz, and since then my bones have hurt me more and more, and my heart hurts—and in general I know I've been dying slowly. I don't mind—except for Anichu. Especially now if you are safe."

"You look old, you look tired. Oh girl, how beautiful you always are!"

"Remember me, will you? Try to remember me clearly when I'm dead."

He smiled, but tears came into his eyes.

"I'll try. May I have some wine?"

"It would be strange if you didn't."

He managed the wine-jug by tilting it with the third and little fingers of both hands. She watched him with pity.

"I'll come and fetch mine," she said. She found her sticks and came to him with her crippled walk. He watched her gravely.

"I always used to think you moved too fast," he said. "Well, he's made us pay, hasn't he? But it was worth a price."

She took her glass, and he picked up his with difficulty.

"What shall we drink to, Antón? To Aragon?"

"No, because you won't be there. I'll give you a better toast. We'll drink to the chime of Santa Maria Almudena."

He drank, delighted with this memory of lost pleasures, lovers' nights; and she smiled back into his mischievous smile. But she thought also, with a reminiscent shiver, of Philip's face under the porch of Maria Almudena.

"How do you manage to ride, with these poor hands?"

"It's torture—but I have to. Gil straps the reins up on to my elbows—you see, they used their devices on my wrists and thumbs—and then I manage to control things with these other fingers and my elbows. I was beginning to get the knack of it just about at Alcala."

"When will you be safe?"

"I don't know about *safe*—they mayn't want me in Aragon, but it's worth trying. We hope to get to Calatayud some time after midday to-morrow."

He took her gently by the arm and drew her near the fire.

"Sit down," he said, and when she did he dropped beside her on the floor. "Oh God, oh God, to stay here! Just to stay here, Ana, and be forgotten, and sleep and sleep—and die some day, when you die!"

He looked about the room with love.

"It's shabby now," she said.

"Yes, I can see that."

"When you confessed—would it not have been all right? I mean, since Philip is now known as your accomplice?"

"No, they were instructed to ignore that. The judge was shameless—everyone saw that all they were taking of my confession was the admission of my own guilt."

"And your letters?"

"They wouldn't accept them as evidence—they said they had enough. And I don't know whether perhaps I couldn't have borne the torture longer—but I was sick of the farce; so I spoke. In any case——" he laughed, "it *was* most damnably painful. And it was only the first degree."

"Eat—you'd better eat something."

"No—I can't. I had food in Madrid, and we have some with us, I believe. But more wine, Ana—oh, more wine!"

He went and refilled their glasses.

"Our time is nearly gone," he said, "and I'm saying nothing. But really I only wanted to look at you again."

"Yes. There's nothing to say, I think, that we both don't know."

"Why did you take me for a lover?"

"On a kind of cold speculation. And you didn't really want me that first time."

"No, I believe I didn't. At any rate, I could have done without you. Yet, it brought us to this—to years and years of pain."

"Yes, it brought us a long way."

"Oh girl, remember me."

"I remember you and pray for you every day of my life. Do you pray?"

"No. I've never prayed, I think."

"Well, I'll be praying for you—here and hereafter. What do you expect from Aragon?"

"A small civil war, at least—which ought to annoy Philip a great deal, I hope. And if the right side wins—there's no knowing! If we lose, I shall have to think again. But do you know who is Governor of Aragon now?"

"No, indeed."

"Your cousin of the lawsuit—Iñigo de Mendoza, now Marqués de Almenara on the titles and lands he filched from you."

"That's not a good omen. He hates me."

"So he's not likely to favour *my* cause. However, I'm appealing to the Aragonese—not to our foreign Castilian governors."

"Are your family safe?"

"The children are already in Zaragoza, I hope. And Juana will leave Madrid to-morrow and join them. Without her complicity I couldn't have arranged this escape. She has been a tower of courage all these years."

"So I should expect her to be."

Antonio smiled a little.

"I've never before made the mistake of talking about my wife to my mistress——"

"But now you *have* no mistress, and you can talk of anything to an old friend."

He came and knelt before her.

"I wish I could embrace you," he said. "These wretched hands! Girl, you're no 'old friend'. You are for ever in my heart my mistress."

She took his head into her hands and kissed his mouth.

"You're a very, very good lover, Antón."

It was a phrase from their past, and he smiled and gave her the old answer:

"If you'd perhaps let me have it in writing?"

There was a soft, steady tap on the door by which he had come in. They both heard it.

"Ah! Then it's time?"

"Yes. Bernardina said she'd knock."

They rose and stood together, looking desolately about the room. Ana took the little leather roll of jewels and said:

"Where can I put these for you? Don't take it in your poor hands?"

She found a pocket in his tunic and slipped the packet in. Then she took the chain and ring from her neck.

"No, not in my pocket, that. Round my neck, Ana."

She put the chain over his head, opened his tunic at the throat and put the ring inside his shirt against his breast.

"Thank you," he said. "It's warm from you."

"Have you no cloak, no spurs or sword or anything?"

"I left them all with Gil and the horses—so as to make less noise."

There was another gentle knock.

"Yes, Berni," Ana said.

Antonio took her in his arms.

"You'll hurt your wrists."

"Oh silly, and why not?"

He drew her hard against him, and kissed her mouth as if in first desire. Ana thought—this is the last embrace of my mortal life; people can't often know when they have reached the last. But I do know. Good-bye, she answered him now with her whole self, with all of strength and gratitude in her possession—good-bye to you, and also to that long-assuaged and quieted me that you alone commanded. Good-bye, dear past, dear sin, and go from me in peace. I loved you and I have atoned and will atone.

Antonio leant back from her to look into her face.

"I don't need to look," he said. "I know it. I've carried it with me a long time."

"Is it the same face, now it's old?"

"It's the same face, and now as then it's young and old," he said and laid his mouth gently against her black silk eye shade, into the hollow of her lost right eye. Then he released her from his arms.

"God speed you," she said. "Let me hear that you are safe."

"There'll be a message." He looked swiftly about the room again and then back to her face. "I must go."

"Yes, you must go, Antón."

He gave a little bow, and walked to the door, but there he turned, smiling.

"I've suddenly thought of Juana La Loca—do you remember, Anichu's old doll?"

She laughed.

"Yes, I remember her. I think she still exists."

"Well, give her my love then—and to Anichu."

They smiled at each other for the last time.

THE FIFTH CHAPTER   (MAY 1590)

I

Anichu came home on Holy Saturday, emaciated from the austerities of the retreat, but very happy. She found Ana well and Bernardina also in good spirits. The three had a happy Easter, not even too much overclouded when they recalled other Easters of Anichu's babyhood; the great processions around Pastrana, the dinner-party for the whole village on the top terrace of the garden, the Monday bullfight at Alcala, supper with the Marqués de Los Velez, and the long drive home and everyone singing all the way. Anichu liked to hear these tales of the splendid, family days she had hardly known.

Ana had told her at once on her return of Antonio Perez's escape from Madrid to Aragon, and of his visit to her on his way.

She looked grave at the news.

"Did he get to the frontier safely?"

"We don't know yet. There'll be a message."

"You must be anxious."

"Oddly enough, I'm not. I'm certain he's safe."

"We'd better pray though."

"Oh yes, I'm praying. You pray, my pet. God will listen to you."

Anichu looked at her thoughtfully.

"You *were*—his mistress?"

"Yes, Anichu, I was."

"For how long?"

"For not quite two years before we were imprisoned."

She saw Anichu's look of relief. No doubt she was thinking of the father she had never known, who had died just after her birth.

"Forgive me for asking you this," the young girl went on anxiously, "but did you have other lovers?"

"No, pet," Ana said. "There was no one else. Only your father while he lived—and then Antonio Perez."

"Thank you—thank you for telling me. I've no right to ask you——"

"You have, Anichu."

"—But, I've heard things said about—the king, and I couldn't help wondering sometimes, he's been so terrible to you——"

"I agree—there's matter for wonder. We were devoted friends, Philip and I, but he never asked me to be his mistress, and the grave things that were said about us were untrue."

"I see. It's all the more puzzling, isn't it?"

"I've given up that riddle long ago."

She seemed now, Anichu thought, as if she had given up most riddles.

On Easter Tuesday a stranger riding west from Aragon called on Jorge, the former *Alcalde*. After he had gone on his way, Jorge, setting out laboriously for Ana's house, met Anichu and gave her the stranger's message. He said that the traveller from Madrid had reached Calatayud in Aragon on the afternoon of Holy Thursday, that he was well and had taken sanctuary in the Dominican house of San Martin. Great trouble was rising in Aragon, he said, and he sent his love to Pastrana. Anichu ran home with the message.

Nunc dimittis said Ana's heart as she received it; and henceforward she composed herself secretly and contentedly for death, which she hoped might tarry now as little as might be. And not because she turned from life in desolation or disappointment any longer, as she had done at earlier periods of her imprisonment. But her sole earthly care now was for Anichu, and for Anichu she desired her death to be hurried forward.

Antonio was gone. While he was in Spain and in the troubles and dangers his love for her had brought upon him, her heart had still tugged back towards life a little, even in bitterest hours of emptiness and loss; she had still desired, against all likelihood, to see him again and also to see some conclusion, for better or worse, put to their story. Now this had come to pass, and he was gone for ever from what was left of her life—gone indeed into danger and inconclusiveness still, but with hands freed at last to fight these, and with a real chance of evading Philip's final vengeance. Antonio's life, divorced from Castile henceforward, was entering a new, strange phase, and her part in it was played and done with.

So there only remained Anichu; and to be with the child in these sweet years of her early girlhood, to have her companionship, so steady, so comfortingly optimistic and young, to love her and enjoy her love, was indeed a poignant consolation and almost a stronger attachment to life than any other she had ever felt. But Ana knew that she took this one great grace of her latter days at a price to Anichu; she knew that the longer they lived together as now, with the child so unself-consciously and generously sacrificial in her love, the wilder and more wounding would be her grief when Ana died, and the harder her return to normal life and to the ways and friends of her own generation. There would be grief indeed—in pity for which Ana shuddered many times each day—whenever death took her from this single-hearted child. There was now no evading that; Anichu had been allowed, unwisely, to devote herself to her one great love, her one fanaticism almost it might be called, and it was no longer sane or kind to talk to her of going away from Pastrana. Their situation as it had grown must now be seen through, and Anichu must be prepared as firmly as love could devise for the slow pain of watching it end. But Ana believed that the younger she was when that end came so much the better. She desired that the child's approaching ordeal should be short, at least, since it could not be escaped. And when it was over, she could still go out young and curable into the sun of the world, able to take its natural comfort again, and forget Pastrana and prison and grief. Ana thought with gladness of the young Count of Tendilla, and sometimes spoke of him lightly to Anichu, who did not repudiate his name, and indeed spoke of him with a gentle interest and goodwill. So watching her and reflecting on her, Ana saw that the best thing she could do was to die very soon. And therefore it pleased her to feel, with Antonio's going, that she was at last completely ready to welcome death.

With the beginning of May she began to feel that she was getting her wish.

The days were exquisitely fair, and she always managed to get to her couch by the great window and lie where the sunlight fell and where she could hear the sounds of life come up from her forgotten village. And because her heart was composed and at peace, because indeed she felt almost gay sometimes, she did not think that Bernardina and Anichu perceived at first the relapse she felt all through her body. She would be glad if they, and especially Anichu, did not. So she lay on her sofa, and said as little as possible about aches and pains; and prayed, and reflected on her life and sins, and watched her daughter's delicate beauty opening to the early summer; and in the sunlight and quiet sometimes almost caught herself being grateful to Philip for having brought her perforce to this readiness and detachment, this calm which saints might envy, she thought, and in which, no saint at all, she did not merit to depart from life.

"I owe the king a great deal," she said to Anichu. "Because I really think he has saved my soul for me!"

"You'd have managed that for yourself," said Anichu. "But he *has* made you something of a philosopher."

"I suppose I've heard the last of him now. I suppose he has in fact forgotten me."

"Does that make you sad?"

"No, not any longer. And I have forgiven him, Anichu. Truly I have. I pray for him every day."

II

On the morning of the twenty-second of May Ana woke early, feeling very ill. But, restless, she got up and dressed, very slowly, more slowly than ever, she noticed; and at seven o'clock made her way in pain to the tribune of the chapel to hear Mass and receive Communion. Anichu and Bernardina were already in their places, and the latter frowned and shook her fist at Ana as she helped her to settle in her *prie-Dieu*.

It was a radiant morning, loud with bird-song, and as the sunlight streamed in on the altar and the priest Ana forgot her aching bones and the feeble thudding of her heart, and prayed in peace and praised God for the beauty of the day.

She stayed in her *prie-Dieu* for a little while when Mass was over and the others were gone. The empty chapel pleased her, so hushed and quiet, and holding many simple and good memories of Ruy and of her married life. She supposed she would find Ruy again after death—the Church taught her that she would, and so though it was difficult to imagine how such meetings might be, she accepted the teaching. Well, if it was true, it made death even easier to welcome, for indeed it would be good to see Ruy again, after all her mistakes and troubles.

She rose with her sticks, dipped her fingers in the holy water font and made the sign of the Cross. And with the morning song of the birds filling her ears she made her way back to the drawing-room.

The morning collation was there, of milk and bread and fruit. Anichu was eating hurriedly, as she had some early classes at the convent. Bernardina looked fussed, Ana thought—even agitated.

"What is it, Berni? Let's sit down and have some milk. I feel quite hungry."

Bernardina looked at her, helped her to sit down and poured her some milk. Anichu smiled at her mother and then glanced at Bernardina.

"Yes—what is it, Berni?" she said sharply.

Bernardina sat down.

"There's something the matter, *chiquita*," she said. "There's something very queer happening—I don't know what it is."

"Go on," said Anichu.

"Well, everyone's disappeared! I had to go to fetch this tray myself, and there's no sign anywhere of old Paca, and it was handed to me at the kitchen door by a soldier! A soldier I've never seen here before. I can't find either of the two usual kitchen-men. And Doña Isabel is nowhere to be seen, and neither is the other governess, Josepha. None of them is downstairs—and the silence, well, the silence is uncanny, *chiquita*."

"There'll be an explanation," said Ana.

"I dare say," said Anichu dryly.

"I don't like it," said Bernardina. "I don't fancy the explanation."

"I'll send for Villasante presently," said Ana, who could hardly bear the look of anxiety in Anichu's eyes. "But let's have some of this lovely breakfast first. We'll need it perhaps," she said with a little laugh.

"I can't," said Bernardina. "I'd choke if I tried. I'm frightened, *chiquita*. It isn't nice—that silence down there."

Bernardina has had too much of all these sinister prison ways, Ana thought in pity. She's breaking up, dear soul. They've almost broken *her* courageous spirit. It's probably nothing—some silly change of plan about the staff.

"Dear Berni! Drink some milk at least."

At that moment they heard the squeaking locks being turned in the iron grill beyond the great door of the drawing-room; they heard the heavy gates scream open, and heard them closed again. In another moment the house-governor, Villasante, was in the room, escorted by four armed soldiers. He looked very grave and self-important.

He bowed coldly to Ana. He had some papers in his hand.

"Your Highness was recently so ill-advised as to abuse the terms of your detention here. Evidence has been received by His Majesty that you admitted an enemy of the state illicitly to your presence, and aided and abetted his flight from justice. In view of this crime, His Majesty is now compelled to alter your house-detention to total imprisonment, and I must request you to offer no resistance whilst we proceed with the necessary arrangements, as instructed by His Majesty."

He bowed again and handed Ana one of the papers he held in his hand.

She glanced at it, saw Philip's signature and laid it down. Anichu took it from her hand and read it. Bernardina sat and stared at Ana. For once, it seemed, she had nothing to say to her gaoler. Neither could Ana think of much to say.

"Are they elaborate, these arrangements?"

"They are, madam. They will include some heavy work by masons and builders in these apartments."

"Masons and builders?"

"Yes, madam. You are to be allowed to occupy this room and your bedroom, and to have access to the chapel. But all outlets beyond that limit, all unnecessary doors and windows are to be built up and barred. And the rooms are, of course, to be stripped of these valuable pictures and furnishings, which would only come to harm in prison conditions. But we hope to have accomplished the work in two days. The masons will not disturb you long."

"I see."

Bernardina roused herself.

"Where are Her Highness's usual servants?" she asked Villasante. "Where is Paca? Where are the governesses?"

He smiled a little.

"They are dismissed, and at present on their way to Madrid, where you will also be, madam, before evening."

"I?"

"Yes. It is the king's stringent instruction that I dismiss you, and all your possessions to-day, and deliver you safely to your husband's lodging in Madrid. You are free and pardoned henceforward, but you return to the district of Pastrana only under penalty of instant death."

He bowed, and handed Bernardina a paper which bore Philip's signature.

Bernardina glanced at it, and stood up.

"I shall not go," she said. "You can tell the king to do what he likes about it, but I'm staying here."

"Berni——"

"No, madam—you are going. You shall not force us into making a martyr of you. You will go this morning under strong escort. You have long been a difficulty and a bad influence here. And in view of your share in the recent outrage of regulations, His Majesty's clemency in setting you free is, may I say, astonishing. Your personal possessions were packed whilst you were assisting at Mass, and they now await you in a coach in the court-yard. Will you therefore be so good as to bid adieu to Her Highness? We shall then, when you are despatched, be able to begin our work on these apartments."

Bernardina looked wildly about the room. She was over sixty now, and unhealthy and tired and fat. Ana thought that she might be going to have a stroke. With difficulty she rose and went to her. She put an arm about her shoulders.

"Berni, Berni! Don't look like that. It's all right, and it can't be helped. We've had a good life together, in spite of all these gaolers. And it's over now and we're both old women anyway, and won't be troubling the king and his servants much longer. So say good-bye, and take my gratitude and a great deal of my heart with you, my dear, to Madrid. And to Heaven, where I'll meet you soon."

"I won't say good-bye! I can't! It's murder, plain, slow murder, to do this to you now! And what *are* they going to do? I'd go mad, I tell you, if I had to leave you to their devilries now! No, I won't say good-bye, I won't, I won't!"

Villasante signed to two soldiers who slipped forward and laid hands on Bernardina. But Ana waved them off.

"Just a moment, please. Berni, for my sake go, and go in peace. After all, you owe it to your poor husband, who has had to suffer so much because of your loyal duty to me. Think of the consolation it will be to him to have you back again for his old age. And——" she put both arms round the *dueña* now, and spoke softly, turning away from where Anichu stood rigid, with the king's order still in her hands—"you know very well that for me it won't be long now, so whatever they're going to do, just bar me in a bit, I suppose, will matter very little. You know I'm near death, and very glad to be. So make it easy for me now. It will be a real comfort to know that you are back with poor dear Espinosa, whom I have wronged so much in taking all your years of loyalty. Do you hear me, Berni? Are you listening?"

"Yes, I hear you, *chiquita*." Bernardina spoke dully, slowly. This last shock was too much and she knew it was. She knew there was no way of resistance for her now, a fat old woman, against armed men and proclamations from the king. Yet she turned once more on Villasante.

"How is she to be looked after? She is, as you know well, a very ill woman. She simply cannot be left without me now! I've taken care of her for years—indeed, it seems like all my life!"

"A female has been engaged who is competent to perform the necessary offices of a wardress."

"A wardress!"

Ana laughed.

"Ah, Berni, what does it matter? Why not a wardress? Perhaps she'll be as amusing as Gypsy Rosa! Do you remember Pinto, and Gypsy Rosa?"

Bernardina broke into helpless, desolate sobbing. Ana held her in her arms, and Anichu came to them, and tried to help her fragile mother to support the dejected weight of her.

"Mother is right, Berni. And it will comfort her to know that you're at home again with Espinosa."

Bernardina was past further speech. She sobbed and shook in Ana's arms.

"Good-bye, my dear, dear friend," Ana said. "Good-bye, my Berni, and God bless and keep you. Pray for me, and I will pray for you."

She signalled to the soldiers, and they came and took

Bernardina gently by the arms. She went with them, blind with shock and desolation. She did not look back, and after the iron grill beyond the door had opened and shut on her and the guards, her choked and formless crying could still be heard—but dying away as she descended the great staircase.

Ana stood leaning on her sticks and looked at Anichu. She wondered with terror what instruction there might be about her.

Villasante looked from one of them to the other.

"What arrangement does Your Highness wish me to make for the young Countess?" he asked politely.

Ana and Anichu looked at each other quickly. Evidently the king had sent no ultimatum about the latter.

"If you wish, we can have her sent under careful escort to the house of her sister, the Duchess of Medina Sidonia, at San Lucar. Or is there any other relative you would prefer her to be sent to?"

Anichu smiled. Ana could see something like radiant happiness taking possession of a face that a moment ago had been rigid with fear.

"Thank you, Don Alonso," Anichu said with a politeness which almost sought to be ingratiating. "Thank you, but I don't wish to be sent anywhere. I am staying here."

It was clear that she understood from his manner that he had no instructions about her, and that therefore he would be unable to force her away.

Villasante looked perplexed. He spoke to Ana.

"I cannot advise such a course," he said. "The Countess is not under arrest, and your conditions here henceforward will be total imprisonment. If she were to stay here, she would have to suffer those conditions also. I can allow no traffic whatever between these rooms and the outer world. And no comforts, nothing more than the standard of life in state prisons, will be permitted. I believe therefore that I shall be obliged to arrange to send the young Countess to her Grace, her sister."

Ana looked at Anichu. The girl intended to stay with her, she knew. And she knew that this time Philip was in earnest, and for her sin in seeing Antonio again, she was to pay the full penalty, and drag out the remainder of her days in the deprivation, filth, darkness and neglect which was the portion of Spain's worst criminals in the crudest prisons. She hardly cared for herself—but it terrified her for Anichu. It would only hurry death to her, which would be good; but it might undermine the young girl's health for ever, and it would leave a great scar of bitterness and sorrow on her soul. And she would have to be alone, more or less, with the ordeal of her mother's death. It was a very dark, dangerous way for a young imagination to have to tread. Yet she believed that for Anichu, who knew so well how to love, the alternative might be far worse. To be sent away by force now into the sun and freedom with nothing to do but try to imagine what was happening in Pastrana—Ana shuddered for what that might do to a spirit like Anichu's.

"You heard what Don Alonso said, Anichu?"

"Yes. And I thank him again. But I am staying here. I understand the terms, Don Alonso, and shall abide by them."

Don Alonso bowed, and frowned.

"I regret your decision, Countess."

Ana sat down again. She suddenly felt most desperately ill and weary. She sat with her elbow on the table and her fingers pressed against her eye-shade. Anichu had chosen the right way for herself, but this strange burden that her fate had laid upon her child was going to be heavier and harder than had ever been foreseen. Oh Philip, Philip, must I forgive you this as well?

"Then, with Your Highness's permission, I will send for the workmen and instruct them. And meantime, we must start on the removal of these pictures and books."

Ana looked up and nodded vaguely. The men began to move about the room. Anichu stood at the other side of the table where breakfast still lay untouched. She sat down now, and leant across and stroked Ana's hand.

"Come, let's have breakfast," she said.

They sat and tried to eat and drink.

Outside the peerless day spread in brightness. The square stirred with its usual gentle, easy signs of life, and the façade of the *Colegiata* threw a peaceful shadow.

"Do drink some milk," Anichu said.

One of the men was taking down the Mantegna. Ana watched him in wonder. They were quick; already the pictures were gone from the long wall. Ruy was gone, and the Clouet head that Isabel of Valois had given her.

There was a clattering sound below—a coach driving out of the court-yard; they could not see it from here. They looked at each other, and said good-bye again to Bernardina in their hearts. Ana listened to the wheels until the sound vanished for ever along the Alcala road.

By the evening of that day they had grown used to the sound of hammering, the clang of iron bars being driven into place, and the tramp and noise of several men working at great pressure all about them.

When they sat eating the mess of supper which their new wardress brought to them, the drawing-room was bare of everything save Ana's couch, two tables and two chairs. The curtains and carpets and desk and all the accustomed furnishings of a whole life were gone with the pictures, and the white walls with their fading and peeling acacia-leaves of gold looked absurd, dishonoured and sordid.

A great wall had been built to cut them off from the staircase which led to the garden. A small iron door was inserted in this, through which the wardress would come to them henceforward, unlocking and locking it with her every move. The landing now where this wall had been built, and Ana's bedroom and dressing-room, where the windows had been built in, were entirely deprived of daylight and ventilation.

After supper they did not light their one candle. The great window was open, and they sat and looked at the rising stars, and smelt the sweet May night. They could see the *Colegiata* door open and shut as people went in and out to say their evening prayers.

Anichu sat on the floor by Ana's couch.

"Talk to me," she said. "Tell me about when we were all little. Tell me things about when you were little."

Ana stroked her shining, dark head.

They stayed very late by the window, and talked of a great many things.

On the second evening of this new imprisonment they had no window by which to sit and talk. The masons had done their work within scheduled time, and the king's instructions had been carried through. There was no light any more in the drawing-room at Pastrana. The great window had been built up, and Ana would never again see the sky or the tower of the *Colegiata*. Nor her daughter's face, save by the light of one candle. Philip's work on her was done now. She could compose herself and wait. Contentedly she realised that she felt very ill indeed. It won't be long, Anichu, her heart said passionately. I promise you, my darling, it won't be long.

EPILOGUE

(JUNE 1592)

PHILIP was tired, and having worked without pause all day at his desk was tempted, when he recognised its handwriting, not to open the last letter of the afternoon's great collection.

It was from the Duke of Medina Sidonia, a loyal man and virtuous, so well-meaning indeed that Philip had had no heart to be other than forgiving and considerate with him over the catastrophe of the Armada. And after all, Philip had acknowledged to himself, that was chiefly his own fault. Yet, though bearing no grudge, he could not bear the sight of Medina Sidonia's writing, for it reminded him of Ana de Mendoza.

He was sixty-five now, gouty and stiff and full of ill-health. His eyes hurt him constantly and were watery and red-rimmed; his once-distinguished fairness of hair and skin had long been a blur of desiccated, neutral grey. But he cared little for his own disabilities and infirmities, so long as he could still work, work for Spain, work with the caution, closeness and tenacity that were all he could give his country in place of brilliance or decisiveness. He was much disheartened now, and pondered questioningly the past for its mistakes. But still he must work, because now he knew of nothing else to do, and because he must keep on trying to redeem some of the failures he had brought on Spain, and on his own reputation as a king.

He had sacrificed Spain's integral greatness to his zeal for Catholicism in Europe—and now it appeared even to him that that cause was lost. The threat of the Armada and its brilliant defeat had roused all England, and settled for ever the Catholic hope in that island; France, with which he was at war, had now a Protestant king, and the Duke of Guise was dead, assassinated; the Netherlands, though William of Orange was long since gone, assassinated also, fought and wrestled eternally still, divided and confused, but intransigent in their refusal to impose Catholicism; they drained his resources and his wits. At home, with Mother Teresa's reformers divided and quarrelling since her death, with the Holy Office as arrogant as always and with Jews and *moriscos* everywhere, he saw the Faith often disgraced and frequently threatened; and overseas the *conquistadores*, though spreading God's message indeed, were doing so at a cost of blood, ships, men, piracy and crime which often made Spain's empire seem to him instead of a glory the source of all her present poverty and decline.

He viewed this picture with realistic depression and regret. He had intended to be a very great king, and had never been less than a conscientious and a serious one. And he had sought God's Will in prayer and self-denial—more and more with every year—and as he thought he read that Will, he had obeyed it without shrinking. But the great scheme had gone wrong somewhere and he knew it, and knew that a vast measure of the blame must lie with him. Yet he could not see how other he could have acted, for he could only be himself and give what he had to give to his high vocation. And that he had done—and the rest was with God, and meantime he must continue, against heavier and heavier odds, to work by his light for Spain and for Heaven's great cause. The thought of Heaven's great cause reminded him now of Granvelle's long memorandum of the war in France which still lay unread and must be discussed within an hour. He turned to look for it—he had better read it. It was undoubtedly dangerous for Spain that Antonio Perez was at the French court, and apparently high in favour with this Protestant, Henry IV. Perez always *had* been liked by the French liberals; Henry III had liked him, and now this Bourbon had taken him up, the renegade. And Perez knew a very great deal, and never forgot anything. It was regrettable that he had escaped from Aragon—and all the more bitter that he did so on the very day that the province yielded unconditionally to Castilian arms. Ironic for Aragon to have lost its ancient liberties in such an unworthy cause, and ironic for him, Philip, to have lost the prey he went to war for. He smiled coldly. He had desired the death of Antonio Perez. Well, it had not been granted. The wrong people died; he had a way of removing the wrong people. Yet it was much to have subdued Aragon at last, to have brought her stubborn nobles as irrevocably to heel as his father had the aristocracy of Castile. The Peninsula was one now, and ruled by one man. Yet the accomplishment had failed of Philip's real purpose— and Perez was the protégé of a Protestant king in France. Ironic. Philip smiled patiently. He was growing used to failure.

He looked about his workroom. It was the end of a very hot day, and he never felt well in Madrid. He did not like the Alcázar, and thought gratefully that at nightfall he would be driving back again up the Guadarramas to El Escorial. There, if anywhere on earth, he found some peace now, and there he saw rising about him—in the library, the schools, the experimental farms, the hospital, and in that great church with its perfect choir and perfect adherence to liturgical symbolism—there in all of these things at least he saw a happy achievement, a carrying-through of his desire. There were his dear children too, Isabel's daughters and the one sickly, precious son who alone survived of poor Anne of Austria's attempts to give him a male heir. Young Philip was fourteen, and it looked as if he would survive and reach the throne. That at least was a comfort.

Philip would be glad to drive home to-night. To-morrow he might have a few hours off and take the boy fishing, to that trout-pool just beyond Carreño Wood. The gardens would be lovely now—he had been away from them for fourteen days, and that was too long in June. He looked distastefully about him, and through the window where across the court-yard and the roof of Santa Maria Almudena he could see Madrid, baking defencelessly in the late afternoon light.

This was the hour when in former days he had liked to rest awhile from work, to leave this cramping room, and be himself awhile and not the king. This was the hour when he had sometimes allowed himself to leave the Alcázar by that gate which he could see from where he sat, and go and idle in the Long Room in the Eboli Palace. The Eboli Palace was closed and empty now.

This memory had overtaken him unawares, and he winced from it and turned back to his table. He thought of Ana seldom and never by his own choice. He had enough dis-comforts in his consciousness; this, his most private, which he had never understood, he buried at its every stirring under the rubble of a long life of anxieties and regrets.

He had loved her, after his fashion. And his love had had much that was tender and brotherly in it, and only in rare moments of impulse to throw off kingship had become desire. And in later life he had been able the more to enjoy those moments for knowing that he would never yield to them. They were a delicate sensuality and sentimentalism of his secret moods, a very private, untroubling grace in a life that had slowly stripped itself of decoration. And he loved her company—rarely though he allowed himself to taste it—and loved with greedy jealousy the flattery of her love, and the hint, the more-than-hint in it that if he had so willed he could have taken her when they were young. She was his preserve, his very private tenderness, and he rested in its reassurance. He liked even to hear her tell how she had thought when she was a little girl that she was to marry him; he liked to think that he had given her some heartache, that she had sometimes been made impatient by the non-finality of his desire for her; he liked to think that he, the king, was what this great and spoilt princess had coveted and never had. It was a day-dream, it was a feather in his cap—and because she gave it to him he gave her great affection. And he admired her, and all the more because he knew that she admired him.

The discovery therefore that in her middle age, while still his friend and dear illusion, she had a lover; right under his blind eyes, and out of his palace, and his closest friend—this shock worked in him slowly and creepingly, like an illness. It wrought effects in him that he could never manage and never face. And he never would face now all that retrospective misery. Against it he had acted, or not acted, by blind, frightened instinct, and in a series of struggles with himself; in a succession of sins against his heart and indulgences of his aching, cancered vanity. There was no law in his reaction, and he had no clue to it. Simply she had disillusioned him, and thereafter he could not, however he sought to, desist from vengeance. And when, regretful, ashamed and weary, he kept the whole tale buried in himself, only hoping that she was at peace in Pastrana and out of mischief and saving her soul—when then, in their old age, the news was brought to him that she was by no means at peace, that she still had her lover, that he had come to her in her prison in his flight into Aragon, perhaps only for the last of many visits, and that she had helped him in his escape—then a last fever of savagery against her invaded him. It was too much gall, this ultimate, unlooked-for opening of an unhealed-wound. He could not resist the passion, the old man's passion of self-pity that invaded him. He could not and he did not. Almost without consulting himself, almost without thought and as if he acted in his sleep, he answered her last flippancy against him, answered it for ever.

But he could not let himself think of her. He hated her dear name. It was carved beside Ruy Gomez's now on their tomb in the *Colegiata* Church of Pastrana. There it must

stand, but in his soul would Heaven in mercy bury it, and let
him never come on it again?

But Heaven was not considerate. Here was this letter from
Medina Sidonia, which could not fail to stir the one forbidden
woe.

Ana was now dead five months. She had died on the second
of February, the Feast of the Purification of Our Lady; for all
that they had told him of her desperate ill-health, she had
lived twenty months in darkness and incarceration. But she
was at peace now in her grave. And in the absence of her son
Rodrigo with Parma's armies, her son-in-law was attending
to the family affairs. Every now and then he deemed it his
duty to report on these to Philip.

Philip opened his letter reluctantly, and read it through
without letting himself concentrate, as if by too close attention he would receive more hurt from it than he could
bear.

It was businesslike and gave details of the disposal of
certain pieces of property. It lamented, as Alonso's other
letter had done, the great depreciation in the value of the
Pastrana estates, the almost-disappearance of its silk trade and
the depression on its farms. Rodrigo would be worried by
the figures, he said, and was pressing for money. Rodrigo,
had His Majesty heard?, was not well. He was developing a
serious weakness of the lungs, and might have to give up
soldiering. The Princess's other sons were well, he understood, and Fernando would soon be receiving Holy Orders.
Alonso heard from his superiors that he was a very promising
cleric. One sad piece of news, however, he had to impart to
His Majesty about this family in which he had always taken so
much interest. His Majesty would recall that a betrothal was
to be arranged this summer between the late Princess's
younger daughter, the Countess Ana de Silva and her cousin,
the Count of Tendilla. This had not been arranged earlier as
the Countess had asked for a little time in which to meditate

and, no doubt, recover from the grief of her mother's death. But, alas, in April the young man had had a fall from a horse, and only a week or two ago had died of his injuries. This was very regrettable in the already sad circumstances, but he the Duke, would have found no difficulty in arranging another equally suitable match for his beautiful and wealthy young sister-in-law. But he heard from her now—and he hastened to communicate the news to His Majesty—that she had returned to Pastrana, and had entered the Franciscan convent there as a postulant. She had said in her letter that this decision made her very happy—so perhaps if it was God's will it would be for the best. What did His Majesty think? . . .

Philip laid down the letter.

He rose painfully from the table and moved without purpose about the room. He came to rest at the window and looked across the court-yard at Madrid outside his walls. A bell was ringing from Santa Maria Almudena. He remembered how much more clearly one heard that bell in the Long Room of the Eboli Palace. Anichu, she used to call the little one, Anichu who did not leave her until the end, and had gone back to her now, gone back to Pastrana.

Philip stood a long time by the window and listened to the bell. His foot was hurting him, but he could not move to return to his chair. It was as if by keeping very still awhile he might master the leaden, deadly pain in his breast. He looked out at the sunlight towards her empty house, and the glare hurt his eyes, and the bell seemed to toll for his loneliness, and the sins that drove him on, for ever further into loneliness.

But he would be at El Escorial by morning, where his children were.

October 1945.   Clifden, Corofin.

The first Virago Modern Classic was published in London in 1978, launching a list dedicated to the celebration of women writers and to the rediscovery and reprinting of their works. While the series is called "Modern Classics," it is not true that these works of fiction are universally and equally considered "great," although that is often the case. Published with new critical and biographical introductions, books appear in the series for different reasons: sometimes for their importance in literary history; sometimes because they illuminate particular aspects of women's lives, both personal and public. They may be classics of comedy or storytelling; their interest can be historical, feminist, political, or literary. In any case, in their variety and richness they promise to confuse forever the question of what women's fiction is about, while at the same time affirming a true female tradition in literature.

Initially, the Virago Modern Classics concentrated on English novels and short stories published in the early decades of the century. As the series has grown, it has broadened to include works of fiction from different centuries and from different countries, cultures, and literary traditions; there are books written by black women, by Catholic and Jewish women, by women of almost every English-speaking country, and there are several relevant novels by men.

Nearly 200 Virago Modern Classics will have been published in England by the end of 1985. During that same year, Penguin Books began to publish Virago Modern Classics in the United States, with the expectation of having some forty titles from the series available by the end of 1986. Some of the earlier books in the series were published in the United States by The Dial Press.